Terms and Traditions

MORGAN TAYLOR GIESBRECHT

Terms and Traditions

A RELUCTANT ROMANTICS NOVEL

MORGAN TAYLOR GIESBRECHT

Cover Design and Illustration by Emily of LoveLitDesign

Edited by L. Taylor Edits

Dedication

For the girls with bruised hearts. The crusty romantics who scoff at romance but secretly want to love big and find their person... yet live with the scars of being hurt again. Whether you were told you were too much or not enough, the right people (platonic or romantic) will love you for who you are. I see you. Here's to finding our people—I pray you find the "staying kind." Don't settle for less. <3

Trigger Warning

This is a light-hearted romantic comedy with the goal of making you laugh. There's no on-page swearing and no sex. However, there are a few heavier themes our characters have to grapple with and overcome. Namely—anxiety attacks, POTS episodes, parental manipulation and abandonment, parent with drug addiction (off-screen), grief (past), cheating ex, and a very vague implication of an attempted sexual assault in the past. While these topics are handled with as much grace and care as possible, please be mindful of this for your own wellbeing going in. <3

p.s. POTS symptoms can vary from patient to patient, so Stephanie's experience may not be everyone's.

Playlist

If you're a music lover and want to enjoy a curated playlist of songs that form a soundtrack of sorts to the book, scan the code below!

And here's the code for Stephanie's special Christmas road trip playlist! Enjoy!

CHAPTER ONE

Stephanie

MANDATORY OFFICE CHRISTMAS PARTIES should be out-lawed, especially for the introverts who planned them.

Why would I want to attend a party I'd literally spent the last four weeks planning when I could be home in my pajamas with a plate of freshly baked gingersnaps—courtesy of my very talented roommate and bestie who stress baked on a regular basis—watching any assortment of Christmas movies? Why indeed.

But if I did say so myself, everything about the party was perfectly executed. From the canapés to the music. Even the festive dress code was a hit. Who knew a bunch of stuffy marketing executives would love the idea of dressing up as their favourite Christmas movie character? (Although the Christmas bonuses our boss, Nash Prescott, always handed out might have explained their enthusiasm.) Neil, one of our graphic design interns, took the prize in my mind with a hideous knit sweater that walked straight out of a '90s movie. But he rocked it. Well played, Neil.

Perfection and costume decisions aside, I, Stephanie Addams, just wanted to go home. And that was before someone spilled cream soda on my sweater dress. While my favourite colour—forest green—hid a multitude of sins, soda wasn't one of them.

But could I duck out early? No. My illustrious boss mandated one last huzzah before the grind of our upcoming software program launch in the new year. So I was stuck there. In the deserted breakroom kitchen. Scrubbing soda stains from my clothing and guzzling a fancy La Croix like tomorrow wasn't coming. Party planning wasn't part of my job description, and if I ever saw another canapé, it would be too soon. Because when the original event coordinator backed out last minute, who did Nash think was the best replacement? You're looking at her. Now we were playing a game of favours and IOUs.

"You are *so* going to owe me for this one, Nash," I hissed under my breath, giving my dress a final scrub.

Nash Prescott, CEO and founder of Genesis Marketing, wasn't a terrible man or a terrible boss by any means, even if I did hate his mandatory festivities participation. I'd worked as his personal assistant for the last two years, and he was generous. A glance at the budget he provided for this shindig proved it. Had he foregone the party (my suggestion) and added said budget to my paycheck, I could have paid rent a few times over.

Not that I was biased about him or anything since we shared a friend group. Which made us friends. Pals. Totally platonic. Well, at least as chummy as a girl could be with her very attractive, very thoughtful millionaire boss. Who was I kidding? I'd watched the man play tea party with his best friend's daughters and rock a baby to sleep. *Just. Friends.*

My phone chimed with ear-shattering intensity, and I slapped my pockets, trying to find it. Since when was my volume on? Not since 2015, that's when. My stomach churned and sweat prickled my skin as I glanced at the name on the screen. Hiram Addams. Dear ol' Dad. *Oh, boy.* I debated opening his message—they were always a harbinger of passive-aggressiveness—but it was family drama or returning to the party. Easy choice. Blowing out a breath, I flicked the message app open and braced myself for his latest rant.

HIRAM

> Stephanie, I want you to entertain Jarrett at the cabin. He's still an asset to Nova and will be joining us for Christmas.

No, no, no! I choked on the mouthful of bubbly water, making my nose burn. This could not be happening. Breaking every boundary and rule I'd set for myself about replying to his messages, I typed out a panicked text.

ME

> No! You are not setting me up with him again. He's a creep. Besides, I have a boyfriend.

What was I saying? I hadn't had a boyfriend in five years, and he'd only lasted a month. The best I'd managed since then was a handful of second dates and one pathetic crush on my boss. But the last time Hiram badgered me into entertaining Jarrett, this "asset" to his marketing company, the guy hadn't taken "no" as an answer. He'd wanted entertainment all right—ugh. Trying to steal a kiss in a dark hallway under nonexistent mistletoe when a girl already said *no* was not acceptable behaviour.

HIRAM

> So you are capable of replying to my messages instead of behaving like a child.
> Bring him. Your job is enough of an embarrassment. Don't disappoint me again.
> It's time you got serious about your life.

And I'd stumbled right into his trap. Hook, line, and sinker. Most of the time, I didn't reply to his messages, but somehow my father—who didn't even deserve the title—figured out threatening me with a creepy date would be an effective topic to break the radio silence. Way to win a dad-of-the-year award. Now I needed a fake boyfriend in less than a week to go and meet my family of five older half siblings and their families. All but one of whom hated me. Lovely.

I'd downed all but the last swig of my seltzer water when unwelcome feminine titters drifted down the hall towards me. *Drat.* I ducked behind a gigantic silver-wrapped gift. Not my finest move, but I needed a breather after that text and to hide the Texas-sized wet spot staining my front. Maybe I could sneak to the bathroom and see if the air dryer would work some magic on my dress. On a regular day, I'd never consider it—have you read how gross those things are?—but this was no ordinary day. And a paper towel wasn't going to cut it.

Plus, I was in no mood to bump into the women moving towards me. While I loved my job as a personal assistant, the environment I didn't love so much. For some reason, being the PA to one of the wealthiest men in Washington State had garnered me the hate of every woman in the office—yay me. The women were catty, and all my attempts at friendship and cordial working relations in the last two years had fallen flat. When I brought a platter of Liz's to-die-for pecan sticky buns? They dismissed them as "too fattening." My lobbying to hear their contributions at the table when we brainstormed ideas? They labeled me as condescending. I was no stranger to the rumours about me floating through the sleek office between cubicles. About how the only way I'd landed my job was from sleeping my way to the top. Gross. It might be the Christmas season, but green jealousy didn't look good on anyone.

I ignored the hum of voices—Samantha and Anika, from the sound of it—as they entered my makeshift sanctuary. Wearing a sweater dress mirroring a Hallmark heroine had been a terrible idea with the thermostat gone haywire, and the sticky residue of cream soda and dampness wasn't helping my overwhelming levels of swampiness. It wasn't until I raised the La Croix can to my lips for the last delicious swig that my brain latched onto the conversation they'd brought into the small kitchen.

"She's the only one who didn't bring a plus one," Samantha commented. "And she planned it all."

Anika tittered. "She's never had a boyfriend as long as I've known her. I doubt she's been asked out since we graduated. The one time I dared her to kiss a guy in high school, he threw up immediately." They laughed hysterically before she added, "Some people peak at graduation and just never realize it. Besides, she's too much of a workaholic to date. Zero work-life balance, I tell you."

I silently resented that because I *had* been asked out. True, only a handful got a rare second date, and there was only one who progressed to boyfriend status—which lasted about a month—but still. *Get your facts straight, Anika.* As for a workaholic... There was some truth to that. Nash was busy, which meant I was, too. But I *did* have a life outside of work, and Anika didn't have to be nasty about it.

Oh, did I mention I knew her from childhood? Yeah. We used to be close friends in middle and high school back in Denver, then we lost touch and ended up in Spokane at the same marketing firm ten years later. Small world.

One of them rummaged in the fridge. Seriously, why were they in here when all the food was out in the conference room? This breakroom was for daily lunches and solitary confinement, not perfectly catered events and gossip hour.

"Any idea why?" Samantha asked.

Oh, boy. My heart stuttered, and a trickle of sweat inched down my back, making me squirm and nearly bump my nose against the shiny paper grotesquely distorting my reflection. Could we get off the love train of Stephanie Addams's nonexistent love life? Please and thanks.

Apparently not, because my former friend opened her big mouth. "Stephanie is... a lot. I grew up with her. I'd know. She's got tons of baggage. Her mom was Hiram Addams's sixth wife, you know, and after she left him, Hiram was never around. Just dumped Stephanie with his parents and moved on."

"She's still an Addams princess," Samantha drolled, then dropped her voice to a whisper. "And what was she thinking, choosing to work here when her family is literally the competition? I should have gotten the job." She sniffed. "Although the look on her face when you spilled your soda on her was the most emotion I've ever seen from her." She snickered. "She's such an ice princess. Guys don't go for that kind of thing."

If I hadn't been so close to tears, I would have snorted. There it was. *Stephanie Addams, the girl who always got left behind. The girl no one wants.* She was right, but I guessed most of her jealousy was fueled by our—unknown to me at the time—rivalry for the PA position. She'd been a longtime employee, and I'd been the newcomer.

I shifted to ease the growing cramps in my calves, silently cursing the strappy black velvet heels my bestie, Liz, insisted I wear. Crouching at this angle threatened to topple me face-first into the shiny silver wrapping paper. Heels were not made for ducking. Or really for any other defying-Superwoman odds. Run in these deathtraps? Not on your life.

Anika laughed, caustic and grating. "Right? She's not the kind of woman any man wants. I don't know what Nash sees in her. He could have the best, and he settled for her? Sure, she's competent, but she's nothing special."

The knife twisted deeper. I was... a lot. Two little words with the force of a wrecking ball. I shut my eyes against the burning tears as they drifted away. At my office Christmas party, I was weird because I didn't have a significant other at my side. I would have brought Liz, but she'd already scheduled a date night with her fiancé. Fundamentally I knew I didn't need a man to be complete or have worth. I *knew* this. Nana had hammered that into me ever since I was small. Nana, with her strong faith, worn Bible, and an answer for everything, had raised me when my mom left and my dad decided he didn't want the responsibility of raising me any more than he'd wanted to raise his first five kids with any of his previous wives.

Your only worth comes from your Heavenly Father, baby girl. No man can ever define you when Jesus already has.

I needed to call Nana this weekend. Her soothing voice always eased my tattered edges. Because despite the strong walls around my heart, the cruel words slithered their way to the still-raw wounds beneath. It wasn't the first time someone decided to comment on my perpetual singleness. Just last week at church, one of the deacon's wives, a genuinely sweet woman, had patted my hand and said with a pitying smile, "You're not getting any younger, dear. There's lots of nice young men around. Maybe you're being too particular."

I was only twenty-eight, and after the life I'd lived, I had every right to be particular. A man who wouldn't walk out on me was my baseline requirement. Funny how married folks talked as if singleness was the greatest evil of the human existence. I'd rather be comfortably single than uncomfortably married to the wrong person.

But the words hit their mark just the same. I wasn't enough on my own. And I was so tired of being alone.

Gripping my empty La Croix, I jogged out of the kitchen, swiping at my blurry eyes. My heels caught on the carpet in the hallway, throwing me off balance. I groped the wall for support, narrowly missing the fire alarm. *Wouldn't that just take the cake tonight.*

"Stupid shoes," I muttered, sniffing hard. I needed to make it to the restroom and assess my makeup before I could plaster a smile on my face and mingle until I could duck out without raising suspicions. Show Nash some team spirit before I went home to my pile of knitting and binging Christmas movies. Solo.

A wave of dizziness gripped me as I neared the corner of the deserted hallway. *Uh-oh.* I'd stood up too fast without giving my blood pressure a chance to regulate. If my emotions hadn't hustled me into such a frenzy, I just—

Oof! I rammed into a solid wall, too warm to be drywall. My bell earrings—a gift from Liz last year—jangled at the abrupt halt of motion. Steady hands gripped my flailing elbows, anchoring me upright.

"Whoa there! Stephanie?"

Humiliation flooded my veins at being caught in such a state, and I kept my head down. I knew that voice... Oh, how I knew that voice. Nothing said Merry Christmas like smashing into the handsome boss you'd been secretly crushing on for two years, only to have him find you with raccoon eyes, running away from his mandatory holiday celebration. Because naturally I hadn't bothered with waterproof mascara since I wasn't planning on crying tonight. Rookie move.

"Nash. I was just... It's nothing." But it sure felt like a whole lot of something. The world tilted, and my eyes slid shut against the sudden wave of light-headedness. I tried tugging away from his grasp, but the blood drained from my head so fast I saw stars. My knees buckled, and I toppled face-first into his chest, his arms snaking around my waist, keeping me from falling.

"Steph!" Panic laced the word, and Nash gripped me tighter. If I'd been more coherent, I'd have basked in the warmth of him using the nickname only my best friends and a few close family members used.

"I'm okay," I murmured against his chest, the soft cotton of his black dress shirt caressing my cheek. Was shirt thread count a thing? 'Cuz his was glorious.

His arms shifted me closer. "I've got you," he whispered in my ear.

"Need... to sit."

Despite my awkwardly limp limbs, Nash guided me to a sitting position on the floor, and I tucked my legs against my chest, belatedly remembering I was wearing a dress. My head drooped against my knees, ears ringing, but I managed to situate my clothing so I didn't flash anyone.

"Just give me a minute," I whispered into my dress, hoping he heard me. "It'll pass." *It always does.*

I heard the soft scuff of shoes and a momentary shuffle before his long leg pressed against mine. One of my hands was encased in his, resting against his soft grey slacks. I didn't remember grabbing his hand on the way down. But I didn't dare lift my head to ask if he minded. Besides, the touch was way too comforting to give up, and if he wasn't protesting, well then, I wasn't going to question it.

In for four. Out for four. I inhaled slowly through my nose and blew out through my mouth. Hopefully this episode wouldn't lead to fainting. Another rookie move, crouching behind that present and getting up too fast. It had been fifteen years since my diagnosis with Postural Orthostatic Tachycardia Syndrome. I knew better than to rush about like a scatterbrained chicken. Slow, controlled movements equaled regulated blood pressure. Too bad my emotions didn't get that memo tonight.

Nash said nothing. Just stroked my knuckles with his thumb and waited beside me while I fought against the paralyzing tidal wave of blackness and gravity's intent to splatter me on the floor like a snow angel—without the snow.

When the overwhelming feeling of the world being a Tilt-a-Whirl faded, I pivoted my neck to glance at him. My millionaire boss, Nash Prescott, was sitting on the ground in a blessedly empty hallway... with *me*. Looking absolutely perfect with his soulful espresso eyes, rimmed by extremely attractive dark-rimmed glasses, and his precisely tousled dark chocolate hair that curled at the ends. *He needs a haircut before the holidays.* I mentally added the task to my checklist.

"Will you be okay here for a minute?" Nash asked, concern infusing his voice when he noticed my staring.

Even though I nodded, he hesitated to release my hand, his eyes flickering with doubt. But he hopped up and his muffled footsteps trailed down the hall. In a heartbeat, he returned, wordlessly extending a stack of damp napkins.

"Thanks." I swiped the first one under my eyes, wincing as it revealed the tell-tale smudges of mascara. A few more damp napkins later, and I was officially raccoon eyes-free.

"Are you all right?" Nash's low timbre was soft and serious, despite our lack of company on the carpeted hallway floor. I might be able to laugh about this someday.

"I have POTS," I said simply. "It makes my blood pressure drop ridiculously low, and my body equates a change in position, like from sitting to standing, to be a strenuous task. Usually it just makes me severely dizzy and my heart pound really fast, but I faint sometimes." I shrugged, straightening my dress over my legs.

Nash blinked in horror before his dark eyes traced my face, like he was filing away this information for later. "How did I not know this? We've worked together for two years and been friends nearly as long."

Friends. Such a hard word to swallow. I twitched my shoulder in a half shrug, making my earrings jingle. "It's not exactly something

I advertise. My case is manageable, so it's not a huge inconvenience. I just have to be smart."

"Like your preference for the elevator over the stairs? Or why you always stand up from your desk slowly and have an aversion to sports?"

I stared at him. He noticed those things? Noticed *me*? And why, instead of feeling embarrassed about it, were my shoulders relaxing? Okay, the sports one was a bit of a stretch. Sure, my POTS affected it a little, but truthfully, I just hated intense physical exercise.

"Is there anything I can do?" he asked quietly.

Only in my dreams. At thirty-three, Nash Prescott was a multimillionaire and just my type... if he wasn't my boss. But I was so far out of his league he would never think of me like that, and after what Anika and Samantha said, I doubted any man ever would. It wasn't just their words that hurt—it was how close their observations lined up with my own fears. If others saw the same flaws in me that I did, didn't that make them true?

To my prolonged silence, Nash added, his rare Texas twang slipping out just a hint, "Anythin', Stephanie. Name it."

Why did he have to be so stinkin' nice? And the way his voice curled over my name... Perfection.

"I need a fake boyfriend to take to Christmas with my family," I muttered then slapped a hand over my mouth in horror. I wasn't supposed to say that out loud. He was probably talking about work accommodations. So why in the Nutcracker realm of Christmas did I blurt *that* out? Maybe it was the way Anika's words gripped my heart in a chokehold. Or the ringing dread in my ears after Hiram's texts. Or the sliver of jealousy I struggled with while getting a front-row seat to my best friend's happily ever after playing out. Or maybe it was just plain ol' lack of oxygen to the brain. Regardless, my heart was tap-dancing in my ribcage, and the words fell out of me without permission. *Abort! Abort! Run!*

"A fake boyfriend?" Nash's dark eyes swam with curiosity and confusion, and he adjusted his glasses. "Wouldn't your real one get jealous?"

Was he... Was he fishing? *Huh.* And whatever gave him the impression there was a real boyfriend in the picture? I would have brought him tonight if there was. My shoulders slumped. "Forget it, it's dumb. I'm not thinking straight right now." And I'd need seven to ten months to recover from my humiliation. To save the last shred of my dignity, I shifted to try standing up without face-planting.

But Nash touched my elbow, stilling my movements and keeping me at his side. Not too tight—I could slip away easily if I wanted, which I didn't. *I am so dead.*

"I'll do it."

Clearly my brain was short circuiting because there was no way he just *agreed*. "Huh?" was my elegant retort to this beautiful man.

Nash smiled, his dimple popping. "You need a fake boyfriend? You got one. You need me to meet your family? Consider it done."

I frowned. Why was he being so blasé—even cheery—about this? He didn't go around doing boyfriend-for-hire gigs any more than I could climb a flight of stairs without getting dizzy. Which was never.

"What about your girlfriend?" I wasn't fishing. Really. As his PA, I knew his schedule. There were no evening dates or dinner plans—how? This guy was seriously a catch. But maybe he'd surprise me, and I wasn't about to cheat.

His eyebrow raised, like he guessed my train of thought. "No girlfriend, Stephanie. You know that."

Yes, I did. I sighed inwardly. He hadn't dated since I'd worked here. Not that I was keeping tabs... Okay, fine I was, thanks to this stupid crush. But I was in no way crossing any HR lines. Because HR made a big deal about that type of thing... I think. At least in the movies. Maybe reality was different from fiction? And yet...

"You're serious?" I asked, probing him for sincerity. Daring him to drop a "Just kidding!" To back out. Hoping he would but praying he wouldn't.

"As a tombstone." Nash didn't flinch under my scrutiny, and my soul shied away from such directness. Even if it made my insides melt like toffee.

"Tomorrow!" I blurted out. "Coffee at Maisie's. Ten o'clock. We can discuss our terms and..." Maybe I should have clarified exactly what this mission covered? Christmas at the Addams's cabin might interfere with his plans. "Um, I should mention it involves spending Christmas with my incredibly dysfunctional, Christmas-obsessed, competitive family."

The smile he flashed me was forty-watt perfection. "We can hash this all out tomorrow over coffee. You aren't scaring me off."

There was no way he could know just how sweet those words tasted after the sting of Anika and Samantha's conversation in the kitchen still prickled in my heart.

Like the gentleman he was, Nash stood before holding both hands out to pull me to my feet. It was a chivalrous move. Thoughtful. Helpful. But when his large, warm hands captured mine, strong and sure, and he slowly tugged me up, I knew I was already a goner.

"If you change your mind, I promise I'll understand," I whispered, studying our lingering joined hands and taking a moment to catch my breath and my balance.

"I'm not changing my mind," Nash said with sincerity. When I tipped my chin up to meet his gaze, he added, "I know what I want." He squeezed my hands again, only stepping away once he was certain I was steady. Straightening his black shirt sleeves, rolled over his forearms, he said, "Fantastic work with the party. You can head out early if you want. You deserve it, and I still owe you."

"Let's call this fake dating my favour and be done with it. You're on your own for all future party planning," I grumbled, crossing my arms to hide the still-damp outline on my dress.

Nash chuckled. "We'll see." He gave me a quick once-over, not in a leering or uncomfortable way, but like he was making sure I was okay. Still, it made my cheeks heat. "What character are you supposed to be?"

I grimaced, tucking a chin-length curl behind my ear. "Just a run-of-the-mill Hallmark heroine."

Questions danced in his eyes, like the concept was unfamiliar.

"You know, those cheesy Christmas movies about every big-city girl ending up in the small hometown she left behind and falling in love with her high school boyfriend again to save the Christmas tree farm?" Pretty sure Hallmark has used that plot model for every movie with one or two minor deviations. Didn't stop me from loving them though.

Nash smiled down at me. "Sounds fitting to me. Till tomorrow." He shot me a parting wink, and the blush instantly raged in my cheeks. Curse my fair skin because there was no way he missed how he affected me.

And as I watched him walk away, I sagged against the wall. *I won't change my mind. I know what I want.*

Oh sugarplums, I was toast—burnt toast.

CHAPTER TWO

Nash

A SACRED HUSH BLANKETED the office as I pressed the power button on my computer monitor and watched it sleepily blink off. Usually, I enjoyed these last minutes of going through the motions of closing down the workplace. But tonight, coming off the high of that party, my usual nightly rituals didn't calm the champagne bubbles in my veins, even though there'd been no alcohol present tonight. If I was being honest with myself, it wasn't the party on my mind while I flicked off the annoying hum of the overhead light and closed my office door.

No, grand as the event was—Stephanie did better than I dreamed and certainly better than the original planner I'd hired—my thoughts were firmly centered around my off-limits PA. Stephanie Addams was a dead ringer for Wednesday Addams with her bouncy jet-black curls, gorgeous hazel eyes, and pale complexion, but we weren't close enough for me to make that comment yet.

Although, based on our conversation in the hallway tonight, I *was* her new fake boyfriend, so maybe that observation would become acceptable between here and... wherever we were going. That minor detail about the location seemed to have slipped through the cracks. No matter. It could be Timbuktu for all I cared. I had the chance to date the woman of my dreams. *Merry Christmas to me.*

Pausing in front of Stephanie's desk just opposite my office, I groaned and scrubbed a hand over my face. It was effortlessly tidy, like always. Stephanie's need for order was rather endearing, though I'd never tell her that. I wasn't a slob, but her brand of neatness definitely brought a whole new level of structure to my life.

I eyed the collection of framed photos lining the desk, nestled between her stapler and a Christmas tree mug full of pens. Stephanie and a burly man in a Marine Corps uniform—her oldest brother, I recalled. Stephanie, a redhead, and a brunette all cheek to cheek at the beach, grinning at the camera—her sister-in-law and cousin. Another frame of Stephanie and four of her nieces and nephews. And the last frame of Stephanie and her three best friends in fancy dresses. Maybe at a wedding, given the white dress? I knew Liz from church and from the friendship she and Stephanie shared with my own best friends' wives. The other two women—Juliet and Paisley—I hadn't met, but I'd heard plenty about, thanks to the way Stephanie lit up when she talked about them. It was ridiculous to be jealous of memories, but I couldn't help wishing I had more photographs of my own I'd want out on display.

My phone buzzed in my coat pocket. It was a text from Stephanie with a link to my online calendar, updating it with a newly scheduled haircut for this weekend. I couldn't help my smile if I tried. Which I didn't because there was no one around to judge me. While handling my appointments was part of Stephanie's job, I was touched when she noticed little things like that. There weren't a ton of people in my life who cared about me for anything beyond my money. Stephanie's thoughtfulness was one of the things I cherished. Along with her rare smile, quick wit, intelligence, the way her presence set me at ease... *Okay, man, pull it together.*

From the minute Stephanie glided into my office two years ago, dressed in smart black dress slacks, a white blouse, and a red blazer, I'd wanted to ask her out. Unfortunately, the moment she marched into my office that Thursday afternoon also meant she was interviewing for the position as my new personal assistant. And asking her on a date would have been an HR headache. A boss dating his assistant. That's how all the sleazy films started out, or so I was told by my best friend's wife, who, as an author, was knowledgeable about these things. No. I couldn't ask Stephanie Addams out on a date until I figured out the power imbalance. I was the boss, and HR technically could have gone for it with a few forms and signatures, but the power dynamic didn't sit right with me. Particularly with who her father was. *Yeah...*

Shooting Stephanie a quick thank you, I blew out a breath and headed for the elevators, leaving the smiling faces behind, frozen in time. Entering the elevator, I punched the ground floor button and waited.

Hiram Addams was Genesis's biggest marketing competitor in the country, and he just so happened to be Stephanie's father. There was a story behind her choice to come work for me when her father was in the same business and employed most of his other children, but I hadn't heard it yet. Only enough to know there was tension and estrangement involved. Looked like I'd be getting a front-row seat to the story this Christmas.

I need a fake boyfriend. Those five words clawed their way through my brain and glued themselves there, repeating on a loop. She was a stunning woman, inside and out. How had no guy seen that? Not that I was complaining because I didn't want that guy to be anyone but me. Still, she was an attractive woman. She'd never brought a plus-one to an event unless it was Liz.

Acting as Stephanie's fake boyfriend meant she had the final say, since I wasn't her boss in this situation, and we were off the clock. A golden opportunity to balance the power dynamic. And meeting to discuss terms was a good plan because I meant it when I said I'd do anything in my power for her. We were already friends as much as our work relationship allowed. How different could fake dating be? *Unless you mess things up and make things awkward after the holidays, and she quits because she can't stand you.*

The frosty air smacked my face, jarring me from my less-than-helpful train of thought, as I exited the main floor lobby. Christmas was definitely on the way, which I both loved and dreaded. Hitting the key fob, I slid into my Jeep Wrangler, the last car in the parking lot—my usual MO—and cranked the heat, blowing on my hands as "Jingle Bells" played on the radio. Could I have upgraded to a nicer vehicle years ago? Sure. But I had an emotional attachment to the old tin wagon. It was the first vehicle I'd bought in college, saving all my own money, and it still ran fine twelve years later. I'd upgrade one day, but for now, it was a good reminder of how far I'd come from the kid who'd worked two jobs in high school to pay for his mom's rent. Just thinking about Mom curdled my gut. *Don't focus on that tonight. You got the chance to date the only woman you've shown a modicum of interest in over the last decade. Figure out how to not mess this up.*

Fishing my phone out of my pocket, I opened the group chat with my two best friends.

THE WISE GUYS TEXT THREAD

I snorted every time I saw the name. It harkened back to the time newlywed Ryan had volunteered me and Emmett to join him as wise men in the church nativity pageant his wife was directing. Our first—and only—stage debut. And the name stuck.

Broaching the subject with Ryan and Emmett equaled opening a whole can of worms. But they were both married, so clearly they were doing better in the romance department than I was. Plus, they knew Stephanie and had seen us interact. Whatever teasing lay ahead might be worth it if I had some help wooing her. *Words I never thought I'd use.* Besides, Ryan's wife, Kelsi, was a romance author, and he was forever spouting off things about tropes and Hallmark. It was a little scary, honestly.

Hmm... Hallmark. Steph mentioned that tonight. Clearly it was a topic I needed to invest some time in researching further.

Two seconds later, my screen lit up as the chaos descended. Wow, that was fast, even for them.

RYAN

It's my time to shine, boys. Fake dating. Defined as a dating relationship that is not real but faked for mutual benefits, but eventually both parties inevitably fall in love.

EMMETT

It's horrifying you know that.

Also, why do we want to know this, Nash?

RYAN

Is there a girl?

ME

"Inevitably fall in love?" You make it sound like a communicable disease.

My point in asking is *why* someone would fake date.

RYAN

To avoid a harassing ex, for the drama, for family expectations, to make an ex jelly.

ME

Never use the word "jelly" again.

EMMETT

Seconded. We will disown you.

RYAN

How about well jel?

ME

Take a step back from the *Jeeves and Wooster* reruns or we will stage an intervention. Kelsi will be on our side.

RYAN

You have no taste. They never used that term on the show. And low blow to include my wife.

ME

Back to the matter at hand.

RYAN

Kelsi knows about this stuff better.

EMMETT

Nash. Why do you care? And why do we care for that matter?

RYAN

I repeat: IS THERE A GIRL, PRESCOTT? SPILL.

ME

Someone mentioned fake dating in conversation at tonight's party. Curiosity killed the cat.

EMMETT

Sounds like a horrible conversation for a Christmas party. My condolences to the cat.

Did Stephanie knock it out of the park?

RYAN

Rightttt. Your crush. And your PA. Send pictures.

Of the party décor and food in case that wasn't clear.

We've met Stephanie and know what she looks like.

EMMETT

Quit before you make this creepy, my man.

ME

I'm sure Stephanie has pictures. She might send them to you if you ask nicely.

And not a crush. What, are we in junior high?

EMMETT

Clearly one of us never left.

RYAN

I resent that.

If you're that invested in the topic, I'll send over a list of films and books Kelsi recommends for a comprehensive study of fake dating.

ME

I know better than to ask if you're kidding.

EMMETT

Does she seriously have that sort of information at the ready?

RYAN

It is a legit part of her job.

Info will be in your email in ten minutes, Prescott.

ME

I'm scared to look. I don't think I'm a Hallmark man.

EMMETT

Don't knock it till you try it.

RYAN

WHO ARE YOU AND WHAT HAVE YOU DONE WITH EMMETT?

Bro, did Danielle steal your phone?

Send proof of life.

EMMETT

Don't make a big deal out of this. Watching Hallmark with my wife doesn't revoke my man card.

ME

True. But you are the man who threw up halfway through *Little Women* on his third date with said wife. I was there. Nothing manly about that.

EMMETT

That was food poisoning. Don't desecrate the masterpiece that is *Little Women*. I saw you reaching for tissues, date crasher.

Nash, you cried over Matthew dying in *Anne of Green Gables*. We have video proof. We *own* you, man. Leave our Hallmark alone.

Gotta dash. Baby's crying, and I'm up to bat. Night, brothers.

I shot off a goodbye text and shifted into drive. The conversation left me chuckling all the way home. I'd known Ryan since high school, and we'd been instant best friends. Emmett had joined our circle in our freshman year of college, and here we were at thirty-three and still going strong. They'd both married amazing women nearly ten years ago and had three kids a piece, leaving me the solo bachelor. If my plans had worked out, I'd have been happily married for the last ten years, too. With a couple of kids and a white-picket fence. A dog. I'd always wanted a dog growing up, but life with my mom was too unpredictable. As for Alexis and me…

She hated your drive but wanted you to be successful. Hated when you focused on things besides her but always wanted more than you could give. You weren't enough for her. Or your mom. Or any woman. Why would Steph be any different?

My tires screeched to a halt as I belatedly recalled a stop sign in my neighbourhood. I was already partway through the intersection, and it was late. Frank Sinatra's velvety cadence singing "Have Yourself a Merry Little Christmas" filled the vehicle. *If only.*

I shook my head to clear the cobwebs. But the thoughts were a chilling ghost breathing down my neck.

I eased out of the intersection. No more reminiscing. Alexis wasn't worth a second distracted-driving ticket. The guys would never let me live it down. But this thing with Stephanie was sending my head into spaces I didn't want to dwell on. Especially not if I wanted something real with her. I had no reason to think we wouldn't be compatible. We'd been dancing around this whole *friends* thing for two years, which included countless get-togethers with Ryan and Emmett's families and Liz and her fiancé. As the odd ones out as a no-couple unit, Stephanie and I often paired together for different events and game nights. I loved the way her nose crinkled when she was hyperfocused and how her eyes sparkled when she talked about her best friends or her nieces and nephews. *Stop worrying.*

Grounded in Frank's melancholy nostalgia, I paid more attention to the road and the perfectly decorated houses flashing past. The neat rows of multicoloured lights. The blow-up Frosty the Snowmans. The song alone was enough to pull me back in time to Christmases past I'd spent with Alexis and her family. Decorating the tree, stringing lights, and driving through the neighbourhood at night to count the number of nativity scenes we found. Just like I used to do with my grandparents once upon a time. But then I lost Alexis, and her family by proxy. Hence my love-hate relationship with the holiday.

Frank finished singing as I parked my Jeep in the apartment complex parking lot. Good thing too—the ache in my chest was almost unbearable. Hearts could be annoying organs. Aching for lost things and holding onto dreams at the same time. I slid out into the nippy night air, absently rubbing my sternum. Lifting a hand, I waved to Mr. and Mrs. Lavoie, my elderly neighbours two units down, as they strolled hand in hand towards the entrance. Maybe bingo ran extra late tonight?

"You got plans for Christmas, young man?" Mrs. Lavoie's warbly voice called across the darkness.

"Yes, ma'am. I'm spending it with my girlfriend." Wow, that rolled off the tongue way too easily, but I couldn't help my grin, despite the twinge of nerves in my gut.

Mrs. Lavoie *awwed*, and her husband grunted, "'Bout time."

We rode the elevator up to the third floor together, and I listened while Mrs. Lavoie told me about their plans to visit their kids in Coeur d'Alene. Mr. Lavoie didn't say much, just grunted occasionally and smiled fondly at his wife. They reminded me of a real-life Carl and Ellie from that kids' movie Emmett's girls were obsessed with.

When I finally slipped into my apartment, I had a container full of Christmas baking, courtesy of Mrs. Lavoie. Helping myself to a pecan butter tart, I groaned. *Heavenly.* This was why I hadn't moved. Mrs. Lavoie's baking was too good to pass up.

After finishing college in Southern California and moving to Spokane ten years ago, I'd roomed with Emmett for a while before buying this two-bedroom apartment. It was simple and well-maintained, meeting my bachelor needs. After Genesis's financial success, I didn't see much point in selling and upgrading when it was just me, simply because I had more money now than I did right out of college. The only difference was I owned the building now—strictly because I liked my neighbours too much to risk losing them. And if Mrs. Lavoie was strategic about catching me in the hall every week to smother me with baked goods, I wasn't complaining.

But as I loosened my tie and dropped it onto my bed's navy comforter, there was a part of my text conversation with the guys I couldn't shake. What had Ryan said? The potential harassing ex. Was someone bothering Stephanie enough to make a fake boyfriend seem like her only hope? I made a mental note to ask her tomorrow. I hadn't even thought about her past exes before now. My friends hadn't mentioned her dating life, which was definitely something they would have spilled because they were nosy imps. My email pinged with a notification. No doubt Ryan's promised materials for all things fake dating, courtesy of Kelsi.

Tonight, I'd do everything in my power to research the role of a fake boyfriend.

Four in the morning. That's when I emerged from the cloud of two Hallmark dramas, four of Mrs. Lavoie's gingerbread men, and Kelsi's latest closed-door, fake dating rom-com. I felt both informed and so out of my depth. But at least I understood

Stephanie's costume choice tonight. Hallmark lived for its coat selections and knitwear.

Ryan's text teased my sleep-deprived mind as I fell into bed. *They inevitably fall in love.* I wasn't new to the dating circle, but I had been out of the loop for the last ten years. Ever since... *her*. I tried to shove the thoughts away, but it was hard to do when hampered by exhaustion. The unwelcome thoughts came with more rapid clarity in the darkness than in the daylight hours.

Was I ready to break my dating ban for Stephanie? What if I wrecked our friendship *and* our work dynamic? What if I didn't measure up to what she wanted in a man? I certainly hadn't been enough for Alexis.

I'd met Alexis in my sophomore year of college and had been immediately intrigued by Kelsi's music major friend, a brunette with smoky eyes and a ready smile. We'd hit it off immediately and started dating. It was nice having a friend group and my first real girlfriend. I hadn't had the time or the connections for either in high school. We'd talked futures, kids, dreams, everything, and when graduation rolled around, I'd had a ring ready to go. Only for me to get down on one knee and have her turn me down flat. She'd met someone else. Someone with drive who didn't make her feel less important than his work. Someone who had more vision for his future. Apparently, she had something against my early dreams of entrepreneurship and took the opportunity to inform me she hated the way I got deeply focused on new projects, among other personal quirks. She knew what she wanted. Someone who, bottom line, wasn't me.

"I know what I want my life to look like, Nash," she'd said with pitying eyes and a sardonic smile. "Chester can give me everything you can't."

Code words for: he had money. *What kind of name was Chester anyhow?*

At the time, I was self-sufficient but nowhere near a millionaire. And just like my mom, she decided, without money, I wasn't worth keeping around.

I groaned and flopped over, punching my pillow. How could Alexis still have such a hold on me all these years later? She'd only chomped on my heart and spit it out. No big deal. But I wasn't going to give her the satisfaction of ruining my life again. I'd shifted my earlier business ideas into what eventually became Genesis Marketing, and I had no regrets about that. No regrets about not marrying Alexis either, since she'd shown her true colours. But I still wanted someone in my life. A partner, a friend... Someone more than just a friend. Someone who saw me—needed *me* and not just my money. I wanted Stephanie.

They inevitably fall in love.

They were the last words I heard as I set my alarm with enough time to squeeze in more than three hours of sleep and still be on time to meet Stephanie at the café .

I did the research. We'll discuss the rules—a mandatory conversation for fake dating, I'd gathered—and promise not to fall in love, which was rule number one apparently. Little did she know, it was too late for that. Now, I just needed to convince Stephanie to drop the fake part and take a chance on me for real.

CHAPTER THREE

Stephanie

DUCKING OUT EARLY FROM the party was the nicest gift Nash could have given me. The tightness in my lungs eased the moment I pulled into the driveway of the cute two-bedroom craftsman-style bungalow, currently decked out in classy white Christmas lights, Liz and I shared on a quaint street of retirees. It was close enough to downtown for work, but suburban enough to see the stars. The South Hill was a nice neighbourhood for Spokane, definitely not one I could have afforded solo. Despite having a billionaire father and a millionaire boss, I'd been raised by my middle-class grandparents, who'd instilled simplicity and frugality into my soul.

Besides, who didn't want to room with your practically-a-sister best friend?

I groaned into the frigid night as my full conversation with Nash looped on repeat. I couldn't believe I said all that. Or maybe I could. When I got nervous, I blurted. I was self-aware enough to know this about myself, and that was half the battle, right? Didn't make it any less humiliating. Maybe I'd wake up in the morning and get a redo. Doubtful.

A spicy sweetness hung heavily in the house when I stepped inside. My body relaxed after the hoopla of the party, and I entered full cave-gremlin mode, donning my flannel pajama pants and oversized United States Marine Corps T-shirt before cozying up on the couch in front of the Christmas tree with hot cocoa, my knitting, and a very capable Dan Stevens extolling the difficulties of writing as Charles Dickens in *The Man Who Invented Christmas.* Oh, and the plate of blueberry Danishes *and* gingersnaps Liz had left me while she was out on her date. I had the best friend in the world and a night of pure bliss.

What was *not* blissful was the blaring volume of my alarm the next morning, playing "Christmas in Killarney." I moaned, hitting the snooze button on my phone and proceeding to stare at the ceiling for a few minutes. Part of POTS meant not springing out of bed at the speed of light when the alarm rang unless I had the urge to kiss the floor. Waking up was a ritual, taking several minutes to go from lying down to sitting to eventually standing. I'd been dealing with issues for most of my life, but the early days were scariest when my fainting spells were more common. It was a miracle I hadn't given Nana a heart attack. But she'd rallied behind me as I'd tried everything from special diets to increased salt intake to finally medication, which helped but still left me having to be mindful of my activity levels.

Once I was relatively certain the floor and I wouldn't be making each other's immediate acquaintance, I tugged my Marine Corps hoodie on and headed for the kitchen, following the aroma of fresh coffee. The hoodie was old and almost decrepit in its twenty-year state, but wearing it was like getting a much-needed hug from my active-duty Marine older brother. Gosh, I missed him. Seeing Gabe, Ivy, and the kids was definitely an incentive to spend Christmas at the family cabin. Add Nana and my cousin Hailey, and that was the only reason I was going.

Liz had set the coffee pot last night after she'd marched my half-asleep hot chocolate sugar-spiked self to bed, bless her heart, so there was a steaming pot to indulge in ready by the time I entered the kitchen.

What I had not bargained on was the catastrophic mess. Flour, everywhere. Red blood splatter—wait, that might be raspberry compote—strewn across the sunshine-yellow walls. And every dish we owned between the two of us either in the sink, the open dishwasher, or on the white-and-grey quartz counters.

Then there was Liz. Crisscross applesauce on the oak hardwood floor like the kindergarten teacher she was, looking positively dazed. Her ditsy floral apron, covering an adorable pair of embroidered denim overalls, was drenched with milk. At least that was my hazarded guess.

"Wha... Liz? What's going on?" I kept my tone light despite the inner panic clawing its way up my throat. I wasn't good with messes or chaos—a product of my unstable childhood. Especially this all-encompassing kind of mess. My skin itched to attack it with a barrage of lemon cleaner and a bit of elbow grease. I winced as the compote oozed down the wall. Did raspberries stain paint? *Deep breath.* It was just food, not toxic family-relationship waste that no amount of mopping could contain. I could handle this.

Liz's honey-brown waves were tangled into a messy bun, wrapped with a pink gingham hair scarf, and her green eyes glimmered with unshed tears.

I touched her shoulder, and she started, as if seeing me for the first time. "Are you hurt? Is it Ben? Did someone die?" Instantly, my mind ran inventory on a list of our mutual friends.

That jolted her into motion. She shook her head fiercely, then scooted forward, revealing a smashed vanilla raspberry-compote layered cake littered across the hardwood.

Greasy. Oily. Slippery. Needs soap and water. Where's the cleaner? Why is she just sitting there? The words tumbled through my mind at the speed of light, but I didn't utter them. My issues were just that. Mine. And I wouldn't make Liz's morning any harder.

Liz tipped her head back against the table leg and sighed. "White chocolate. I'm out of white chocolate for the frosting, and I was trying to get this done today."

I stared at her, trying to reconcile the disaster on the floor with the sudden need to have a cake baked. "Why today? Was there a party I missed hearing about?" *Please say no.*

"No. I was stress baking."

"Which caused more stress?" I asked, glancing around.

Liz shot me an unamused look. "Not helping, Steph."

"Right. Sorry." I rubbed my forehead, inwardly bemoaning the delay to my morning caffeine fix. But first things first: solve the mystery of the now-deceased dessert.

"I still need to make the marzipan for the cookies I'm making for you to take to the cabin. I was in a hurry and"—Liz flailed her hands at the smashed cake—"it slipped! Ben's mom has texted twenty times already about wedding opinions, and, Steph, I'm *done*. It's barely 7:30 in the morning! I just wanted to marry the love of my life and have a bunch of cute babies. There's still three and a half months until we walk down the aisle. I did *not* sign up for wedding mania. I always laughed through *Father of the Bride*, but right now, I'm ready to elope!" She was panting by the time she got all the words out, hands braced on her knees.

I eased down beside her, greasy floor and all, and leaned my head against hers in solidarity. "First, Steve Martin is hilarious in that movie, and it's worth laughing over. Maybe not right now, but one day. As for the white chocolate, I'll grab some after my meeting this morning. Wafers, right? Text me a list of anything else you need. I'll even help you make the marzipan. You said I can't mess up something that simple. And about Carey—" I broke off, trying to figure out how to nicely phrase what I needed to say about my bestie's future mother-in-law. How did you describe a woman who most commonly resembled a harpy? It was like she was going for gold on every stereotypical mother-in-law problem. But she was a decent woman to everyone else, which made things ten shades of awkward. "Have you talked to her about it?"

Liz pulled back slightly with a stink eye. Stupid question. Liz was an excellent communicator. As a kindergarten teacher, she had to be.

I sighed and nudged her shoulder. "Talk to Ben. Part of marriage is navigating difficult family members, and there's no better time to start than now. He's your champion and can help invoke some boundaries that need to take place. You're partners in this."

Liz laughed shakily but hugged me. "You should have been a counselor." She side-eyed me. "And maybe take your own advice sometime."

I rolled my eyes. "So you'll talk to Ben, then? And not elope in Cancun over Christmas?" I said, half teasing.

Her laugh was stronger this time. "I'll talk to Ben, and I promise not to elope in Cancun." She held her fingers out in a Mockingjay salute because she was a *Hunger Games* nerd. "Besides, we'd elope in Victoria, not Mexico."

Figures. Since Liz had all but fallen in love with Butchart Gardens the one time in college we'd ferried from Seattle to Vancouver Island, British Columbia, for spring break. "That still your honeymoon plan?"

Liz grinned. "Yup. Just in time for the cherry blossoms, tulips, and dogwood to be in bloom." She sighed dreamily, caught up in her floral daydreams before her face fell. "Provided we actually get married."

"Are you having second thoughts?"

"No." Liz rubbed her forehead and puffed out her cheeks. "Just overwhelmed with all *this* stuff. I know they say it's about the marriage, not the wedding, but I at least thought the wedding planning would be fun." She huffed a sigh. "Foolish child, I was. But I'll talk to Ben, and we'll work it out. It'll be fine." Glancing around the kitchen, she bit her lip as if seeing it for the first time in all its apocalyptic glory. "After I take care of this mess. Gosh, it's bad, Steph. I'm sorry."

"Don't worry about it." I struggled to my feet, bracing a hand on the table for a minute as a wave of dizziness flooded my veins. I shut my eyes, tightly, breathing slowly. *Mornings are the worst.*

Liz grimaced sympathetically as she offered me a steaming mug of coffee, doctored perfectly with cream and sugar.

"Thanks." I accepted the proffered beverage and sipped the creamy liquid. "Perfection."

"Let me tackle this." Liz motioned around the kitchen with a wide flap of her hands. "You go enjoy that and then we can discuss breakfast."

I glanced at the clock. I had a few minutes to sit and enjoy my coffee before jumping in the shower. "Why did you stress bake? Did something happen on your date?"

Liz guffawed and balled up her soiled apron. "No, it was peachy. We went ice skating downtown in Riverfront Park, then Ben took me for steak. Oh! And we drove through the Candy Cane Lane neighbourhoods to look at Christmas lights. Somehow they're even better this year. Hey! You and I should go one night this week before you leave. Maybe tomorrow?"

I plugged in the Christmas tree lights before trudging to the worn leather couch and settling in. "Works for me, but you didn't answer my question." Careful not to spill a drop of liquid gold, which was disappearing far too quickly, I draped the fuzzy red-plaid sherpa blanket over my legs and sighed contentedly as I soaked in the magic of the twinkling lights.

Dishes clanged, and I could have sworn something broke. "I'm fine!" Liz called.

"Liz. Why the cake?"

She poked her head into the living room. "It wasn't anything major, I promise. I just woke up early feeling jittery, and Carey's texts didn't help so I thought, why not bake?"

"Only you," I said fondly, smiling over the rim of my cup.

Laughing, she returned to the kitchen, and I heard the tap running. "Who are you meeting on a Saturday? Isn't it your day off?"

Busted. I hadn't planned on telling Liz about my... proposal until after I'd hashed out the details with Nash. She knew about my crush and would have plenty to say about my no-doubt idiotic scheme. "Just a friend. I'll tell you about it later."

Liz bounced back into view, hands on her hips. "Uh, I know you aren't meeting a friend, because hello? I'm right here."

I arched an eyebrow. "I have other friends, Liz."

"I know, honey. But Danielle's girls are down with the flu, and I talked to Kelsi yesterday, and she didn't mention going out with you. So... who's the hot date?"

"Not a date." I choked on the last sip of coffee and set my cup down on the side table. "I need to grab a shower."

"Steph!" Liz hollered after me, but I just laughed and shut the bathroom door with a decisive click to avoid further questions.

Under no circumstances would I be late to meet Nash... That was, if he decided I wasn't insane and actually showed.

"No, no, no, *NO!* Come on!" I cried out in frustration, giving my steering wheel a slap. The one day I desperately didn't want to be late, my car died. On the road. Thankfully not in the middle of the intersection, like last time. I loved my little silver Toyota Matrix, affectionately named The Flea because, for all her quirks and threats of dying, she was impossible to fully kill.

Plunging out of the warmth of the vehicle into the stinging cold of outside, I muttered threats to the temperamental automotive. "Next time I fill your tank, you only get eighty-seven octane. If you're going to act this bad on ninety-two, I'm just wasting money." The old girl hated the winter cold as much as I did, but I didn't see the need to replace her with a new vehicle for five months of the year. My job paid well but not *that* well.

By the time I got the hood up, fiddled with a few things, and admitted defeat, I was five minutes away from being late to meet Nash. Gabe had ensured I learned car basics, but whatever was going on exceeded my skill set. Time to call an expert.

I punched in Ben's number—perks of having my bestie engaged to a mechanic—and he promised to come take a look at it on his lunch break AND swing by the store to grab the white chocolate for Liz. The gem of a man. *Thank you, Lord, for giving my bestie a mechanic fiancé.* After locking the car, I trekked down the slushy sidewalk. I was now officially late and still fifteen minutes away on foot.

New problem. Did I text Nash and tell him I was running behind? What if he didn't plan on showing and my text guilted him into it? What if—

"Stephanie Addams, pull. Yourself. Together," I scolded, huffing with cold. My fingers numbly fumbled for my phone in my purse because, of course, I hadn't planned on needing gloves.

ME

> I'm so sorry. I'm going to be about 15 minutes late. Something came up, but I'm on my way.

The reply was immediate, like he'd been waiting for me to reach out.

NASH

> No worries. I've saved us a table.

Okay, so he wasn't standing me up. Why did that have my nerves twitching more than if he had?

Normally I'd have enjoyed a jaunt through downtown Spokane, taking the time to fully appreciate the seasonal décor and the whimsical, winter-themed window paintings, which always reminded me of Paisley, one of my other besties, a librarian who moonlighted as an artist. I tried to hurry since I was in danger of turning into a popsicle and didn't have the time to linger, but the window art for Mad Hatter Wonders, my favourite bookshop, was too beautiful to ignore.

I snapped a quick picture of the Who Village and Mt. Crumpet and shot it off to Paisley.

ME

> Missing you. *kissy face* This should totally be your next library window painting.

PAISLEY

> Ha! Too bad my boss would totally take it personally. Miss you, too. With all my grinchy heart.

ME

> We both know you're Cindy Lou, and Juliet is the Grinch.

PAISLEY

> Haha, truth! Love you.

Paisley and Juliet, who completed our best friend quartet, had each other and their husbands in Serenity Springs, Idaho, and Liz and I had each other here in Spokane. I missed the days of us living together in the same town, but that hadn't happened since college, and I didn't have time to linger at the windows with my thoughts any longer. Nash awaited, and I was without proper winter attire. The only thing going for me was that I'd had the sense to wear boots, so my feet, if nothing else, were warm. But I nearly cried with relief when the faded royal-blue of Maisie's Café appeared, a beacon in a sea of red brick, as I stumbled around the corner onto W 1st Avenue.

Finally, the end was in sight. I flung the door open, letting the warm air and yeasty cinnamon-bun aroma wash over me. Now to find my new fake boyfriend.

Chapter Four

Nash

Panic wasn't a familiar feeling for me. But when ten o'clock rolled around and Maisie's bustled with the usual midmorning rush with no Stephanie in sight, I got a rapid-fire introduction to the emotion.

Stephanie was a rarity. The woman was a colour-coded machine of capability. If I'd had a PA as competent as Stephanie earlier in my career, I could have been a millionaire much sooner. Smart, capable, and steady under pressure—my ideal assistant. Foreseeing needs and effortlessly working behind the scenes. She was quiet and didn't linger around the water cooler. If I had to hazard a guess, she probably dealt with some sort of anxiety she kept under wraps. But in a business setting, she was a rock, levelheaded and... Yeah, she was gorgeous. I was only human after all. Point being, in our two-year history, her being late had never entered the realm of possibility.

Relief tasted sweet when my phone chimed with a text, and her apology about being fifteen minutes late eased the nerves in my stomach. I wasn't sure which had me more terrified—that Stephanie had never been late before or if I didn't want to admit to myself I was afraid she'd back out of needing a fake boyfriend. Of needing me.

Taking advantage of the few minutes I had to wait, I shot off a quick text to Emmett. He was head of finance at Genesis and was one of the only employees who missed the office party last night.

ME

How are the girls feeling this morning?

EMMETT

Two out of three ain't bad. I've never seen kids get the flu like dominos. One after the other within twelve hours.

Projectile vomit is something no one pre-pares you for as a parent.

ME

You are dangerously close to being TMI.

Need me to swing by with anything?

EMMETT

We're good, but thanks.

Bummer about missing the party last night.

I can feel your devastation from here. *eye roll*

Let me know if you need something. Give my love to the girls.

Thanks, man.

When a frazzled blur stumbled through the doors, I glanced up quickly and slid my phone back into the inner pocket of my coat draped over the chair next to me.

Relief mixed with regret flashed across Stephanie's wind-chapped face as we locked eyes, and I stood quickly.

"I'm so sorry," she gushed, her boots squeaking on the tile as she hurried towards me. The rush of words stopped when I tugged out the chair opposite me for her, and she glanced curiously between me and the chair. "Oh, thanks."

It wasn't the first time I'd done that. My Texan mama, for all her flaws, had raised a gentleman after all. I cleared my throat, trying to dislodge the uncomfortable lump that always rose when I thought of my mother. I'd been out on my own for fifteen years and hadn't seen her in person in the last decade, but it still hurt to think of her.

Once Stephanie slid into the chair, the flurry of words continued. "You didn't have to wait. I'm sorry I was so long."

I resumed my seat opposite her, waving aside the apology. "Don't worry about it. Did something happen?" I tried for levity, adding, "You've never been late before. Is this a fatal flaw I should know about your nonwork life?"

Redness that wasn't from the cold flamed her face. Oops, I wasn't trying to embarrass her. "I... I had car trouble and had to walk," she said.

Trying not to fluster her further, I said quietly, "You could have called. I'd have picked you up."

She shook her head fiercely. "It's fine. Have you already ordered?"

Okay, we were moving on. "Not yet. How does a peppermint mocha sound?"

"Perfect, but you don't have to—"

"Steph." I smiled at her. "Just sit and catch your breath for a minute. I've got this." Then I winked at her. From her slack-jawed reaction maybe I shouldn't have, but the flush of her cheeks when I did it last night was too tempting to avoid getting a repeat performance. Giving the table a quick rap with my knuckles, I strode towards the counter.

"What can I getcha?" The goth teen behind the register loudly snapped her gum.

Before I could give her my order, a scolding voice hollered from the back storeroom. "Jazz, what did I tell you about chewing gum on the clock?" It was Maisie, the owner and queen croissant maker this side of France. And she must have had bat-level hearing to notice the bubble blowing over the hiss of the steamer and the upbeat rendition of "Deck the Halls" playing over the speakers.

Maisie's silver head popped into view, nose scrunched. "Take his order, then spit it out. And don't let it happen again."

Jazz ducked her chin, so her jet-black hair hid half her face. "Sorry, Ms. Maisie," she mumbled.

"It's like dealing with toddlers," Maisie muttered, giving me a wave before disappearing back into the storeroom.

"One peppermint mocha with extra whipped cream and an Americano. Both for here. And a cinnamon bun and a chocolate croissant." Pulling out my wallet, I paid the bill, then slid a twenty into the tip jar when Jazz turned away to make the drinks. I'd been raised by a single mother and knew a thing or two about going without because money was tight. And while I knew Maisie's paid well, generosity never hurt anyone.

As I walked back to our table with our drinks, I could see Stephanie had discarded her burgundy wool coat over the back of her chair, exposing a cream-and-forest-green Fair Isle sweater. She was focused, hunched over a black leather journal complete with colour-coded tabs I recognized as her notebook. She never tackled a meeting without it, but her expression was decidedly less frazzled than when she'd walked in. Work-mode Stephanie had entered the building, and, attractive as she was, it cooled my ardor when I remembered this wasn't really a date but a business meeting. As desperately as I wished it could be a date.

Stephanie smiled up at me as I set the peppermint mocha in front of her. Taking a sip, she hummed with pleasure. "Thank you. How did you know what drink I wanted?"

Because I paid way too much attention to her. Not willing to admit that out loud and sound creepy, I cleared my throat and twisted my cup on the table. "I've never known you *not* to get a peppermint mocha at Christmastime. The taste of Christmas in a cup, you said."

She bit her bottom lip, distracting me, but I forced myself not to focus on it. "Guess that's one thing we can mark off the list of things we need to know about each other. Our coffee orders." She slashed a line through one of the columns on her spreadsheet with a flourish. "You always go for the Americano."

"Always prepared, aren't you?"

Her smile froze like glass. "Are you sure you're okay with this? We haven't even discussed what *this* is. You could hate—"

"I'm here, aren't I?" When she didn't relax, I continued. "Tell you what. Lay it all on me. The good, the bad, the hideous secrets. Then when you've given me every ugly detail, I'll tell you I'm still in. Sound good?"

Her shoulders dropped from their battle-ready position, and she fiddled with her pen. Always black. Always a ballpoint. Classy.

Just like her.

"Here ya go." Jazz slid the two plates of pastries onto the table. Sans bubble blowing.

"Thank you." I nodded to her, and she offered a lazy salute before sauntering back to the counter.

"You didn't have to do that," Stephanie said, eyeing the frosted bun.

"It was purely selfish," I admitted, picking up the croissant. "I didn't want to eat alone, and I've been dying for one of Maisie's pastries."

"You've got quite the sweet tooth for a man who drinks his coffee like an ashtray."

"You got experience with drinking ashtrays, Steph?"

"Forget it. Thank you for this." She gestured to the bun, then fiddled with her pen again. Contemplating. "All right." She sipped her drink and glanced out the broad front windows overlooking the bustle of holiday shoppers milling around W 1st Avenue, seeming to gather courage.

"Hey," I said quietly, trying to set her at ease. "I already know who your dad is. Everything else should be uphill from there, right?"

She snorted, which was hilariously adorable. "You have no idea."

CHAPTER FIVE

Stephanie

I BLEW OUT A breath. Nash was being entirely too accommodating about this, but also SO. NICE. I wasn't used to that from guys. Or rather, I wasn't used to niceness without strings attached. Particularly when it came to possessing a last name like mine. My one and only boyfriend thought I was his ticket to a job at Nova. He had no idea my father and I weren't on good terms. Involving Nash like this might blow up in my face and maybe I'd lose my job and have to figure out another way to pay rent—no big deal—but I was going to risk it all. Wow, I sounded like a bad TV host.

I fiddled with the handle of the snowflake-etched pottery mug and admired the Christmas tree in the corner. Here went nothing. "My family's a mess. I'm sure you've heard the gossip about Hiram Addams's latest woman. I have five older half siblings, all from different mothers. We're all scattered across the US, but Christmas is the one thing that brings us together every two or three years.

How much of that is familial love and how much is placating our father in hopes of not being written out of his will is anyone's guess."

Nash raised an eyebrow but said nothing as he took a bite of his croissant. He knew my dad in a business capacity, so this couldn't be a huge surprise to him.

"I'm talking a five-day family vacation at a cabin in Jackson, Wyoming. Skiing, Christmas, family reunion, the whole nine yards wrapped into one holiday event."

Nash nodded and sipped his Americano, looking completely unfazed. "I can ski."

Of course he can. "Well, I can't but... that's beside the point. My family is insane at Christmas. There will be screaming children, no less than six arguments about, well, anything, ridiculously spiked eggnog you need to avoid at all costs. Oh, and assume every adult on the premise—well, except for Nana, my cousin Hailey, my brother Gabe, and his wife Ivy—will hate your guts on sight. Because, you know, I work for the enemy."

Nash blinked before a smile curved his lips, exposing that southwest dimple through his five o'clock shadow. Like he forgot to shave this morning. "Sounds like you're trying to scare me off, Miss Addams."

Nervous laughter bubbled through me. "More like giving you a chance to gracefully bow out of this insanity. There's no shame in running for the hills. Seriously, I have no illusion of this going well, and I wish I didn't have to go. But family is family."

His gaze steadily held mine. "I'm not running, Steph. Whatever you need, I'm here."

Ugh, his words did something to my insides, and I liked the sound of my nickname on his lips way too much. I smoothed the paper in front of me to tamp down the flutters in my stomach before sliding it across to him. "This is the itinerary for the week of December twenty-fourth through twenty-eighth. We'd have to leave early on the twenty-third to travel since it's a nine-hour drive. I've never bothered to fly since it's so close, and it's a hassle to have someone pick me up on the other side, but... does that work?"

Nash silently scanned the paper before he smiled softly. "You know my schedule better than I do. But yes, this is fine."

"Did you have Christmas plans? I shouldn't have brought this up without asking."

He shook his head slowly as if measuring his words. "I don't have family around, so usually I spend holidays with Emmett's or Ryan's family. They share custody of me like I'm a child in a divorce case." He laughed lightly, but tension lingered around his eyes. "But they'll understand this year. In fact, they might love that Uncle Nash isn't there to rile the kids. With them both married, it'll be nice not to be the odd man out for a change."

Yeah, I knew the feeling, and I wasn't sure why he hadn't been snatched up already. Besides the tall, dark, rich, and handsome vibe he had going, he was incredibly kind and attentive. Whether you were a business partner or a waitress, he treated you the same. Don't think I didn't notice the twenty he slipped in the tip jar, despite how discreet he was. That was just Nash.

"So, the terms of this arrangement," I squeaked out before hastily sipping my drink. Man, that was good. "To be fully upfront, I don't have a lot of dating experience, so I'm not sure I'll be any good at this, but..." My words trailed off, and I wasn't exactly sure where I was heading with them in the first place.

Nash touched my hand, strangling the pen. Oh. I slackened my death grip, but he didn't move his hand. "Whatever makes you comfortable, okay?"

"I'm not gonna sleep with you," I blurted.

Nash jerked back, eyes wide, and I realized I'd never seen him flustered before. It'd be cute if I wasn't about to perish from embarrassment.

I groaned. What was wrong with me? Could I sink through the floor immediately? Why had I gone straight to *that*? There were a hundred different alternatives I could have landed on besides that. I needed to channel calm, cool, collected Steph, not the usual anxious mess I presented outside of my work environment. This was *just* work after all. A business arrangement. The repayment of a favour for planning the party.

"I..." Nash spluttered before getting a hold of himself. "No. I'm not that sort of man and you've never struck me as that sort of woman. I have standards and convictions. True, I've dated in the past, but it's been a long time. And that's a line I never intend to cross until I've married my wife."

My face burned with the heat of a thousand candles, and I couldn't believe I was actually having this conversation with Nash Prescott in the middle of a coffee shop. If it wouldn't draw so much attention, I'd fan my furnace of a face. Instead, I swallowed a too-large swig of my drink to fortify myself and stared out the window for a solid minute. *Breathe for a minute and focus. This is business. You're good with business. Don't make it personal.*

The hiss of the steamers and the squeak of wet shoes on the tile floors grounded me. So did the taunting smell of the cinnamon bun, sitting untouched in front of me. My stomach churned too much to even attempt a nibble right now. When I trusted myself enough to not blurt out anything else embarrassing, I said, "All right then. That's out of the way." I straightened the napkin beside my snowflake mug and sighed. "Most of my family members aren't believers and don't share those convictions, so they will assume that we're…" I gestured vaguely between us. "You know. But I'll have Nana make sure there's an extra room for you."

Nash nodded, and there was no mistaking the swath of red creeping across his cheeks. But the man had the audacity to hold back a smile by the way his lips twitched. "And how about PDA?" He extended his hand across the table to me, palm up. "According to my research, it's a necessary thing to sell the story."

Slowly, I slid my hand to meet his, and his thumbs brushed my knuckles. I arched an eyebrow even as the light touch threatened to short-circuit my brain. "Research?" I croaked. *Smooth, Steph.* I swallowed hard. What in the sugarplum fairy castles was in our coffee? Was it spiked? Because I was jittery and warm and ready to follow him barefoot in the snow with the look he was giving me. This was ridiculous. I'd kept a tight leash on my emotions for the last two years, and now five minutes in his presence like this was going to be the death of me. I was a brilliant actor when it came to hiding my feelings, but allowing the *real* to come out and merely pretend it was fake? In front of my family? Could I do it?

"Yes, research." Amusement curved Nash's lips. "You think I was going to do this unprepared? I'm going to be the best fake boyfriend you've ever had. You won't want to get rid of me."

"Only fake boyfriend." As for not getting rid of him... Forever sounded good to me. *Not going there!*

Nash grinned boyishly, eyes crinkling behind his adorable glasses. Had I mentioned how much I loved those glasses? "Semantics. This okay?" he asked quietly, still running his thumbs over my knuckles.

I cleared my throat. "Yup." Oh boy, I sounded like a prepubescent junior higher being asked out to prom. "Holding hands, hugging, it's fine. As for kissing..." Was it just me or was it getting hot in here? I tried to discreetly pinch the front of my sweater for airflow. Maybe we should have grabbed an outside table for this conversation. Forget the below-freezing temperatures and the lightly spitting snowflakes. I was about to combust.

His mouth twitched, but he waited for me to continue—clearly enjoying this way too much to bother helping me out.

"If it's needed. When we're in public," I clarified. "I know how fake dating works. Particularly because my family is crazy obsessed with mistletoe. It's everywhere. Be sure to watch out for Great-Aunt Edith, especially after she's hit the eggnog. Just..." I heaved another sigh, then groaned and leaned my forehead against my balled fist. "It's been a while, okay? I... I've only had one real boyfriend before. So..." Anika's story about the guy who threw up after I kissed him in high school flashed through my brain in 4K clarity. Not relevant, but still, it messed with my confidence. "Forget it. Is there anything you want to add for rules?"

I'd shocked him into silence because it took two throat bobs for him to recover himself. My kissing history wasn't something I was ashamed of. Apart from the disastrous kissing challenge, I didn't kiss until a third date, and in light of my two-date only curse, I'd only had one of those—who turned into the aforementioned boyfriend for a month. Until he'd hit me with the "I need to take some time to work on my relationship with God" line after his job aspiration to work at Nova didn't pan out, and he dumped me. Only to have a blonde on his arm by the end of the month. Yeah. And Jarrett the creep didn't count. If no one had wanted to kiss me—or simply want me for myself—there must be something wrong with me.

Samantha's words echoed from last night, and I glanced out the window to keep Nash from seeing the fine sheen pooling in my eyes. *She's not the kind of woman any man wants.* No. I was the woman nobody wanted. Not even my parents.

"You're in charge here," Nash said at last, his low timbre drawing me out of my spiraling thoughts. "I've got you."

His protective words smoothed the sting of Samantha's. *I've got you.* I smiled before adding, "Nana will be the hardest to convince. And maybe Hailey." Not that Gabe and Ivy were going to be a walk in the park either, but on the scale of nosiness, Nana and Hailey were cut from the same cloth. They treated it like an extreme sport.

"Why's that?"

"Because I talk to them almost every week, and I never mentioned we were dating. I mean! Fake dating." *Get your head in the game, girl.* "Fake dating because this isn't real. Of course."

Something flickered across his face, but it disappeared before I could name it. "So, none of them know about me?"

Uh... more like they knew about him as the object of my crush. They knew too much. I cleared my throat. "They know about you as my boss, just not about... us."

Nash's grin widened, his mouth twitching mischievously. "Us," he practically purred. "I like the sound of that."

My eyeballs were ready to fall into my lap. He... what? He was either a fantastic actor or... nah, he definitely wasn't into me. That'd be ridiculous. Fantastic actor it was.

"My turn?" he asked with a smile that was dangerous for my health.

"Go ahead." Picking up the fork, I prodded the plump cinnamon roll. Maisie never skimped on the icing.

"I'm proposing that we not fake date."

My fork clattered, and my jaw dropped. "What?" After that whole conversation and my life story—at least part of it—was hung out to dry, he thought, "*Let's not fake date?*"

Nash held up a hand, accurately reading my internal freak out. "What if we actually dated? For real?"

"I... you... Why would we do that? That literally breaks Rule Number One: don't fall in love." I'd already broken that rule, but semantics.

"I'm not hearing a no," Nash teased. "I'm not a huge fan of lying for one. So, what if starting now we dated for real. That is... if you consider me someone you would date?"

"I... I..." *I would. I have. I do.* I could say any of those things and mean it. Hope fizzled in my chest like champagne bubbles. It was everything I wanted. But those niggles of doubt from last night were louder, and my knee-jerk reaction to panic kicked into gear. "I'm not your type."

His espresso eyes sharpened slightly. "You have no idea what I want, Steph, and it's you. I know our work dynamic brings a level of complexity to this relationship, and I'd never ask you to do something you're uncomfortable with. But if you're willing, can we try this for real?"

I chewed on a mouthful of the decadent pastry, breathing in the aroma of coffee and spices to ground my parading nerves. "A holiday trial run full of Christmas magic before the bubble pops?"

Nash grinned. "Getting into the spirit of the season, I see." He leaned back in his chair, totally at ease.

I was upturning his holiday, and he sat there like it was the best gift I could have given him. Meanwhile my insides were shuddering with electric shocks of anxiety knotting my stomach. "I... I'm not sure," I whispered. Was it everything I'd ever wanted? Yes. But was I brave enough to reach out and grab it? *He's out of your league. He'll leave. Everyone does.*

Nash's smile flickered, but he nodded. "The offer stands. Think about it, and if you change your mind, let me know." His throat bobbed as he took another sip of coffee, his expression clearing.

Like I hadn't just dragged my feet through his offer of real dating. What was wrong with me?

Before I could whisper my apology, he was already moving on. "I'll pick you up on Friday morning then, yeah? We can play twenty questions of getting to know your fake boyfriend on the drive up. You said Jackson's nine hours from here?" He fished his phone out of his coat pocket and tapped a few things on the screen. "That's not bad. We can stop in Butte for lunch. It's about halfway."

He wasn't offended? If he was, he was hiding it well. But I knew Nash and that wasn't his style. He wasn't a brooder. And he was planning the route? My planner heart fell in love a little harder. Theoretically. My mind instantly started racking up the cost of gas and the current undriveableness of my car. "I'll pay you for the gas, or we can take my car. Uh... if it's fixed by then."

Nash smiled serenely. "Don't worry about it. I'll pick you up."

Just like it was a date.

He sipped his drink then cocked his head to study me. "Wait, so this is an extended Addams family holiday?"

I winced, not missing the emphasis on my surname. It had been the brunt of jokes for decades. And the mirth flickered in Nash's eyes as he draped an arm over the chair next to him. If it were me sitting there... nope, not going there.

"Any relation to the actual Addams family?"

"You've met my father. What do you think?" I snorted. "Word of advice, my family drama makes Morticia and company look like a cakewalk."

Nash grinned, dark eyes crinkling behind his lenses, dimple deepening with amusement. "Bring it on, sweetheart."

I shouldn't have liked the sound of *sweetheart* coming from his mouth with that rare Texas drawl he let slip out as much as I did, but it was still echoing in my ears days later.

CHAPTER SIX

Stephanie

WHEN I'D COME HOME from my meeting with Nash, Liz had the kitchen sparkling and her baking accomplished, except the marzipan. Because I'd offered to help, she'd naturally saved it for me. I didn't even like the stuff, but she said it was too easy of a recipe for me to ruin, and it was for *my* family get-together anyways. Apparently Liz was making Christmas cookie deals with Nana behind my back, and I got saddled transporting the goods.

Cookies completed, Liz proceeded to drag every detail of the meeting from me while I unearthed my suitcase from storage. Except the offer of it being real. I didn't know how to tell her that yet.

"Girl! Are you serious?" The deafening shrieks accompanying Liz's question left my ears ringing. "You asked him to fake date you? What were you thinking?"

"Oh, I don't know. Somewhere between *don't pass out* and *how sweet, he's sitting on the floor with me*, it just popped out."

Instant concern bathed Liz's face. "You had another episode?"

"Almost," I clarified. "I didn't faint so it's fine."

I stared at the clothing hurricane in front of me on my bed. Usually, I threw what I needed into a suitcase and called it good. But the idea of going with my fake... or not-so-fake boyfriend if I agreed to Nash's proposal had me second guessing every wardrobe choice. Were leopard print pj's too much? Better stick with the red plaid ones instead. Not that Nash would see them. *But what about Christmas morning?* I tossed the folded pair into the suitcase. I needed Christmassy.

Wait. I dug through my drawer until I found a pair of flannel pants with llamas in Santa hats, singing fa-la-la-la-llama. Perfect. They'd been a gift from my cousin Hailey last Christmas, and she'd get a kick out of my actually wearing them.

I still had nearly a week before we left. Was it too soon to pack? Never.

"Take another suitcase," Liz counseled from where she was lying on my bedroom floor, her legs propped up against the wall. Apparently, there were health benefits attached to the position?

"I don't want to take another suitcase," I grunted as I wrestled the zipper around the first corner. Victory would be mine. "What was I thinking?"

"Answer me this. Does your reluctance to take the second case have anything to do with the very handsome, very attractive Nash Prescott, your newly hired fake boyfriend?"

The zipper snagged, and I groaned before turning to her, hands on my hips. "First, handsome and attractive are the same thing. Second, it has everything to do with him. And third... Was there a third thing? Oh, right, I did not hire him. That makes it sound ten shades more sleazy than it is. There is no sleaziness happening."

"Oh, honey, you've got it bad." Liz's face—upside down at this angle—softened with compassion. "Are you sure this is a good idea? You've had a crush on him forever."

I huffed in a breath and gave my suitcase a small kick. It was an absolutely terrible idea that my anxiety-addled brain blurted out, thanks to the cocktail of insecurity mixed up for me by Hiram's text and my former childhood friend's words. I didn't need validation from a man or even need a relationship to be fulfilled. I loved my life... most of the time. But I couldn't go back because... well, having Nash's full attention like that was heady. "It's not a crush, okay?" I finally said. "That sounds so juvenile."

"Yeah, well, the powers that be haven't come up with a different term for pining over someone at nearly thirty, so we're working with what we've got."

I rolled my eyes. "Fine, I'll bring the second suitcase. He can think I'm a diva all he wants."

Liz dropped her legs from the wall and rolled over to face me, chin propped in her hands. "You're not a diva, and if he thinks that, he's an idiot. But seriously, Steph, are you going to be okay with this being fake?"

Folding my favourite mulberry cable-knit sweater, I pasted on a smile. "Of course. I've worked for the man for two years. I'm an expert actor." *Lies.*

"Except this time, you have to *show* you're in love with him, not hide your feelings." Liz was quiet for a moment, which was a rarity for her. "Why are you really doing this? Are you lonely? Or did something happen? Because you're not the desperate sort or rash like me."

Stephanie is a lot. The words reverberated through my skull with so much force I sucked in a breath.

"Steph?" Liz popped up vertically, concern lacing her tone.

"It's hard to explain." I chanced a glance at my laptop stowed on my dresser where *White Christmas* was playing. I had about thirty-seven seconds to spill my guts before Danny and Bing danced their way across the screen lip-syncing "Sisters," which Liz and I would, of course, belt along to. It was a leftover tradition from college when the four of us—Liz, Juliet, Paisley, and I—would watch it together before winter break after finals.

Liz gave me the stink eye before jabbing the space bar, freezing Danny's face in an unnatural contortion. Pausing the movie *before* our favourite song number. This was serious. "Spill," she demanded with all the ferocity she needed to wrangle kindergarteners all day.

"Nash asked to date me. For real," I whispered, clutching a third knit sweater to my chest. Was there such a thing as too much knitwear? I thought not.

"He did?!" Liz bounced on the bed with a squeal, knocking a cascade of fuzzy socks over the edge. "Steph, that's amazing! You—"

"I said I wasn't sure!" I blurted out, shoulders sagging. "Because this came from Hiram last night." I slipped my phone from my jeans pocket and opened my messages.

"I thought we weren't replying to him." Liz's face puckered like she caught a whiff of roadside carrion.

I smiled faintly at the way she included herself. "We weren't supposed to but just read it."

Liz scanned the message and let out a strangled scream. "Seriously?" She punched my single throw pillow for emphasis. "He bullied you into answering by threatening you with that cretin who tried to assault you?" Jumping up, she paced my cream rug.

"I thought Nash was better than Jarrett," I tried to joke, but it sounded hollow. I sagged down onto my cream comforter. "At least Nash and I have terms for kissing instead of being cornered in a dark hallway."

Liz propped her hands on her hips, staring me down. "You could have asked me to come. Ben would have understood."

"No," I said firmly. "You guys need this, and I need to figure out my own mess." Liz had come with me to the cabin three times already, which was more than any best friend should sign up for. Besides, this was her first Christmas with Ben as a couple.

Liz pursed her lips. "So you're doing this to appease your dad? Showing up with his rival as your romantic partner is a weird way to do it."

"I'm not," I said through gritted teeth. But a sliver of me knew she had hit the truth. I'd been chasing Hiram's approval for decades. Then I told her the rest. About Samantha and Anika's conversation in the breakroom last night. My own doubts and fears.

Liz didn't interrupt the tidal wave of various ramblings I poured out, but when it was all out, she wrapped her arms around me and squeezed. "I want to smack that so-called friend of yours so hard she won't see straight. What even happened between you two for her to be so nasty? By the time I met you, she was already a piece of work."

I laughed at her violent wishes. Liz had a protective streak Mississippi River wide, and I'd almost pity Anika if she got caught in her wake. "I wish I knew. One day we were okay, the next, she just... ignored me and turned our mutual friends against me." I shrugged as if it didn't matter. But truth be told, the events of over a decade ago still bothered me. If I'd had closure, it wouldn't have hurt so bad, but the never knowing why I wasn't worth staying friends with... Well, it didn't do great things for my mental health. Just one more person who decided I wasn't worth sticking around for. "High school sucked until I met you."

"Right back atcha, sister." Liz plopped down beside me on the bed.

"But what if Samantha and Anika are right?" I whispered, tugging at my sweater cuff. "What if I am too much? I have a ton of baggage, and I'm working on it, truly. I thought I was past this, you know? But then—"

"Steph." Liz's tone sharpened, and her eyes were serious. "Don't give their words credence over the voices of those who know and love you best. You're not too much. Your standards aren't too high. If anything, you could expect a little more from people. I'm saying that. Me, Liz Kelso. Your Nana says that. And most importantly God says that. You're exactly the person He created you to be. Growing like the rest of us but made perfectly in His image. He likes you as you are—loves you. So do I. Don't let their bitter words rob you of a peace their acceptance could never give."

I leaned my head on her shoulder. "Thank you."

"Of course." Liz paused. "And do you want it to be real? With you and Nash?"

The *yes* was thick on my tongue, but I couldn't force it out. So, like a coward, I shrugged and stared at my hands. "I want... I just..." Past memories flashed to life with rapid clarity.

My parents had divorced when I was five, and Hilary—I didn't even remember calling her Mom—left without a second thought. I hadn't seen her since. Hiram had shuffled me off to my paternal grandparents in Denver and became a passing phantom, only showing up for Christmas or birthdays, if he remembered. I was the youngest of the Addams brood, and while I loved my grandparents, that early abandonment had shaped my world. My earliest memories were of my parents arguing. Screaming loudly one night in particular.

Hoping for some comfort, I'd crept into my oldest half sister Zoe's room, since it was her weekend to visit Hiram. But Zoe had just scowled at me when she popped off her headphones at my interruption, and with all the jaded wisdom of a thirteen-year-old child of divorce said, "All adults fight. Get used to it. Everyone leaves eventually."

Not the comfort my five-year-old heart wanted to hear, but I'd believed her. Despite the love of my grandparents and brother and sister-in-law, I'd spent the next twenty-three years waiting for the other shoe to drop. If the ones who were supposed to love me the most left, why would anyone else want to stay?

"Oh, Steph." There was understanding and a little disappointment in Liz's tone, which hurt, but I couldn't blame her. With a little sigh, she gave me a final squeeze before hip bumping me.

I hated letting my fears win, but I wasn't brave enough to open myself up to that kind of hurt. Nash Prescott didn't strike me as the leaving kind. *But everyone leaves eventually. It's safer this way.*

"Now fill the second case and don't overthink it. I'll be praying for you all week because I'm worried about your heart." Liz handed me a folded pair of jeans, a small frown wrinkling her forehead.

You and me both, sister. But as I finished packing, we belted out "Sisters" (with choreography, of course) and the world seemed a little less dark.

CHAPTER SEVEN

Text Thread

LATER THAT NIGHT…

NASH

You mentioned skiing… is it something you don't do or can't?

STEPHANIE

Let's just say a bad ski instructor as a child, a propensity for fainting from low blood pressure, and a run-in with a hyperactive puppy scarred my ten-year-old-self.

NASH

Noted. Would you be open to a different instructor sans puppy?

STEPHANIE

No promises, but maybe? I'm not known for my balance. As you are now aware.

And before I forget, ugly sweaters are a must for Christmas Eve, and Christmas Day dinner is formal, nearly black tie.

NASH

We talking tux and bow tie?

STEPHANIE

Most of the guys just do a suit and tie. Maybe your charcoal one with the pinstripes?

NASH

I won't read into the fact you know my closet so well. *winky face*

STEPHANIE

eye roll Bring whatever you want. Do you need me to find you an ugly sweater? I can add it to my list for Monday.

NASH

I'm not your boss. I'm your fake boyfriend, Steph. I'll handle it.

And shouldn't a boyfriend know what colour dress his girlfriend is wearing so his tie will match? *smirk*

Why do you sound so gleeful? I'm the one benefiting from this arrangement, and you get the short end of the stick.

Time spent with you is never a downside. It's an upgrade.

My dress is red. See you Monday.

CHAPTER EIGHT

Nash

MONDAY MORNING, THE OFFICE buzzed with the last week of work energy before the holidays. I couldn't say how productive those hours were for anyone, including myself, because Stephanie's desk was in my line of sight when I glanced out my open office door.

Late morning, I slid off my glasses and rubbed my eyes. After three straight hours of staring at the computer, I was desperate for scenery not burning into my retinas.

"Knock, knock." Stephanie poked her head in the half-open door and frowned. "What's the matter?"

Perfect timing. I popped my glasses back on and gestured at the computer. "Just some light reading."

Approaching my desk, Stephanie set down my black coffee. Like she did every day like clockwork. But then she surprised me with a new move. Coming around to my side of the desk, she leaned down slightly to view my screen, her hazel eyes scanning the news article with speed.

I remained where I was. Her shoulder brushed mine as she hovered over my back. With our height difference, we were nearly cheek to cheek. A delicate whiff of vanilla filled my nose, familiar and sophisticated. Wholly Stephanie.

"Are you worried about Nova Designs?" Stephanie said at last, pulling me from the vanilla haze of my imagination.

"Hmm? Oh. I don't know." I sighed, leaning back in my chair as she perched on the edge of my desk. "I try to keep tabs on them. More so than our other competitors, and this article resurfaced about the allegations of them stealing information from SkyLark. No way to prove it as there wasn't a paper trail, but SkyLark was planning their launch for three weeks after Nova swept in with theirs."

It hadn't been the first time such allegations had followed Nova either. Nova Designs, headed by none other than Hiram Addams, Stephanie's dad, was our biggest national competitor in the marketing world. Speculations, hearsay, and accusations of bribery littered the papers when it came to winning bids on projects. Nearly as much as the gossip magazines were filled with Hiram's latest conquest on the potential marriage market. His name had been attached to nearly every prominent socialite or actress between the ages of twenty-five and fifty.

"And it feels like more than coincidence." Stephanie's forehead wrinkled in a frown. "I wouldn't put it past him. But it's hard to take precautions against a ghost if there's no proof. Are you worried about interference with the spring launch?"

"I don't know. It's just a weird feeling." I groaned, scrubbing a hand over my jaw. Stephanie's insight and honesty were things I loved about her. She was an excellent listener and had a way of drawing me out of my head, helping me see the big picture. More than once she'd served as my sounding board, even if it wasn't in her immediate job description. But I valued her thoughts, and she had good instincts.

Oblivious to my ponderings, she smiled wryly and nudged the coffee towards me.

That smile was a gut punch after her reluctance to agree to real dating. But I could be patient and play the long game. Prove to her I could be the guy for her. That didn't mean it hadn't stung when she shot me down, though. But I hoped it was more fear than repulsion that made her hesitant. That it wasn't me she was against dating, but the dating concept itself that had her glitching. For half a second, the moment in the café had taken me back to Alexis's rejection. *But Stephanie isn't her. Her reaction wasn't artificial; she was genuinely nervous.*

Taking a sip, I sighed, refocusing on the present conversation. "It doesn't matter what I think. Vigilance is key." I drummed my fingers on the desk absently. "We've all worked too hard for me to let him ever sweep in here and try to pull one over on us."

"We won't let that happen," she announced with a nod, something like anger burning in her eyes.

I appreciated her confidence and loyalty. I had no reason to suspect Hiram of interfering in our upcoming software program launch as there were no hints of it. But having those articles pop up this morning gnawed at my gut in a way I couldn't shake.

Stephanie rose. "Five minutes till your eleven o'clock." At the door, she paused. "I dropped your dry cleaning off this morning. Anything else before your meeting?"

I shook my head. "Thanks, Stephanie. I should be done by lunch."

"I'll have it waiting for you."

I swiveled back to my computer and pulled up the virtual link for my meeting. As a marketing firm, we worked with businesses to give them a polished branding package and presence. But there were plenty of small businesses and entrepreneurs who weren't looking for our big corporate packages and wanted a small-scale approach, which was where our new software program slated for spring came in. It fit a small budget and offered creators more supportive do-it-yourself and design options than were available to them anywhere else on the current market. Kelsi, Ryan's wife, had been the one to propose the idea over dinner one night last year. As an independent author, she was responsible for all her own marketing and design, which was a big job on top of writing. She'd test run the program and all but begged me to make this a reality. The balls were all in motion, and after the new year, we'd head into our final phase before launching in early March.

Hovering my cursor over the *Join Meeting* button, I rolled my shoulders. It was go time.

I LOGGED OFF JUST after noon and stretched with a groan. We were on track and according to plan.

"Hey, Stephanie, is the big man in?"

I froze when I heard the familiar upbeat voice. *He wouldn't.*

"Ryan, Emmett, hey. Yeah, he's back there now."

Apparently, they both would. I heard her shuffle a few things on her desk, no doubt checking my calendar like the diligent worker she was. She'd know I had finished my meeting.

"He's free. Head on back. Oh, and take him this, will you? I'm out for lunch."

Usually, she would have paged me and asked if I was taking visitors, but she knew they were my best friends. Why wouldn't I want to see them? And it was my lunch break after all.

Except they were the last people I wanted to see right now because I'd been avoiding their texts all weekend like the mature man I was. Not for any particular reason, but I wasn't sure how to act around them after my meeting with Stephanie on Saturday. I wasn't egotistical enough to think she'd jump at my offer to date for real just because I'd asked. But I had thought there was something there between us and that she might at least consider it. And she *was* considering it—she'd been uncertain, not given me a flat-out rejection. That was something.

My door flung open, and Ryan marched in, grinning like the Cheshire cat himself. He broke every stereotype of being a staid high school history teacher, and some days I questioned the mental state of whoever decided to put him in charge of impressionable teens, but his students loved him like he was a second John Keating. Meanwhile, Emmett's hulking, silent presence slipped in behind him. The man was an accountant who could pass for a bearded lumberjack bodyguard. *I'm dead.*

"Nash, I see you haven't perished from off the earth," Ryan said too loudly, flinging his arms wide like he was welcoming home a long-lost brother from war.

I glared at him, not rising from my chair. "If you're going to be obnoxious, shut the door so my employees don't have to know I have such deranged friends."

Ryan slapped a hand over his chest dramatically, but Emmett closed the door. That was why Emmett was my favourite. The strong silent type. Solidarity, brother.

"You converted to Hallmark yet?" Emmett asked, setting down a brown paper bag on my desk. No doubt with the soup and sub Stephanie had ordered.

Scratch that. Emmett was *not* my favourite friend. I would disown both of them and be in the market for new friends if I thought there was hope of finding replacements. But once you hit a certain number of years in friendship, you didn't get rid of your friends. They knew too many embarrassing stories and secrets. "No."

"So defensive," Emmett tsked with a wry chuckle.

Ryan dropped into one of the overstuffed leather armchairs and crossed his ankles. "We've been talking—"

"You've been talking," Emmett grumbled, leaning against the far wall. "Like always."

"Right. Like I said, *we* have been talking," Ryan continued, "and we've decided it's about Stephanie, isn't it?"

"Is what?" I asked slowly, crossing my arms as I reclined in my chair.

"The fake dating question." Ryan pinned me with a glare, adding to Emmett, "Back me up."

Emmett just shrugged and watched the standoff.

"The nature of my relationship with Steph will stay between the two of us," I said firmly. "I'll be meeting her family for Christmas, though, so I'll be out of your hair."

Oh boy. We hadn't discussed talking about the complexity of our arrangement with our friends. This was something we definitely should have planned for. At least I should have, with my level of nosy friends. And yes, I said friends because Emmett was the biggest sap for gossip, even if his gruff and grumbly exterior dissuaded all manner of confidences.

Ryan's eyes sparked with glee.

Yeah. This was definitely something we should have talked about.

"That's not a no, and meeting the family already?" Ryan crowed, throwing his head back. "Dude, you're so gone!"

Emmett smacked the back of Ryan's head—something I sorely wanted to do myself at the moment—then fixed his steely grey eyes on me. "Christmas. With her family. Hiram Addams's princess, yeah? Isn't this all rather sudden?"

I had a sudden sympathy for all small animals being hunted by a deadly jungle cat. Wow, I did not think this through well enough. But neither was I expecting to be ambushed at work by my soon-to-be former best friends. As if I could get rid of them. "She's not his *princess*," I growled. From the moment Stephanie applied for the job, she'd been upfront about her father. The kingpin of the rival marketing company to my own, Genesis. Nova Designs and Hiram Addams were the equivalent of cuss words in the Genesis office.

Ryan perked up. "Yeah. On Friday you protested that she wasn't even your crush, and you never said anything about a girlfriend. What gives?"

"Can't a man have a few secrets?" I fiddled with the cuff of my navy dress shirt, wishing I had left my suit coat on in a power move, but alas, the thermostat was still on the fritz, and a suit coat would have been the sweaty death of me.

Emmett grunted. "Not in this group apparently."

"Think about it this way," I said. "You both get a Christmas free of a third wheel. Whatever will you do without Uncle Nash there to rile up your kids?"

Ryan nodded solemnly. "We owe Stephanie our thanks." He tossed a teasing wink at me over his shoulder as he left the room.

Emmett hesitated at the door, clearly warring with himself on whether he wanted to say whatever was brewing in his mind.

With how long Emmett tended to deliberate over things, I'd be here till New Years if I left him to it without some encouragement. "Spit it out, Mitchell. I can take it."

But Emmett didn't smile. "You didn't do this because of us, right? We didn't make you feel unwelcome?"

The thoughtfulness—and uncertainty—in Emmett's question surprised me. Ryan was a goof to his core but could be serious when the situation demanded it. Emmett though... He didn't do feelings stuff if he could help it—which was particularly amusing to watch as he had three young daughters, one of them a preteen. That meant this really bothered him.

I offered him a half grin. "Nah, man. As much as I'd like to trade you in for new friends when you get on my back about Hallmark, I couldn't ask for better ones. This is..." I hesitated, trying to find the words to explain it. "This is for me. For Steph. It's been a long time coming." As long as the week didn't burn up any chance I had of convincing her to make this real.

Emmett studied me for any hint of a lie. But he must not have seen one because he relaxed. "She's good for you. Better than Alexis ever was." He dipped his chin slightly. "She sees *you*."

Tension coiled my muscles, and my jaw clenched till it ached. But I forced myself to take a slow breath. "Yeah. Right."

Emmett nodded apologetically before slipping from the room. It'd been years since either of them had mentioned the name of my ex-girlfriend-almost-fiancée from a decade ago. I hadn't dated seriously since her, despite the guys' attempts to wrangle me into blind dates on a handful of occasions. And she was the reason I'd started my company in the first place.

But when it came to Stephanie, I'd considered breaking my no-serious-dating rule. And I could only pray she wouldn't break me like Alexis did. Whether it was real or not, despite all my past hang-ups and doubts... I was already in, my heart on the line.

CHAPTER NINE

Stephanie

Sweet relief was palpable when I finished my last day of work on the 22nd. All week I'd been as nervous as a Christmas cracker ready to explode. Because even though Nash was my fake boyfriend as of tomorrow morning, he was also still my boss, and we had boundaries in our friendship. The only thing that had changed was the frequency of our off-work-hours texts. He had questions about the schedule and my family. I fired off as many warnings and cheat sheet items as I could, giving him a crash course in all things Addams family.

There are six siblings—Gabe, Zoe, Elijah, Veronica, Austin, and me. All of them are married or have significant others who will also be there.

Gabe and I are the only siblings who don't work for Hiram.

All of my nieces and nephews are pranksters. Watch your shoes.

Nana, Hailey, Gabe, and Ivy are your only safe zones. Every-one else is a land mine.

In my last bit of office housecleaning, I powered down my computer and quickly scanned my office. It was snug but sleek, done up with a soft neutral colour palette and sage accents and boasting of just a desk and two chairs along with my filing cabinet. Nash's office connected to the back of mine, our desks in each other's line of sight when the doors were open. As I grabbed my purse, I heard his murmured undertones through the closed door. Must be a phone call.

With one final scan to triple-check I hadn't forgotten some-thing, I stepped out into the open concept of the cubicles, which were decked in garland and leftover lights from the party last week, ready to embrace the holiday madness. The office was already deserted, and I couldn't bring myself to feel guilty that I hadn't said goodbye to anyone. They hadn't made an effort to say goodbye to me either, and the platter of gingerbread men I'd had delivered at lunch would suffice.

My cell vibrated as I started down the hall towards the eleva-tors, and I smiled at the caller ID. It was my sister-in-law, Ivy. "Hey, hey, hey, Ives!"

"It's Jackson, Auntie Steph!" a young boy's voice corrected.

I laughed. "Does your mother know you're calling me?"

"Yes. I only have five minutes, though."

"You guys already on the road?" I checked my watch. It was just after six.

There was a scuffle in the background, then Jackson replied, "Yup. Dad said we just passed Mesquite. We're almost in Arizona."

"Making good time," I teased. It was a long trek from San Diego to Jackson, Wyoming, with four kids. As much as I loved my nieces and nephews, I didn't envy Gabe and Ivy those fifteen hours in the car. "What can I do for you, kiddo?"

"Did you see the game last night? It was *amazing*! Cal Satterfield nailed that goal in the third period. Did you really see him at Thanksgiving?"

I should have expected this. Jackson was obsessed with Idaho's Caldwell Chargers, a prominent AHL team in the hockey world, particularly with their right defender, Cal Satterfield, who just happened to be the older brother of my best friend, Juliet. Anytime Jackson called me, it was usually related to hockey and to ask if I'd had any new encounters with his hero. Cal was a great guy, no doubt about it, and great role model material. But I was an honorary little sister and thus not obligated to think he hung the moon like most of his fans.

"Yes, I really did. No, I did not sit beside him, but he played Settlers of Catan with the girls and me." I winced at the deafening screech of excitement.

There was a scuffle and then a different bright voice came over the line—this one decidedly not Jackson. "Hi, Auntie Steph! I just finished my dishcloth! There's a few holes, but I did what you said and kept going."

I smiled at my niece Ava's enthusiasm. The last time I'd seen her, I'd gotten her started on knitting dishcloths. Nice and easy for a beginner. "That's great, lovey! Did you start something else?"

"Yup, I'm making a scarf with some Christmas yarn Daddy got me."

That sounded very much like my older brother—big strong Marine but a total softie for his girls—but before I could get another word in, another scuffle crackled the line, and I yanked the phone away from my ear with a wince. It sounded like it was clanging through a rock tumbler.

"Ava, it's *my* turn to talk to Auntie Steph!" from a disgruntled Jackson.

"But I needed to tell her about my scarf!"

"Ava, hand the phone back to your brother and ask permission next time." That no-nonsense mom voice was impossible to mistake for anyone but Ivy.

"Bye, Auntie Steph," Ava grumbled.

"Bye, sweetie." Not gonna lie, it was pretty sweet to have them argue over me.

"Sorry," Jackson apologized, when the phone was back in his possession. "Dad said next time the Chargers play in San Diego he might take me to see them!"

"That's great, kiddo!" What he didn't know was that his Christmas gift from me was tickets to one of Cal's home games in Caldwell right after Christmas. "Listen, I gotta run. Last-minute Christmas stuff is calling. But I'll see you soon."

"Okay."

"Love you, Jack-Jack."

He groaned at the nickname like any ten-year-old boy would but rattled off a goodbye and "love you too" before hanging up.

I pressed the down button on the elevator and waited for it to arrive. Mentally, I sorted through the remainder of my to-do list. Packed? Check. Food? Mostly check. Text Nana about the room? Eh... I'd chickened out about that so far. If I told her right now I had a boyfriend, she'd have questions. Dropping it on her felt more doable. But about the room... There was no way Nash and I were sharing. We were not one-bed troping our way through this fake relationship. No way.

I pulled out my phone before my courage died.

ME

> Hey, Nana! I know it's last minute, but I'm bringing a friend for Christmas, and they need an extra room. Can you swing that?

No three little dots appeared telling me she was typing back. I sighed and slipped the device back into my purse as the elevator chimed, the doors whooshing open.

"Hold the elevator!" a familiar tenor voice called from behind me, muffled footsteps jogging my direction.

I stepped inside and held the door as Nash tumbled in after me.

He waited till the death trap rattled into motion before smirking down at me. "Trying to duck out on me, Steph?"

The shortened use of my name was a new thing for us, but I secretly loved hearing him say it, like the sap I was. I rolled my eyes. "You were on the phone, and I have... things to do tonight."

A twinkle lit his molten eyes, and he leaned closer. "So mysterious. What kind of things?" He put the last word in air quotes. "You're the kind of woman who had her bags packed the day after we made our arrangements."

I bit my cheek to keep from smiling, even though my face heated a little. The seventy-eighth downfall to dating your boss—he knew how organized you were. "True," I confessed, leaning against the metal bar that dug into my lower back.

"I heard you on the phone, and I believe the name Cal Satterfield was uttered more than once." Nash's eyes danced. "Should I be jealous?"

"Honorary little sis, remember?" Cal was objectively good looking but not my type.

Nash chuckled. "So it was Jackson calling to debrief after the game last night? It was a good one."

I groaned, tipping my head back against the mirrorlike wall. "Don't tell me you're a fan of the Chargers, too?"

"Guilty."

"Figures," I groused. "And yes, it was Jackson. He calls without fail because, apparently, being friends with a famous hockey player's little sister makes me the cool aunt."

"You hate hockey, don't you?" Nash stepped closer to me in a dare.

"Hate is a strong word. But—" My phone vibrated loudly, and I froze, my heart skipping a beat.

"Is there something you're not telling me?" Nash asked, eyebrows raised. The elevator jiggled, making my stomach swoop, before it halted and flung the doors open. He motioned for me to step out ahead of him.

"There's plenty of things I haven't told you," I huffed, adding under my breath, "including whether or not you'll have a roof over your head for the next week."

We waved to the night security guard before the automatic doors blasted us with the frigid December air. I shuddered and flipped my woolen coat collar up against the chill, but I couldn't do anything about my nylon-clad legs. I really needed to invest in those fleece tights Paisley swore by—a necessity for Idaho winters when you wanted to wear a skirt or dress, she said—or just not wear pantyhose during the five months of cold weather Spokane always got.

"You ready for tomorrow?" Nash asked as he walked me across the parking lot to my car—rather Liz's car because she let me borrow it since she was on Christmas break.

Ben said I needed a new transmission, and that extra two grand wasn't in the budget before Christmas, even if he was cutting me a deal. The Flea really might be resting in peace this time because it was almost cheaper to buy a new vehicle instead of doing the repairs.

Ready? Was I ready to sprinkle the metaphorical blood in the water and let the sharks circle around us? "Of course," I chirped like the idiot I was for living under the delusion that this would go over well and that the persistent buzz of my phone wasn't Nana losing her ever-loving mind.

After I unlocked the driver's door, I faced him. "I think the real question is, are *you* ready?"

Nash smiled, that southwest dimple popping in the dim light of the streetlamps. It was just starting to snow and the small flakes landed mesmerizingly on his dark curls—freshly cut. He leaned forward and opened the door for me. "I'm nowhere near as organized as you are. That's why I have you."

"Not what I meant, but I'm glad for the job security." I laughed and slid into the seat, dropping my purse onto the passenger seat and ignoring the persistent hum of my phone. No doubt Nana would be calling any minute.

Nash paused for a second, leaning down to peer at me. "You don't need to worry about me, Steph. I can handle your family. I can handle you, too. Crazy doesn't scare me."

The sincerity of his words hit me in the chest, and pesky tears burned my eyes. I so desperately wanted to believe him, but I'd believed other guys who had promised to stick around only to ditch me when I didn't fit in their plans anymore. Would Nash be different? He was the one who wanted things to be real between us. Well, I did, too. More than I was admitting out loud—especially since I'd told him I'd think about his offer. But would this be the Christmas my crush died because reality and my family's insanity crashed down around us? Or the year I was finally brave enough to reach out for what I wanted?

Gently, Nash reached out and lightly tugged one of my curls, breaking the tension. "And I hope you're bringing your A-game because I found an ugly sweater to top all ugly sweaters."

I snorted. "If you can give Nana a run for her money, you'll have half the family in love with you."

His grin was hypnotic in the shadows. "Good thing I'm only concerned about one member of the Addams family being in love with me, then. That might be too much pressure otherwise."

I stared at him, dumbstruck. But my mouth dried at his words, my tongue refusing to work. Was he... did he just... flirt? Were we at that stage? Man, I was rusty.

Nash winked. "I'll pick you up tomorrow morning at 6:30. Drive safe." Then he closed the door and waved before strolling across the parking lot towards his Wrangler like he hadn't just dropped the biggest bomb.

Turning the ignition, I cranked the heat and let Liz's Christmas music flood over me—you could never go wrong with the Jonas Brothers. While I waited for the car to heat up, I snuck a look at my phone, which sure enough, Nana was blowing up.

NANA

A friend? How delightful!

Are you bringing Liz again? We haven't seen her in forever!

She didn't mention coming when I asked her to send some cookies with you. I thought she was spending Christmas with her fiancé?

NANA

But if it's Liz, why do you need an extra room?

Wait.

Are you bringing a MAN?

STEPHANIE MAE LOUISE ADDAMS.

I wasn't sure what the all caps were supposed to convey, but yeah, Nana was too sharp for her own good, and I'd been far too optimistic to hope she'd not see through my sham request.

ME

I'll explain everything later. Just tell me there's an extra room. Please.

NANA

There is.

And you can bet your Christmas karaoke medal that you and I will be having a nice long chat the minute your rear lands up here.

ME

I love you. Thank you. And make it the second minute.

Oh, goody. Here I was, twenty-eight years old, and my nana would be giving me the grilling of my life. But Nana's words faded on the drive home, replaced by Nash's words in the parking lot.

I'm only concerned about one member of the Addams family being in love with me.

Oh, sugarplums. Shoot. Me. Now.

CHAPTER TEN

Stephanie

"You ready?" Liz asked, perching on her bed as she opened her laptop later that night.

I set the artfully arranged charcuterie board on her *Little House on the Prairie* plaid comforter and glanced at the assorted bottles of nail polishes on her nightstand. Inhaling deeply the pine tree and vanilla aroma bubbling from the diffuser on her dresser, I nodded an affirmative. "I think we got everything. Let's do it."

Her laptop chirped as she placed the video call, and we waited for Paisley and Juliet to join us. The four of us had met at the University of Washington in Seattle ten years ago. Our meeting was nothing short of miraculous. Paisley was running from the horrors of foster care after aging out. Juliet was looking for the best law program within a day's drive of home. Liz and I were a package deal after she'd become my next-door neighbour in Denver. Her parents were newly divorced after nearly two decades on the mission field, and Liz was livid. We'd hit it off, and when it came time for college applications, she'd begged me to come with her as she tried to put miles between her and her parents' disastrous marriage fallout. I hadn't been sad to leave Colorado—just Nana.

After graduation, work and life split us up between southern Idaho for them and eastern Washington for Liz and me. Paisley and Juliet had both married amazing guys, and we'd kept our friendship strong with once-a-month girls' nights via video chat, complete with snacks, nail polish, and life advice. These women had my back at every moment, and I'd be lost without them in my life. Rooming with Liz was like rooming with a sister, and having Paisley and Juliet so far away after four years of college together hurt. But they were happy, and so were we. Tonight was our last catch-up before Christmas, and let's face it, so we had nice nails for the holidays.

When the video chat failed to connect, I grabbed my phone and shot our group chat a quick text.

ME

> We still good for tonight?

It took a minute before Paisley messaged back.

PAISLEY

> Yes, sorry. Give us a sec. Jules needs to be surgically removed from her husband. Are all newlyweds this bad?

Liz leaned back against her pink floral pregnancy pillow, which she swore saved her back, and chomped on a sweet potato chip, laughing as I tilted my phone for her to read. "She's one to talk! Do you remember how smitten she was—both times?"

We laughed a little uncomfortably. Paisley's first husband wasn't a topic we discussed often, because... as Nana often said, sometimes the nicest thing you could say about someone was nothing at all. But she'd found love again—with a good man this time—in Greyson Satterfield. Yes, Cal Satterfield's twin and another one of Juliet's endless supply of older, rather attractive brothers. He was a veteran Marine turned mechanic. Our friend group clearly had a thing for mechanics, first with Paisley and Greyson and now with Liz and Ben.

"You and Ben get things sorted out with Carey?" I asked, popping a grape into my mouth.

Liz shrugged. "Maybe? It's a work in progress, but Ben and I are on the same page." A dreamy smile spread across her face. "You should have seen the way he stood up to his mother, defending me. 'She's my first priority, even from you,' were the words he used." Liz fanned herself. "A girl can get used to that kind of knight in grease and coveralls."

I laughed with her before leaning over and wrapping her in a hug.

Liz's laptop chimed with an incoming call, and I scrambled to accept it before she tried to use her toes to click the touchpad—gross. But when Juliet and Paisley's familiar faces flooded the screen, nothing else mattered. We were together again for a night.

"Hey!" That bright smile could only be Paisley's, next to Juliet's usual storm cloud. From the looks of it, they were in Paisley's cozy living room tonight. She had a killer eye for making a space welcoming.

"Myles keep you too long, Jules?" Liz teased, biting into a cheese cube.

Juliet glared through the screen, her already-flushed face reddening. "I'm not apologizing for finding my husband attractive, especially after his epically hot goalie moves in the net tonight."

"Yeah, yeah, go Chargers," Paisley drolled, then impishly squished Juliet's cheeks together so she looked like a fish. "We're very proud of our boys."

Juliet swatted at her and rolled her eyes, but the hint of a grin tugged at her lipstick-smudged bright pink lips.

Liz and I snickered at their antics. "Glad you're with us," I said. "You got snacks?"

"Chocolate mint tea, candy cane cookies, Nanaimo bars, and artichoke dip with crackers," Juliet said, nudging Paisley. "None of which she burnt."

"Hey, I *can* cook!" Paisley protested, crossing her arms. "Maybe not as well as Liz, but I haven't actually burnt something since before I was married. That counts for something."

We all busted up laughing, remembering some of her earlier cooking disasters—we were talking firefighters-being-called mishaps. I picked up two bottles of nail polish. *Hmm... red for festive or silver for subtlety?*

"All right, ladies," Juliet said, taking charge. "Do we have our colours picked?"

"Seductive Wine for me." I jiggled the bottle of deep burgundy. "Who names these things, seriously?"

Liz swiped the silver from me. "Silver Bells. Ooh, I like that!"

"My usual," Juliet said, fluttering her fingers. "Black French tips. To match my heart apparently."

Paisley nudged her. "And yet we still love you, Grinchy. I'm not painting mine because I don't have any nails long enough to paint." She ducked her head sheepishly.

"Things been stressful, Pais?" I asked, uncapping the base coat polish to get started on Liz's nails.

Paisley shrugged, adjusting her position on the couch to sit cross-legged as she started on Juliet's. "The holidays are always insane at the library, but not more than usual. I'm just... maybe a little unsettled." She chewed on her lip as she said nothing for a few moments. "I thought I was pregnant."

"Oh, honey," Liz said sympathetically.

"I was kinda hoping, you know? We've been married three years now. But... I don't know, at the same time, I was scared I might be. I don't know how to be a mom since my mom didn't either. Sure, I had some great foster moms, but..." Paisley shrugged again.

"You'll be a great mother," Juliet said with a no-argument tone. "Whatever that looks like—biological or adoption."

"Didn't Gabe and Ivy adopt?" Paisley asked me.

I nodded. Because Greyson and Gabe were both Marines, they knew each other. Before Greyson retired a few years ago, he'd been stationed at Gabe's last base. "Yup, all four. And you'd never know those kids weren't their biological kids, besides their looks."

We were quiet for a moment before I added slowly, "Speaking of the Carson clan, they'll be in town for the Chargers' home game right after Christmas."

The tension eased in Paisley's face at the conversation shift, and her laugh was bright, albeit a bit brittle. "As if we could forget. Cal is about to burst his buttons about finally meeting Jackson and the rest of the family."

"And Myles keeps reminding him they're there to see the whole team, not just him," Juliet cut in, referring to her goalie husband, who also played for the Chargers, as she balanced a cookie on her knee.

"Don't laugh," I warned Liz, gripping her hand. "You'll smudge my hard work."

Doing her best, Liz still managed a cackle. "Never did I think I'd see the day where two grown men would be competing for the attention of a ten-year-old fan."

Juliet snorted and chomped on her cookie. "You have no idea. If they weren't besties, they couldn't handle this rivalry."

"Do you call them besties to their faces?" I asked curiously.

Juliet rolled her eyes. "Cal calls them that. Those men, I tell you."

"Steph has news!" Liz offered in a singsong voice.

My hand slipped, smearing polish across her skin. "Seriously?" I muttered. "Can't you develop a subtle bone in your body? Just this once."

She cackled again. "You're stalling. I gave you time to bring it up."

"Oh, Stephie!" Paisley cooed, green eyes bright behind her wire-rimmed frames.

I huffed. There was no way I could wriggle out of this now. *Thanks a lot, Liz.* "Fine. I... I'm dating someone. Kinda."

Paisley cheered, and Juliet eyed me through the screen. "How do you *kinda* date, Steph?"

I cleared my throat and swabbed nail polish remover over Liz's fingers. "I may or may not have asked someone to be my fake boyfriend for Christmas with my family."

"Which one is it? May or may not?" Juliet dared. She was intimidating when she wore her scary lawyer face. But she had to be scary since she worked with bulky, hulking hockey players all day as part of the Chargers' legal counsel.

"Can I plead the fifth?"

"No!" my friends all chorused.

I half growled, half screamed. Was that a thing? "Fine. I asked Nash, and he agreed."

"Your boss?" from Juliet.

Paisley clapped her hands. "Nashanie! I totally ship you! Wait, you said fake? Why, Steph? You've crushed on him forever."

"Yeah, Steph." Liz drew out my name with all the finesse of a mother getting her kid to talk.

I glared at her. "Because he's my boss. And that's that."

"Is he not interested in you then?" Juliet asked, her voice softened slightly. Well, soft for her.

"Uh... he might have asked for it to be real?" My voice squeaked on the last word, which was all it took for my friends to pounce.

"Might have?" Paisley challenged. She was spending way too much time with Juliet.

"Fine. He wants real. So do I, but I panicked and said no. Or I wasn't sure yet. Happy?"

"No," Juliet deadpanned.

"Do you want to talk about it?" Paisley asked gently.

I shook my head. Then shrugged. "I'm just... I can't..." The words I needed wouldn't come. They knew my story. My dating hang-ups. My strained parental relationships. "Hiram texted," I said lamely.

Paisley gasped, and Juliet muttered, "That no-good slug." They'd come to the cabin for Christmas with me once while we were still in college, so they knew what an Addams family holiday entailed.

After I told them about the text and my frenzied idea of asking Nash to be my fake date, I sighed. "If Hiram hadn't gotten into my head, I think I could have said yes."

"He threw you," Juliet said quietly.

"Yeah." I scrunched my toes against the quilt, grounding myself. "All of this stuff I thought I'd worked through is just boiling over, and I hate it." Hated feeling unmoored. Hated being left behind.

"It's part of the grieving process," Paisley said. "And that's okay. Give yourself some grace, but don't get stuck. Maybe you and Nash will turn into more. Who knows. But pray about it, Steph. Be open to embracing the scary." She shot me a look. We both knew I loved my comfort zone. "And we'll be praying, too, okay?"

The words cloaked me like a hot cocoa hug. "Thanks, Pais."

"And definitely keep us posted," she continued, "because we all know the first rule of fake dating is not falling in love, and I'm pretty sure you've both already broken that rule, so... genre expectations."

Juliet blinked at her, half-eaten cookie in hand. "You're weird sometimes, you know that?"

"You fell in love with your older brother's best friend, so you're one to talk," Paisley shot back.

I laughed weakly and let Liz start on my nails. Relief flooded me when Paisley, bless her, redirected the conversation.

"Speaking of new things, we got a puppy! Well, not an actual puppy. She's eighteen months and needed to be rehomed."

"Ooh, what kind?" Liz asked.

"Golden retriever. We named her Rosie Cotton."

We all blinked at her owlishly, and she groaned. "You know, Samwise Gamgee's wife from *Lord of the Rings*? Tell me you remember this."

Juliet snickered, poking Paisley's shoulder. "We're not all nerds like the pair of you."

And it was true. Paisley and Greyson were the biggest *Lord of the Rings* nerds I'd ever met. It was how they fell in love—all starting with a themed trivia night. Never get between them when it comes to trivia.

"To tell you that would be lying," I said apologetically. "But she sounds adorable. Is she with you?"

"Nah, Grey took her out tonight. I'll send pictures!"

After another hour of talking, we reluctantly hung up the video call. Liz dragged the leftover food to the kitchen and started washing up the few dishes we'd used. I slipped a Bing Crosby Christmas vinyl onto my record player in the living room, and we worked in companionable silence, my mind full of news and bits of life from Idaho against the soothing background music.

"Hey, I'm sorry if I pressed too hard and made it weird for you to tell them," Liz blurted out as she rinsed the charcuterie board before handing it to me to dry.

"You were fine. I wanted to say something. Just didn't know how to start." I slid the board onto the wood shelf we used to display our platters.

"Are you happy, Steph?"

The abrupt change in topic startled me. I swiped the water droplets from Liz's "I'd Melt for You" snowman mug with deep concentration, conflicted on how to answer such a question. Happy? *Was* I happy? At last, I said, "I think happiness is fleeting... but I'm making my way."

"Steph." Liz shut the water off and turned to face me, ignoring the rest of the dishes in the sink. "Real talk."

"What do you want me to say?" I huffed. "That I'm lonely, miserable, and terrified of ending up alone while all my best friends get their happily ever afters, and I have to find another roommate to pay the rent? Because I'm not miserable, Liz. I promise. I'm just..." My shoulders deflated as I tried to find the words. "I just think it'd be nice to have my own person. To be someone to come home to—someone's first choice—ya know?"

Between my three besties, I was the last single woman standing. Paisley was on her second husband, Juliet had married Cal's best friend, and Liz was engaged to an amazing guy she'd met not long after we'd moved here. Leaving little ol' me behind. I loved my friends and the awesome guys they had at their sides, and they never made me feel like a third—or seventh—wheel. But I knew firsthand it was possible to be so thrilled for someone else while also secretly mourning the ache in your heart because your own guy hadn't entered the picture.

What about Nash? I swallowed hard and swiped extra hard on an already dried dish.

Liz's gaze softened, and she tugged me into a hug—a classic Liz move. "You're an absolute catch, Stephanie Addams—beautiful inside and out—and I think you're amazing. And if Nash is worth his salt, he'll see that, too."

I hugged her back and swallowed the lump in my throat. But I couldn't voice my swirling thoughts. That I was too scared to even give Nash a chance. Worried that he would see the real me and decide I was an inconvenience... not enough. My mother didn't want me. My dad abandoned me for most of my childhood. My best friends were moving on with the loves of their lives. *Everybody leaves eventually.*

CHAPTER ELEVEN

Nash

ARMS FULL OF PRESENTS, I staggered up the stairs of Ryan and Kelsi's house. I missed the last step, nearly face-planting and upsetting the entire load. I groaned and shifted the gifts. No doubt Ryan would get a kick out of this playback video when he reviewed his door camera footage.

I gave the red door three light kicks with my foot, signaling my arrival. As late as it was, I didn't want to risk the doorbell waking the boys—especially the baby.

"Saint Nick came early!" my hyperactive friend cried, throwing open the door and simultaneously pulling me through it as he tried to grab every present I carried.

"Hey!" I pivoted, avoiding his grabby octopus hands—seriously, how were they everywhere at once?—but he followed me like a persistent puppy.

"Ooh, is that my name?" Ryan tried to swipe another gift—green-papered this time.

"Stop it!" I growled, shoulder checking him. "Kelsi, come distract your husband, won't you?" We might be grown men, but we still had the ability to turn into teenage boys at a moment's notice. Or at least, Ryan brought that particular flaw out in me. Must be a side effect of his spending so much time with teens.

I jumped as a ginger-haired woman just *appeared* at my elbow. Gingersnaps, how did she do that? Twenty years of theatre experience no doubt. She tugged Ryan away from me, drawing him into a kiss. Then two. Then a longer one.

Okay, then.

I scooted around them into the living room and set down the assortment of packages, taking a moment to admire the newest cinnamon-stick ornaments the boys had added to the tree. I glanced over my shoulder, but they were still making out, so I settled on arranging the gifts neatly around the tree skirt, being careful to place all of Ryan's out of sight. Petty? Maybe.

Another shoulder glance. They were still at it. I cleared my throat. "Get a room, guys. I said a distraction, not a show." Don't get me wrong, I was thrilled for my friends and their happy marriages. That didn't mean I wanted a front row seat to their lip locking. Emmett and Danielle were rational creatures who kept PDA to a respectful amount in company. But Ryan and Kelsi did PDA like the world was on fire and kissing was the only way to stay alive.

Apparently taking pity on me, Kelsi pulled away first, and Ryan groaned dramatically. "That wasn't for your benefit, Nash." She smirked, patting her husband's chest before disappearing into the kitchen.

"You already been to Emmett's?" Ryan asked, stuffing his hands in his pockets and eyeing up the tree. No doubt already trying to find his name.

"Stopped there first. Can't have the girls thinking Uncle Nash forgot them."

"Should I be offended you picked him first over me or take it as a sign you saved the best for last?"

"He literally lives fifteen minutes closer to my place than you do."

"So best for last then." Ryan laughed when I shook my head in defeat. "All ready for tomorrow?"

I flicked through a mental checklist. My suitcase was packed. My ugly sweater was ready to go. And I'd spent way too long trying to decide on a gift for Stephanie. What I had picked I wasn't sold on. Was a necklace too personal for a fake relationship? "As ready as I'll get."

"And you have no concerns about this whatsoever?"

Kelsi handed us both a glass of sparkling juice. Peach from the smell of it. She leaned up and kissed Ryan's cheek. "I'll let you two talk. I've got one more deadline to meet before the holidays start. And for now, the baby's down."

Ryan reeled her closer, stealing a quick peck. "No rest for the gorgeous." He waggled his eyebrows at her.

Kelsi rolled her eyes, but a smile touched her lips. To me, she added, "Merry Christmas, Nash. We'll miss having you this year, but I'm glad you and Steph are *finally* giving this a go." She gave me a hug.

"Yeah?" I was stuck between a rock and a hard place here. Not admitting it was fake because I didn't want to embarrass Stephanie, but also not admitting it was real because she hadn't decided yet.

Kelsi barked a laugh. "We're not blind, Nash. Pretty sure everyone noticed the chemistry between you two. You're not exactly subtle."

Just to Stephanie, I guess. I chuckled. "Merry Christmas, Kels. Not sure how this guy lucked out with you."

She grinned saucily, winking at Ryan. "I keep telling him the same thing."

After she disappeared up the stairs, we sank down on the leather couch, silently enjoying the drink, the enchantment of the twinkling tree lights, and the crackle from the fireplace.

"So, you have no worries about this?" Ryan prompted. "Because it takes guts walking onto Hiram Addams's home turf. And I'm not sure you'll have any guts left when he's finished with you."

I grimaced, eyeing him. "Your pep talks need some work." I wasn't worried about myself in this situation. If anything, I was more concerned about Stephanie. From the vague comments she occasionally dropped about her father, I gathered they weren't close. Absentee dad it seemed. Walking in with me on her arm might put more of a target on her back. But I'd stand with her.

Protect her. Stephanie was the best thing that had happened to me, and I wasn't taking this glimmer of a chance for granted.

Chapter Twelve

Nash

At precisely 6:28 the next morning, I parked on the curb in front of a single-story craftsman-style bungalow. Even in the predawn shadows, it held a charm, with its buttery-yellow colour, cream trim, and shutters. Just the sort of sunshiny house I'd expect Stephanie to live in. The girls—or probably Ben—had hung white Christmas lights along the roofline, adding to the character of the house.

It hadn't snowed too hard overnight, so the driveway was still mostly clear. I noticed the snow shovel on the porch and made quick work of clearing the thin layer just in case it froze or rained and turned to slush. I didn't know what Liz's plans were for the holidays, but shoveling was the last thing she needed to worry about.

I'd just finished the driveway and was starting on the porch stairs when the front door flew open, revealing a very casual Stephanie.

I usually only saw her in business or church attire. Jeans occasionally when we hung out together with friends. But now she was in maroon joggers and a black oversized hoodie with the Marine logo on it. Huh... That's right, her oldest brother was a Marine, currently stationed in San Diego. He and Stephanie were close, I knew that. The only sibling she was close to. And I was positive the hoodie looked way better on her than it ever had on him. *Move on, Nash, it's a hoodie.* Her tousled black curls looked like she'd just popped out of bed—and it was adorable. I could definitely get used to seeing her like this every morning, if she'd let me.

"What are you doing?" Stephanie hissed, flicking on the porch light and nearly blinding me.

I grinned brightly. "Good morning to you, too."

She grunted and crossed her arms, clearly trying to look fierce, but she had more resemblance to a puffed-up kitten than a menacing porcupine with her puffy eyes still half shut.

I chuckled to myself at the mental image. "Just making sure Liz didn't have to worry about ice or slush," I said simply. "Where's your luggage? I'll load up."

"I can get it," she offered, relaxing her stance. "And thanks for doing the driveway. It's one less thing for Ben to insist on taking care of."

"Not a problem. Is this it?" I asked, stepping into her entryway and draping a garment bag over my arm before I hefted up the two medium-sized matching navy suitcases.

"Is it too much?" she called after me.

I laughed. "You worry too much. Two suitcases is nothing. Got anything else?"

"Just my purse and the cookie tins."

"Bring your purse, and I'll grab the cookies." I popped the trunk of my Wrangler and Tetris-ed the luggage inside between my case and the garment bag holding my suit. When I got back to the door, Stephanie already had her boots on and her purse slung over her shoulder. "This it?" I asked, motioning to the two large clear plastic containers filled to the brim with assorted cookies.

"Yeah. I think." She blew out a breath. "Sorry if—"

"Ah, ah," I cut in. "No more apologies, okay?" I softened my tone. "For this to work, you need to be comfortable around me. You're a strong and competent woman, Steph. Just breathe. You're all good."

Her deep exhale tugged at a protective feeling in my chest. Yeah, I couldn't have been too far off about the anxiety. I wasn't used to seeing the unsure side of Stephanie Addams. At work, she was always so organized and in control. But as I took in her leisure wear, sleepy expression, and the dark circles under her eyes in a noticeable absence of her usual makeup, she looked... softer and more vulnerable than I'd ever seen her. There was never a doubt in my mind about Stephanie's strength—but I could get used to seeing her like this, even if she needed to apologize every few minutes. *Lord, help me to help her feel comfortable in her own skin. Even if this thing between us doesn't work... help her find her bravery so she doesn't feel the need to be so small.*

A yawning Liz materialized in the foyer, wrapped in a fuzzy blanket, her hair in a messy topknot. After waving to me, she hugged Stephanie long and hard before handing over a small white envelope. "For Christmas morning." She yawned again. "I forgot to sneak it in the suitcase with the other gifts."

Stephanie laughed. "You're the best. Thank you. Yours are under the tree."

"Thanks. You have everything?" Liz asked, readjusting the blanket around her shoulders. "You got the food? Your dress? The gifts?"

"Yes. Yes." Then Stephanie jolted. "Wait, I forgot—" What she forgot was lost as she shuffled down the hall, disappearing into a room on the right side.

"Step in," Liz invited. "No sense heating the outside."

I chuckled and kicked the snow off my shoes before stepping into the entryway and shutting the door. "My grandmother used to say that."

"Used to?"

"She passed when I was in college." I stiffened slightly, surprised that information had just dropped out of me so willingly. Especially because Liz and I weren't exactly close. Friends, sure. But... she had that effect on people, I guess. As a teacher to young impressionable minds, I was sure she was a master of ferreting out information. Probably good at keeping it, too.

Liz's face pinched with sympathy, but before she could say anything, a landscape photograph in a distressed wood frame caught my eye on the entryway wall.

"Wow," I breathed, leaning in to examine it. "Where is this?"

Liz paused beside me. "Glacier National. Steph has a good eye. It was the last trip us girls took all together right before Juliet and Myles's wedding a bit over a year ago."

"Steph's a photographer?"

Liz nodded. "A good one, too. But she rarely does it anymore. Just the occasional shoot, like she did for Ben and me for our engagement."

I'd seen a few of those photos online, and they were magical. Airy and light with a storybook-magic haze to them. Almost like '90s nostalgia. Stephanie had all this talent, and she'd studied business? "Why—?" but I was cut off by Stephanie's reappearance.

If she caught me studying the photo, she didn't comment on it. Just smiled tiredly and jiggled a pill bottle. "Ready."

And then something crystallized in my mind. I knew exactly what I wanted to give Stephanie for Christmas. I would need Liz's help, but that would have to wait till we were on the road.

"May the odds be in your favour, Nash." Liz saluted me with a *Hunger Games* salute before smothering Stephanie in another hug. "The Addams are something else. Keep our girl safe."

"Yes, ma'am." Resting my hand on Stephanie's lower back, I guided her down the cleared driveway. It was a simple gesture that felt natural.

Once we were in the car, I held out a coffee thermos from the cup holder. "Peppermint mocha, m'lady."

"You got me a coffee?"

Technically I'd made her the coffee at home, but she didn't need to know that. "What sort of boyfriend would I be if I didn't bring you a coffee at the ungodly hour of 6:30 in the morning?"

Stephanie laughed and snatched the thermos from me, sighing contentedly after the first sip. "You're too perfect," she whispered, and I wasn't sure if it was about me or the coffee.

I discreetly pulled out my phone as I keyed the ignition and shot Ryan a quick text.

ME

> Need a favour. Can you get me Liz Kelso's number from Kelsi? I'll babysit one night if you do.

Babysitting bribery was Ryan's love language, and if I was going to pull off Stephanie's Christmas gift, I needed some help.

The quiet neighborhood fell behind us. "You got a road trip playlist, or did you want to jump headfirst into the twenty questions? Or catch a few more winks?"

Stephanie snorted. "I'm not much of a morning person. I feel you should know that."

I stole a glance at her. "I got that impression. That's fine, though. Plug your phone in and crank up the music or sleep if you need to. We've got a long drive."

She hesitated. "Are you sure you don't want to pick the music? What if you don't like my taste?"

"Won't know until I at least hear it," I countered. "Besides, I'm sure your taste is just fine." And when Elvis Presley crooning "Blue Christmas" filled the car a minute later, I started to sing along in a thoroughly bad pitch, which made her laugh as she snuggled deeper into her seat, still cradling her coffee thermos like a dragon hoarding gold.

Against the backdrop of Elvis, Sinatra, and Crosby, short sentences slowly ebbed into full conversations by the time we were halfway through the Idaho panhandle. The sun peered over the mountains on the horizon, reluctant to show its face. Snow dusted the evergreens and the dead grassy fields we passed, and the morning light shimmered on the lake, edging along the side of I-90.

A lone moose, tall and majestic against the patches of snow, watched as I merged into the left lane, adjusting my visor to counteract the glint off the road trying to blind me. "Nothing like winter sunshine."

"Mm-hmm." Stephanie groaned a little as she stretched and readjusted in her seat. She dug around in her bag and pulled out a wad of needles and yarn. It was a nice navy colour, though I was lost as to what it was supposed to be. Was that an arm hole? "I feel like I should know if you're one of those crazy people who loves winter or sees it as a necessary evil before we get back to spring and summer?"

I tapped the wheel lightly in thought. "I never minded winters growing up. Texas was mild compared to Washington. So was Southern California. But I do prefer the warmer months."

"Same. The only mild winter I experienced was when I visited Gabe in Hawaii one year. Growing up in Denver wasn't exactly a mild winter experience."

I snorted. "Definitely not. Now, Gabe. He's the Marine. Married to Ivy with... four kids, right?"

Her face softened. "You remember all that?"

I shoulder-checked before changing lanes. "Of course. You talk about them often. And Nana and Hailey. They're important to you." I gestured to her hoodie. "Besides, you don't seem like the boot camp type."

Stephanie smiled, the knitting needles clicking in a soothing rhythmic cadence. "Yeah, I stole it from him one year. With his deployments, they don't always make it to the cabin for Christmas, and some years they're with Ivy's family, but this year they're gonna be there." She blew out a breath. "Truthfully, that's the only reason I'm not skipping this year. Them and Hailey, because her folks are out of town."

"You miss him." It wasn't a question. Her tone practically bled with her affection.

"Yeah. Gabe's the only sibling I'm close to. We're not even blood relatives technically, since Hiram is his stepdad—his stepson from his first marriage—so we're half siblings. Maybe? There's no blood connection. So, I don't know how that works, but he's always been there for me." She abruptly cleared her throat and glanced out the window.

Nat King Cole's soothing lilt in "O Holy Night" filled the space between us, and I hummed along softly, giving her a few minutes to collect herself. My phone pinged, and I recognized Ryan's chime. We were due for a quick restroom stop soon to stretch our legs and maybe grab another coffee. I could sneak a peek at the message then.

But for now, we still had several hours of driving and way too many details to iron out between us. It was time to steer us back into lighter waters. "I saw your picture of Glacier at your place. I didn't realize you were a photographer."

Stephanie bristled, her knitting movements becoming jagged and exaggerated. "I'm not."

"C'mon, Steph, I saw the picture. And don't even get me started on the engagement session you did for Ben and Liz. You have a gift. Why don't you use it?"

The clack of needles stopped, and she inhaled sharply. I'd clearly hit a nerve, but why?

"It wasn't a surefire success plan," Stephanie said at last, blowing out a breath. "I thought about studying photography and media, but business marketing and administration was a safer venture. Solid job options. Stability. Even if it did feel like I was following in Hiram's shoes."

I nodded, tapping my fingers lightly against the wheel, keeping time with the background music, and not totally sure what to say to that. "Do you... miss it? The creative aspect?" I asked once the next song started.

She shifted in her seat, turning to face me. "Why are you asking this?" It wasn't exactly accusatory, more defensive with a hint of curiosity.

"Well, originally I thought it was a safer conversation than your family, but I evidently stuck my foot in my mouth," I said with a self-deprecating laugh, which made her mouth twitch in a smile. "But honestly, it's because you make me curious. I've gotten to know a side of you for years. But I want to know more. I want to know what matters to you. What you value. What makes you tick. And you evidently have a passion for photography. I could feel it as a viewer."

Stephanie's cheeks flushed as I finished. Maybe I'd said too much, but I wanted honesty between us.

"Sorry. I didn't mean to snap." She sighed. "I do miss it. Capturing the moment. I want to do it again one day. I just need to be brave enough." Resuming her knitting, she muttered, "Story of my life these days."

Now it was truly time for a lighter subject. "Nick, Joe, or Kevin?" I said after "Like It's Christmas" finished playing.

She stared at me and then burst into laughter. It was music to my ears. Someone should bottle that sound up. It'd be worth millions.

"I honestly never thought about it," she wheezed. "All of them together is what makes the music sound good. Is this what I get for squeezing one boy band song into a playlist of classics? It wasn't even me—Liz added it."

"Keeping you on your toes. Now, what's our story?"

When she didn't reply, I stole a glance at her and noticed the pink in her cheeks again. Huh, interesting.

"Well, we should probably stick to the truth. We had mutual friends but didn't realize it till after I started working for you," she said slowly. "But we should probably underplay that."

"How long have we been dating?"

She winced, dropping her head back against the headrest with a thud and a groan. "Nana's gonna kill me."

"I didn't sign up for murder, Steph."

She laughed again. "It's just that I talk to her every week. There's no way I would have kept my dating life from her. So it can't be too long, or she won't believe me, but not too short because who brings a week-long boyfriend home for the holidays?" Her voice cracked with tension.

"Well, we've been friends for a while," I said slowly, not wanting to scare her with just how long I'd been interested in her. "Friendship is a good base for any relationship, and once there were sparks, we just knew."

Stephanie shifted to study me, considering. "That could work. I talk about you often enough." The subtle pink staining her face shifted to a deep crimson, and it shouldn't be this appealing. "I mean, you're my boss. I tell her about work, obviously. So yeah, she should believe that."

I shouldn't find her awkwardness so endearing, but this side of Stephanie was so different from what I was used to. It was addicting. "Okay, we wanted to make sure we weren't just better off as friends before meeting the family. That sound about right?"

She relaxed into the leather seat, sipping from her water bottle. "Yeah. Nana wanted to meet you anyway. This will be my Christmas gift to her." She snorted. "This, plus the vinyl collection of Shania Twain's greatest hits."

We shared a laugh and eased back into the companionable silence. It wasn't forced or awkward or heavy. It was the kind of quiet where you could sit and just... be. There was no pressure, no uncomfortable tension to break. Just two souls comfortable with the presence of the other. I'd felt this way with her before, but now... it was more poignant.

We stopped at a coffee shop in Missoula for a restroom break, and I finally had the chance to check my phone while I waited for Stephanie. Ryan had come through with a number, thanks to Kelsi, and a demand for answers on why I needed Liz's number. I'd tell him later. For now, I had a handful of minutes before Stephanie would reappear.

ME

Hi, Liz. This is Nash. I hope you don't mind that I got your number from Kelsi, but I need your help with a Christmas gift for Stephanie. I wanted to get her something photography related, if you think she wouldn't hate it?

I wasn't expecting an immediate reply, but I got one anyway.

LIZ

Oh my goodness, you're a gem. There's a lens she's been eyeing for years, depending on your budget.

ME

No budget.

Don't let her know that. She's allergic to spending money on herself. Okay, here's the link.

The link came through to a sleek 70-200mm lens. Ideal for portraits and macro shots, according to the product description.

Thanks. I owe you one.

Keep our girl safe from the vultures, and I'll call it even.

You got it.

I quickly ordered the lens and had it express shipped to the cabin. In Gabe's name. I was hopeful he wouldn't mind. I'd just clicked "Confirm Order" when my phone rang. My gut clenched at the caller ID. Mountainside Rehabilitation Center. *Lord, please no. Not again.* With a deep breath and another hasty prayer, I answered.

"Hello, Mr. Prescott, this is Julia from Mountainside Rehabilitation Center. I'm sorry to have to tell you this, but—"

"She checked herself out again, didn't she?" I cut in roughly.

Julia's breath hitched. "Yes, sir."

We'd done this dance before, and no doubt my mom would be calling me any time between now and New Year's to ask for money. Depending on her current boyfriend, it might be a month or two.

"She was only two weeks off of completing her program, wasn't she?"

"That's right, sir." Julia sounded tired, and I couldn't blame her. I'd hate having to make calls like this, too.

I'd paid for four stints of rehab for my mother to get clean from the drugs she insisted on using, but twice she'd checked herself out before even finishing the program.

I rubbed my forehead. "Thanks for calling, Julia. Have a merry Christmas."

"You, too, Mr. Prescott." She hung up.

I stared at my phone's blank screen, the hum of the coffee shop and the heady aroma of nutmeg blurring my senses. Why now? She was so close. By New Year's she would've been clean.

"Everything all good?" Stephanie asked as she came around the free-standing shelf of roasted coffee beans and mugs.

I jolted and slid my phone back in my pocket. "Yup." I tried smiling, but it felt stiff. Mechanical. "Christmas isn't the time to ask questions. Want another coffee?"

She shook her head slowly, eyeing me like she saw right through my sham. "Maybe after lunch. I forgot to take my medication earlier, and it needs to be away from caffeine."

I nodded. "All right then. Let's hit the road." Up till now, I hadn't been open about my past with her, and if we were going to make this work, I needed to be. But not right here in a dimly lit coffee shop with a mounted elk head eyeing us up.

"THIS IS IT?" I asked in wide-eyed appreciation as I parked the car in the broad driveway. It was just after four in the afternoon, and the sky was already a deepening hue of shadowed periwinkle.

Stephanie smiled wryly. "Yup."

As I stared at the timber monstrosity before us, I quickly got the picture of why she wanted to change out of her sweats and hoodie at the gas station and into dark jeans and a wine-coloured cabled sweater. I thought she'd looked great in the sweats. Better than great actually. But apparently, loungewear was for lounging only at the cabin.

The timber and stonework emanated stately prestige from where it sat on a slight ridge, overlooking the expansive swath of the snowcapped blue-hued Tetons and flanked by a shadowy sentinel of evergreens. Strings of white-and-red Christmas lights capped the gables and wound around the front deck railing. Warm light spilling through the expansive front picture windows dazzled the darkening sky. "I think calling *this* a cabin is majorly underselling it. The fact that we were going to Jackson should have been my first hint."

Stephanie huffed, tugging on her sweater sleeve. "Hiram has expensive taste, so for him this is a cabin." She raised an eyebrow. "And you're one to talk, Mr. Millionaire."

Maybe, but I didn't own ritzy woodland cabins big enough to house a few football fields in a high-end elite town. I hadn't been born into money, and I didn't see the need to change my way of life extravagantly just because I had it now.

Stephanie blew out a breath. "You ready?"

"You trying to scare me off? Because it's too late for that."

She bit her lip and sighed. "They're ruthless, Nash. Like sharks smelling blood in the water. Watch your back. Remember, Nana, Hailey, and Gabe and Ivy's family are the only allies once you step in those doors."

I offered her a lighthearted salute to make her smile. "Aye, aye, Captain. I've alerted my lawyer for my last will and testament should I not make it back alive, and Emmett and Ryan will inherit the company."

Stephanie rolled her eyes. "So dramatic. And Ryan doesn't even work for you." But her lips twitched, so I called it a win. "Oh… and I should mention…" Her eyes were full of apologies as she looked up at me. "This is my first Christmas with my family since I started working for you."

"Making me public enemy number one?"

She winced, but I took her hand, lacing our fingers. A bit of warmth compared to the nippy breeze. "Don't worry, Steph. I figured this might be a bit uncomfortable, but we've got this. I'm in your corner. It's why I'm here."

In a flash, Stephanie was up on her tiptoes—height difference was a thing for us—brushing a kiss to my cheek. "Thank you."

Words ceased to exist in my brain, and all I could do was squeeze her hand. Stephanie was a petite woman, and her hand was small in mine. Nerves and hope danced across her face as she peered up at me. I smiled reassuringly. I'd face a lot more than my business nemesis on his home turf to have her thank me like that again. But for now, it was time for our Christmas performance. *Because it's fake. For now.*

"Showtime, darlin'."

It took two trips to the door with luggage and then we just stood there. Hesitating. Like whatever was on the other side couldn't hurt us from out here.

"Nash," Stephanie whispered, her hand hovering over the doorknob.

"Yeah?" My name sounded far too appealing on her lips.

"Welcome to the Addams Family Christmas." She flung open the door, and my ears instantly rang with the noise.

CHAPTER THIRTEEN

Nash

THE BUZZ OF THE house was electric, seeping out from every corner. If I hadn't already decided *cabin* was a generous term for the place, the open-concept layout with an expansive mezzanine above confirmed it. And the décor... Wow. It was like someone took all the décor of nostalgic '90s Christmas movies and splashed it into one house. Garland, green and gold, warm incandescent lights, and was that tinsel? No minimalistic beige here, and nothing at all like the billionaire cabin chic I expected from Hiram Addams. Let that be a lesson to me on judging by appearance.

It was cozy and familiar. And was that...? I sniffed. Yup, definitely potpourri and hot mulled cider. For a brief moment, I was transported back in time to another Christmas. When, for a few years, my mom and I lived with her parents. Their Christmases were like this. Magical and... welcoming.

A wintery cartoon played on the living room TV, entertaining a gaggle of children clustered around it. I squinted—huh, an animated snowman singing about summer. I had so many questions about that. Two kids pelted up the stairs, shouting, "Humbug, humbug, humbug!" Okay, they were clearly Scrooge fans in this house.

But against the homey backdrop and the delicious heat from the monstrous grey stone fireplace, heated arguing boiled out from the kitchen at the back of the cabin. That was more what I'd expected from the Addamses.

I rested my hand on Stephanie's lower back in a show of solidarity and support, ushering her ahead of me. And not a moment too soon because I barely caught a breath before a shrill shout erupted. "Auntie Steph!"

Before I could blink, Stephanie was mauled by four kids—two boys with wheat hair and azure eyes, a dark-skinned girl with dozens of small braids, and an olive-skinned toddler with her shiny ebony hair pulled into two fountain pigtails. All four chattered over each other, throwing their arms around their aunt. I'd seen Work Mode Steph the last two years, Friend Steph over dinners and board games with our friends, and Casual Steph in the car. But Family Steph? Her hazel eyes sparkled as her nieces and nephews clamoured for her attention. She ruffled hair, kissed cheeks, and entered into their world with such ease I could barely believe this was the same woman who lived in heels and pencil skirts.

"Stephie!" a booming voice called. A tall man built like a linebacker approached us, and I immediately recognized him as the Marine from Stephanie's pictures.

Still swarmed by kids, Stephanie managed a saucy salute. "Captain Carson. At your command, sir!"

Gabe rolled his eyes. "Dork."

The four kids squealed and released their aunt just in time for Gabe to sweep Stephanie into his arms, his tanned face full of affection.

Her laughter bubbled out as she returned the embrace with equal fervour, although her petite frame practically disappeared next to his. When he set her down, she patted his biceps. "Still keeping up the big guns, Staff Sergeant sir?"

He winked at her, smirking. "Ivy appreciates it."

"Gross!" Stephanie faked a gag, but she was smiling.

Gabe's eyes locked on me, and I stood a little straighter. We were the same height, but he was broader, and his bearing was definitely military. He held out a meaty hand to me. "Gabe Carson."

"Nash Prescott," I said, returning the shake firmly. Being in business told me you could tell a lot about a person by their handshake, and Gabe had a good one—solid. I expected nothing less from a military man, even if I was a little lost as to his ranking right now.

Gabe glanced between me and Stephanie. "Your boss?"

She looped her arm around mine and beamed up at Gabe with a doe-eyed look I'd never seen her use. "Boyfriend."

Gabe opened his mouth to say something when the youngest girl, no more than two, tugged on his jean-clad legs, and his smile softened as he lifted the youngster into his arms. She wrapped an arm around his neck and hid her face against his chest as she stole glances at me with her dark almond-shaped eyes.

Stephanie had her free arm around one of the blond boys talking a mile a minute, and since I caught the word *hockey*, I assumed this was Jackson.

Clearly thinking better of questioning his sister in the foyer, Gabe said, "Ryder, Jackson, bring the cookies to the kitchen. And no snacking. Nana will know what to do with them."

The boys—blond, blue eyed, and looking like twins—each hefted up a plastic container and called out, "Cookies coming through!" as they hustled across the living room towards the kitchen.

Gabe shot his sister a meaningful look that meant business. "I have so many questions."

Stephanie scrunched her nose, lightly squeezing my bicep. "You always do."

He chuckled and kissed her forehead before toting off his two girls.

"Stephanie? You came?" a blonde woman with royal blue streaks in her hair eyed Stephanie with disgust, her lips pressed into a sour pucker. When her gaze flicked to me, she gaped like a fish. "And is that... you wouldn't?" Her icy blue eyes could have flayed off flesh with their cutting edges. A crude swear fell out of her before she screamed, "Zoe, get out here!"

Stephanie let out a strangled whimper from the back of her throat and pressed closer to me.

I wrapped an arm around her waist. While I knew she could absolutely hold her own, I wasn't about to let her get mauled by the circling vultures just because I was here.

"Why wouldn't I bring my *boyfriend*, Veronica?" Stephanie practically purred, placing a hand on my chest, making me straighten up instantly. "Isn't this what everyone always wanted? Poor pathetic little Stephanie to 'get serious' with her life?" Sarcasm dripped off her words.

Boyfriend. It gave me a little bit of a thrill… until I remembered that this was only fake. And this was just a performance. *She's not Alexis, who only used you until you didn't serve a purpose anymore. You're both getting something out of this. She needs you in her corner, and you need the chance to help her feel safe enough to let things be real.*

"Him?" Veronica's eyes bugged out comically like a cartoon, and she yelped when the wine glass in her hand shattered as it hit the floor. More swearing.

The room suddenly lost its nostalgic charm. The walls felt closer. More eyes swiveled to us, probing. Questioning. And was that… judging? I knew coming was a risk—Stephanie had all but told me that—but I wasn't prepared for *this*. A few jaws dropped before the volcano erupted.

"Is that *the* Nash Prescott in our living room? With *Stephanie*?"

"Is she out of her mind?"

"What was she thinking?"

"Some nerve you have showing up, Stephanie. And bringing this—*swear*."

"You never could behave like the rest of us. What a loser."

"What in the world is going on?" a platinum-blonde woman demanded, storming into the room, hands on her hips. This must be Zoe. Her hazel eyes raked over me and Stephanie, and her lips curled in a snarl. "You better start explaining yourself."

Stephanie pasted on a smile, fake as tinsel, while the words (abundantly littered with curses) flew at her. With her conference room voice, she announced for the room to hear, "Everyone, meet Nash Prescott, my boyfriend."

The noise level died for all of three seconds. Okay, maybe they'd take this better than I—

The bomb went off.

And the scientific community needed to do a study on the noise levels produced by the Addams family. I could have sworn it broke the laws of nature, *The Guiness Book of World Records*... and a few windows.

CHAPTER FOURTEEN

Stephanie

MAYHEM. THE VOICES CLAMOURED. Accusing. Shouting. Swearing. None of them thrilled. The solid press of Nash's arm around me was the only thing anchoring me to the present, and he squeezed me closer as if sensing I was ready to bolt. How did he know me so well? I was more than ready to ding dong ditch the Addams, hightail it out of the state, and change my phone number. Anyone have Witness Protection's card? Because I was dead meat.

A shrill, intense whistle cut through the room, silencing the commotion, which I swear made the crystal chandelier ring. (Yes, this otherwise rustic cabin did have crystal light fixtures.) And I breathed a prayer of thanks for Gabe's stellar lung capacity and take-charge presence as the pandemonium dimmed. I might give him a hard time, but I adored him, especially in this moment.

"We've all got questions," Gabe said, firm and even, eyeing me with a look that told me I was so in for an interrogation later.

"Whatever your opinions, there's no excuse for rudeness. Nash, welcome. Merry Christmas."

Gabe's speech earned him several withering scowls—from all four of my other siblings—but his hulking size had garnered him enough reverence in the Addams clan that no one contradicted him. They might not like him anymore than they liked me, but he at least could make them listen. Perks of being the eldest instead of the baby, I guess. *Lord, thank you once again for intimidating big brothers.*

Ivy rushed over, gushing as she threw her arms around me. Which was awkward for a second since Nash was still holding onto me. But after the untangling of arms and limbs, I sank into her hug. Ivy was the big sister I'd always wanted—and completely unlike the older sisters I had. She'd married Gabe when they were still teenagers, and I was only seven years old. The gentler counterpart to Gabe's strait-laced nature and a peacemaker at heart, she'd always been a steadying force in my life. And her hugs, a comforting blend of fresh detergent and baby powder, always felt like home.

When I pulled back, because she never let go first, Ivy shook Nash's hand and gave him a once-over, her sharp green eyes beneath tortoiseshell glasses assessing him.

I found myself sweating a little because her opinion mattered to me.

Ivy twisted a long auburn curl around her finger thoughtfully, then speared me with a smirk. "Your boss?"

I flushed. Because.... Okay, I had talked about Nash more than I let on to him in the car. And maybe more than I had admitted to myself. "Yup, this is Nash. Nash, this is Gabe's wife, Ivy."

Nash flashed her his million-dollar smile that never failed to win him clients.

But Ivy was unfazed. She returned the smile warmly and patted my arm, leaning in to hiss, "We are soooooo talking about this later."

Ha. Take a number, sister.

"Stephanie Mae Louise Addams!"

I winced. Being full-named was as terrifying at twenty-eight as it was at eight. There was only one person who got away with using my full name at that volume.

Ivy snickered, backing away with her hands raised. "Good luck," she mouthed, her auburn curls retreating into the lingering crowd, who insisted on spectating like we were in the gladiator arena.

I glared after her. The coward. It was showtime. I grinned ecstatically, then toned it down, so I didn't look like the Joker, baring way too many teeth. That wasn't a good look on anyone. "Hey, Nana! Merry Christmas Eve Eve!"

My nana—Charmain Russo Addams—was a five-foot, American-born Italian firecracker. Her bright white hair was always permed within an inch of its life, and I never saw her in anything other than rainbow, bright colours and chunky jewelry. Oh, and she didn't glide through life. She marched. Currently clad in a red gingham apron over a burnt-orange cardigan and navy slacks, she jabbed her wooden spoon at me.

I jumped back to avoid it, smacking into Nash. His hands gripped my waist, holding me upright as I leaned against him. By this point I was as rosy red as Nana's signature lipstick colour.

Nana jerked to a stop in front of us—me with a mottled face and Nash's fingers still warm at my waist through my sweater. She raised a sculpted feathery eyebrow. I had inherited my short stature from her, so we were eye level. "Care to explain, Stephie?"

No. I really didn't. But it wasn't a question. It was an order. Besides, this was why we were here.

Before I got a word out though, Nash smoothly extended one of his hands to her, the other still resting on my hip. "Mrs. Addams, it's a pleasure. Stephanie speaks very highly of you. I'm Nash Prescott."

Nana harrumphed but shook his hand. She was too well-bred not to. "You're the millionaire boss she talks about all the time." She eyed him from the curl of his hair to the loafers on his feet. "You're right, Stephanie; he is a looker."

I covered my face with my hands. Why did I ever tell her such a thing? If I thought I was red before, the fire department was about to be called because I was officially on fire with embarrassment. And *all the time* was a big stretch. "Okay, Nana, that's enough. What rooms are we in? Separately. Because, you know, together is not happening."

Nana snorted. "Nash can take your luggage to the Mistletoe. You'll be bunking with Hailey." She pointed to the right staircase, and I instantly relaxed because Hailey was my favourite—and only—cousin. "And you"—Nana jabbed a finger at Nash—"will be staying in Cedar." Her finger jerkily shifted to the left-hand staircase. "And there will be no hay rolling on my watch."

"Nana!" I shrieked.

She grinned saucily, swatting at me again with her wooden spoon. "Join me in the kitchen, baby girl, while your man totes up the luggage." She patted his arm. "He's got enough muscles for it, and we'll catch up."

The sweet words were a decoy, a pretty package harbouring devious intent. "I told you she would murder me," I hissed to Nash as she sashayed away.

He glanced between me and Nana's retreating march. "Are you safe alone with her?"

I laughed. His concern was touching. "Safer than you. Just remember I want blue roses and thumbprint cookies at my funeral."

Nash chuckled and nudged me towards the kitchen. "I'll see you soon."

"You better." Without thinking, I blew him a kiss over my shoulder.

And what did the man do? He caught it. And winked.

Darn his dimples.

Now to face the dragon of the family. It was time to catch up with Nana.

I was toast.

"Stephie."

"Nana."

We were in a standoff. Nana had dragged me into the walk-in kitchen pantry where a shelf was now digging into my back as I stared at the bag of flour over our heads. Who thought that was a good idea? One small shake and *poof!* Death by flour sack.

"Out with it, girl."

I thought about waiting her out. Standing my ground. Making her sweat out her questions. But this woman had raised me for the majority of my childhood and teen years, and her stubbornness was the stuff of legends. So, I caved. "We're together," I said simply.

"Mm-hmm. And you decided Christmas was the time to spring this joyous news on us?"

"He doesn't have family nearby and usually spends Christmas with friends. So I thought..." It was a low blow, but appealing to Nana's inner devotion to family—even one as dysfunctional as ours—had the desired effect when she deflated from samurai warrior to kindly grandma ready to adopt the world. I didn't have the full scoop on Nash's family situation. Just that he never talked about them. Overhearing him mention a grandmother to Liz this morning in the entryway was the most I'd learned in the last two years. And I was trying to not be jealous he'd told her and not me. But Liz had that effect on people—they told her everything.

"And you're sure about this between you two?" Nana asked, smoothing the front of her apron.

My shoulders hunched. "Nana, I'm not sure of anything these days. But we're dating. To see if we're compatible and I... I like him a lot, and I want you to like him, too." *No lies there.*

She was quiet for a minute—an eternity really, miracle that—before she nodded slowly and gathered me in a hug. "All right, baby. If you're sure, we'll give him a chance. Well, some of us will." She squeezed me tight, smelling like her signature lilac perfume and freshly baked cookies. "Though bringing that man into this family speaks volumes on his character. And I don't know if I should congratulate you on your cunning or lament your insanity."

I huffed. "Maybe a little of both."

"Besides," Nana reached out and cupped my cheek, smiling warmly, "I've been worried about you and praying the Lord would bring the right person to you. You've been alone too long. Hopefully that bit of eye candy you brought is the answer to my prayers."

"Nana, you can't say things like that!"

She shrugged, waggling her feathery brows. "Always appreciate the beauty the Good Lord creates."

I had to laugh, but at the same time, I relished in the comfort of her hug and the security of her prayers. Nana was legendary as a prayer warrior—I was in good hands, hers and the Lord's.

CHAPTER FIFTEEN

Nash

STEPHANIE WASN'T KIDDING ABOUT the Christmas fanatics. I hadn't even toured the whole place, and I'd already counted four trees between the living room, entryway, and the two Charlie Brown trees on the upper mezzanine floor leading to the sleeping wings. And I had no doubt there were more.

Across from a palatial washroom, I found the Mistletoe Room. It had one of those fancy lacquered brass nameplates on the door with the name. And judging by the Pine, Juniper, and Holly rooms I'd passed on the way here, forest themed seemed to be the order of the day.

"Who in the Kris Kringle of Christmas are you?" an extremely feminine voice that sounded vaguely familiar demanded as I awkwardly tried to wrangle Stephanie's luggage into the Mistletoe.

Whirling around, I caught a glimpse of the unseen voice. Curly brown hair, wild and free with snapping hazel eyes, much like

Stephanie's, and a hefty volume of literature in her hand. Was that Shakespeare or a Bible? Both would hurt upon impact.

"Uh…" I stammered, unsure of myself. Why did this woman look so familiar? *Nana* had *said Mistletoe, right? And why am I mentally referring to her as* Nana? *That's Mrs. Addams to you.*

"Well?" the woodland pixie snapped, prepared to wallop me with her tome of choice.

The light clicked in my memory. *Cousin Hailey.* I cleared my throat and offered her my hand, slipping into business mode. "You must be Hailey. I'm Nash Prescott, Stephanie's boyfriend. I was told to bring her luggage here—"

Hailey's shriek shattered whatever hearing I had left after the initial Addams family mega blast. "Oh my goodness! *Boyfriend!* Stephie Lou!" she screamed, bolting from the room.

I inhaled deeply and pinched the bridge of my nose. *One week. One week of noise. For Stephanie. For us. I can do this.*

More shrieking erupted downstairs, and I'd wager a guess the energetic sprite of a woman had found Stephanie. The… complicated welcome of Stephanie's family wasn't lost on me. She was clearly beloved and despised at the same time. But the welcome of those who loved her… wow. I'd been alone most of my adult life, excepting Ryan and Emmett. My grandparents had passed in my teens, and my mom… I'd lost any version of her around the same time.

Once Genesis started up and grew rapidly successful, she started contacting me again, asking for money. I'd funded four stints of rehab, and it stuck for a while, until she found a new guy who drew her back into the drugs. I hated her choices, and my heart broke a little more every time I heard she wasn't clean anymore.

Now I just dreaded her phone calls when she'd ask for rent money and promise to do better. But they were empty words. I'd heard them all my life. And I hated the fact I was only worth something to her when she needed the money.

So I was alone. Alexis, my college girlfriend, was my first and last serious relationship. And that had ended in a dumpster fire of a disaster. It'd just been me and the guys, and by extension, their families. This level of familial connections and community was as foreign as snow for Christmas on the Texas Gulf Coast.

Realizing I shouldn't be caught standing in the middle of Stephanie's room, I slipped back out into the hall. But I wasn't ready to face the exuberance and tensions below after dwelling on the weighty chapter of my past. The way my thoughts turned back to my childhood Christmases, my grandparents, and how alone I felt made me uncomfortable.

A small nook tucked into the panelled wall sat nestled at the end of the hallway, overlooking the star-studded sky and the silhouetted shape of the Tetons. I stood there for a moment, lost in thought. Praying I wouldn't mess this week up beyond repair.

I tried to imagine that the Addams actually wanted me here. Or that Stephanie and I were a real couple. Maybe I should be honest with her about my past. She was certainly giving me a window into her world this week. Maybe it was time I returned the favour. Not because of a bargain, but because I wanted to open up. Maybe.

You'll never be enough for her. You weren't for Alexis. I shoved the thoughts away and hurried back towards the stairs. I might have been ready to take on my familial past, but I wasn't ready to battle the lies from a former girlfriend right now. The enemy camp was preferable to the war with a ghost inside my own head.

Chapter Sixteen

Stephanie

"WHAT IS THIS, AN intervention?" I sat cross-legged on the quilt-covered bed, opposite my cousin Hailey, who was grinning like the Cheshire cat, while Ivy perched next to her and Gabe stood blocking the closed door, arms folded and stern lines guarding his expression—like this was a military mission... More like I was the mission, and he would be taking no prisoners.

We had a brief pocket of time before dinner, and my closest relatives decided *now* was the ideal time to undertake a debriefing. No one asked if *I* thought it was a good time because, for the record, I did not. I was hungry, and whatever Austin was cooking smelled *divine*. Perks of having a brother who was a professional chef. He was the most decent of my siblings who worked for Hiram. Maybe because Austin didn't technically work for Nova—he worked for the catering company Hiram owned.

And I was nervous leaving Nash alone with only Nana downstairs, since the rest of my main allies were all holed up here with me. Too bad Aunt Robin and Uncle Jim, Hailey's parents, were on their anniversary cruise to the Caribbean. They'd have been a helpful buffer compared to the rest of the vipers downstairs. But Nash would be fine. Right?

Ivy pushed her tortoiseshell glasses up her nose and raised an eyebrow at me. Wow, she'd really mastered that mom look. "Boyfriend, girly pop? Spill it."

"And leave out no details," Hailey cut in, batting her lashes and clasping her hands under her chin dramatically. "Is he a good kisser?"

Gabe let out a strangled gurgle. I tossed a buffalo-plaid throw pillow at Hailey's head, but she ducked with ease, cackling like a cartoon villain. *Cousins.* But it was impossible to be angry with her because Hailey was a lovable, vibrant soul without the Addams last name to weigh her down.

"Your boss?" Gabe prompted gruffly.

Ooh, that's the unimpressed voice mixed with—am I a dad or a brother in this situation? I puffed out my cheeks, letting my head drop back against the wood-panelled wall. What should I tell them? I was still sorting through the idea of dating Nash for real, so for now this was part of a bargain. The fulfilment of a debt. I organized a Christmas party; he would pretend to date me. Suddenly I was wondering how he got the raw end of the deal.

But these were my people. The ones in my corner. They'd shown up again and again. *Until the day they don't. Everyone leaves,* the dark voice in my head, that sounded exactly like Zoe, whispered. I doubt she ever thought those harsh words spoken from the heartache of her own teenaged self would have gripped me so deeply. I shoved the words—and the memory—away but still tasted their bitterness.

"We're dating," I said at last, opening my eyes and meeting their gazes. "He knows about all of you. I keep pictures on my desk, and he asks about the kids and Gabe's deployments and Hailey's music"—I pointed at her—"he loves your newest album by the way. Why is our relationship so hard to believe? Am I that out of his league?"

I tried not to sound defensive, but Samantha and Anika's words from the office party did more damage than they'd ever imagined. My insecurities were coming out to play hardball, and I was still in the minor leagues.

"No!" Hailey practically shouted, bounding off her bed and onto mine. Her arms squeezed me tight in a Hailey-hug that never failed to make me feel better. Pulling back, she pinned me with a firm look. "You're a total catch. And for the record, I'm Team Steph all the way. If he shares your values, makes you happy, and treats you right, you've got a keeper."

I leaned my head against her shoulder and glanced expectantly at Gabe and Ivy. We had a unique relationship. There were twelve years between me and Gabe. Since my dad was absent for most—read: *all*—of my growing up years, I lived with Nana and Papa and then later with Gabe and Ivy for a while. Ivy was a year younger than Gabe, making it an awkward balance at times to straddle the brother and sister dynamic with the stand-in parents' role they played in my teens.

"We're glad you brought him home, Steph," Ivy said at last, her voice gentle. Ever the diplomat and peacekeeper. This wasn't her first time refereeing between us, and I doubted it'd be the last. "You just never told *us* you were dating. This is new, yeah?"

"It's not like he's a stranger," Hailey added. "We've only been hearing about him every other week for the last two years."

Okay, maybe I overestimated when I told Nash that Nana would be the hardest sell. Clearly, I talked about him more than I'd realized to my favourite relatives. But they were nosy, and I loved them for it. Except for maybe right now when they were standing between me and dinner.

"Yes. It *is* new," I confessed. "I like him, and he feels the same about me. So I don't want you scaring him off with your bad-guy routine." I glared at Gabe with all the heat I could muster.

Gabe still didn't say a word. This wasn't a good sign because Gabe's poker face was impossible to read. Hello, military training. Which left me no choice but to deploy my own training. A little something I called Operation Dollface. Which I hadn't used since I was sixteen and trying to soften him up to let me go to prom with a boy. The same guy who Anika dared me to kiss, but Gabe didn't know about that, and I'd take that news to my grave. This was almost the same thing. Kinda.

Slipping out of Hailey's hug, I crossed the room and paused in front of Gabe. At over a foot taller than my five-foot frame, he towered above me, which worked to my advantage. Lightly gripping his folded forearms, I leaned into him and gave him my best soulful, wide-eyed pleading expression—the same one his daughters now used. As a youngster, I'd discovered I had Gabe wrapped around my finger and only had to flash this look at him to get him to cave. It had worked the last time I used it for prom, but I was twenty-eight now. Were the odds still in my favour?

Gabe's cheek twitched, and the firm muscles under my hands relaxed. Oh, I had him.

"Please understand?" I added for good measure. "He's a really good man."

The military stance crumbled, transforming him into my squishy big brother with a heart of marshmallow fluff. "Fine."

Score! I bit my lip to hold in my laughter. I hadn't been sure it would still work, but man, I was good.

As if he could read my thoughts, Gabe flicked my forehead lightly.

"Hey!"

"I'm only agreeing to this because I'll get to keep an eye on him for the week, and if he hurts you, he'll have my guns to answer to."

I patted his biceps and cooed, "So you did this for me, too, and not just Ivy?"

Gabe swatted my hand away with a grunt. "Not those guns."

"Chill out, big brother. I said no bad-guy routine."

"You should have thought of that before you pulled that ridiculous stunt. Your eyes look weird when you do that."

"More ridiculous than you still falling for it?"

"Dork." But the word didn't sting as Gabe chuckled and kissed my forehead. "You're a good judge of character, Steph. No one's questioning that. We're just surprised you sprung this on us."

"But we're happy." Ivy stood and hugged me. "Truly."

"Thanks." I shifted uncomfortably, trying to find the words to tell them how much they meant to me. How much their trust and opinions mattered. How much I wanted them to love Nash like I did. *Whoa, there. We're not at love yet, girl. Not if you can't even commit to not-fake yet.*

Hailey squeezed my hand. "We've got you, Stephie."

Roaring laughter erupted from the floor below, and there was absolutely no telling what sort of torture the rest of the Addams clan was inflicting on Nash. This family played low and dirty, particularly with the enemy. And if they were laughing, chances were high it was at Nash's expense.

"Now if you'll excuse me," I said, grinning through my apprehension. "I have a boyfriend to save."

IT WAS SO MUCH worse than I thought.

Nash was cornered between Great-Aunt Edith, the mistletoe, and the punch bowl. A triple trifecta of a bad idea.

Someone had the brilliant idea to go all out on the mistletoe this year—whoever you are, you are dead to me. But it was probably Nana, since she was in charge of assembling a team to decorate the cabin. But Zoe did interior design on the side so... maybe it was her? I did a quick scan of the crowd for my oldest half sister—her expensive platinum hair as bright as a lighthouse beacon—but I didn't see her.

Moving on. I had bigger flames to put out.

Great-Aunt Edith was a scary woman on a good day. But catch her at Christmas in a bah-humbug mood that included spiked eggnog, and you'd better run for your life.

But Nash clearly didn't have the same level of self-preservation skills because he engaged her in conversation, all the while slowly moving backwards in the direction of a sprig of mistletoe.

Great-Aunt Edith was no fool. She knew exactly what she was doing, luring her prey with senile complacency. And Nash was about to become her victim.

I rudely shoved my way across the room, tripping over someone's foot. And a random elbow clocked me in the temple so hard I saw stars. Pretty sure that one was on purpose. My knees nearly buckled, and I grabbed the sofa back for support, but I needed to rescue Nash. Fainting could wait. Rushing up to him, I gripped his shirt front and hauled him towards me.

The momentum startled him, and he grasped my waist tightly. Questions swirled in his eyes as he glanced between me and the enemy... er, elderly relative.

"Hi," I said breathlessly, my mind blanking on what exactly my escape plan was. I was no Marine and clearly no Great-Aunt Edith either. I'd gotten him away from her clutches, but now what? We couldn't stay here all night.

Nash was under no such compulsion as he didn't seem to mind. Leaning forward, his warm breath tickled my ear as he whispered, "To what do I owe this pleasure?"

I shoved at him, trying to tell him to behave, but still clutched his shirt with one hand. Plastering the most benign smile I could summon, I faced Great-Aunt Edith. "I've got to steal him away. Thanks for making him feel welcome."

Her wiry eyebrow arched, calling me out. "Selfish girl, hogging such a nice man. Even if he is the enemy. Hiram will hate him." She grinned manically. "And won't that be a treat. I'll tell Charmain we'll need popcorn for that showdown."

I dragged Nash away from her, through the crowded living room and down a quiet hall into a small den. Only once the door was closed behind us did I heave a sigh of relief. How she and Papa were siblings baffled me. Papa had been the nicest man in the world. Great-Aunt Edith was a garlic-breathing dragon with questionable morals.

"Not that I'm complaining," Nash said smugly, "but care to share why I was just hauled into a dark room with my girlfriend?"

I glared at him. "You have no idea how close you came." I nearly laughed at his bewildered expression, but Great-Aunt Edith was no laughing matter. "I warned you about her, and you just about fell into her clutches."

"You said avoid the spiked eggnog," he clarified.

"The eggnog and Edith are a package deal. You were standing between them. What's worse is the mistletoe. You were about two feet and three seconds away from being mauled by an octogenarian who chomps on raw garlic every morning."

Nash actually turned a bit green. "But I have a girlfriend. Why would she...?"

I snorted. "That doesn't mean much to Edith. You could have a ring on your finger, and she'd still make passes at you." Collapsing into a brocade armchair, I dropped my head into my hands, the bump on my temple smarting. This was all too much. Apart from Nana, Hailey, Gabe, and Ivy, I didn't exist day-to-day with the rest of the Addams family. Just got roped into family holiday occasions like this. Sometimes—when Hiram wasn't bombing me with texts—I could forget just how much the outcast I was with the rest of them. Coming back was like getting a front row seat to a horror movie.

"How is Hiram?" Nash finally asked, easing down on the ottoman across from me.

Excellent question. How was dear old Dad who gave me his name, ditched me at five years old, occasionally dropped in to flash around expensive gifts on major holidays, and effectively disappeared from my life the rest of the time? "As manipulative as always." I swallowed hard. "He threatened to set me up with a certified creep, but I told him I already had a boyfriend."

His thoughtful expression turned downright murderous, and my heart warmed several degrees.

Before I got the job, I'd disclosed to Nash I was the daughter of his biggest competitor. Honestly, I thought it might have cost me the position, but to my surprise it seemed to be the thing to seal the deal. Keep your friends close and your enemies closer, I guess. But I wasn't out to steal company secrets, and Nash seemed to know that. No. I was dead determined to live outside my father's shadow, and if working for a rival company was the way to do that, so be it. I was a trailblazer.

My therapist used other words, but that's a different story. I didn't hate my dad. His abandonment stung when I was younger, and if I was honest, still did. What kid didn't want their dad's attention and approval? To not be shuffled off to another relative because she was inconvenient? Instead, I got Louis Vuitton shoes for birthday gifts and a pony for Christmas. And I didn't even like horses. Money was no object with Hiram Addams, but all I wanted was the thing I never got—his attention. His love was too big a thing to ask for. At eighteen, he offered to pay my way through college, and I turned him down. I paid for it all myself and never took another dime.

He forgot my birthday, but when it came to Christmas, he still tried to buy my loyalty to maintaining the family image with lavish gifts. Hiram Addams was a prominent figure in the social world—his family had to act accordingly. But the expensive gifts didn't mean anything. They didn't fit in my world. And I didn't fit into his, between his work and his woman of the week.

"Does he know I'm the boyfriend in question?" Nash asked roughly.

I fell back in my chair, laughing. Not a cute laugh or a giggle but a deranged honk. One of my siblings had probably ratted me out already, but I didn't bother mentioning it.

Nash cracked a smile, like my moment of insanity amused him. "I'll take that as a no."

"I'm sorry." I straightened, shaking my head. "I should have been more upfront about why I asked. Snap, I shouldn't even have asked. This is insane. Totally my fault. Absofreakinglutely—"

Nash's hand squeezed mine gently, cutting off the flow of verbal nonsense spewing from my soul. "No. Don't apologize. Your dad should have never put you in this situation." His free hand brushed against my temple. "Did you get hurt?"

"I'm okay," I whispered breathily.

Nash's fingers lingered a minute, then dropped away. "I don't have extended family," he said slowly. "I was raised by a single mom, and for a short time, her parents until they passed when I was in my teens. I never knew my dad. It's not even on my birth certificate. At nineteen, I was completely alone in the world, familywise."

I swallowed hard. Nash had always been incredibly tight-lipped about his past and never talked about his family connections. But I desperately wanted him to open up, share more. He was getting a front-row seat to my mess. Something I was regretting by the second. "I'm sorry. Were you close to them?"

He stiffened, avoiding my gaze and drawing his hand, still holding mine, back.

Come on, open up. You saw what we walked into. Can't I know more about your family than what fits on a postage stamp?

"It doesn't matter now."

I frowned. "Of course it does. If you—"

"We were no Addams family," he quipped, motioning towards the door. "Seeing all that, I have no protocol for normal family dynamics because I may not have your typical American family, but even I know that isn't normal, darlin'."

I loved when he let his twang slip. And *darlin*? Melt me. But I knew what he was doing, deflecting from his own family. And it stung. In the car, he said he was curious about me, wanted to know things. Why, then, couldn't he return the favour and be open with me? "Normal is overrated," I deadpanned.

Nash grimaced. "You Addamses may have gotten more than your fair share of the toxic family genes, but they don't scare me. Okay, your nana scares me, but I like her. Gabe seems cool. Ivy and the kids are great. I can already tell I've won Hailey over. What I can see, though, is that they *love* you. That's the thing that matters. We can handle the naysayers together."

Tears pricked in my eyes, but there was no way I was crying in front of this man. I wasn't sure what hurt more—how sweet his words tasted or how desperately I wished he let down a few of his walls for me.

"We made a deal. We're good. Save me from Aunt Edith is all I ask."

He might live to regret those words, but for now, I brushed a kiss to his cheek in thanks. It was quick—a butterfly touch—and I pulled away quickly.

Nash stared at me, and I blinked. I shouldn't have done that. We had rules, and we didn't have an audience, so... My stomach picked exactly that moment to rumble, and I pressed a hand to my middle, biting my lip. Lunch in Butte had been great but way too long ago.

Nash chuckled, breaking the tension. "Let's get you fed. Whatever Austin—it is Austin, right?—is cooking smells amazing."

Smiling at him, I added, "Final warning: It's karaoke night."

CHAPTER SEVENTEEN

Nash

ADDAMS FAMILY KARAOKE NIGHT should come with a warning label. Because this wasn't karaoke. This was war.

I was starting to get the impression that everything Stephanie's family touched wasn't family fun as much as a family competition. Like there was an invisible scoreboard for favourite Addams sibling. Hiram wasn't even present yet, and they were already out for blood.

Austin whipped up a fantastic assortment of homemade pizzas unlike anything I'd tasted before and had me seriously missing my college metabolism. Then in my satiated pliability, I was crammed onto a tan plaid couch—I swear it walked off the set of every '90s sitcom I watched growing up—right beside Stephanie, who had Gabe and Ivy's youngest on her lap. The toddler eyed me with suspicion seeping from her dark almond-shaped eyes. Eden,

I recalled her name was. Given that none of the four kids looked anything like their parents, I bet they were adopted.

Hailey wedged in on Stephanie's other side and was more than happy to spill all the details about her cousin, much to Stephanie's horror. Hailey Bishop was a valuable ally in the venerable lions' den. We chatted briefly about her music—of which I was a huge fan—and I got a sneak-peek hint at her new release coming in the new year. She hadn't earned the title of America's Country Sweetheart for nothing.

Nana—or Charmain, I wasn't sure what I was supposed to call her—stood in front of the living room television, clipboard in hand. Fingers to her lips, she gave a shrill whistle, and the cacophony died down. So that's where Gabe got it from.

I'd gotten a quick head count over dinner and there were twenty-five Addams relations in this palatial mansion. Noise just came with the territory.

Nana squared her shoulders and surveyed the room, like a general assessing her troops. "Everyone ready? Rules are the same as usual. The team divisions are known only by the judge"—she grinned ferally—"that would be me. Each performance will be voted on by the audience, so keep your score cards handy. At the end, the performance totals will be tallied, and the team with the highest score wins."

I leaned into Stephanie. "This is blind karaoke?"

Eden's elbow dug into my gut as she rearranged herself to recline more comfortably against Stephanie. Cute kid.

Stephanie's lips pinched. "We're Addamses. Did you expect anything different?"

I chuckled softly. "Ryan would love this, and Emmett would hate it. I might borrow this for a payback plan."

"If you do, invite me because I'd *pay* to see Emmett do karaoke."

"First performance!" Nana announced, then her eyes homed in on me like a heat-seeking missile. "Stephanie and Nash!"

Murmurs slithered around the room as Stephanie shifted Eden onto Hailey's lap and stood up. Reaching out a hand, she tugged me up after her, leaning against me for a brief moment to catch her balance. "Let the initiation begin," she whispered.

I kept hold of her hand as she led me to the front of the room. Was I going to humiliate myself? Very likely. But I could see the spark of determination in Stephanie's eyes. As much as her family dynamics wore on her, she was still trying to enter the spirit of the occasion. And I wasn't about to let her down. Although...

"Is now a bad time to mention I can't carry a tune?" I murmured in her ear as we took the proffered mics from Nana.

Stephanie tossed me a cheeky smile. "Everyone needs a handicap. Levels the field."

I could get addicted to her smile. When I caught Gabe's stare, I refocused on the task at hand instead of daydreaming about his sister, which I was certain he wouldn't appreciate.

"Do we pick the song?" I asked Stephanie.

She bit her lip, trying to hold back a laugh. "That would be too easy."

"I'm beginning to realize your family loves torture as much as your namesakes," I grumbled, waiting for the television screen to roll the words. Then I panicked. "Wait, we do get the word prompts, right?"

"We're competitive, not sadistic, Nash." That wasn't an affirmative. But the cue words popped up on the screen, a dark green background with a Christmassy border. How festive. When the music started, I easily picked out the tune of Mariah Carey's "All I Want for Christmas is You."

Hailey moaned from the front row and covered her ears. Clearly not a Mariah fan since I hadn't even opened my mouth yet. But Eden laughed in Hailey's lap, bouncing to the beat.

Tough crowd.

Stephanie swayed rhythmically to the music and began to sing. Her voice was soft and soothing. Not cultured like Hailey's but breezy and light. I was so busy watching her, I nearly missed my cue, and it probably would have been a good thing because the minute I opened my mouth, a muffled snort erupted from the audience—my money was on Gabe since he was recording my public humiliation. Stephanie didn't miss a beat, but as she met my gaze, the mirth danced in her eyes. I could make a joyful *noise* unto the Lord all right because no one was mistaking what came out of my mouth for music. Did that stop me from belting out the bridge like I was Mariah herself? Absolutely not. I clutched my pearls to make a Southern grandma proud and let the music pound out of me.

Halfway through, Stephanie stopped singing, doubled over at the waist with laughter. I wasn't used to being the brunt of the joke—that was more Ryan's style—but I loved her laugh. And if horrible karaoke was the way to coax that rare sound out... bring it on.

We finished the last verse strong, hitting our stride. But at the final chorus, Stephanie's face paled, and the words died on her lips.

The unnatural ashen shade of her skin made me quickly step towards her, gripping her arm. Was this another POTS attack? I had done some reading after she had told me about it the night of the office party—in between researching the pros and cons of fake dating—and I racked my brain trying to figure out if karaoke was somehow a trigger. Lack of oxygen caused dizziness, but did it lower blood pressure? I'd seen her take her meds in the car, but did she need more? The music cut out.

"What a mercy," Veronica muttered. "I think my ears are bleeding."

A single clap of applause came from the back of the room.

That's when I focused on my surroundings. And I saw exactly why Stephanie suddenly resembled a sickly Victorian child in need of a seaside vacation.

Hiram Addams was in the house.

Chapter Eighteen

Stephanie

I WAS PRETTY SURE deathly paleness wasn't a symptom most adult children experienced when in the presence of their father figure. But after those light moments of singing karaoke with Nash, seeing that smooth face (thanks, plastic surgery), more pepper-than-salt hair (thanks, Turkish "vacation"), twisted smile, and a blonde bombshell on his arm (wife number seven to be exact), I remembered I hadn't prepared Nash for this exact moment of an Addams family nightmare... er, Christmas.

I'd brought him into enemy territory and thrown him to the literal sharks. If he thought Great-Aunt Edith was bad, Hiram Addams was another story.

Oh, they had met before. On opposite sides of the board room and a marketing war. And as of two years ago, I'd been caught in the middle.

I'd stopped taking Hiram's calls, but passive-aggressive texts still pinged my phone occasionally. Like at that crazy office party. We hadn't had a face-to-face meeting in over two years, and now we were doing it with Nash present. Lovely.

"What do we have here?" Hiram tilted his head thoughtfully, but with a dark, cunning gleam in his hazel eyes as they darted between Nash and me. Hazel eyes... The one predominant feature we shared. Everything else I inherited from the mother I could barely remember.

Nash's hand gently squeezed my arm. Right, he was still holding onto me. He bent his head to my ear. "You okay?"

Blood whooshed in my ears, but I nodded and flashed him a small smile, hoping he read the apology in my face. "Dad." The word felt rusty on my tongue since I never used it. "Nice to see you." I glanced at the young blonde woman beside him. She didn't look more than thirty-five, but between the make up and the... *lifts* I couldn't be certain. She was young. That much was obvious. Could even be Zoe's age. *He's old enough to be her father. Ugh.* "And you must be..."

"Zara!" the woman cried enthusiastically. "We were married just last month. Hiram, what a cute little family you have!"

Zara—who ironically shared a name with one of my nieces—didn't talk, she gushed. And this family was anything but small. As for cute... Sure, the kids were. Everyone else was a piranha. Mostly. And currently watching the showdown in smug intrigue.

"Prescott," Hiram growled, ignoring Zara's trilling voice and grip on his arm with her clawlike hot pink nails. "What are you doing in my home?"

My heart thundered in my ribcage, begging to take flight, and I sucked in a raspy breath. "He's here with me," I said with a firmness that surprised even me, taking a step closer. "Nash is my boyfriend." Every nerve and muscle was taut with strain, ready to go to battle. I felt like one of those early medieval rulers granting sanctuary to an enemy. Claiming him as my business.

Hiram's eyes sharpened, followed by an ugly curse. "It's not enough that you humiliated us by agreeing to work with him, but now you sully our name further by sleeping with him of all people?"

Embarrassment burned my cheeks. "That's not... We're not—"

Hiram flicked a hand, silencing me. "You told me you were bringing a suitable guest. He is not welcome in my home. You're a little—"

"Don't insult her," Nash interrupted in his commanding boardroom voice, making half of my siblings gawk at his audacity. He shifted protectively beside me. "I know I'm not worthy of your daughter, and whatever choice words you have for me, fine. But leave her out of it. She's a fine woman—one to be proud of. I know I am."

Um... *swoon.* I gaped at him. *Fake. This is fake.* But when Nash met my gaze and kissed my forehead, it sure didn't feel like it.

"Leave them alone, Hiram," Nana snapped, smacking her clipboard for emphasis and cutting into my short-circuiting spiral of emotions. "She brought a date, as you asked. They're your guests. If he goes, so does she."

Ignoring his mother, Hiram hummed to himself, patting Zara's arm. "Children and their little rebellions." He blinked at me. "You've disappointed me yet again, Stephanie." To the rest of the group, he waved, adding, "Carry on. We'll get settled and cleaned up"—he eyed Zara, frowning slightly at her jeans and blouse—"into something more... suitable, and then we'll come join you."

Once they were out of earshot, Great-Aunt Edith threw a handful of popcorn in the air. "Woo-hoo! Now that's what I'm talking about!"

Nana instantly jumped back into karaoke mode, calling for the next pair—Hailey and Ivy. With Hailey being a professional singer, she was always a guaranteed win. *She should have been paired with Nash.*

But I barely heard the duet as Nash steered me towards the couch, settling in with his arm draped lightly over my shoulders. I tucked my legs under me to counteract the dizziness swirling through my veins, and the slant of the sofa tilted me towards him. I couldn't find it in my heart to care that I was almost plastered against him as the adrenaline drained from my body.

His fingers gently caressed the side of my neck, loosening the tight muscles. I wanted to fight the sensation. Fight the urge to relax. But I was too tired. Too... everything. Giving in, I let myself sink against him, dropping my head against his chest. Listening to the steady thrum of his heartbeat.

"You regretting coming?" I muttered. Not that anyone could hear me over the sweet sound of the women singing "Winter Wonderland."

Nash's chuckle rumbled under my ear. "Not a chance." His soft words tickled the hair at my temple. "I'm exactly where I want to be. Chilly reception notwithstanding. I'm not here for them. I'm here for you, Steph."

The words warmed my soul more than the cozy blanket he tugged over our laps and were twice as sweet as hot cocoa topped with marshmallows. His eyes softened in the glow from the Christmas tree, and his lips tipped up in a grin.

Steph, stop staring at his lips. This is FAKE, girl. I blinked rapidly and refocused on the duet, clapping as Hailey and Ivy bowed dramatically. But not before Nash chuckled again and tipped me farther into him. He had noticed me looking at his mouth, and no doubt my thoughts were way too obvious in neon lights above my head. *It could be real though.*

Liz had been right to question my acting abilities. This was going to be a long week.

CHAPTER NINETEEN

Nash

OUR TEAM WON KARAOKE. Based on the team groupings revealed in the end, most of the score was thanks to Hailey and the cute kid duets. It definitely wasn't thanks to Hiram, who after his "see you soon" holed up in his quarters the rest of the evening. Zara joined us, fidgeting with the ends of her loose curls, saying he was on a "work call." I felt bad for her, getting thrust into a ready-made family without anyone in her corner. She deserved better than that.

After getting the kids down for the night, Stephanie's siblings and their partners, except Gabe and Ivy, cracked out the alcohol and were enjoying the hot tub on the enclosed back deck, judging by the muffled raucous laughter. Which left Hailey, Stephanie, and me in the living room with the enchanting glow of the light from the tree, hot mulled cider in hand. Nana had yawned loudly about twenty minutes ago and excused herself for the night, saying an old woman needed her sleep, but she was as spry as the rest of us, so my money said it was a ruse. But Hailey regaled me with stories of her and Stephanie growing up. They were close, despite growing up in different cities and often different states. It was easy to see that with their shared comradery, the "remember when..." stories, and the uninhibited laughter.

"Remember when I'd sleep over with you at Nana and Papa's, and we'd be up till midnight talking? And Nana kept coming in and threatening to separate us if we weren't quiet?" Hailey asked.

Stephanie snickered. "Yeah, but it was your idea to keep smuggling toys under the covers until there was a big lump between us in the middle of the bed."

"You were older! You should have stopped me!"

"Would you have listened?"

Hailey's head dropped back against the sofa as she shook with laughter, nearly spilling her cider. "Point taken."

The ease between them made my chest twinge. I didn't have these close sister-cousin type relationships of my own growing up, but watching them reminisce had me aching for my own kids to have these close connections one day.

Whoa, buddy. Brakes on. We're not at the kids' stage of this relationship yet.

I knew this and yet... somehow seeing Stephanie surrounded by her nieces and nephews clamouring for her attention flashed a mental picture to life. Her with a passel of kids with our looks combined, swarming me when I came home. Her big eyes sparkling as she smiled at me with a baby on her hip... Yeah, that felt way too easy to picture as real.

The topic of conversation shifted to karaoke, and I learned these two were the perpetrators for starting the tradition of tonight's suffering.

"It was all you." Hailey wagged her fingers at Stephanie. "You got me obsessed with *High School Musical*, and we had to make home movies of our singing every single track."

Stephanie didn't deny it. "Hey, our rendition of 'Gotta Go My Own Way' practically got you your first audition. Besides, that franchise is golden."

"I agree," I slipped in casually. "They don't make them like that anymore."

Both women gaped at me, wearing identical wide-eyed expressions. Side by side, it was easy to see how they were related, especially with those hazel eyes and facial mannerisms.

"You know the song?" Hailey demanded.

"You've *seen* all *three* of them?" Stephanie gasped.

I shrugged. "Ryan—" Glancing at Hailey, I added, "—one of my best friends, had a phase in college. He was trying to impress a cute—his words, not mine—theatre major who loved the shows. Emmett, our other best friend, and I never quite recovered from that binge watch weekend." I chuckled.

"Did it work?" Hailey asked, leaning forward in anticipation. Like needing to know if this couple got together over ten years ago was necessary to her current happiness.

I shrugged. "He married her."

Hailey clasped her hands together, sighing moonily like it was the most romantic thing she'd ever heard.

"And I totally need to see these home movie versions," I added.

Hailey's grin was devious as she whipped out her phone.

Stephanie lunged at her cousin. "Don't you dare!" she shrieked. "And since when did you make digital proof?"

Hailey shushed her. "Remember the children!" To me she mouthed *Later*, giving me a conspiratory nod. Stretching, she added, "As fun as this has been, I've gotta get to bed. Nana's got a food list a mile long, and the annual snowball war is tomorrow. And skiing on the twenty-sixth. I'm tired just thinking about it."

"Snowball war?" I asked. "You Addamses can't do anything easy, can you? Why have a fight if you can have a war?"

"Now you're asking the right questions." Hailey smirked then glanced at Stephanie. "How much did you prepare him for this experience?"

Stephanie groaned, eyes sliding shut as she sagged against the back of the plaid couch. "Clearly not enough. Great-Aunt Edith just about got him earlier."

Hailey shuddered with horror. "You're a lucky man, Nash Prescott."

"For escaping Edith?" I raised an eyebrow.

Fondness touched her smile when she glanced at Stephanie. "Sure. But also your taste in women. You picked a keeper."

"Hail," Stephanie warned, but Hailey jumped up before the throw pillow Stephanie tossed at her could do any damage.

Halfway up the stairs, she paused to blow a kiss and waggle her fingers. "Behave yourselves now! Don't do anything I wouldn't do!"

Stephanie tried to splutter out a reply, but the cackling pixie was already gone.

I only chuckled and draped an arm along the sofa back, lightly touching her shoulders. "She's good for you. I'm glad you invited me."

The suspicion on Stephanie's face told me she thought I was kidding, but I wasn't. Rising, I held out a hand to her. "Let me escort my girlfriend to her room for the night. Something tells me we're going to need all the rest we can get for this war tomorrow."

She grasped my hand, letting me pull her upwards. Till we were standing close. Too close. I could make out the smattering of freckles on her cheekbones. Adorable. The flecks of gold in her hazel eyes. Funny how I'd never noticed them before. She gripped my hand, setting her free hand against my chest as she swayed lightly on her feet, eyes slipping shut.

I lightly grasped her waist, waiting a moment for her to catch her balance. Her eyes blinked open again, and a man could get lost in their depths, twinkling with sparkling lights from the Christmas tree. The softness of her smile...

"Oh, sorry!"

We jumped apart at the chagrined voice. Zara lingered at the edge of the room, her bright pink nails fidgeting nervously with the belt of her blush-pink silk bathrobe. Without the makeup, she appeared more normal, and weariness drooped her smile as she adjusted the clear framed blue-light glasses she wore.

"Hey, Zara." Stephanie offered an awkward wave.

Zara's smile brightened. "I didn't mean to interrupt, just came to get some water but got a little turned around."

I laughed lightly. "It's an easy thing to do around here."

She glanced between us. "It's Nash and Stephanie, right? There are so many names. I'm trying not to mix everyone up."

Stephanie nodded. "That's us."

I had to admit I was impressed by the woman. Hiram may have been a class-A jerk, but his newest wife at least had some humanity left in her.

"Are you joining us for the snowball war in the morning?" Stephanie asked.

Zara tittered lightly. "That's one initiation I'll be happy to participate in as a spectator."

"Probably safest." I shrugged with a chuckle.

Again, Zara studied us, likely trying to unravel the knot of how her husband's biggest competitor ended up as his daughter's date. A story for the ages.

When another peal of riotous laughter followed by a curse blanketed the room from outside, Zara glanced towards the noise wistfully. Guess she hadn't been invited to join them. She yawned. "Well, I'm beat. See you two in the morning. Oh, and which door is the kitchen?"

Stephanie pointed down the short hallway. "Down and on the first right."

"Thanks."

When Zara disappeared into the kitchen, I led Stephanie up the stairs to the sleeping wing. She was quiet until we stopped outside her door, and she paused, glancing back at me.

I slid my hands in my pockets, not wanting to make her uncomfortable, and smiled. "She seems nice," I commented blandly.

"I know. Not many of them try to learn our names." Stephanie sighed. "Makes me sad for her. She's one of the decent women Hiram's collected like a participation trophy—like he does with his kids—and yet he'll just drop her when he gets tired of her."

"What makes you think she won't leave him?"

Stephanie snorted. "Because of the fourteen times he's done this, only two ditched him. Even though he only married seven of them, he's statistically more likely to do the leaving. I would know."

The hurt in her voice tugged at my heart, and I wanted to wrap her into a hug. But the way she held herself, arms around her middle and head bent, made me think the gesture wouldn't be welcome just now. So it was time to make my exit. "Thanks for inviting me. I had a great time."

"You mean that?" she whispered.

Slipping a hand free, I braced it on the door frame and bent closer to her ear. "I'm not a fan of lying, Steph."

She bit her lip, her eyes wide and glossy, and I hoped she was remembering our last conversation about lying—the one about us being real.

I pulled back marginally to give her space, not wanting to push too hard too fast. "Good night. Rest well."

Stephanie nodded, almost dazed. Then her soft hand gripped my shoulder as she leaned up and brushed a kiss to my cheek. "Thanks, Nash. For everything," she whispered in my ear, and then she was gone. Disappearing through the door and leaving me alone in the dark hall with that third butterfly kiss burning my cheek.

I stood there for a minute, staring at the closed door like an idiot, the softness of that kiss flooding my senses. It wasn't even a real kiss, and it hadn't been for an audience—not that I was complaining about that—but it was poignant. The stuff of dreams and legends. Giving my head a small shake, I retreated slowly to my room on the opposite end of the sleeping wing.

The Cedar Room, again courtesy of a fancy gilded nameplate, was the marriage of luxury and hominess with the wood-panelled walls and plaid accents. And that view of the Tetons out the window was worth a fortune. I couldn't see it in the dark, but the glimpse I'd caught earlier was breathtaking. Almost as much as Stephanie's picture of Glacier National.

As I tumbled into bed, lights off, the hum of voices, music, and laughter from the back deck seeped through the darkness. My room was directly above them from the sound of it. Closing my eyes, I replayed the events of the day. Sleepy Steph. The drive when we teased and bantered. The look on her family's faces when we walked in the door. That kiss... And by the time I fell asleep, I still felt that ghost of a touch on my skin. And I desperately wanted another one.

CHAPTER TWENTY

Nash

Apparently, "morning people" genes did not run in the Addams family. Breakfast was a late affair at just before nine o'clock, but it was worth the wait. A buffet of Belgian waffles with an entire topping bar—everything from whipped cream to sprinkles—bacon, two flavours of sausage, four kinds of fruit, eggs Benedict, and avocado toast was the stuff of dreams. Almost enough to distract me from the impending war.

Almost.

When all the plates were cleared, war was declared. Teams were picked—guys versus girls—goodbyes were said, and terms of surrender were drawn.

Like I said before, the Addams family didn't have a snowball fight—they turned it into World War Three. Short of convening the Hague and filing a war crimes complaint that was.

The majority of the family assembled on the snowy lawn, decked out in snow gear. The only ones missing were Nana, Great-Aunt Edith, and Hiram. True to her word, Zara sat bundled up in a powder-pink snow set on the front deck beside Hailey, who held a still-sleepy bundle of Eden on her lap. The air was crisp and fresh, the grey sky heavy with low-hanging clouds. More snow threatened to fall, but there was an undercurrent of stillness in the air amid the chattering children and war assembly.

Stephanie sauntered up to me and bumped my shoulder. A mischievous sparkle dazzled her already gorgeous big eyes. "You ready for this?"

"Oh, bring it on." I smirked, crossing my arms. "You brought a snowball champion into your midst."

"Yeah?" Her gaze dragged over me with a slow perusal, warming me more than the thermal layer I was wearing. "Emmett's girls took pity on you and let you win, huh?"

A bark of laughter escaped me. "Ouch! Anyone ever told you you're competitive?"

She shrugged, adjusting her scarf. "You've met my family. What do you think? It's survival."

"All right." Gabe's commanding voice cut through the noise and our conversation, demanding attention. "Listen up!"

Stephanie's eyes widened as I leaned down into her space, halting with my lips just above her ear. "Good luck," I whispered, "You'll need it." I bussed a kiss to her cold cheek and walked backwards away from her, watching the surprise on her face with amusement. Then for good measure, I threw her a wink.

"You know the drill," Gabe boomed as I rejoined my team. His voice carried over the snow-covered lawn to where the girls' team lined up opposite us. "Both teams have ten minutes to construct their snow fortress and three minutes to prepare snowballs—"

"We all know the rules!" an all-black-clad stick figure called from my right. Elijah, I think Stephanie had called him.

Gabe frowned at him. "We've got new faces this year. A refresher never hurts."

Elijah muttered a curse with Stephanie's name attached, eyes dark with disgust.

Gabe reacted before I could. "Hey!" His voice turned frigid, giving me a glimpse of the drill sergeant military man underneath his family face. "Not in front of the kids. You got a problem, Eli?" Elijah's cheek twitched at the name. "Take it up with me later or sit this round out. Your choice."

Elijah took the hint and crossed his arms. "Loosen up. It was just a joke."

Gabe's eyes shot upwards, like a silent plea for patience before he continued. "No snowball prep can be done during fortress building. Once the war begins, if you're hit, you're frozen for ten seconds. Which means you can't throw any snow, but others can still hit you. All hits have to be below the head. If you hit someone in the face, you freeze for ten seconds." He eyed the group firmly. "Are we all clear on that? Any questions?"

A chorus of "No" and "Let's get on with it already" rippled across the lawn.

Gabe nodded to where Hailey sat with Zara, thermos in one hand and Eden curled up on her lap. "Hails, the timer."

She raised her arm, phone in hand. "Addams Family, build your walls!"

I watched as Gabe's boys, Jackson and Ryder, along with their cousins of a similar age, Cayden and Ollie, immediately dove into action, amassing snow to form a shield wall. Austin and another man—I was losing track of which partner belonged to which sibling—assisted as the boys gave orders.

Across the lawn, Stephanie and Ivy huddled together as Zoe, Austin's wife—I hadn't caught her name—and several nieces pushed snow into large heaps. For half a minute, I wondered about Stephanie's blood pressure. This wasn't risky for her, was it? She was smart and wouldn't do something dangerous. Besides, this was a family ritual from what I'd gathered.

Gabe tossed me a shovel. "Give me a hand, will you?" Together, we started shoveling snow into a pile close to the snow fort foundation.

When I let myself steal another glance at Stephanie, Gabe paused and followed my line of sight. "Regretting the initiation?" His voice sounded amused.

I chuckled, throwing another load of snow onto the pile before Jackson scurried towards it and started pounding it against what would become the front shield wall. "More like relishing the moment."

Gabe's intense gaze bored into me. Weighing my words. Let him probe all he liked. Despite his gruff routine, he didn't intimidate me. He loved Stephanie and wanted what was best for her. I couldn't fault him for that.

"We need more snow on this side, Dad," Ryder called out.

Moving to the other side of the building project, Gabe started chucking snow with ease. Seriously, the man wasn't even wearing gloves.

"How long have you been in the Marines?" I asked.

"Twenty-two years." Gabe grunted as his shovel hit a rock, jolting him. "Enlisted right out of high school and never looked back." His mouth tipped down and a line furrowed his forehead.

"You thinking about getting out or staying in forever?"

The line deepened. "Ivy and I have been discussing it. Leaving."

I wasn't sure if it was his words or the fact that he was telling me this that surprised me more. Particularly in the middle of a snowball war of all places. "Does Steph know?"

We both glanced towards his sister, who stood with Ivy and several of the younger girls clustered around her, giving directions. Shifting to observe my own team, I noticed Ryder, Gabe's eldest, and his similar stance. Then it hit me. What I had regarded as Stephanie's natural take-charge attitude and organizational skills were a family trait. One only had to look at her father, Nana, and Gabe to see those same tendencies.

"Not yet." Gabe's tone was low and guttural. Like this was something he'd wrestled with again and again without a clear outcome on what to do.

"I take it this decision has something to do with her." I didn't want to pry. I barely knew the guy personally, except through what

Stephanie had told me over the years. But he was a good man. That much I did know.

"I've always worried about her." Gabe skirted around me with another shovelful. "Nana and Papa had the bulk of raising her, but Ivy and I helped, too. Nana's getting older, and we want to move closer to Colorado to be there for her more permanently. Full time. But we want to be there for Steph, too." He cleared his throat. "I had a front-row seat watching what she went through with an absentee dad." He rubbed the back of his neck, glancing at his sons piling snow mounds higher and higher. "I saw how hard it was on her. And this job... I love it. I love the rush, the guys I work with. But the moving, the deployments." He blew out a breath, the puff hanging in the air in the low temperatures. "I don't want my kids to grow up the same way. I don't want to miss any more milestones."

"I can't presume to tell you what to do," I said thoughtfully, watching as Stephanie helped Ava pack snow into the snow shield. "But I do know that from what Steph's mentioned, there's no way you're anything like Hiram."

Gabe barked a laugh, then shot a glance in Zara's direction, but she was preoccupied with chatting with Hailey. "That bar is stupidly low. Hiram Addams is a lot of things, but a present, attentive father was never one of them."

I nodded. "I know what it's like to grow up without a dad, and from what I can tell, you're a great one." I clapped his shoulder, then tossed another scoop of snow.

He didn't say anything, but he didn't have to.

"Time!" Hailey hollered from the porch. "Gather your ammunition in three... two... one... go!"

Gabe and I joined the fray of creating an ammo pile. The snow was the perfect consistency for packing into tight snowballs.

Ryder produced a handheld snowball maker with a grin. "No one said they were against the rules." He high-fived his dad and started squeezing out snowballs like there was no tomorrow.

"Who usually wins these things?" I asked, adding another ball to the pile. After my smack talk with Stephanie earlier, I realized this might have been helpful information to have had. And Stephanie wasn't too far off the mark with her comment about Emmett's girls taking pity on me.

Jackson snorted with all the derision a ten-year-old could manage. "The girls for two Christmases straight, but we're gonna get them this year. We got a secret weapon."

"Oh?"

He flashed a buck toothed grin at me. "You, Mister Nash. Auntie Steph is the best thrower they got. You just gotta get her twitterpated and then we got this thing in the bag."

Oh, the confidence of childhood. And the conniving. This youth with barely a decade of life behind him made me part of the war strategy to seduce the rival team's best thrower to win the game. This kid was going places. But what did I expect given his family? I imagined someone would come away maimed if they ever tried Dutch Blitz. I made a mental note to never mention the idea to Stephanie. It had been bad enough when I'd broken a finger in college playing a round with Kelsi and Ryan. My first and only broken bone. Never again.

"And what makes you think I can get her twitterpated?" I asked, raising a solemn eyebrow.

Jackson scoffed. "Because she looks at you like Nala looked at Simba, and she goes red."

Only because Emmett's youngest daughter was a *Lion King* lover did I understand that reference. But I nodded solemnly and saluted him. "Aye, aye, Captain. I'll take one for the team."

Jackson held out his hand, and I shook it. "I've got your back," he promised.

"Dad, you're the best long arm," Ryder said, giving orders. "Uncle Austin, you're in charge of keeping the snowballer going." He handed the machine off to his mustached chef uncle. "Everyone else, spread out and stay low. Auntie Steph is Mister Nash's target, and Jackson will be his backup. We clear?"

"Sir, yes, sir!"

"Time!" Hailey screamed from the porch, standing and perching Eden on her hip. "Ladies and gentlemen, friends and enemies, let the 5th Annual Addams Family Snowball War begin..." She paused and glanced at Zara. "Would you do the honours?"

Zara's face, perfectly intact with makeup this morning, beamed. "NOW!"

I locked eyes on my target and moved into raid position. Jackson hovered in my shadow, awaiting my move. The kid had a lot more faith in my twitterpating abilities than I did.

Ivy flung a ball in my direction, and I dodged left. It went long, and Jackson grunted behind me. The girls' team cheered. Guess I was on my own.

"Hey, Steph!" I called out, sidestepping another missile. "Looking good!"

She paused, mid-throw and glanced at me. "You sweet talkin' me?"

Her attempt at a Texas drawl warmed my chest. Man, she was adorable, bundled up like a snowman in her white parka and burgundy pom-pom knit hat.

"Is it working?" I prowled closer, tossing a missile towards Ava. It splattered on her knee. Score. I get she was only seven, but I was taking every win I could manage here.

Stephanie arched her ball at me. I ducked, but the wind rustled past my ear. The guys weren't kidding. She was fast and accurate.

"And you thought *I* needed good luck?" She sniffed, a smile tugging at her lips as she flung another snowball, nailing Gabe. She whooped.

I edged closer. "Well, I kissed you, so I assume that helped your performance." I heard a childish snort crossed with a gag behind me. Oh look, I had my shadow back. "This was your idea, Peter Pan," I hissed over my shoulder, and Jackson laughed again.

Stephanie dropped the ball she'd scooped up, slack-jawed. "I... you... what?"

"Now!" I charged the remaining ten feet towards Stephanie, flinging a snowball at her.

She scrambled backwards, her boots slipping as she tried to gain traction. But my legs were longer, and with Jackson at my back, I was shielded from oncoming projectiles. One of my snowballs hit her in the midsection, but she didn't stop moving.

"Cheater!" someone called, but I pursued her. When she was just in front of me, she stopped on a dime, sidestepping. Then I fell. My arms flung out, snagging Stephanie on my way down.

She screamed, and I twisted to avoid landing on her. And man, that snow was deceptively hard. The air whooshed from my lungs between the impact of the ground against my spine and Stephanie half on top of my chest. Silently, I congratulated myself on the foresight to be wearing my contacts instead of my regular frames.

"You fight dirty, Steph," I grunted when I could suck enough oxygen in. Sweet fresh air and the smell of vanilla.

Stephanie lifted her head from my chest, raising an eyebrow. "Oh yeah? Using my nephew as a shield and sweet talking me doesn't count?"

I shrugged, one arm still wrapped around her waist. "Strategy. You tripped me after I tagged you out."

She squawked, smacking my chest. "I did no such thing. You're clumsy and can't admit it."

"That the story you stickin' to, darlin'?" I rasped, eyes boring into hers. Daring. Our faces only inches apart.

Stephanie's cheeks reddened, even as her eyes softened. "Maybe. I don't hate how it ended up." Her gaze dipped down to my lips.

She was attracted to me. I wasn't imagining this tension between us. The way she looked at my lips. The moment Zara interrupted last night. The things I liked in Assistant and Friend Steph were the same things I liked in Girlfriend Steph. And looking into those big hazel eyes, I saw a future. *My* future. "Steph," I whispered her name and cupped her cheek with my gloved hand. Her eyes fluttered shut, and I probably would've kissed her except—

SPLAT!

Cold. My face stung with the sharpness of a thousand needles, and I grunted when Stephanie's elbow jammed into my ribs as she scrambled off me. I was blind, my skin burning as I tried to brush the rogue snowball off my face. But my gloved hands refused to cooperate. Another set of hands shoved mine away before gently scooping the snow from my skin.

"Who was that?" I growled, ready to rain down justice on the sneak who broke the rules and ruined my kissing plans. When I could sit up, I loosened my scarf. Man, I hated snow running down my neck.

Stephanie giggled—something I'd never heard before—her cheeks still pink. As much as I hated snow to the face, I hated our moment being interrupted even more.

"Oops," Jackson said without an ounce of apology in his blue eyes and buck-toothed grin.

"So much for a wingman," I muttered, standing and holding out my hand to Stephanie.

She slipped her hand in mine, letting me pull her to her feet. "Was I your mission?" she asked, glancing between the two of us and crossing her arms.

"I believe the words used were…" Leaning closer, I whispered, "Snowball seduction." Louder, I added, "Twitterpate Auntie Steph to distraction. Right, Jackson?"

"You little sneak!" Stephanie stepped towards Jackson, but she wobbled.

I snagged her around the waist, tugging her back to my chest. "Ah, ah, careful," I whispered in her ear, relishing the moment.

She tried half-heartedly to tug out of my loose grip, but she was too busy using me to regain her balance to offer much of a fight.

"You were hit. That means you're frozen. Tripping is extra time."

Stephanie scoffed, shoving at my arm. "I didn't trip you! You fell!"

"You tripped him," Jackson affirmed with a solemn nod, scooping up more snow and packing it into a sphere.

Stephanie pinned him with a glare. "And you face-washed my man. You better run."

Jackson's eyes flew open, and he dashed pell-mell across the carnage of the battlefield without a backwards glance. Clearly he considered this as no idle threat.

"Your man, huh?"

Stephanie twisted in my arms, giving my chest a light shove. "Snowball seduction?"

"Gotta take one for the team." I shrugged. "Not that they had to twist my arm or anything." I leaned in, since she was still tagged out. "Game on, sweetheart."

IF I WASN'T ALREADY convinced this was the weirdest Christmas I'd ever experienced, the Addams Christmas Eve schedule confirmed it. After the buffet-style breakfast and snowball war, which the guys' team won thanks to the snowball seduction technique—stuff of legends, that—we had a pocket of downtime before the official festivities started at three o'clock.

And by official, I mean more food than an entire team of hockey players could eat and an ugly sweater contest.

I tugged the sweater over my head and checked the small mirror hanging on my bedroom wall. It was terrible. Hideous really. And I couldn't wait to see Stephanie's reaction. A light tap came at the door, and I did one final check before facing my hopefully-more-than-fake girlfriend. This level of ugliness might be a deal-breaker.

I swung the door open with a flourish, leaning my forearm against the frame and smirking.

Stephanie's mouth puckered into a perfect O as she took my sweater in. It might have stoked my ego if I thought she was checking me out, but no. This was a look of horrific revulsion. Unease skittered through my veins. Had I gone too far? I had bowed to the decisions of five kids under the age of twelve when it came to fashion design after all.

I mean, that might not have been my smartest decision. But were dozens of Elf on the Shelfs duct-taped to a scratchy red-and-green knit pullover with tinsel and fairy lights hot-glued onto it to complete the ensemble beyond the scope of this game? I thought the kids were onto something.

Stephanie shoved me back through the half-open door and shut it. Leaning against it, she covered her mouth, shoulders shaking.

"Steph?" The suspense was worse than the loose thread tickling my neck.

She snorted. Actually snorted, and then the laughter rang out in peals as she tried to muffle it with her hand.

Okay, maybe I was on the right track after all then.

"What... What did you do? And what do you have against tinsel?" Stephanie gasped for air, holding her sides. "Are those... elves?!" The last word came out with a wheeze.

I rubbed the back of my neck, feeling a bit sheepish. "I may have enlisted the help of the guys' small fry for this."

Her eyes softened, and the laughter faded into a quiet echo around my room. "You're really involved with them."

I shrugged. "They're family."

Stephanie smiled knowingly. I'd never been super vocal about my past family relationship—it was hard to bring it up to people who didn't care about me beyond my success in business. Every interview focused on my business successes, and I never answered questions about my personal life. But if I told her... something told me she'd see down to the real me.

"I wouldn't judge you, you know," she said softly. "Whatever it is, you're clearly avoiding telling me about your family." She shifted nervously, fiddling with the hem of her sweater. "Look around." She gestured absently. "I know a thing or two about complicated, okay?"

I cleared my throat and glanced at her sweater, which wasn't all that ugly beyond belonging to a hideous designer in the '90s. She made it look much better than it would alone. "Thanks. I know you wouldn't, I just…"

The assortment of half a dozen ties hanging over the footboard of my bed caught my attention, and I grabbed at the subject change. "Oh, while you're here, which one matches your dress for tomorrow night?"

Stephanie followed my motioning to the bed, and her eyes widened. "You brought all these ties?" she asked, running a finger lightly over each.

"Well, you weren't exactly forthcoming with the shade of red, so…"

She held a burgundy tie with white Swiss polka dots to my chest and tilted her head. "This one."

I swallowed hard and took it from her. Realizing we were standing a little too close in my bedroom, I cleared my throat. "Great. Shall we?" I motioned to the door.

She fished her phone out of her jeans pocket. "Selfie first. This moment needs to live in infamy."

"You just want to send it to the guys," I grumbled.

Stephanie laughed. "Tempting, but no. This is for us." She nestled into my side as my arm draped over her shoulders. With the height difference, she didn't quite hit my collarbone. Handing me the phone, she added, "Your arms are longer. Wait, move to the left, the lighting's better."

That was the photographer in her speaking, I was certain, making me even happier that my express shipped package had arrived this morning and was currently hiding under my bed. I chuckled and snapped a few shots, being sure to capture our sweaters. Loving her bright smile and dancing eyes. The way she fit perfectly against me.

She took her phone back and snapped another picture of me with a laugh. "I'm sorry. It's too terrible."

"Send them to me at least." I rolled my eyes as we slipped into the hallway. "Think I have any hope of beating your nana?"

She snorted again. "With that getup, you better."

"Are you embarrassed to be seen with me?" I asked in mock horror. "Steph, I'm crushed."

"I think your ego can handle it."

"Handle losing or your embarrassment?"

Stephanie shook her head, stomping ahead of me. "There's money if you beat her, Prescott. Don't let your guard down."

I smirked, hurrying to catch up and lace our fingers together. "Good thing only one Addams has to love me then, huh?"

I counted her attractive blush as a win.

IF I THOUGHT STEPHANIE'S reaction was priceless, her family's were even more so. In true Addams form, they were loud about it, especially little Eden, who promptly burst into tears, thanks to the number of elf eyeballs I was wearing. I'd make it up to her later. My main mission now was crushing Charmain Russo Addams. Wow, that Addams spirit was really rubbing off on me.

Stephanie kept her arm lightly hooked around my bicep as we wandered around the living room taking stock of the competition because we'd be voting on who had the ugliest sweater. Once we'd seen everyone and filled out our secret ballot, Stephanie led me into the kitchen. It was humming with activity. Trays and platters of desserts and appetizers littered the counters. Austin basted two baking dishes loaded with chicken wings—barbeque and honey mustard—before popping them back in the oven. Zoe adjusted the stack of poinsettia-print napkins and paper plates with preciseness. Nana twirled her spatula, saying something I didn't catch, but it spurred three bodies into action. It was mayhem. And it smelled like heaven.

Hailey materialized beside us and dragged Stephanie after her. "Time for bruschetta. It's tradition!"

I wandered after them, watching as the two cousins stood hip to hip at the counter and piled the creamy mayo, cheese, tomato, and olive bruschetta filling onto sliced baguettes, laughing freely. I rubbed my sternum absently as if I could ease away the gnawing sensation their banter created. How could I miss what I never had? Since losing my family, my closest relationships had been with

Ryan and Emmett and their families. It had been enough, and I was incredibly blessed by them. But now... I wanted more.

As Hailey shuffled the first two trays of bruschetta into the second oven, Stephanie glanced around until she caught my eye, then she smiled. It was a forever kind of smile, a hundred words conveyed in a simple gesture... and something inside me clicked into place.

I'd been reluctant to date for the last ten years, determined to not let another woman break me the way Alexis had. I'd convinced myself I was happy where I was, content... and I was. But I could also admit I wished for more. Despite all my defenses, all my reservations, Stephanie Addams had shown up, and without me even fully realizing it, she'd waltzed into my heart and taken up shop.

I was gonna marry this woman. If only she could be convinced to take a chance on me, too.

CHAPTER TWENTY-ONE

Stephanie

NASH SHOULD HAVE WON the ugly sweater contest.

And I wasn't just saying that out of loyalty. The man taped *elves with eyeballs* to his body. Willingly. Shudder. He deserved a medal. But no. Four of my siblings decided in a show of displeasure to rig the contest with enough votes to not have Nash win. Ugh. Family politics.

As everyone clustered around the kitchen island waiting for the crowning glory of an Addams family Christmas Eve—the bruschetta—Nash confessed to having Ryan's and Emmett's kids assist him.

Ryder, overhearing, nodded his head way too wisely for a twelve-year-old, looking like a mini version of his dad. "I've got to meet these kids. They're going places with ideas like that."

Nash patted his shoulder. "Y'all might be too powerful together."

It wasn't often Nash's Texas twang slipped out, only when he was really comfortable. Watching him with my nephew made me smile. He was great with kids. *He'd be a great dad, too.* I pumped the brakes on that thought. This was Christmas with my family, not a marriage proposal.

But would I be so averse to that? I'd crushed—for lack of a better word, as Liz pointed out—on Nash for the last two years, despite my own dating qualms. With an unstable childhood, every part of me craved stability. And the guys I'd gone out with on occasion over the years couldn't give me that. I'd always been the dumpee and then told I was too picky, too high-strung. But was wanting a man who believed in "till death do us part," not "until the next shiny thing catches my attention and I dump you for her," so bad? In Gabe and Ivy and Nana and Papa, I'd seen real, true love. The kind that stays. As secure as I was in their love for me, that little-girl part of my heart still huddled in the corner, crying as she was passed off to another relative to raise. Those feelings of insecurity and inconvenience threatened to choke me right there in the kitchen.

I desperately wanted to love and be loved, but that weight of not being worth staying for smothered those thoughts like water fizzing out a wildfire. I was a successful woman with loving family, supportive friends, and a solid grasp on my identity in Jesus. I had a version of stability, even if it felt counterfeit compared to watching my friends find their happily ever afters.

Yet, I'd turned down Nash's offer of real, why? Because of fear. And Hiram's manipulative mind game. *Everyone leaves. What if Nash leaves, too?*

Nash touched my elbow, and I jolted, finding his warm eyes searching my face with concern.

"Sorry, did I miss something?" I asked, trying to gather my scattered thoughts from the realms of the four winds.

"You okay?" he asked softly, his thumb rubbing light circles over the fabric of my sweater.

I pasted on a phony smile. "Sure." But I wasn't convinced and neither was he.

He lifted his hand, brushing my cheek with the back of his fingers. "You look like you're alone in a room full of people."

That was exactly how I felt sometimes. Like an outsider looking in. Like I was here but didn't fully belong. Because I was the family pariah, waffling between loved and ignored. "You seem familiar with the feeling."

Nash grimaced. "Very familiar. Did something happen?" He scanned the noisy room briefly as if looking for someone who'd hurt me. Protective Nash was an attractive thing to behold.

I shook my head. "Just zoned out and got lost in my thoughts."

"Some thoughts are better shared. They lose their power to hurt after you say them out loud."

Maybe he was right. But I couldn't give voice to these ones... not yet. And besides, bruschetta was calling. I tugged him back towards the hubbub. "True, but bruschetta waits for no man or woman."

His face pinched, like he was going to press. Counteract my false brightness. But he didn't. Just slipped his hand in mine, lacing our fingers and squeezing gently. "I'm here, whenever you need me, okay?" His whisper brushed my ear.

Pausing, I studied him. "So am I, Nash."

WHAT THE REST OF the world called White Elephant, my family dubbed the Fifteen-Dollar-Gift Game. Simple, straightforward, and without any nonsense about albino Proboscidea animals. And quite a mouthful.

The premise was the exact same as White Elephant, just with a spending budget—currently set at twenty-five dollars, but that didn't roll off the tongue as nicely—and an age restriction. Only kids twelve and up were allowed to join the adults in "stealing" gifts. If your number was called and you weren't old enough, Nana just gave you your gift bag and you got to open it without anyone threatening to steal your hopes and dreams.

The rest of us were subjected to cutthroat highway robbery. Because, while we may have set a budget (we weren't all millionaires after all), we also had to set a stealing limit. Three times and no double stealing—if your gift was stolen, you couldn't steal it back until your next turn.

In another era, my family would have been an elite Victorian thieving gang because the stealing part seemed to be the cherished event of the evening. More so than actually opening gifts. Alliances were forged between turns with hand gestures, eye contact, and vigorous facial expressions. My family was anything but subtle.

Like everything else we Addamses seemed to touch, this was another call to perform and outshine each other. And we took no prisoners.

This year was special because Ryder, Gabe and Ivy's oldest, was finally of age to play with the adults, and he was ready to burst his buttons with that grin.

No one was supposed to know who each gift on the coffee table belonged to. Gotta keep the battlefield—I mean, playing field—fair. But Jackson immediately scooched between me and Nash on the couch and whispered to me which one was Ryder's. The large golden wrapped box with a silver bow.

"You'll want that one, Auntie Steph," he insisted, with all the conviction of a ten-year-old boy handling national secrets.

I adored my nephews. Should I have known better than to have believed that innocent smile and boyish charm? Absolutely. Did that mean I didn't fall for it? Absolutely not.

Nana passed around a bucket full of folded sticky notes with numbers, and we each took one. Once our number was pulled from the second number bucket, it would be our turn to pick a gift.

"I happen to know there's a few extra special gifts under there this time. We'll see who deserves them," Hiram announced with a smirk, and there was a titter of excitement. Which probably meant there were a few more-than-twenty-five-dollar items. Despite the price limit, Hiram had his own way of doing things. I think he got some sick satisfaction out of his offspring's antics in trying to outdo the others. Like an emperor watching his very own gladiator game.

Zoe's number was called first and the cycle began. She shimmied her shoulders and plucked a poinsettia-papered gift off the table.

I recognized the paper. It had Nana written all over it, and I was pretty sure it had been in our wrapping paper bin under the stairs since I was in high school.

Zoe must've recognized it, too, since she shot Nana a sardonic smile. To be fair though, Nana always contributed pretty epically hilarious gifts for under twenty-five dollars. This year was no exception as Zoe unwrapped a clothing bejeweller, scrunching her perfect nose as she showed it to us.

Zara—not Hiram's, but Zoe's eight-year-old daughter—cheered. "You gotta keep it, Mom! I *love* it."

"I love those things, too!" adult Zara said, beaming at the girl.

Hiram chuckled without any real humour. "Why settle for fake diamonds when you have the real thing?" he said, lifting his wife's hand to admire the monstrous rock on her slim hand. He glanced at his granddaughter. "You'll be old enough to appreciate class soon enough, if your mother raises you right."

The happiness of young Zara's face faded faster than twilight.

"Didn't these things go out of fashion in the '70s? I had no idea you could still get them," Hailey asked, redirecting the conversation. Bless her.

Nana shrugged. "What goes around comes around."

Elijah's number came next, and he picked one of Hiram's gifts. Because there was no way *that* name-brand wireless speaker was anywhere close to twenty-five bucks. That was definitely going to be a hot ticket item.

When Hailey, who was always Nana's assistant, called my number—lucky number thirteen—Jackson whooped and sprang from the sofa like a jack-in-the-box.

"Tell me which one!" He ran to the table and picked up Ryder's. "This one! You want this one."

"Jackson." Gabe's voice was level but gently chiding. "Let your aunt decide for herself."

Jackson set the gift down and rocked back and forth on his heels in barely contained glee.

I stole a glance at Ryder, sitting directly across from me beside Nana. His smile was subdued compared to Jackson's, but his eyes were bright with excitement. I sighed inwardly. Who was I to deny this child?

"Bring the gold one, Jack-Jack."

Jackson snatched Ryder's gift and lugged it to me. "It's not too heavy," he announced before dropping it in my lap and half of Nash's beside me.

Nash's low chuckle skittered across my skin. "The exuberance of youth."

I laughed and tore through the shiny golden paper, uncovering a plain brown box... completely encased in clear packing tape. And on the top was a note:

NO SCISSORS ALLOWED.

Oh, boy. I gave Ryder the stink eye across the room, but he just laughed, leaning back in his chair to enjoy my suffering. The punk. "Are you serious?" I waggled my Wine Seduction polished fingertips, fresh from girls' night. "I just did these!"

Ryder rolled his eyes, heaving the sigh of an eighty-year-old man dismayed at the priorities of a younger generation. "If you must."

"Here." Nash handed me a small pocketknife—did all guys have a secret stash of knives on them at all times?—and winked. "Knives weren't prohibited after all."

Ryder huffed. "Whose side are you on?"

I grinned cheekily. "Mine, nephew dearest." Leaning in, I kissed Nash's cheek, much to my nephew's dismay.

But Nash? He stilled under my touch, his steady gaze enchanting me. This was pretend. We were pretending. Playing a part. Selling a story. But the warmth in his espresso eyes, the quirk of lips holding back a smile had me feeling like this was too real. Like this was our future. Bantering with my nephews. Surviving family holidays. *I'm not running, Steph.* The words were a soft caress to my mangled heart. And oh, how I wanted to believe them.

I shook my head to clear the foggy thoughts, using the blade to carefully slice through the top of the box. I handed the knife back to Nash—safety first—and opened the present.

To find packing peanuts. Mint and bubble-gum pink.

Scooping out the mounds of fluffy Styrofoam, I dug down until my fingers brushed a smooth object. "Do you mind holding the box?" I asked Nash.

"Sure." He pivoted and adjusted the box farther onto his lap, tilting it so I could grasp the new item.

And what did I pull out? Another box. This one wrapped in a black garbage bag and secured with endless duct tape. It was official. I'd received the gag gift of the game. They weren't common anymore, after several siblings who shall not be named overdid them in a battle to outdo each other. Competitive even about gag gifts. But Ryder had heard the stories of each brand of crazy and had witnessed at least one or two in the past. Now, on the cusp of his initiation into the game, he was bringing things to a whole new level.

Everyone was laughing at my ill-fortune by this point. Hiram even slapped Ryder on the back in approval as he walked past, bringing a plate of goodies with him from the kitchen. While none of them wanted to be in my shoes right now, they were all getting a kick out of it in the meantime.

Zara reached for a lemon tart from Hiram's plate as he settled back beside her, but he tilted the dish away. "Probably enough carbs for tonight, my dear," he said.

I picked at the duct tape, listening. They weren't talking loudly compared to the high energy of the room, but I still caught the pointedness of his words framed as a suggestion.

"Oh. Right." Zara's face shattered a little, but she recovered quickly and nibbled a baby carrot.

Nash offered me the knife again. "You'll be needing this."

And he was right. Because after the duct tape came another atrociously taped box.

"So that's where all the tape went," Ivy commented wryly, eyeing her eldest over the rim of her glasses.

"And the hours you spent holed up in your room, hmm?" Gabe mused, tossing another log on the fire, his amber eyes twinkling with amusement.

Ryder only grinned with secret knowledge.

Thankfully, that box was empty with an envelope inside. Breathing a sigh of relief, I opened the envelope and read the computer-typed note aloud:

FINISH THE CAROL. FIND THE CLUE.

"There's a song in the air!
There's a star in the sky!
There's a mother's deep prayer and a baby's low cry!
And the star rains—"

I smirked at Ryder. "Was this tailor-made for me, buddy?" He'd chosen my favourite Christmas hymn, and I finished it easily.

"its fire while the beautiful sing,
for the manger of Bethlehem cradles a King!"

Going to the mantle, I picked up the baby Jesus from the nativity set Nana brought with her from Colorado every time she trekked up here and turned it upside down. Sure enough, a small piece of paper was taped to the manger. It unrolled to read:

TO EARN YOUR NEXT CLUE, SIT ON THE KNEE OF THE PERSON NEXT TO YOU AND SING A VERSE OF JOY TO THE WORLD.

The person next to you... Glancing at the sofa, I noticed that Jackson had conveniently vacated the premise, leaving Nash the only other person on the loveseat. Oh, sugarplums. I could feel my cheeks melting off my face with embarrassment.

Great-Aunt Edith wolf-whistled, wagging her spidery eyebrows. "Back in my day, that was as good as a marriage proposal."

Could my face be any more red? Slowly, I approached Nash. He didn't move as I perched on his knee, face flaming, and glared at Ryder—who only had the audacity to look smug. This was fine. This was okay. This was... *Abort. Abort.* I was going to kill my nephew—with kindness and wet willies.

Taking a deep breath, I sang the required verse as quickly as possible. Nash didn't say anything. Just smiled at me and gently squeezed my knee before I popped back up again.

"Happy?" I demanded of my scheming nephew, even though there was no way he could have known I was bringing Nash. Although... he knew about the clue and could have had Jackson convince me to pick his gift *because* Nash was sitting next to me. I would dissect Ryder's potential espionage plans later. I had a gift to win.

Ryder handed me another envelope. This one thankfully only required me to name all of Santa's reindeer correctly before I was instructed to find a small gold box under the living room Christmas tree. Nestled in the branches of the fake tree (we weren't a real tree family) was a fist-sized package in the same gold foil as Ryder's original Trojan horse.

"Is this the end?" I begged, half desperately. A girl could only take so much mortification.

Ryder laughed. "That's the gift, don't worry."

Thankfully, this wasn't outrageously wrapped in tape and instead opened to a wad of tissue paper. Lifting it up, I gasped. Because underneath were the two most gorgeous glass cut snowflake ornaments I'd ever seen. I held one up gently, letting it sparkle as it caught the light.

"Ryder…" I breathed. "These are beautiful."

He beamed with pride, sitting taller.

The air in the room sharpened. Tangy and electric. I winced. *Uh-oh. I shouldn't have mentioned loving these.* My siblings smirked with far too much cunning. Great, just because I liked something meant they'd pounce on the opportunity to take it from me. Ducking my head, I tucked the box near my feet.

Hailey announced the next number, but I didn't catch it as I was too focused on the ornaments. My nephew had superb taste, and he knew me well enough to choose that package for me. That lodged a lump in my throat.

Two turns later, Zoe stole my ornaments. She offered me a sardonic smile. "These will go perfectly in my collection." Sure, Zoe.

Nash's turn was next, and he stole them from Zoe. I beamed at him, leaning close. "You're my hero right now," I whispered. "But they've already decided I won't get them."

He smiled down at me. Eyes tracing my face, assessing. And dare I say, appreciating?

I bit my lip, feeling this was new territory for us, but not hating it. "Anything you want me to steal for you?"

"You've already stolen from me," Nash whispered, glancing towards the group as Hailey called another number—Ivy's apparently as she opted to open a fresh gift.

"What's that?" I asked, puzzled.

"My heart," he murmured, and I swear I misheard him in the clamour of the group. But from the steadiness of his voice and the truth in his eyes, I couldn't find a lie.

I didn't win the ornaments. Since Zoe started the game, she got the final turn, and she snatched them from Ryder, who'd made a valiant attempt to snag them for me. I couldn't blame her—they were gorgeous—but she didn't have to be so callous about it. And maybe, just maybe, she'd trade with me. Because, yes, after the game ended, we traded gifts if we so desired. I had a power drill up for grabs, but I didn't see that convincing my older sister. I could have handed her cash, and I doubt it would have made a difference. And it didn't matter what Nash had, she wouldn't trade with him on *principle*.

Sure enough, Zoe laughed in my face when I ventured to ask. "Dream on, little sis." What could have been an endearing name was chalked full of vitriol derision. She had a way of making me feel two-inches tall.

However, Elijah's long-term girlfriend wanted the drill, so I ended up with a heavy-duty flashlight and a coffee shop gift card.

Couldn't complain. Nash traded with my niece Millie—Veronica's daughter—giving her the stationery set in exchange for a Nerf gun.

When I asked how he outmaneuvered Ryder in that deal, Nash only shrugged. "He wanted the throwing knives." Of course he did. "And I've got some adopted nephews and nieces at home who will love Uncle Nash for bringing this around. And their parents will hate me for it. So, I'm calling it a win."

CHAPTER TWENTY-TWO

Nash

"How scandalized would you be if I told you I'd never seen *It's a Wonderful Life*?" I whispered in Stephanie's ear as we smooshed together on the sofa, the beginning credits starting to roll. "Oof!" I grunted as she bolted upright, jamming her elbow into my ribs.

"Are you kidding me?"

I chuckled at the absolute horror in her tone and tugged her back down to lean against me. Purely for her family's benefit, of course. "Not at all. I'm afraid old movies have never been high on my radar."

She snorted, settling back into my arms. Vanilla blanketed my senses as she tucked her head against my neck. Like she belonged there. "How have you managed to live this long without this essential piece of Christmas culture?"

"Guess it's a good thing I've got you then." I kept my voice light and low, but I caught her barely suppressed shiver all the same. "And you guys watch this every Christmas gathering?" I asked, keeping my gaze on the black-and-white film—apparently the recoloured version was an anathema according to Hailey.

"Mm-hmm. Frank Capra's masterpiece and puzzles round out the evening." Stephanie nodded over to the two low coffee tables, where two groups—headed by Elijah and Zoe respectively—were sorting puzzle pieces into edges versus middle. "The goal is to finish the puzzle by the end of the movie and beat the other team."

"How many pieces are there?"

"I think they're trying a thousand pieces this year since we beat the five-hundred-piece record last time."

A chuckle rumbled low in my chest. Never had I met a more competitive family. They turned holiday traditions and puzzle solving into a contest. "I had no idea y'all were so cutthroat. I mean I did, from a business perspective, but this..." I frowned. "Constantly competing for attention and recognition is a hard way to live."

I felt Stephanie's eyes on me before she whispered breathily, "You should do that more often."

"What?"

"Let your drawl out."

"I do not have a drawl."

Her lips twitched, distracting me. "Whatever you say, cowboy."

I rolled my eyes. We'd had this conversation before about stereotypes. "Not all Texans are cowboys. Particularly not this one. Horses and I are not friends."

"Would you prefer me to say you're a Texan tycoon then?"

"I can live with that."

We slipped into silence, and I found myself immersed into the story unfolding before me on the screen. The story of a man who gave up everything for others, including his dreams, and in the end still stood to lose everything to the point his life seemed worthless. Only to have the chance to see his life through the lens of if he'd never existed. What a rare gift to see the impact of your life from an external viewpoint.

Eden crawled onto Stephanie's lap around the time George Bailey got himself hitched, and soon after, her breathing leveled into soft snuffling snores. She was a cute kid, but how she could sleep in this level of commotion—and after the six gingerbread men I'd witnessed her scarf down—was beyond me. The puzzle people alternated between smack talk and quoting the movie lines as they played on the screen. There were very few films I knew well enough to quote lines from, so colour me impressed.

"How's the puzzle going?" Stephanie asked Hailey when she dropped onto the floor in front of us, leaning her head back against Stephanie's knee.

"Remind me that if anyone *ever* suggests a one-thousand-piece puzzle again I will have no part of it. Also—" Hailey tilted her head to look up at us. "I was not built for that level of meanness. Somehow I forget how bad they get."

"Sorry, Hails." Stephanie sighed softly, running a hand over Eden's hair as she slept. "I take it we won't be beating the record this year?"

Hailey huffed. "I was on Zoe's team, and we barely got the border together. Have I mentioned she scares me? Last I checked, Elijah's team wasn't doing much better. It wouldn't have been so bad if it wasn't a mystery puzzle, but *no.*"

I tore my attention away from the screen, suddenly clueing in. "Wait, y'all don't even have a picture to reference what you're putting together?" When they shook their heads, I groaned. "Has anyone ever told you your family is—"

"Insane?" Stephanie smirked.

"Mad as a hatter?" Hailey deadpanned.

"I was going to say intense, but those work, too."

Stephanie patted my knee. "Says the man who's never seen *It's a Wonderful Life.*"

Hailey actually gasped before slapping a hand over her heart. If she were a Southern grandma, she'd be clutching her pearls. "How have you never seen it? You're practically old."

Stephanie kicked her cousin with her foot, making me chuckle. "Thirty-three isn't old, Hails. He's only five years older than me. He's younger than Ivy. Are you calling her old?"

Hailey raised her hands in surrender. "Sorry, Nash, but you've got ten years on me. And how did you miss out on this cultural moment in childhood?"

"I've never been a fan of old movies," I confessed. "But this one has my attention."

"So shhh," Stephanie told her cousin, giving her head a little pat, before stealing a chocolate-covered peanut butter ball from my plate. Did I care? Not in the slightest. This woman had my heart, my future. She was welcome to my food and, hopefully one day, my last name.

By the time George Bailey ran home from the bridge and sang "Auld Lang Syne," I may or may not have had to clear the lump in my throat. Not that I was going to admit that and give the guys more ammunition against me. "I think I have a new favorite Christmas movie," I said simply as the final credits played.

Stephanie beamed up at me, Eden still cuddled against her chest, and Hailey cheered with a fist pump.

"Movie's over. You finish the puzzle?" Hailey hollered over to the table of puzzlers.

"Shut up," Elijah growled, continuing to finagle pieces together.

Hailey stuck her tongue out at him. "Cool it, string bean, and use real words."

Zoe moved between the two low tables, studying them sharply. "We were closer," she announced.

"No way!" Veronica retorted from Elijah's table, flipping her blue-streaked hair away from her face.

"Maybe get an unbiased opinion," Ivy suggested from where she and Ava were cuddling in the recliner with their hot cocoa and matching reindeer Christmas socks. But it was too late.

I never expected a bunch of grown adults to start fighting over puzzles, but here we were. One of the tables was flipped. Swearing broke out. One of the kids shrieked.

Hailey watched in wide-eyed horror, but Stephanie's shoulders drooped with weary resignation, and she covered sleeping Eden's ears.

"That's enough!" Nana yelled, and to my surprise, the noise lessened. "Clean up this mess now, and if I hear another word from any of you—" she jabbed a finger around the group—"Well, I guess you'll just have to find out, won't you." Her gaze shifted over to us, and she softened when she landed on Hailey. "Come help me for a minute, baby."

Hailey didn't need to be told twice before she scampered after Nana towards the kitchen.

Stephanie nudged me, being careful to avoid jostling Eden as we were left in a pocket of quietness, amid the mumbling. "So you're a convert?"

Okay, so we weren't talking about whatever that was then. I leaned my head back against the sofa cushion, weighing how to put into words the ways I sensed a kinship to George Bailey. I'd spent my life bailing on my own dreams to try and save someone else's. Working two after-school jobs in high school to pay the bills while my mom promised to do better when she was in between boyfriends. Giving up interests and opportunities to integrate myself into Alexis's life only to have her dump me with the words, "I need someone with more to offer me." Like the dreams we'd made together meant nothing.

"You ever wish you got a chance to see how much of a difference your life made?" I asked instead. I felt the heaviness of her gaze, sorting through my words and weighing a response.

"Yes," she said slowly. "I think most of us do at some point. That's what makes George relatable. But I don't think we were built to know that. To know the nuances of someone else's story. That's what will make Heaven so amazing, finally seeing the tapestry God wove. With no mistakes." To my surprise, she rested her hand on my knee and squeezed it lightly. "For what it's worth, my life certainly got better with you in it."

"Me or the job?" The bitter words tumbled out before I could stop them, tasting like ash on my tongue. I didn't miss the shock Stephanie quickly masked. I hated that. Hated that a woman who left me ten years ago still had a grip on me. I knew Stephanie wasn't Alexis or even my mom. They couldn't have been more different than this sweet woman at my side.

"Sorry to interrupt, but I've got to get this munchkin to bed." Gabe appeared before us, amused. Like he relished interrupting our moment. Little did he know I was about two seconds from spilling my soul—not kissing his sister.

Stephanie sighed and kissed Eden's silky raven hair. "Night, lovey." She shifted, leaning into my side as Gabe bent forwards, and they maneuvered the sleeping toddler.

Eden roused slightly as Gabe cradled her against his broad chest, but she settled instantly, her face nestled into his neck. Watching the tender moment sent a pang through my chest. I wanted that. The whole package.

Once Gabe was out of earshot, Stephanie whispered, "It's only ever been you, Nash." Her shoulders curled in, and I hated that I'd done that. "You know the money's never been an incentive. I'm not her."

Wait, what? I stiffened. How could she have known about Alexis? Or my mom? If Ryan or Emmett told her, I would... "Who told you?" I growled.

Her smile was sad but gentle. "You just did."

Sitting in her family's busy living room on the cusp of another fight threatening to break loose, if the whispered curses and razor-sharp glares were any indication, wasn't where I envisioned having this conversation. Part of me wanted to shove it away, leave it in the past. Weren't buried things better left that way? Not according to my therapist.

Stephanie touched my forearm. "Please let me in," she whispered.

My body deflated, and I scrubbed a hand over my face. "Wanna get out of here?"

She glanced back at the bickering group. "Follow me."

Chapter Twenty-Three

Nash

Wordlessly, we slipped on our coats and snuck out the front door. The wind in Wyoming was no joke, and I tugged my gloves on.

"This way." Stephanie tilted her head, guiding me across the front deck and around the corner where it wrapped around the side of the house to a private enclosed area with the hot tub. She flicked a switch and small white lights winked to life overhead. This part of the deck was nestled against the house, sheltering us from the directness of the wind. It might not be strong, but it was nippy. Another switch kicked on the free-standing patio gas stove.

Aha. This was the hot tub deck. It was built up on a custom platform with wooden edging and stairs. Boosting herself up onto the platform edge, Stephanie patted the seat beside her, inviting me to join her.

I obliged, letting my eyes adjust to the dimness of the night and the distant smudges of the Tetons. Taking deep breaths and praying I wouldn't mess this up. "I'm not sure where to start," I confessed.

Stephanie didn't say anything for a minute. She slipped a ChapStick from her pocket and applied it quietly, and I half envied her because that dry wind was chapping my lips like crazy. The benign movement settled something in me, though, giving me a minute to collect my thoughts. When she slipped her gloved hand in mine, threading our fingers, I was ready. "I'll listen to whatever you want to tell me," she said, the sincerity of her words burrowing deep in my heart.

Here went nothing. "Alexis was my college girlfriend for three years. We were serious, or I was. I bought a ring and proposed right after we graduated." I huffed softly, remembering the moment. "She looked down at me with pity as I knelt in front of her, then she snapped the ring box closed and told me she was moving on. She'd met someone else, a guy with deeper pockets and more potential."

"She cheated on you?" An unearthly, strangled growl came from the woman beside me, and I turned to see Stephanie's face dark with rage, eyes flashing in the soft twinkling lights. She shook her head. "The woman is an idiot!"

"It's what inspired me to start my own company. Prove to her I could be something." I tried to laugh it off, but it sounded a little bitter in my ears. "Things worked out, and I made more money than the man she left me for. Now money is the only thing women see when they show an interest."

"Did she try to win you back?"

"How'd you know?"

Stephanie shrugged. "'Cuz she made the mistake of a lifetime, and she'd have been a fool not to have tried, even if it was for the worst reasons ever." She side-eyed me, swinging her legs. "What happened to starting a company because, and I quote, 'I saw a gap in the market I could fill?'"

I smirked. "Can't a man be multifaceted?"

"Meaning you didn't want to talk about Alexis and wanted your privacy. I get it."

"Yeah? You don't seem surprised by this."

Ooh, an eyebrow raised. "You're thirty-three and look like that." Stephanie waved her hand in the general vicinity of my body. "I assumed there was at least one woman who thought you were a catch. And as for the privacy, I do get it because one whiff of heartbreak and you'd have every woman from Washington to Texas lined up to date you. Heartbreak makes a man more attractive for some reason, but when it's a woman, she has baggage."

"Just to Texas, darlin'?" I teased, sensing she wanted to move away from the heaviness of the conversation.

Stephanie patted my knee. "Easy there, cowboy."

"Not a cowboy."

She tipped her head back and laughed, and it echoed softly off the distant hills. "Right."

We sat there, hand in hand, just watching the gently floating snow and the hypnotic dance of flames from the patio stove. This was the most comfortable I'd ever been with another person, and I wasn't in a hurry to head back into the madhouse.

"What about your family?" Stephanie asked softly.

"What about them?"

"I'm sure you have one."

"Had." I grunted then sighed. "My dad was never in the picture, so my mom raised me alone. We spent most of my childhood in Texas and lived with her parents for a few years before she packed up and carted me off to Southern California, just before my sixteenth birthday." I could remember Grandad teaching me to play chess and checkers. The bolts upon bolts of fabric in Gran's sewing room. She was a quilter, and I'd had one of her quilts on my bed for years, until Mom lost it in the move. "Mom went no contact with them, but I secretly kept in touch. Grandad called me just before I graduated high school and told me Gran had passed. Mom didn't even care when I told her."

I swallowed hard, focusing on the distant darkness while I tried to rein in the wave of anger at my mother even all these years later. "Grandad was the whole reason I went to college. He helped pay my way after Mom kicked me out at eighteen, tired of being saddled with a kid. And then just before I went to spend a summer with him after my freshmen year, I got the call he'd passed, too. I never got to see either of them in person again." But I could still hear Grandad's easy laugh and smell Gran's vanilla perfume. It reminded me of home.

"I'm sorry," Stephanie whispered, squeezing my hand and leaning into me. "I know how hard it is to lose a grandparent. I can't even imagine losing both."

I nodded. "My mom's a drug addict. She's tried on and off for years to get clean, but it never sticks. That was the call I got at the coffee shop in Missoula. The rehab center was letting me know she'd checked herself out—again—even though she only had two weeks left."

"Oh, Nash." Stephanie wrapped her free hand around my arm, hugging it close. Whether for my comfort or because I could feel her shivering, I wasn't sure, but I appreciated the gesture. "And here I was, going on about my family problems—"

I touched a finger to her lips, stopping the words. "Don't. Don't compare our family pain and decide you have it better, Steph. That's not how it works. We both had pretty rotten things thrown at us. What matters is how we grow from it. How we let God use those trials to shape us. I haven't always done the best job with that." Alexis's face flashed across my mind. Yeah, letting her rejection rule my dating life for the last ten years wasn't my strongest point. But maybe that was what brought me to Stephanie.

"Neither have I," she confessed, lips brushing my gloved finger. "Thank you. For letting me in."

"I'm sorry I didn't do it sooner."

She shook her head, her glossy curls bouncing. "Don't be. I get it."

Letting my finger fall from her lips, I cupped her face in my hands. "Steph, you need to know that—"

An ugly swear cut through our cozy cocoon, shattering the bubble. Seriously, would this family ever let me kiss this woman?

Startling, Stephanie inched back and eyed Elijah, standing at the balcony door, still in his signature funeral garb, lips curled in a snarl.

"Get in here, shrimp. And bring your boy toy."

Stephanie glared. "Boyfriend, Eli."

"Save it for someone who cares." Elijah slammed the door with a rattle.

She growled in frustration. "I'm sorry for that."

"Why don't they like you?" I asked, easing off the hot tub platform and offering a hand to help her down.

Stephanie accepted and her boots thudded softly on the wooden slats underfoot. "I'm the youngest and the most convenient scapegoat. They all despise Hiram for leaving their mothers and moving onto the next woman. Which is why they hate each other. But since Hiram holds the purse strings, they've all decided I'm the convenient one to hate if they can't hate him and have to work together."

"That's messed up, Steph."

"I know. It's why I hate coming here, especially alone. Don't get me wrong, Nana, Gabe, Ivy, and Hailey are great. We're just outnumbered." She scrunched her nose. "But we should get in there. No sense stirring the pot even more."

Backtracking to the front door, we shed our winter layers, and the warmth never felt so welcome. The puzzle remains were packed up, replaced by a table with Monopoly (how was that a good idea?),

Hiram popped a wine bottle, and the newest cartoon version of *The Grinch Who Stole Christmas* played on the TV for the kids.

Stephanie made a beeline towards Hailey, who was curled up in the corner on a low beanbag chair, nearly obstructed from view by the Christmas tree and the mounds of blankets she was under, an e-reader in hand.

I followed, but before I caught up to Stephanie, a shadow sailed above my head. "What was that?" I jumped and twisted around, trying to identify the object.

"What?" Stephanie asked, looking back at me confused.

"There was—" My words were cut off by an excited cheer, and several people pointed just above my head.

I tilted my head up, nerves taut and dread pooling in my gut. I wasn't ready for another Addams torture chamber after just spilling my guts to Stephanie like that. Sure enough, nine-year-old Ollie, Austin's son, stood on the mezzanine floor above us, with a fishing pole in hand, dangling a sprig of mistletoe over our heads.

"Are you kidding me?" Stephanie grumbled beside me.

Right, her nieces and nephews were pranksters. "I take it this is a new addition to the initiation rites?" I was now more bemused than dread filled. An irritated Steph was an amusing Steph.

"Who brings fishing poles to a ski lodge?" she huffed.

"Found them in storage." Austin offered a mustached smile. "Get on with it, Polly Pocket."

Unlike Elijah, Austin didn't sound hostile but still condescending, and I could tell he was relishing making Stephanie uncomfortable. Nicknames were weaponized rather than endearing with this crowd.

Stephanie's eyes locked on mine as the chanting grew louder: *Kiss her. Kiss her.*

I slipped a hand on her waist, tugging her closer. Leaning in, I whispered in her ear. "We giving the people what they want?" And here I was, complaining minutes ago about Elijah's interruption.

I expected her to laugh. Blush. Swat my chest even. What I wasn't expecting was for her to fist my Henley and drag me into a kiss. Her lips brushed mine, soft and hesitant. Like she was suddenly regretting her momentary boldness.

But I was not.

One hand still on her waist, the other threading into her short hair, I tilted my head, deepening the kiss. Something clicked inside me as her fingers teased the hair at the nape of my neck, like two souls meeting. I couldn't breathe, but I didn't care when the woman in my arms tasted like forever. *And peppermint ChapStick.*

Remembering our audience with young eyes, I pulled back, leaning my forehead against hers. Stephanie's cheeks were a becoming shade of pink, her hazel eyes sparkling. She appeared all-around thoroughly dazed—I smirked knowing I'd done that to her.

A wolf whistle pierced the air. I'd bet money on that being Great-Aunt Edith, but I didn't turn away. Just focused on the woman in my arms. *Finally.*

"Hey," I whispered.

"Hey." Her voice was breathy.

Her family faded away, the noise softening to a distant hum as they moved on to torture another relative with the kissing pole.

"Maybe you'll let me kiss you for real sometime," I said, tucking a loose curl behind her ear.

Her eyes widened like sparkling snow globes. I'd always loved her big, expressive eyes. "That kiss felt plenty real."

I chuckled softly, still holding her against me. Our gazes held, and she kept her hands resting on my chest. Could she feel how fast my heart was beating right now? "Maybe, but I never intended our first kiss to be for show."

Stephanie swallowed hard. "You... You've thought about kissing me then?"

I smirked a little sheepishly. "Probably more than I should have."

She bit her lip. A hundred thoughts danced across her face before she tugged out of my grip. Grabbing my hand, she dragged me down the hall after her. We bumped into Veronica—our original welcoming committee—when we turned a corner towards the kitchen.

Veronica swore loudly, eyes narrowing on our joined hands. "You should—"

But Stephanie didn't stop to engage. Just hauled me—her willing captive—into a blessedly deserted kitchen, marching us towards a frosted glass door in the corner and yanking me inside after her.

The room was small, mostly dark, and most definitely a pantry.

"We don't have an audience now," she said softly, flicking a switch, causing the small incandescent lightbulb overhead to cast unnatural shadows over the shelves.

I glanced around. No, we most certainly did not. I studied the jam jars on the shelf above her head. "A pantry, huh? Very romantic."

Stephanie rolled her eyes. "Oh, forget it."

I laughed, grabbing her arm and tugging her towards me as she tried to open the door. "Never said I didn't appreciate the sentiment, Steph. Pantries can absolutely be romantic. Care for some flours? White or whole wheat?" I motioned to the bags overhead with my free hand.

She eyed the overhead bags warily. "I told Nana those were a death trap."

I leaned down, nudging her nose with mine. "What a way to go, though." I could see the gears in her head, whirling a hundred thoughts a minute. Overthinking and overcalculating. "Steph, we don't have to do this," I said simply. "I'm here for the long haul."

Stephanie fisted a hand against my chest then smoothed it out, meeting my gaze. "Yes," she said simply.

"Yes?"

"To this being real. I... I want to try us for real. Not faking it. If... if you still want that?"

"I do," I rasped, hardly believing all my dreams were coming true in a kitchen pantry with jam and flour for witnesses.

Stephanie swallowed hard. "I want a real kiss, Nash. Not for my family or for show." Her voice fell to a whisper. "For me."

Who was I to deny that sweet wish? "Yes, ma'am."

Chapter Twenty-Four

Stephanie

Who was this daring woman asking for a kiss? Even as the words came out of my mouth, my anxiety started to climb. This was bold, especially for me. What if he—?

Nash brushed a kiss to one corner of my mouth, then the other, short-circuiting my spiral. "I've got you." The words were as soothing as his caress. I could fall; he'd catch me. Who was I kidding? I'd already fallen hard and fast.

"Nash," I whispered, and he caught my plea with his lips, cradling my face in his hands. I felt... safe. Cherished. The kiss for my family had been wonderful, mind-blowing. This kiss was softer, sweeter. For us. Time slowed as the kiss lingered, giving and taking. Nash took charge, and my racing thoughts bled into the background, anchoring me in the moment. I was breathless and yet for the first time, I could *breathe.*

Pantries were absolutely romantic material, highly recommended.

My lower back lightly bumped against one of the shelves, rattling the jars. But I ignored it, winding my arms tighter around his neck. He groaned with approval when I wove my fingers through his hair, which was absolutely as soft as I'd imagined. And would be properly tousled when I was finished with it.

The shelves shook again and then *THUD!*

I gasped, pulling away from the kiss as a shower of white powder flew through the air, coating us. "Was that...?"

Nash didn't let me go, just glanced behind him before resting his forehead against my neck and laughing softly. "Flour. Of course it was the flour."

His chest rumbled as he held me close, and I joined in the laughter. The bag had missed our heads, but the fine sheen of powder blanketed the entire pantry and our clothes. "There's no hiding the evidence that we were in here," I whispered between gasps.

Nash tugged his Henley over his head, leaving just his white T-shirt.

"What are you doing?" I hissed. There was no pantry stripping on the agenda.

"Relax." He chuckled and shook his head, ruffling his hair to dislodge the white film. "We can't track this all over the house. I'll go grab some paper towels."

I grabbed his elbow, his skin warm under my touch. "Make sure the coast is clear."

"Aye, aye." He winked over his shoulder before cracking the door and peering into the kitchen. "Let's go."

I felt like a teenager, slinking through the deserted kitchen after making out in the pantry. Something I'd never done before, but that was beside the point. I couldn't meet Nash's gaze without blushing. He'd kissed me for real, no fake agreements between us. After two years of dancing around the truth, we were doing this. And as we wiped up the flour explosion, I knew I couldn't go back to being just friends, where these quiet, heartfelt moments between us vanished. Those light touches and sweet kisses.

And as I watched Nash kneel on the floor, mopping up the mess, I knew deep down this was right. I'd been brave enough to leap and trust the fall wouldn't break me. *Lord, please don't let him leave, too.*

NOT LONG AFTERWARDS, NASH headed upstairs to grab a shower. There were plenty of washrooms and hot water on demand to go around, but it was still a bit of Russian roulette at times. After saying goodnight—with a goodnight kiss, of course—he left me to mingle with my family alone.

I helped Nana in the kitchen—dutifully avoiding eye contact with the pantry—before finally dragging myself towards my bed. As an introvert, too much socializing drained me, and I was ready to recharge in solitude while I finished the last touches of my knitting project. The one I needed to have wrapped and ready for tomorrow morning.

I hugged Ivy at the bottom of the stairs as she ushered her three kids out of the crowd still gathered in the living room and up to bed, since Eden was already asleep. "Merry Christmas," I murmured, squeezing her tight.

"Merry Christmas. Love you."

"Love you more."

"Stephanie." Hiram's abrupt voice cut through the haze of Ivy's hug and my post-kisses bliss, making me tug away. He rarely addressed me directly, so this was new. "A word." He tilted his head down the hall towards the same small room I'd dragged Nash into the day before after rescuing him from Great-Aunt Edith. Without even waiting for my acknowledgement, he disappeared into the room. Expecting my compliance.

I couldn't help the way my body tensed instantly and the sinking feeling in my gut that made me feel small. I was tired and not really in the mood for whatever he had to say. The curious, burning gazes of my siblings watching from the couches didn't help either.

"You can say no," Ivy whispered.

I smiled at her wearily. "Yeah, but might as well get it over with." There was no way I wanted it hanging over my head tomorrow either. Giving her an extra squeeze, I trudged after Hiram. I loved how protective she was of me. I may not have been her actual kid, but she could go mama bear for me if the situation called for it.

Stepping into the room, I closed the door behind me and mentally assembled my armour for battle. As much as I would rather be dwelling on Nash and those kisses, I needed my head in the game for this conversation.

"What is this scheme of yours?" Hiram asked coolly, eyes taking me in from where he stood perfectly relaxed by the small corner bookshelf. From the disdain in his expression, I'd been found wanting. Again.

I frowned, adjusting my stance. Being short had its disadvantages when dealing with a powerful individual. Although... Nash's height didn't make me uncomfortable. I felt safe with him. *Focus!* "Scheme?"

"Bringing the enemy into the fold. You told me you had a suitable partner, not some—" He dropped a curse that had me cringing. "Were you jealous of Zara and me? Trying to upstage our announcement for attention?"

I should have gotten an Olympic medal for refraining my eye-roll. "I didn't even know about you and Zara before you arrived. Guess I missed that wedding invitation. And Nash and I are dating, so it made sense for him to spend Christmas with me. That's what boyfriends do, right?"

"Maybe if he was like Jarrett. You need a man worthy of this family. Of the image we represent. I have several important contracts coming up, but you'll be the ruin of us if you insist on this petty rebellion. Do you know what people think when my own daughter works for my biggest rival? He's not worthy of us. But—"

"But nothing. Nash is completely suitable. Regardless of the rivalry your companies have going on, he's here because I asked him to come, and that's that. It's not a question of if he's worthy of rubbing shoulders with the Addams. Or even being worthy of me. He's entirely too good for me." Anxiety burned in my veins as I finished my spiel, and my limbs buzzed like I'd had too much caffeine. "And Jarrett tried to assault me. I don't care that he was a potential big win. After his behaviour, you shouldn't either."

"So dramatic. I'm sure it was nothing that bad." Hiram waved dismissively. "You encouraged him."

Excuse me? Trying to steal kisses when a woman said *no* was not nothing or encouragement. Jarrett was lucky to be alive, since it was Hailey and not Gabe who'd found me cornered in the hallway. She'd still managed to give him a nasty concussion with a trusty Sanderson tome.

Hiram continued. "After all I've done for you, this is the thanks I get. You're just like your mother." The words reeked with derision. "You have no idea what it means to be an Addams, to carry the honour of the family name. You had the best of everything. Name-brand designers. A pony. A new Mercedes at sixteen. Who do you think paid for your high school trip to Europe?"

After all he... what? Thanks to my frayed nerves, the laughter spilled out of me in deranged cackles. "I never went to Europe, Dad. That was Veronica. And Zoe got the Mercedes. You haven't had an active part in my life since the day you dumped me off on Nana and Papa when I was five years old." My voice cracked slightly, and I hated the show of weakness, but I pressed on, the words I'd repressed for years tumbling out of me. "You gave me *stuff* that never fit into my world. Stuff we sold because it wasn't like you gave Nana and Papa any compensation to raise me. I get it. I'm the family disappointment, who never fit into your vision for the perfect Addams image. I'll never be good enough for you, no matter what I do or have done. It was never enough! But don't you *dare* try and make this my fault."

I was panting once I finished. I needed air. *Out. Get out.* Stomping to the door, I hesitated with my hand on the doorknob. "I wish you all the best with Zara, and I truly mean that. She's a nice woman. Better than you deserve." I lifted my chin to meet his gaze, those hazel eyes a mirror of my own as he stood there, watching me. How the man had the audacity to look disappointed in me was astounding. Was he really so clueless as to his parental failure? Or did he just not care enough? As long as he kept up the image, who cared about the foundation? "I hope with her at least you realize the treasure you have instead of chasing an illusion."

Heart pounding like a bass drum and dizziness threatening to overwhelm me, I stumbled up the stairs and locked myself in the bathroom, grateful it was free at that moment. I sank down to the cold tile floor, my back pressed against the door, and buried my face in my knees, tremors rattling my limbs. Emotional fireworks ricocheted in my brain as I felt like laughing and crying at the same time. I'd stood up to Hiram verbally, finding my voice, for the first time in my life. Before this, my decisions were mostly action-based, like declining his offer to pay for college and the complimentary job offer to Nova Designs every Addams sibling received upon graduation. Getting out all the words I'd said to him in my head for years was freeing, but it still made me nauseous. I was exhausted, and his accusations hurt. He didn't refute anything I said. How could he?

Some hopeful—or delusional—part of me had hoped we could have existed in civility. But it had been too much to dream of, and something inside me snapped. I couldn't force someone to accept me or even treat me with respect. And I was done reinventing myself into a more palatable shape for someone else's convenience. I didn't know what that fully looked like going forwards. But if I'd accused Hiram of chasing an illusion, I was just as guilty of chasing his affirmation. I had a Father who loved me, who'd affirmed me as His child. *My beloved daughter.* Chasing a flawed man's acceptance would never be enough. I already had my Heavenly Father's love and approval. I didn't have to earn it—it was freely given. No strings attached. *Thank you, Jesus.*

I inhaled slowly, trying to ease the tension in my chest and the burning of my lungs. This wasn't how I imagined the holiday would go. Wasn't how I wanted this chapter to end.

And it wasn't until I brushed my teeth after disassociating on the floor for twenty minutes, I noticed the tears trickling down my cheek.

Chapter Twenty-Five

Stephanie

"So…" Hailey dragged out the word when I entered our room after scrubbing all traces of tears from my face and finishing my nighttime routine in the washroom across from the Mistletoe. "That was some kiss." She wagged her eyebrows in mischief from where she sprawled across the double bed opposite mine, her chin propped in her hands.

I dropped my flour-bedazzled clothes in the laundry bag I'd brought along and spun around to face her. "How did you know?" I touched my cheeks, no doubt burning peony pink on my vampiric skin.

She blinked and closed the fantasy book open in front of her. "Uh, I know the world fades away when you kiss and all that, but you did smooch in the middle of the living room, and we were all witnesses. Unless…." She bolted upright, springing from the bed and jabbing a finger in my direction. "You're thinking of another kiss. He kissed you again! Steph!"

I groaned and collapsed face-first onto the red-and-green plaid quilt on my bed, but I couldn't keep the silly grin from my face if I tried. And I didn't bother denying it. I needed this bit of lightness after that conversation with Hiram.

Hailey squealed and pounced onto my bed. "Tell me everything!"

"This feels very awkward, you know," I protested. While I'd been on the receiving end of girl talk and hearing my friends recap their dates and relationships, my mostly dateless existence hadn't prepared me for this.

Hailey shoved a pillow at me. "Stop stalling and spill."

There was no way I was admitting to Hailey this had started out fake. Not with the precious newness of its realness. So I reluctantly shared about the pantry kiss and the flour bomb.

Hailey cackled loudly like one of those deranged Disney villains.

"Quiet!" I hissed, shoving my hand over her mouth.

She composed herself, propping her chin in her hand as she sat cross-legged opposite me on the bed. "I've told Nana several times that flour is dangerous on the top shelf. Never did I think it would have kissing ramifications." She chortled again before smiling widely. "I'm happy for you, Steph. You're great together."

"Yeah." It was a small admission, light and breathy. There was a steadiness to Nash that was heady. Compelling. Maybe it was our friendship, or the way he'd been such a trooper about my family's craziness, but things didn't faze him. He showed up and kept showing up. That was what I lo—liked about him. It was too soon for the other L-word. *Was it though?* "Hey, where's Cam? I thought you were bringing him."

The light dimmed in Hailey's face, and she shrugged, tugging at the cuff of her crimson silk blouse. "We broke up after Thanksgiving."

I blinked at her. I hadn't been home to Nana's for Thanksgiving this year, spending it with Liz and the rest of Ben's family instead. But I thought Hailey and Cam had been cute together. "And you didn't tell me?"

"Like you didn't tell me about Nash?" she shot back, a slight bite to her tone.

Yeah, this definitely wasn't a great breakup because Hailey was *never* sharp. I arched an eyebrow, and she mirrored me. "Touché."

"It was mutual. We're fine. He has his singing career; I have mine. Can we leave it at that for now?" Hailey yawned, stretching her hands over her head. "I'm going to catch a quick shower."

"Hey." I stopped her once she reached for the doorknob. I knew deflection when I saw it. "I'll listen when you're ready."

Hailey nodded and slipped out into the hall, pajamas draped over her arm.

Once she was gone, I reached for my phone. After Nash, that kiss, Hiram, and my bathroom breakdown, I needed my friends. In the faint light of the bronze touch-lamp with idyllic forget-me-nots printed on its frosted glass shades, I tapped the button for a four-way video call.

Liz was the first one to connect, her hair curled up into two space buns and looking adorable in a silvery wrap dress. And was her lipstick smudged? "Steph, are you okay?"

Just hearing her calming voice eased my tight breathing. "Hey, yeah. I just…" Just what? I bit my lip and snuggled under the covers. "Did I interrupt something?"

She laughed. "Just a bit of mistletoe. I'm still at Ben's parents. Did something happen?" There was a small scuffle on her end, a whisper, and then it was quiet again.

"I—"

"Hey, what's going on?" Paisley's face filled the screen, her slightly too-large glasses dwarfing her delicate face as she shoved them up the bridge of her nose. "Merry Christmas Eve!"

Rosie barked in the background, but before I could answer, Juliet joined. Only… it wasn't Juliet. It was a very awkward angle of her… ceiling?

"Jules?" I said.

"Uh… no," said a very masculine voice that was decidedly not Juliet. "She'll be a minute."

Liz cackled. "Oh my gosh, Myles!"

"It's not what you think," Myles groused. "She's finishing gift wrapping and asked me to answer while she's putting the presents under the tree."

That tracked since Juliet was a notorious Christmas Eve gift wrapper. But I had to laugh, clearly picturing the Caldwell Chargers' quiet goalie with his man bun in the epitome of discomfort at having to answer a girls' video chat. It wasn't like we were indecent or anything, but comical nonetheless.

"Thanks, babe!" Juliet sang followed by a definitive kissing noise. She was a grinch for all but that man.

"Jules," Paisley groaned.

"Sorry, give me a minute." Her background changed from the ceiling to the pink-themed Christmas tree in her living room. "What's up, Steph?"

"Nash kissed me. Or I kissed him." Technically that living room kiss was on me. But the pantry... Yeah, he started that even if I asked. That sent the fireworks off.

"Are you serious?" from Paisley.

A piglet squeal imitation—definitely Liz.

"Wait, that was what you wanted, right?" A very Juliet question. And given what they knew about Jarrett, a fair one.

I sighed softly. "Yeah. It was a mistletoe kiss in front of my family."

"Oh." Liz hummed softly. "So it was for show."

"Kind of." I blew out a breath, pinching the bridge of my nose. *Maybe one day you'll let me kiss you for real.* Those words etched into my brain on a loop, and I recited them to the girls, followed by the pantry saga.

"Wow, Steph..." Juliet mused. "I know I was reluctant about this in the beginning, but he's good for you. Like, really good."

"I just wish I could see all this cuteness firsthand," Paisley sighed dreamily. "It's so much better than a rom-com."

I raised an eyebrow. "I'm not a public kisser."

"That mistletoe kiss says otherwise," Liz cut in. "I'm going to find a bunch before you get home and plaster it everywhere. Ooh, maybe Kelsi can help me smuggle it into the office. I know better than to ask Emmett."

"One, you're hardly a mastermind if you're telling me your evil plans, and two, that's an HR fire waiting to happen."

Liz groaned. "Spoilsport. Fine, just our house then."

"Are you sure that isn't just for your and Ben's benefit?" Paisley asked slyly.

Liz groaned. "Three and a half months. Do you know how hard that is?"

"Yes!" Juliet and Paisley chimed in, and we all laughed.

We chatted for a few more minutes about blasé things and trading Christmas family escapades. Liz was in good hands with Ben and his family for the holidays, and I missed those few Idaho Christmases we'd spent with Juliet, Paisley, and the rest of the Satterfield clan. Soon after, Paisley and Juliet said their good nights first, but Liz stayed on the line a minute longer.

"You know how you said to be careful about my heart?" I whispered.

Liz was quiet for a moment. "Yes."

"I think it's too late."

"Do you love him, Steph?"

Did I? It felt too soon for that word. We'd been fake dating for less than a week. True, we'd been friends longer than that, and I'd admired him for years. But love? "Isn't it too soon? It would be crazy, right?"

Liz snorted. "You've had two years to think about it, honey. Crushes fade. If this hasn't, maybe it's because it's the real thing. Let me ask you again. Do you love him?"

"Yeah," I whispered. "I think I do."

"Falling in love can be scary, especially when you haven't done it before," Liz said soothingly. "But if he's the one God has for you, it'll work out. Are you feeling anxious?"

"That he'll decide he can do better than me," I whispered.

"Steph, not everyone will abandon you like your dad or those stupid guys you've gone out with. I'm still here."

For now. I shoved that aside and confessed, "He makes me feel safe. Like I can breathe. I've never felt that way before."

"Then I think you should see where this goes. Thoughtfully. Prayerfully. Don't let fear hold you back."

I silently offered a prayer of thanks for such a friend, who could celebrate my joys while also calling out my self-sabotaging tendencies. "Thanks, Liz. And thank Ben for letting me borrow you. I'll get out of your hair and let you get back to smooching." The conversation about my dad could wait for a different time. I wasn't in the mood to rehash it all again.

She laughed. "You saved him from a round of charades. Trust me, he's your biggest fan right now."

Exhaustion pulled at me as I joined the laughter. I'd won the friendship lottery with a friend who could make me smile no matter how close I was to tears. "Love you, Liz."

"Love you right back."

After hanging up, I pulled out the knitted garment I had been working on and finished stitching together the final seams. Nash's gift was done with no time to spare. I tucked it into the gift bag I'd brought before burrowing back under the covers.

I barely heard Hailey come in a few minutes later. And after a mumbled good night, I rolled over to face the wall, a smile touching my lips, and fell asleep dreaming of Christmas morning, pantry kisses, and a dark-eyed handsome man with adorable glasses holding my hand.

CHAPTER TWENTY-SIX

Text Thread – The Wise Guys

LATER THAT NIGHT

EMMETT

> The girls want to know if your hideous self won the ugly contest.

> No, that wasn't a typo.

NASH

> You're just jealous you couldn't have pulled that sweater off and won.

EMMETT

That spawn of the underworld was the stuff of nightmares. I'd rather not have the childhood trauma of small children on my conscience.

NASH

Your children helped create the aforementioned trauma.

RYAN

So you won?

EMMETT

So nice of you to join us.

NASH

They rigged it out of my favour because of spite. #publicenemynumber1 But according to Nana, there was no contest. Tell all the kids thanks. The elves especially were a crowd pleaser.

RYAN

Pretty sure my kid came up with that one.

EMMETT

You wish. It was my Sadie.

NASH

Team effort.

EMMETT

Why you ever wanted five kids to decorate it for you, I'll never know.

NASH

For precisely this reason.

EMMETT

All these years and you still surprise me.

NASH

Keeps the friendship alive.

RYAN

I'm back. Baby's not settling tonight.

You're obviously still alive on enemy turf and all that.

NASH

I've been put through the initiation rites and run the gauntlet.

EMMETT

No guts, no glory.

RYAN

And things are good with Stephanie?

NASH

Yup.

RYAN

Yup? That's all we get?

EMMETT

You aren't the nonverbose friend in this trio. I have the monopoly on that role. Talk.

NASH

Later. Gotta run for the night. Merry Christmas, guys.

RYAN

Gotta get that good-night kiss from his lady love.

EMMETT

Dude. Shut up.

Nash, you can run, but you can't hide.

RYAN

Love you, bros. Merry Christmas.

CHAPTER TWENTY-SEVEN

Stephanie

"Merry Christmas, Steph!"

I groaned, pulling the quilt over my head as Hailey's chipper voice cut through the haze of sugarplum dreams. "Go away," I mumbled, burrowing deeper into the nest of blankets.

She plopped down on the edge of the bed, making it dip. "There's a handsome man at the door with a special delivery."

"I will not be bribed," I muttered, flailing a hand out and giving her a shove.

"Don't keep the man waiting—Oof!" She thudded to the ground. "You've been working out."

I grunted, ignoring her. Hailey was worse than my nieces and nephews when it came to being bright-eyed and bushy-tailed on Christmas morning. Few Addams relatives were morning people. She'd evidently picked up the bad habit from her dad's side of the family—the Bishops.

There was a light tap on the door, then the voice from my dreams entered my sleepy reality. "Steph, I brought something that might help."

I ran a hand over my face, shoving my messy curls aside as I sat up. Dizziness rattled my brain, and black splotches danced across my vision. *Slow down.*

Hailey scoffed. "Ha, I see how things are. I wake you up, trying to do a nice thing for you, and I get shoved off the bed. Mr. Dreamy over there says a handful of pretty words, and you're primping."

"Shut up," I growled, slipping my Marine hoodie over my oversized T-shirt and shuffling to the door as she cackled, like the deranged woman she was.

"You're lucky I love you," I muttered to her, opening the cracked door to reveal a smiling Nash. I took him in through half-open puffy eyes. He wore the blue-and-red plaid flannel pajama pants and black hoodie well. His hair was sleep rumpled, but his eyes were bright behind his glasses. Goodness, he was adorable in the mornings. "Ugh, you're a morning person. That might be a deal breaker."

Nash laughed, holding out a gorgeous sight. A Christmas mug full of steaming hot coffee with a pillow of whipped cream. "You're a delight in the morning, sweetheart."

I growled and made grabby hands at the mug, catching a whiff of peppermint. But before I captured my bribe, the momentum of standing caught up to me, and I pitched forward.

Nash caught me against his chest. "Whoa! Hailey, can you grab this?"

I shut my eyes against the swimming sensation plaguing my senses and shamelessly nestled into his hoodie. "You smell nice," I whispered, squeezing my arms around his waist, letting him take my weight after he passed the coffee off to Hailey.

His chuckle rumbled under my cheek. "So do you." He rubbed my back lightly. "You okay?"

I nodded against the fabric. "Got up too fast."

"I see you're falling for me," he teased. "First in the hallway and now this."

That cheekiness deserved a smack. Which I felt strong enough to deliver to his shoulder.

After a minute, I reluctantly eased out of his arms, no longer a gangly newborn colt. Nash rescued the coffee from Hailey and handed it to me.

Two swigs in, I hummed appreciatively. The man brewed good coffee, I'd give him that. I stifled a yawn. "Thank you. Merry Christmas."

He leaned down, pressing a kiss to my forehead. "Merry Christmas. You ready to open presents?"

"No." I grumbled, taking another sip of my mocha. "But apparently, I can be bribed with coffee and forehead kisses from a cute guy in nerdy glasses. Let's go."

Hailey spluttered behind me, and Nash laughed as he draped an arm around my shoulders, pulling me into his side. No complaints here as the delightful citrusy scent that always accompanied him filled my nose. "My glasses do it for you, huh? Man, I'm loving this Early Morning Steph with no filter."

I snorted, taking another sip of coffee and cuddling into his warmth. Don't judge me—I was cold. "My filter doesn't kick in till cup number two."

"Noted."

CHRISTMAS MORNING HELD A special kind of magic. Maybe it was the children's laughter. Or the winking lights from the tree. Or the cozy ambiance from the fire in the hearth. Or just maybe it was cuddling with your new boyfriend on the sofa in Christmas pj's and sipping the most decadent coffee while watching a bunch of kids open presents. Definitely the snuggling. Highly recommend.

Every family had a different way of opening gifts, and we were the one-at-a-time type or a couple of kids together if it was a group gift. Savouring the moment and reducing noise levels were the ultimate goals.

But first. Stockings. Which was an all-at-once affair. After stockings came homemade shortbread, mandarin oranges, and coffee.

Gift giving was one of my love languages and finding the perfect gifts each year was one of my favourite parts of the season, even if I started planning a year in advance sometimes. This year, Jackson's gift was my personal favourite accomplishment because—

"CAL SATTERFIELD!" Jackson's shriek was deafening. His whole body shook with excitement as he waved the navy-and-silver jersey overhead. "And it's signed!" He ran a finger over the bold, scrawling script of Cal's signature. "He's the best player in the AHL. His scoring average is the highest for his position in the Pacific Division. With his talent, he's wasting it in the minor leagues."

"Should I pass along your assessment to the man himself?" I asked, biting back a smile, even if the last part of his speech stung uncomfortably. Cal had his reasons for sticking to an AHL career. I'd have to chat with Jackson after.

Jackson flung himself into my arms, half landing on Nash beside me as he went in for a bear hug. "I forget how cool you are sometimes when your best friend is Cal Satterfield's sister."

I squeezed him a little harder, soaking up the moment before I ruffled his hair. He was growing up so fast—they all were. Soon he'd be too cool for hugs from Auntie Steph. Then came graduating high school, dating, marriage. Ugh, I couldn't go down that trail of thought. *Stay little a little longer.* "That's right, I'm the cool aunt." What I didn't tell him was that there was a second half to the gift. When I had Cal sign the jersey, he offered me a few special tickets for Gabe and Ivy to take the kids to a home game in Caldwell on their way back to San Diego.

Jackson slipped the jersey over his pajamas and flashed me a toothy grin when it came down to his knees. "You're the best, Auntie Steph."

"My turn! Here." Ivy handed me a small burgundy-papered box, tied with a silver bow.

"I thought we weren't exchanging here," I murmured. Christmas morning was mostly for the kids and Hiram. Because most of my siblings and I didn't exchange gifts. Only Gabe's family and me.

And we preferred to do it in quiet pockets of time over the course of the day.

Ivy smiled knowingly. "It's something small. Go ahead."

Untying the ribbon, I tore into the box and carefully lifted the tissue paper. Happiness bubbled in my chest, and I laughed. Inside were the ornaments from last night's White Elephant. "Did Zoe have a change of heart?"

Gabe scoffed. "Hardly. She's—"

"We bought an extra set," Ivy cut in, shooting her husband a warning look. "Just in case you lost them in the game. I had no idea they were going to start a fight."

I snorted. "Your son has excellent taste."

Ivy cocked an eyebrow. "And who do you think suggested them?"

I reached over to side-hug her, smooshing our faces together. "Have I mentioned how much I love you?" I glanced at Gabe. "You, too, Gunny." It was practically my duty to annoy my brother with every Marine title except the one he currently held.

Gabe shook his head and sipped his coffee patiently. "You're like having another kid."

"And you love it. Your life would be empty without me to temper that ego of yours."

"I think my ego would be just fine."

Beside me, Nash snorted and stage whispered, "You sure that filter kicked in after cup number two?"

Gabe laughed, actually laughed. Which was rare for him but also, rude. Whose side was he on?

I stuck my tongue out at Gabe. "My filter is just fine."

Nash's arm snaked around my shoulders, and he pressed a kiss to my temple. "And I like you just fine," he whispered against my hair. He was so perfectly snuggable—could you blame me for cuddling further into his citrusy warmth?

Then it was Hiram's turn to shine. Gifts were doled out liberally on a performance basis. Much like how a boss awarded holiday bonuses. The better you did, the nicer your bonus. For Hiram, the better you toed the family line, performed in the family empire, the nicer your gift potential. Which was why, as much as my siblings had a common dislike for how Hiram had treated their mothers, even if they themselves were always treated well, they danced to the puppet master's strings. Because none of them wanted to be written out of the will.

Gift wrapping flew in a hundred directions, uncovering Kate Spade purses, Louis Vuitton shoes, new smartphones, keys to an ATV, Tiffany gift bags, and more. Gifts in Hiram's world were awarded on merit or bribery. Gabe and Ivy received a couples' gift, some sort of gift card. They were apparently still in Phase Bribery, since the rest of my siblings were high-end merit receivers.

Then it was my turn. Hiram plopped an icy-blue snowflake-patterned box into my lap with a veneered smile. Honestly, after last night, I was expecting no gift. But apparently he still thought I could be bribed?

I shifted uncomfortably, struggling to hold eye contact. "Thanks." The paper even *smelled* expensive when I tore it lightly.

Please don't be another pair of designer shoes. A girl could only sell so many pairs.

My fingers brushed luxurious buttery fabric under the creamy tissue paper lining the box. My pulse stuttered. Was this... clothing? I shot Hiram a confused look. He'd never bought me clothes before, only accessories.

He smiled benignly, waving me on. "Something suitable for tonight."

Tonight? Still lost, I gently lifted the silky puddle of sapphire fabric, and it fluttered down into a shape. Oh. *Oh!*

It was a dress. A very fashionable, expensive designer dress. And tonight was our formal family dinner. So, this was what he meant by *suitable*.

Talk about anything *but*. It was... slinky, bordering on risqué. *How is this formal family dinner appropriate?*

The slit was in dangerous territory, and the skirt was murderously long. I was five feet on a good day, not a supermodel. There weren't heels high enough to save me from tripping. As for the top half... The company must be making budget cuts with the alarming lack of fabric, since the designer forgot the entire back. And no one should entrust that much faith in those skimpy straps.

I cleared my throat and tried to speak, but nothing came out. The weight of everyone's eyes on me—most amused, others uncomfortable—squeezed my chest. I didn't dare look at Nash next to me as the tsunami wave of embarrassment flooded my veins. After clearing my throat again, which sounded like a cat hacking up a hairball, I pasted on my professional smile. "Uh, thanks, Dad. It's... a nice colour."

What else could I say about it? I wouldn't be caught dead in that dress. It was so far from my comfort levels of attire, and I was pretty sure it was worth several months of my salary. I tucked the fabric back into the box, jaw clenching.

I glanced at Zara in her cute teal silk pajama set. Maybe I could soften this disaster with a deflective compliment? "Pretty sure this gown would look better on you. You've got the lovely height for it."

Zara brightened in pleasure. "Aren't you sweet?"

"Nonsense. It'll wash her out horribly," Hiram cut in. "She already has the perfect dress." He smiled at his wife, but she'd already withered.

I didn't miss the word *perfect* or the way he believed I was clearly less than. My middle siblings tittered. Hot tears scalded my eyes, but I refused to let them fall. What I wouldn't have given for it to have been just another pair of stupid shoes. At least I could sell those without feeling slimy.

There was no way I could wear that gown. And if Hiram had known me at all, he'd have known that. Maybe that was the whole point. He never had.

The grandkids were spared most of the mind games but still received pretty cool gifts. It was something of a sore point for Gabe and Ivy because they were trying to instill values in their kids that other family members weren't. And lavish gifts with tons of battery toys and screen time wasn't their approach to parenting.

During a lull in the noise, Nash leaned over and whispered in my ear, "Ready for your present?"

I jolted, eyes wide. "You got me something?"

"Would've looked odd if I hadn't, don't you think?"

"We didn't talk about it." I shrugged as he stood and rustled the gifts under the tree. "Oh! Grab that gift bag, please. No. The other one." I laughed, motioning to the left. "Nash, the red truck one with the red tissue paper. Yes!"

Nash chuckled and hurried back to me, gift bag in one hand and a neatly wrapped square box in the other. He gently set the box on my lap and smiled. "Go ahead."

Arching an eyebrow, I lifted it, assessing. "Kinda heavy."

"Just open it, woman," he teased.

"So impatient," I tsked, but I undid the ribbon and popped the lid off the box. Lifting the tissue paper, I gasped. Nestled inside was another box, a camera lens printed on the side. The 70-200mm I'd been eyeing for years but never justified buying because I hadn't treated my photography as more than a hobby. "What?" I croaked, feeling the sting of tears in my eyes. "Why?" I knew how much this cost, and the thought of him buying it for me...

Nash smiled softly. "For when you're ready to embrace your gift and soar again."

This man. I cradled the new lens in my hands at a loss for more words. I'd pushed back against making photography my main occupation because the lack of security scared me. I needed a solid income, somewhere to land. Even though I loved my job, I didn't *love* it. Organization didn't fuel my soul the way looking through a camera viewfinder and capturing a hundred moments that would last a lifetime did.

"Thank you," I whispered. The words were a paltry compensation for the emotions swelling through me, but I smiled up at him, trying to infuse all my gratitude into the look.

Nash nodded, then lifted the gift bag in his other hand. "This one for me?"

"Yeah." I fidgeted with the cuff of my worn hoodie. Compared to his lavish gift, a handmade sweater seemed like a pittance. I loved giving gifts and planning surprises for other people, but after his grand gesture, knitwear was pathetic. *I* was pathetic. What business did I have pursuing a relationship with this amazing guy? He was so far out of my league.

Oblivious to my mental spiral, Nash grinned up at me in boyish excitement as he crouched at my feet, pulling on tissue paper. My heart sank when he lifted the navy-blue knitted sweater. But his dark eyes softened as he brushed a hand reverently over the cabled detailing. "Steph... you made this?" His voice was low with awe.

I smiled mechanically, flexing my fingers. "Right under your very nose."

He inspected it again. And again. Finally, his gaze locked on mine. "You were working on this in the car."

"Yup." I tugged at one of my curls. *Okay, maybe he didn't hate it.* "I've never knit a sweater so fast in my life."

"How'd you get my measurements?"

"I may have snooped in your closet when I dropped your dry cleaning off last Monday."

Nash chuckled. "Clever girl." Standing, he tugged his hoodie off and eased the new sweater over his white T-shirt. "Perfect fit." He spun in a circle, striking a pose.

I laughed and stood to smooth a hand over his chest. "I didn't get it fully blocked yet because I ran out of time, but after I do that, it'll drape better."

Nash smiled before bending down and wrapping his arms around my waist, pulling me into a sturdy hug. "Thank you, Steph," he whispered into my hair. "This is the nicest thing anyone's ever given me."

I wasn't sure I believed him, but I squeezed his neck, feeling a little woozy. Whether that was the man or my blood pressure, I wasn't certain. "Thank you for believing in me. Merry Christmas, Nash."

"Merry Christmas, darlin'."

CHAPTER TWENTY-EIGHT

Stephanie

AFTER A QUICK BREAK so Austin and Nana could stuff the turkey and pop it into the oven, more gifts exploded across the living room. But when I caught a glimpse of Jackson, I knew I needed to have that chat with him from earlier.

"Hey, kiddo, can you wait a minute?" I called to Jackson as we headed towards the main living room for more gifts. The allure of shiny wrapping paper was a siren call, but I didn't want to postpone this conversation either.

"Sure." He paused in the hall, still decked out in snowman pj's and his new hockey jersey.

"I'm glad you like your jersey."

That infectious grin flashed at me again. "Best gift ever!"

I couldn't help smiling back because his smile really was contagious. The words I wanted to say clawed at my throat, but I needed to phrase this carefully. "Did you know Cal Satterfield has a little girl?"

Jackson's blue eyes bugged out. "He has a kid?"

I bit back a laugh at his expression. It wasn't super public knowledge, since Cal liked to keep his private life private. "She's a little older than Eden now. But the thing is, her mom died three years ago."

Jackson instantly frowned. "That stinks. She probably doesn't even remember what she looked like."

"You're right, it does stink." I paused, gathering my thoughts. "Do you remember when Cal got sent down from the NHL?"

"Yeah, about three years ago. Oh."

I saw the instant the lightbulb clicked in his head. "Yeah. Cal had an attitude problem and that's on him. But around the same time, his wife died. Being in Idaho, even if it was a punishment of sorts, meant his family was there to help take care of his little girl. When he had the chance to go back to the NHL, that meant uprooting Khia. Or leaving her behind when he was on the road for months at a time."

Jackson stewed over the words, looking too mature for a ten-year-old. "I guess I was wrong. He's not just a great hockey player. He's a good dad. And I think that's better." He scuffed the rug with his bare foot. "'Cuz, I know I miss my dad, even if he's a hero."

I tousled his hair, aching to pull him into a hug, but I could see he wasn't ready for that. A brave boy trying to be a man. "I know the feeling, kiddo."

He studied me for a minute then added, "Yeah. You deserve a better dad." And with those words, he disappeared down the hall.

All I could do was stare after him, even after he vanished. Out of the mouths of babes. Was my dad's manipulation obvious to even my young nephews? Everyone always said blood was thicker than water, but maybe family was what you made it. Sure, I had an absentee dad and strained sibling relationships, but I had a great nana, a strong bond with my brother and sister-in-law and their kids, a sweet cousin. I was blessed, despite the heartache. Like Nash said last night, it was all about how we let God use the hard times to grow us. *Lord, I need your help in the growing department. I haven't done so well lately.*

"Did you take the stars out of his eyes?"

I jumped at Gabe's voice behind me. "Jeepers, don't do that!"

He smirked. "It never gets old."

I slugged his shoulder, but it hurt me more than him because he was crafted of iron, granite, and carbon fiber. I wrung out my stinging hand. So unfair.

Gabe only laughed and slung his arm over my shoulders. "Did you tell him about the real Cal Satterfield? Single dad?"

"How much did you hear?"

"Not a word. But I know you."

I smiled wryly. "Cal may be a hotshot athlete, but he's something of an honorary brother which means I don't have the same level of hero worship as y'all and don't mind dropping him a few pegs to keep him humble."

"He has my condolences then." Gabe chuckled, sidestepping my attempt to swat him. "Jack looked pretty somber."

I hummed. "It happens when heroes lose their shine, but I doubt that's what's on his mind."

"Oh?"

"I'm not your snitch, my dude."

He nudged my shoulder. "I'm not asking for a snitch, just my sister's insight on my kid."

"You don't always like what I have to say."

"Doesn't mean I don't need to hear it."

I sighed, wondering where to start—with Jackson's thoughts on his dad or his grandfather. "Is Hiram's... differential treatment obvious?" I bit my lip and snuck a glance at my brother. "Towards me?"

Gabe's expression morphed into flint as it often did whenever Hiram's name came up. While his own relationship with Hiram hadn't initially been terrible, it had soured after I came along and Gabe joined the Marines. Gabe had no patience or respect for the man who'd abandoned his own daughter. "Did Jackson say something about it?"

I shrugged. "Just that I deserve a better dad than I got." My voice was light, almost breezy because my defense mechanisms were kicking in. The walls I used to be a professional at work. To keep my heart from getting beat up by my dad's abandonment. To ward off the sharp words from the siblings who never thought I fit the Addams family mold. But it was harder to maintain today with the whispered vines of Hiram's words last night choking my memory.

"It's... noticeable to those who have their eyes open," Gabe said slowly. He met my gaze frankly, his expression soft with understanding.

"I'm sorry your kid had to pick up on that at ten years old."

Gabe's hand cupped my shoulder. "Hey, don't deflect on me. I know it bothers you. You don't have to pretend otherwise. Not with me."

Hot tears burned my eyes, but my smoldering relationship with Hiram wasn't worth crying over. It wasn't even smoldering. It was... gone. We shared blood and nothing else. For twenty-eight years, I'd fought to be someone my dad could be proud of. I'd reinvented myself so many times to try to be the version of Stephanie Addams he could approve of, brag about to his friends, and show up for. Instead, I got passive-aggressive criticism, late birthday cards (if they ever came at all), extravagant gifts, and a therapy bill. I didn't hate him, even if I wanted to sometimes. I just wanted him to choose me for *me*. One time.

"Do you ever think about not coming back here?" I whispered, swiping at a rogue tear sneaking out from my lashes. *Stand down, soldier. No crying.*

Gabe hauled me into a hug, the perfect balance of gentleness and security. "We've talked about it. Stepping out to do our own thing with you and Nana and Hailey's family. Like we've done on off years sometimes when we're not with Ivy's folks."

"Hard to do when you never know where you'll be sent though, huh?"

The hall echoed with silence, the murmur of voices in the distance a hundred miles from the moment. He was quiet. Too quiet, even for Gabe.

"Gabe?"

"I won't be renewing my contract. Once my time in San Diego is up, I'm out."

WHAT? I yanked back, nearly toppling over as I studied him, searching for the joke but not finding one. "You're serious? But you love the military."

Gabe nodded, his half smile sad. "True, but I love my family more. It's been over twenty years, and I want to be more involved with my kids. As for branching out on our own for Christmas..." He sighed. "Maybe it's overdue. Family is family. But..."

At what cost? "Family is what you make it, not what you're born with."

He huffed softly. "Something like that." Hesitating for a moment, he added, "You going to be okay?"

My laugh was weak and watery, but I nodded and eased out of the hug. "Of course."

Gabe fished his phone from his pocket and tapped something on the screen before refocusing on me. "Any other insight on my son?"

"Let's just say that you have a little boy trying desperately hard to be a man... who misses his dad very much."

Something flickered in Gabe's face, but I couldn't name it.

"I can't tell you how to parent," I quickly added, "because I'm not one. And I wouldn't have dreamed of telling you to give up the military because I'm so proud of you. But I'm excited for you guys and this next chapter."

Gabe pressed a kiss to the crown of my head. "Thanks, Stephie-Lou. I hear you."

Something about the way he used my nickname and paired it with the words he used to tell me as a teen—his way of telling me he heard the words I said as well as the ones I didn't—broke the dam on my tear ducts. But instead of hugging me, Gabe shifted out of my peripheral, and a new smell filled my nose. Something citrusy and... like *home*.

Nash's presence cocooned me in safety as he led my crying self towards the west alcove, closing the door softly behind us as I fell apart in his arms. I didn't question how he'd gotten there—Gabe probably—or why. Just let myself feel the tsunami of emotions that I'd kept walled up behind my façade.

I cried the tears of the little girl who didn't understand why her friends had moms and dads and why she lived with her grandparents. The tears of the teenager who shuffled between her nana's house and her brother and sister-in-law's house in the middle of grief and loss, never feeling like she belonged in one place, though she knew she was dearly loved. The tears of the young adult who walled off her heart to all thoughts of her father, convincing herself that she didn't care that he didn't want to be a part of her life. The tears of the adult woman terrified to love a good man and take a chance on him because the people in her life who should have loved her and stayed decided she wasn't what they wanted. If her mom and dad hadn't wanted her, why would Nash?

I cried until I couldn't cry anymore. Nash just held me, securely and tenderly. Stroking my hair as I heard murmured snatches of words. Was he... praying? For me? Somehow that made me cry harder. But in this moment, I was content to break in the arms of a man who insisted he was the staying kind while he brought me to the feet of my Heavenly Father, who already loved me beyond measure.

"You wanna talk about it?" Nash asked when my tears lessened to muffled sniffles.

I felt like a wrung-out dish rag. Emotions were heavy things. Did I want to talk? Oddly... yes. To him. I swiped my nose with the sleeve of my hoodie. "It's not pretty."

"Heartbreak never is."

I tried to breathe through my nose, but my clogged sinuses were having none of it. Gross. "Bet you didn't expect to spend Christmas like this?"

"With a beautiful, clever woman in my arms?"

"Who just used you as a human tissue."

Nash brushed his thumb gently over my cheek, wiping away the last rogue tear. "There's nowhere I'd rather be." His gaze skittered over my features, taking me in—red nose, puffy eyes, and make-up-less. Like I was the most enchanting thing he'd ever seen. I felt the warmth and steadiness behind the look all the way down to my toes, and part of me wanted to cry again, so I opened my mouth and let the story fall out of me instead.

"My mom, Hilary, was wife number six. When I was five, my parents divorced, and she left. Moved to Paris, restarted her life, and never thought about me again." I sniffed hard. This wasn't the first time I'd told my life story. The girls had gotten it out of me during our dorm-room days. But standing here in Nash's arms on Christmas morning in pajamas, messy hair, and no makeup scraped me raw with vulnerability. *What if my mess scares him away?* This was new territory for us, but something in me craved to let him in. I was tired of being alone.

"I found out as a preteen that she remarried and had three more kids."

"She never reached out to you?" Nash's arms tightened a fraction.

"Nope. I tried connecting with her my freshman year of college." A fresh wave of tears stung my eyes. "I thought maybe she'd want to know me. But she told me she'd moved on and wanted nothing to do with that, and I quote, 'unfortunate chapter of my life.' Then there's Hiram." I let out a bitter laugh. "He's never been a stable presence. He handed me off to his parents and lived his life, occasionally popping in and out of my life between women. He was never around for everyday things like school plays, but Christmas and birthday presents—when he actually remembered—were always extravagant. I waffled between being appeased by the items and hating his absence.

"Papa died when I was thirteen, and that's when I was shipped off to Gabe and Ivy's for the first time. Nana was struggling to cope and needed hip surgery around the same time. She was grieving

and scared and didn't want to put that weight on my shoulders."
My throat caught. "I'd have given anything to have stayed with her.
Anything to keep my life from upending again. But…" I glanced
out the nearby window where the morning sun bathed the pure
white snow, dazzling with a million diamonds. "Once I got older,
I realized she was trying to protect me while she was falling apart.
I knew it was from a place of love, but I felt… passed around and
inconvenient."

Nash hummed quietly, gently rubbing a hand up and down my
spine. He didn't push me to go on with the story, but now that I'd
started talking, it poured off my lips like a waterfall.

"Military life was unstable and unpredictable. Because Gabe
and I are twelve years apart, there's a weird, not-quite-fa-
ther-but-not-quite-sibling relationship between us. Gabe was de-
ployed for the first part of my stay—he was based in Arizona at the
time—and Ivy was a saint for putting up with me. Though she says
it was the other way around." I paused, remembering.

The truth was Gabe and Ivy struggled with infertility and had
just gotten devastating news before I arrived in Arizona. So there
we were. Ivy, the woman who desperately wanted to be a mother,
and me, the budding teenager unwanted by either of her parents
and heartbroken about losing her grandpa. I'd always loved Ivy
since she'd been a part of my life practically forever, but those three
months before Gabe came home from Afghanistan bound us in
a way nothing else could have. Years later, Ivy had apologized for
leaning on me too heavily at a young age, but I never saw it like
that. Maybe it was because for the first time, someone needed *me*.

I wasn't just the youngest sister who needed protecting. But that part of the story wasn't mine to tell, even though Gabe and Ivy's choice to adopt was no secret.

"How long did you live with them?" Nash's low voice brought me back to the small nook where his arms still looped around my lower back, holding me securely.

"Eight months the first time. Then depending on where they were stationed, I spent summers with them until I went to college, especially after they adopted the boys. They're bio brothers. The girls came a few years later."

"Did Hiram ever make an effort after that?"

My shoulder twitched in a half-shrug. "He offered to pay for my tuition, like he did for all of us, but I turned him down. Honestly, he still thinks of me as a child who can be pacified with toys and luxury. But I can't be bought, and he hates that. Yet he still tries."

"Like the dress?"

"Yeah. It's an image thing. How he wants me to look. Act." I groaned just thinking about the monstrosity and hid my face against his chest.

"I'm sure working for me didn't help."

I snort-laughed, and it was real. "I saw your job listing by accident, and I've never been so conflicted. I was terrified that all you would see was my dad when I walked in."

"It took guts to tell me who you really were. I admired that."

My palms were a bit sweaty as I remembered our first meeting, when I'd waltzed into his office with more bravado than I felt. I'd been immediately struck with Nash's attractiveness, but I was already a fan of his business ethics. The decision to apply wasn't some misplaced rebellion or a chance to "stick it" to my father, but I wasn't cut out for the rat race of the family business and wanted to be valued for my skills, not just because of my last name.

"Was that all you admired?" Excuse me, *what*? Who was this flirty woman? Thy name was not Stephanie.

Heat flashed in Nash's dark-chocolate eyes before he leaned forward until his lips brushed the shell of my ear, his voice low and raspy. "I think you know the answer to that."

I shivered and gave him a playful shove, returning us to lighter footing after my emotional breakdown. "Can't blame a girl for trying."

Nash smirked, but the seriousness didn't leave his eyes.

Lightness eased through my limbs, and I stifled a yawn. Who knew emotions were so exhausting? When I couldn't resist the next yawn, I let my head drop back against his chest. He rested his chin on my head, and we stood there in silence for several moments.

"Thank you," Nash said at last.

My head popped up like a jackrabbit. "For what? We already established the human tissue."

He ignored my jab of humour. "For trusting me, Steph. For letting me in."

"Oh." It felt like an odd thing for him to be thankful for. Shouldn't I be the thankful one—and I was—for him holding me together while I fell apart and letting me snot all over his shirt?

Thanking him for not running for the hills? Yet hadn't I appreciated it when he opened up to me last night? Sharing the load?

He must have thought I needed extra convincing because he crooked a finger under my chin and gently tilted it up. "I'm no stranger to heartbreak, and I know taking that first step to let somebody see the mess, the fractures, and the broken parts of you is the hardest part. Thank you for trusting me with that. It's an honour to share pain, not a burden. And it's okay to grieve a relationship that didn't turn out the way it was meant to."

Why was his face going blurry? Oh, I was crying again. Relationships required communication to work, even when it was uncomfortable. When all your broken pieces and ugly edges were held up to the light by another soul. But there was a beauty to being known. Being truly seen. Scrubbing my sleeve over my eyes, I whispered, "Thank you for staying."

"Always."

And somehow, I believed him.

Chapter Twenty-Nine

Nash

STEPHANIE CLUNG TO MY hand the rest of the morning as we sipped coffee in the breakfast nook with Nana and Hailey and stuffed our faces with Liz's homemade shortbread. Watching Stephanie fall apart this morning broke something inside of me. In trusting me with her story, I got a clearer picture of the woman I'd called a friend and employee these last two years.

For the first time, I saw past the colour-coded planner, meticulous notes, and obsessive need for order as personality quirks to catch a glimpse of the little girl underneath, grasping to order an unstable world that hadn't chosen her.

As the gift-giving wound down, the leftovers from Christmas Eve emerged onto the kitchen island, people wandering in and filling a plate at will. Austin, professional chef that he was, commandeered the kitchen preparations. He assigned jobs and tasks with precision, and once again, I witnessed that Addams take-charge attitude.

Stephanie and I were paired together peeling a mountain of potatoes. From the catlike gleam in Austin's eyes, I was betting this was a bottom-of-the-barrel job. But it gave me time to watch family interactions. The teasing and banter. And interestingly enough, the work talk. Nova Designs truly was a family business, and even Austin, who didn't work for the company directly, still worked for Hiram's catering business. Between tension and subtle jabs, they projected a front of moderate camaraderie. One Gabe and Stephanie were clearly excluded from. Gabe was hard to flat-out ignore—I mean, look at the guy. But Stephanie? Unless they were throwing shade her way, it was like she didn't exist.

Like she'd handed them the ultimate betrayal in disgracing the Addams name by working for the enemy and bringing him onto their home turf for Christmas. Sorry, guys. I intended to stick around for a good long while.

Once the food preparations were underway and close enough to finishing, we scattered to prepare for dinner. Because, of course, the Addams family did black tie.

My hands shook as I wrapped the burgundy tie with the white Swiss dots around my neck in my third attempt at a Windsor knot. Why was I nervous? I didn't do nervous. I'd negotiated multimillion-dollar deals without batting an eye. But escorting a beautiful woman to dinner with her family had me—and my tie—in knots. Once I was satisfied with the result, I shrugged on my suit coat—the Armani grey pinstripe Stephanie had suggested—and strode downstairs to wait.

At the foot of the stairs, I fiddled with my silver monkey's fist knot cufflinks. *Get a hold of yourself.* It wasn't like I'd never seen Stephanie in formal attire. I had a couple times when Genesis hosted gala events, but this was different. She'd said *yes* to dating for real. This was the first time I'd get to escort my girlfriend to dinner, and I wouldn't even get a dance out of it.

A throat dramatically cleared behind me, and I whirled around, my blood thrumming with anticipation.

Hailey grinned down at me—probably in a nice dress, but I didn't notice. She swept aside, making a motioning arch with her arms. I waited and then my breath caught.

Chapter Thirty

Stephanie

I smoothed my sweaty palms over the velvet skirt of the dress as I stepped forward, and Nash's gaze washed over me with appreciation and a smile. Scooping the floor-length skirt up in one hand, I trailed my free hand over the polished wood of the banister as I descended. Nash's eyes locked on mine. Utterly transfixed.

"Hi," I said, stopping on the last stair so we were nearly eye level, and smiled shyly.

"You're beautiful," he said simply, pushing his glasses up his nose.

"You like the dress?" It was one of my favourites. A floor-length burgundy velvet gown, designed with the illusion of a wrapped dress in the bodice with short puffed sleeves and an A-line skirt. And, of course, a strappy pair of black heels that added a hint of loftiness to my five-foot frame.

Nash scanned me up and down once more, like he was just noticing the dress. That made me feel more confident than I could have ever been in that skimpy sapphire number upstairs under my bed. "Yes, of course. But *you're* beautiful. The dress is just a bonus."

I reached out, straightening his tie—an impressive Double Windsor knot, if I wasn't mistaken—and patted his chest. The man knew how to wear a suit. His wavy hair was stylishly tousled and very distracting. But the way his tie perfectly matched my gown sent a flutter in my stomach. It was couple-y, and I loved it. "You look pretty dapper yourself."

He kissed me softly before holding out his arm with an elaborate bow. "Shall we, my lady?"

I laughed and tucked my hand into the crook of his elbow. "With pleasure."

The dining room sparkled as we entered, among the last to arrive. Zoe had outdone herself on the decorating. The table was beautifully dressed. Greenery and holly snaked through the center of the distressed wood, interspersed with golden candlesticks, their pure white tapers flickering with welcome. Golden-rimmed china plates and a narrow-fluted glass marked every place. It was a feast for the eyes as much as for the nose.

All the food was piled in steaming dishes on the table. Buttery, fluffy rolls neatly arranged in a linen cloth basket. Roasted turkey overflowing with dressing. Honey-glazed ham. Brazed carrots. Creamy confetti corn. Roasted Brussels sprouts drizzled with balsamic and topped with hazelnuts and pomegranate seeds. A heaping punch bowl of ambrosia salad.

Eager faces clustered in groups, laughing. A bonus table off to the side housed a gaggle of kids.

Against my will, my eyes pinged to Hiram, like a heat-seeking missile, and I saw the exact moment he noticed me. His face iced over in disapproval as he took me in, head to foot. In my festive dress, I was formal dress-code appropriate.

Just not molded into the image Hiram Addams wanted to control.

"You weren't kidding about formal," Nash whispered, re-claiming my attention as he held out a chair for me. "From snowball wars to ugly sweater contests to the red carpet, y'all go big. Can I assume there will be family glambot pictures afterwards?"

"Just selfies." I laughed, settling my skirts as he pushed me in. "And the unexpected seems to be a theme for us."

"Us, huh?" he smirked, dropping into his chair. "Consider-ing we haven't even had a proper date yet."

I glanced around, worried someone might overhear, but Nana had everyone laughing, granting us a bubble of privacy for now. "Maybe we're just untraditional?"

"I plan on remedying that."

"Is that so?"

"Most definitely." Nash grinned easily, eyes crinkling with mirth and warmth as he squeezed my knee lightly. Leaning in till his shoulder brushed mine.

I swallowed hard. *He's not like Hiram. He doesn't think you're too much.*

Nana stood at the foot of the table, her kelly-green gown commanding notice, and clapped twice. "All right, attention, everyone."

"*Everyone*," Gabe drolled across from us, flashing me a wry look as he fiddled uncomfortably with his tie.

I flushed, ducking my head and lacing my hands in my lap even as I bit back a laugh. One of the good things to come from this fake-turned-real relationship was the opportunity to annoy my brother a little bit. None of my dates had ever met him, not even my boyfriend of a month, so Gabe seeing his sister get lovey-dovey with a guy was new territory for both of us. And I loved seeing him, big strong Marine that he was, squirm just a bit. Little sister perks.

Nana's lips twitched when she glanced my way. *Busted.* "Gabe, if you'll say the blessing."

Gabe obliged, ignoring the murmurs of disapproval. Outside of the family close to me, none of the rest were religious, although not from lack of exposure. But Nana insisted on family grace when it came to holiday meals.

Nash reached out under the table and entwined our fingers. Family drama aside, this was the best Christmas ever. Good food, people in my corner, and a forever kind of guy.

Over the evening, plates were passed, toasts were offered, and laughter bathed the table. And I let my guard down a fraction. I thought about what Nash said earlier—it was okay to grieve a relationship that didn't turn out the way you wanted. Looking around the table, I understood that better. Joy and grief were intermingling dinner guests.

CHAPTER THIRTY-ONE

Stephanie

THE DAY AFTER CHRISTMAS, we skied. Correction. Those who weren't challenged with a lack of grace strapped poles—boards?—to their boots. Me? Absolutely not. But I wasn't averse to sitting in the lodge, La Croix in hand and not freezing my nose off, while watching Nash take a few runs down the slopes. Nope. He cut a good figure on skis, clearly being a favoured one with athletic giftedness.

Warmth curled in my stomach when he grinned brightly as he chatted with my oldest niece, Veronica's daughter Millie, before giving her a few pointers on how to go down. She hung on his every word, looking every bit as smitten as I was. *I know the feeling, girly.* But she was only thirteen, and hero worship could only go so far.

Nana hip-checked me as she came to stand next to me by the broad windows overlooking the ski hill. "You been avoiding me, Stephie? I've barely seen you."

I ducked my head. "Not avoiding. This year's just been... different."

She glanced out to where Nash was giving young Ollie a hand off the magic carpet. Sure, Nash was a different part of this year but not the whole part. Nana was whip sharp and wasn't deterred by my attempt to get her off the true scent.

"Your first Christmas back home after joining Nash's company. Your father's an idiot. I shouldn't be saying that, but I swear, my son doesn't use the brains the Good Lord gave him when it comes to family and women. Business, sure he's a success, but when it comes to family..." She sighed heavily and her straight shoulders hunched, the issue wearing on her like a weighted vest.

I wrapped an arm around her waist. The delicate lilac of her perfume grounded me in nostalgia and childhood. Some things never changed—Nana's perfume was one of them. "We talked on Christmas Eve."

"Oh?" She sounded far too benign.

"Did you hear us?" I asked suspiciously, shifting to look her full in the face.

Nana grimaced, suddenly looking far older despite the vibrant fuchsia of her ski jacket. "I did. Not everything, but a few things." She patted my back. "I'm glad you found your voice, but I'm sorry, too. As much as I love my son, I could shake him. And I have, many times, for all the good it's done." With another sigh, she shook her head. "I should have protected you better."

"Nana, no." I reached out and squeezed her hand, infusing all the love I could into the gesture. "You and Papa took me in and gave me the best you could. I don't resent that." The words clogged in my throat as memories of Papa flitted through my memory. Grocery shopping and backyard barbeques. The way he loved buying me an Easter dress every year. Or the time he dropped handfuls of coins in the backyard and sent me and Hailey—she was five and I was ten—out with the metal detector. "You gave me everything," I whispered around the lump in my throat. "And I thank God for that every day."

Nana crushed me into a hug. "You know better than to make me cry with a face of makeup on," she scolded, but there was no heat to the words, and we both sniffed.

"I miss him," I whispered.

"Me, too, baby." We held each other in silence. Remembering a good man. Drawing strength from a shared loss and a promise of being reunited with him.

"Gabe mentioned doing things differently going forward. Instead of playing to Hiram's whims," I said into her shoulder after several minutes.

When she faced me again, Nana's hazel eyes sparkled, all signs of tears vanquished. "Excellent. I've been thinking about it myself. Half of this family isn't bad apples, but the rest..." She shuddered. Then she studied me and waggled her eyebrows. "And you might have a husband of your own next Christmas to take into account."

"Nana!" I squawked, and she only cackled like the impudent grandmother she was.

"He's a keeper, Stephie-Lou. Men like him are rare."

Didn't I know it. But because I couldn't give in to her too easily, I snarked back, "What, tall, dark, and wealthy?"

Nana swatted at my behind, but since this wasn't my first rodeo, I dodged her, laughing. "He's easy on the eyes, girl, but he looks at you like you're his world. He sees *you*. Not just the version you show to the rest of us. He brought your sparkle back." She patted my cheek. "He's the staying kind, baby girl. Who isn't intimidated by your mess, doesn't bat an eye over getting up with a colicky baby in the middle of the night, and brings you closer to Jesus, not further away. He's a treasure worth hanging onto." She gave me a meaningful glance before hurrying away, leaving me speechless.

What was I supposed to say to that? *Sorry to dash all your hopes and dreams, Nana, but this was just fake? Until it wasn't.* Happiness sparked in my chest like the bubbly water I sipped, and I offered a silent prayer of thanks for Nash.

"I hope you're happy with the choices you made," Hiram said from behind me, instantly plunging me back to earth.

My pulse skyrocketed, and I gripped the edge of the side table beside me. A sturdy mahogany thing. Perfect for concealing nail marks from my death grip. "And why's that?"

He studied me, his expression giving nothing away. His poker face was almost better than Gabe's, and that was saying something. "Sometimes we live a lifetime to regret the mistakes we make. I'd hate for that to happen to you."

"Is that a threat?"

"Friendly concern."

Friendly, my Christmas cookies. I tilted my head, gripping the table tighter as I swayed. "Maybe. But the real testament of character is making a life despite those mistakes. Not wallowing or making those mistakes your whole personality."

"Is that what you think I've done?"

I shrugged. "I can't assume your motives. But I know you're in love with the idea of love. Maybe it's time to realize perfection isn't the goal, but a beautiful partnership—ups and downs included—is."

Hiram's gaze moved beyond me to the motion on the slopes out the window. Shifting, I could see Zara in her lavender snowsuit set giggling with a couple of the kids.

When his gaze drifted back to me, determination smoldered in his hazel eyes. "We'll see, won't we. Goodbye, Stephanie."

And in his wake, I was left wondering about the sincerity of his words and hated that I had to even consider the mental gymnastics of psychological warfare coming from my father. Maybe he heard me, maybe he didn't. I'd said my piece. There was nothing else left to say. His choices were his own, and his life in the hands of One far more capable than my own.

"IF EVERYONE WOULD ASSEMBLE in the living room, I've got an announcement," Hiram said when we returned from the ski run. Knowing Hiram, this could be anything from a new business venture, a new real-estate acquisition, or a new wife. Given he and Zara were just over a month into their marriage though, and she was here for Christmas, I didn't see marriage being the new truth bomb. Besides, I actually liked her. Unlike the last few romantic liaisons, she was trying to enmesh herself into our lives. I wished her all the best since she was saddled with a man like Hiram. But after our conversation at the ski lodge, I was a little on edge.

"Any ideas what this is about?" Nash whispered to me as we came downstairs together after changing out of our winter layers into more comfortable jeans and sweaters. He was wearing the one I'd knitted him, and it hugged his shoulders just right.

"Steph?"

Oops, I hadn't meant to get distracted. "Not a clue."

I gave Ava a few knitting pointers while we waited in the living room for the rest of the family.

"Stab it, hang it, cut off its head," Ava announced, going through the motions with her needle with an intensity that had her glossy corn braids bouncing. The saying was a little dark coming from a seven-year-old, but hey, it worked.

"You got it."

Hiram stood in front of the tree and tapped a glass of... was that champagne? Weird choice for the middle of the day. Besides, it was for toasting and celebration. Was I wrong about the marriage thing?

"I had some exciting news to share, but with the unexpected guests this year, I had to seriously consider whether it was the best time to share company details." His hauntingly familiar hazel eyes lingered on me and Nash, hard and blank.

I wanted to squirm under the blatant disapproval, but Nash laced our fingers, resting our hands on his thigh for all to see. Completely at ease. I inhaled deeply, trying to borrow his nonchalant attitude.

Hiram continued. "In the end, it's too important to let a few setbacks interrupt."

Oh, I was a setback, was I? Not far off from the *mistake* he had hinted I was earlier.

"Nova is getting ready to launch our biggest venture yet," Hiram boasted.

I wanted to roll my eyes but refrained. He sounded like a sleazy businessman giving his schtick with all the "never been done before in history" stuff spewing from his mouth. Hiram was smart. No one could accuse him of being otherwise, and he could work a room to his advantage. And looking around this crowd, I'd say he had half of them enthralled already. Of course, half the family actually worked for him, so... not exactly an unbiased opinion when he was signing their paychecks.

"... a new marketing software focusing on more accessibility for small businesses."

I froze when Hiram's words yanked me out of my zoning out. A new feature? Instantly, I glanced at Nash before I could even figure out why, and our gazes locked. Nova's new software program sounded an awful lot like Genesis's... and why was Hiram announcing it with us here if it was? Was this a power move?

I'd seen couples give each other *the look* and communicate with their eyes. I'd seen Gabe and Ivy do it. Nana and Papa over the breakfast table doing crosswords before Papa died. The silent exchange Nash and I shared was filled with unspoken words, questions, and reassurances. When he squeezed my hand, my heart squeezed, too, as the clawing panic ravaged my insides. I wasn't alone in this, and it was nice being someone to somebody else—part of a team.

But what in the world was going on?

Chapter Thirty-Two

Nash

I WAS FURIOUS. MORE than furious. My blood simmered as I paced my room, phone to my ear and hating that I had to interrupt my legal team the day after Christmas. But I needed answers. How had Hiram gotten something so similar to our program? And how were they so close to launching—and potentially beating us to market?

You couldn't copyright ideas, but corporate theft was a thing. Did Genesis have a mole? A well-connected mole?

The possibility of Stephanie being the one behind it crossed my mind, but I quickly dismissed it. Call me a fool, but I knew deep in my bones it wasn't her.

I raked a hand through my hair and shoved my glasses back into place. I *would* get answers. I wouldn't fail my employees by letting a snake like Hiram win. But I was going to need a miracle to fix this. We were still three and a half months from launch. If Nova was closer...

Tension infused the rest of the evening. I finally got a hold of one of my lawyers, and he promised to start an investigation into the legal ramifications. The hard part would be getting proof and trying to find the potential mole. Another call to IT, and they had launched a full system work-up on our communication servers.

I doubted they'd find incriminating evidence in bold print announcing, "It's me. I'm the perpetrator." But I needed something. Anything.

I couldn't let my people down. Couldn't let Stephanie down.

Dawn broke bleak and dismal. I'd received very little information from my team since last night, but I made another call while packing up my suitcase. We were leaving a day early, which was hard to explain when we weren't showing panic but needed to get back to Washington. Hiram knew. He had to.

"You better have a good reason for this, Nashville," Emmett said, groggily.

I glanced at the clock and winced. It was just after six in the morning, but I'd forgotten we were an hour ahead of Spokane which meant... Five o'clock was a brutal wake up call. If I thought Stephanie wasn't a morning person, Emmett was worse. And if he was pulling out the Nashville nickname, he was royally ticked.

"Sorry. I got word of potential corporate espionage on our new software." I gritted my teeth just saying the words.

"Nova?" Emmett immediately sounded more awake.

"Yeah." I blew out a breath. Just talking about this out loud with a friend had my chest easing a fraction. Emmett worked as my chief financial officer at Genesis. He might not be able to solve the problem, but he would be invested in the issue and would be a good sounding board, since Stephanie wasn't up yet. Best let her sleep and avoid this nightmare a while longer.

After I explained Hiram's new proposal, Emmett growled in frustration. "Is there any proof someone in the office leaked it?"

"I've got IT on it, but Hiram is slick. A few drinks and conversation between whoever it might be and his liaison, and this is all hearsay."

"What's his angle, do you figure?"

"Honestly? Probably the fact that I showed up to the family Christmas with his estranged daughter."

Emmett hummed. "Estranged?"

"It's a long story and not mine to tell, man." I blew out a breath. "But it isn't pretty."

"Is she a liability for the company?" The question was a blow to my gut.

"I'm not firing her, Emmett."

"Not asking you to. Just asking if she's a liability. You're responsible for other people's livelihoods."

"Don't you think I know that?" I snapped, pausing my pacing to stare at the predawn hue of the Tetons and sprawling snow-covered meadows and woodlands between us. "I realize I might have fallen in love with the one woman who's most inconvenient to love from a business perspective, but I'm not jumping ship on her just because it's complicated."

Emmett had the audacity to chuckle.

I held the phone away from my ear, staring at it confused. "Care to share why you're laughing? There is nothing remotely funny about this."

"Oh, I know. I just never thought the day would come when you'd finally get over your insecurities and commit to a woman. You've let Alexis live in your head for far too long."

"We're dating, not married."

"I know. But Stephanie is the only woman who tempted you to break your no-serious-dating rule, despite Ryan and I setting you up on blind dates. She's the first woman you've fought for at the risk of your company. The company's been everything to you, Nash. Now you've found someone worth fighting for. Don't mess it up."

Emmett's words stuck to me like pesky burrs while I finished packing up my suitcase and scanned the room, checking for any last items I'd forgotten. Little did he know messing things up was my chief concern.

A jaunty knock came at the door. "Coming!" I called, half hoping it was Stephanie, though the hour was a bit early.

Nana stood in the doorway, a grim expression on her face. A rare look from everything I'd learned about the vibrant woman so far this week.

"Nan—Charmain, what can I do for you?"

She waved me off. "Nana is fine, young man. I'm hoping you wouldn't mind a stowaway for your drive back to Washington."

I blinked in surprise. Had I heard her correctly? "You're coming back to Spokane? Does Steph know?"

Nana grinned, a little ferally. "She probably forgot, but she'll remember once she wakes up. I cleared it with Liz."

In her bright orange fleece cardigan and houndstooth slacks, Charmain Russo Addams was a formidable war strategist I had no desire to argue with. Besides, having her around might be good for Stephanie right now. "Of course. I'll make sure the seats are all clear."

She eyed me with a smirk. "You don't strike me as a man to have to make sure. That vehicle is spotless."

I chuckled. "You caught me."

"Good." She snapped off a quick nod. "When are you planning on leaving?"

"Around ten. Steph's still sleeping."

Nana snorted. "That girl could sleep through an apocalypse. She's no morning person."

"Don't I know it, but I want her to get as much rest as possible. We're in for a long fight."

Curiosity lit Nana's sharp hazel eyes, so much like Stephanie's I realized. "You're standing by her."

"As long as she'll have me." This woman was it for me. In an uncertain world, I was certain about that.

Reaching up a hand, Nana softly patted my cheek with her wrinkle, age-spotted hand, decked in a turquoise ring. "You're a good one, Nash Prescott. An old woman can tell." She tottered off before I could say anything. "I'll be ready by ten!" she called.

STEPHANIE RAPPED AT MY door half an hour later, two coffees in hand. She scanned the hallway as I opened the door before hopping inside and bumping the door shut. "Coast is clear. Any news?"

Apart from the dark crescent moons under her eyes, I had no indication of how she was handling all this.

She offered me the dark blue pottery mug and cradled the remaining white mug in her hands, inhaling the soft steam.

I took a swig of the coffee for fortitude. "Not much. Nolan promised to call when the legal team had something, and IT is still doing their thing, so..." I waved a hand vaguely.

She nodded slowly from where she leaned against the closed door. Given whose territory we were in, we were trying to keep our voices down. "It wasn't me, Nash. I swear."

I sipped my coffee again, relishing the boldness and body of the flavour. I'd have to ask Nana about the brew she used because I might have just converted. "I know that."

Stephanie reared back as if offended I *hadn't* suspected her. "I'm not sure if I should be relieved or concerned that you're so trusting."

I shook my head, sinking down on the edge of the queen bed. "I'm not trusting by nature, Steph. My dating life should make that clear. But I know you. You're loyal to the bones." I forced a smile. "Besides, if you were reluctant to date me because I'm your boss, somehow I doubt selling company secrets to the enemy would have accomplished that bridge between us."

She huffed a little laugh. "You think, huh?"

"Just a hunch." I winked at her over the rim of my cup. "You okay with leaving around ten? I know we're cutting things short."

"Yeah, everything's packed."

"One hiccup," I said slowly. "Nana's coming back with us."

She stared at me. Blinked once. Again. "She... what?"

"Seems she cleared a visit with Liz—"

Stephanie groaned. "I forgot. How could I forget that?"

I frowned. "Forget what?"

"She usually spends New Year's with either me or Gabe's family. Since they're headed to Idaho for the hockey game, it's my year." Stephanie stiffened. "And she doesn't know about..." Her head fell back with a thud against the door. With a sigh, she motioned between us.

"About what? That we were fake but not anymore? I don't see how that matters." I shrugged, shoving my hands in my pockets as I approached her. "Gives me the chance to take you on a real date."

Her face shuttered like she'd donned a mask. It was the professional mask I often saw at work or when she was blocking out comments from her siblings and dad, but I hadn't seen it around me this week. It was almost alarming to see how seamlessly it slid into place now. "Maybe," she said quietly, shifting her weight from foot to foot. "See you in a bit?"

Even though we were only an arms-length apart, the chasm was widening. She was inching away from me. I wanted to reach out, rescue her from the spiraling thoughts I could see behind those dazzling hazel eyes. Wanted to push and ask her why she was shutting me out. Why the word *real* suddenly had her backpedaling faster than I could blink. But I did none of those things. All I said was, "Sure thing."

Real brave. But I wasn't sure I could handle any of the answers right now.

CHAPTER THIRTY-THREE

Stephanie

GABE HELPED NASH LOAD up the Jeep, and I checked our rooms for the third time. *Just to be sure.* My brain was running a hundred miles an hour with five hundred browser tabs open. An itchy feeling of forgetting *something* nagged at me.

Goodbyes were my least favourite part. The veneer of politeness felt more stark in the light of Hiram's big reveal. Stiff hugs and polite nods were doled out with the enthusiasm of going to the dentist.

Gabe and Ivy's cohort along with Hailey followed the three of us out to the vehicle, the kids trying to squeeze in as many last-minute conversations and hugs in as possible.

"Steph, is there anything I can do?" Ivy asked when it was her turn for a hug.

"I'm fine," I lied because the truth was too big to come out of my mouth. My mind was too loud and messy for driveway confessions.

Her green eyes scanned my face when I pulled away. "I know you're not." She glanced at the small crowd milling around us and lowered her voice, "I won't press. Not now. But call me, okay?"

I nodded, pasting on a brittle-as-spun-sugar smile. "Thanks."

"I'm going to come see you before I go on tour again," Hailey said, squeezing the air out of me. I loved Hailey hugs. You could feel the way she pressed the love into you. And if my emotions weren't so numb right now, I'd probably cry.

"You're always welcome."

Nash helped Nana into the back seat of the Wrangler. She refused to take the front seat, and honestly, I was too tired to argue and prolong my inevitable loss anyway.

"Stephanie!"

My head snapped back towards the cabin, to where Zara hurried down the front stairs waving a purse. One that looked exactly like mine. Wow, I really was losing it. *I knew I forgot something.*

Zara paused a few steps away. "I think this is yours." She held it out to me.

I rifled through the inside. Yup, that was my medication, phone, and wallet. "Thanks. Not sure how I missed this."

Her smile was kind. "Sometimes I feel like I'd forget my head if it wasn't already attached to me." She laughed softly, and I couldn't help smiling back.

"It was really nice to meet you," I said, meaning every word.

"You, too." To my surprise, she wrapped her arms around me in a tentative hug, like she wasn't sure I'd welcome the gesture. But I hugged her back. Once again praying that Hiram, for all his mistakes, wouldn't mess things up with this woman.

"I tucked a couple things in there for you." She motioned to my bag, giving me an almost pointed look. Huh, that was kinda weird, but I filed it away to examine later. "Take care." She shook Nash's hand then wandered back towards the cabin, pausing at the door to wave before she was swallowed back into the madhouse.

"She's nice," Ivy commented.

"Hopefully she'll stick around," Hailey said with resignation.

"More like, hopefully he keeps her around," I muttered, then threw myself into Gabe's open arms and let his hug soothe some of my rough patches.

He didn't say anything, just kissed the top of my head before Nash opened the passenger door for me, and I climbed inside.

As we drove down the long driveway, I waved until the passel of shadowed figures grew smaller, then vanished as we turned the corner onto the road. Leaning my forehead against the cool window, a hot tear trickled down my cheek. Then another.

This mess is all my fault.

I STUMBLED UP THE familiar worn stairs of the bungalow, lugging Nana's suitcase. Never in the history of the world was I so glad to be within my own four walls. Behind me, Nash had one of my suitcases in one hand and Nana hanging off his free arm. There wasn't any fresh snow, but the ice hazard was no joke, although Liz or Ben had clearly salted the walkway. Before I reached the top step, Liz flung the door open, emitting the telltale aroma of fresh sourdough. But I couldn't even muster up the desire to eat.

"Oh, honey." Her voice dripped with compassion as she took me in, and I wanted to burst into tears. But I had an audience and didn't feel like answering questions, however well meaning they might be.

So I pasted on a placid smile as Nash and Nana followed me inside. Liz took charge of Nana, hanging up her coat and ushering her into our small living room with promises of tea and dinner, while Nash disappeared back outside to grab my last suitcase.

I kicked off my boots and hung my coat on the peg. My body was going through the motions of mundane things, but inside I was numb. Or maybe I was feeling too much. My emotions were churning with no outlet. I needed my knitting or a rage room. I wasn't picky either way. Anything to shake the pent-up-soda-bottle feeling inside me.

The framed picture of Glacier National Park on the entry wall caught my eye. The same one Nash had seen. But when I saw it, I saw my failure. My failure to do what I loved. The way I got lost in my head. The fear holding me back. I scrubbed a hand over my gritty eyes, overcome with the urge to smash the glass into a million pieces. What was wrong with me?

Nash slipped back inside and silently followed me down the hall—me with Nana's luggage, he with mine.

As we entered my room, I was hit with the keen awareness that I'd never had a man in my bedroom before who wasn't related to me. A quick scan relieved me that there was no embarrassing evidence. Liz had already changed the flannel sheets and from the looks of it, dusted, leaving a flickering beeswax candle on my dresser, emitting a warm glow and a soft cinnamon aroma. The sage-green walls with neutral accents were my sanctuary. I didn't love people in my room—it was my safe spot. But somehow Nash's presence didn't feel like an intrusion. Maybe because like for so much of our relationship, he'd been quietly showing up and knocking down my defenses. But I needed those walls back tonight.

Nash set the suitcases down at the foot of the double bed and faced me. "You were pretty quiet on the drive back."

I snorted. None of us had much to say the entire trip. Nana had tried from the back seat where she insisted on sitting, and I'd feigned sleep. "How can you be so calm about this? This is terrible. We're dealing with possible corporate espionage wrapped up with a bow of familial blackmail. Hiram is going to ruin you, because of *me*! And—"

With quiet quickness, Nash stepped into my space, his citrusy scent washing over me. He cupped my face with his hands, thumbs gently brushing my cheeks. "Hiram's choices are on him," he growled, low and serious. "You can't take the blame for his decisions. We'll figure it out, Steph. I have a meeting with the lawyers first thing in the morning. I promise you, this will get sorted out."

I swallowed hard as I met his gaze, taking in the shadowy scruff he'd let grow. The weary lines around his eyes beneath those charming frames. I was doing this to him. If I'd never brought him to the cabin for Christmas, never let Hiram trap me in his mind games, never proposed a fake relationship, never entertained the idea of us being real like he wanted—like I wanted. Never asked for it to be real. For him to kiss me like he meant it in the pantry...

"I should just quit," I whispered. "I'm more trouble than this is worth. If I leave, there goes his leverage."

Nash's dark eyes flashed. "If you leave, he wins."

"Then fire me!" I cried, shoving his hands away. "Do something to make him think I don't matter to you! He'd believe it since I don't matter to him. Why would I matter to anyone?"

Nash shook his head, running a hand through his hair. The chaotic strands would be comical if this wasn't so serious. "I can't do that," he said patiently. "And you brought me to your family Christmas. Talk about conflicting messages. Besides, I'm not a convincing liar, and you mean too much to me for me to lie about it."

My body sagged with exhaustion, but my limbs vibrated with tension. I hadn't slept well since the news dropped. I was emotionally, mentally, and physically drained. And the soda-can mocktail inside of me exploded. "I'm not worth this hassle, Nash!" I spat out. Then the tears started because not only was I an ugly crier, I was an angry one, too. Covering my face, I turned my back to him.

But he didn't let me walk away. He hauled me against his chest, arms holding me fast and his hand cupping the back of my head.

I hated crying around people, even my best friends and closest family members. To cry in front of Nash on multiple occasions now was beyond embarrassing, but also... under the anger and exhaustion I realized I felt safe enough to cry in his presence. The swelling ride of emotional upheaval didn't feel so daunting encased in his steady embrace. The walls I'd so carefully built tumbled down. If he chose to leave like I begged, it would break me. Worse than anything else because I loved him. I *loved him*. But was loving me worth the risk of him losing everything?

When the tears lessened, Nash pressed a kiss to my hair. "I need you to trust me," he said quietly. "And I need you to hear me. You matter, Stephanie Addams. To me. And to a lot of other people. I'm not going to leave you because it's convenient to avoid discomfort or would make my life easier. I'm staying because *you* are worth staying for."

He said all the right words. The words I'd ached for a lifetime to hear a man say and really mean. And yet... "I don't know if *I* can stay," I whispered, so broken I barely recognized my own voice. "I can't do this to you. You're in this mess because of *me.* This was just fake... a Christmas dream. We had a bargain. That's all."

"That's all?" Nash echoed, stiffening, like his own armour was locking into place to keep out the pain of my words. He chuckled mirthlessly and stared up at the ceiling. "Then I guess that's your choice, isn't it? But don't make decisions for me, Stephanie." He pulled away, careful not to let me sway as I readjusted to standing on my own. He raked his hand through his unruly hair again. "Trust, Steph. That's what I'm asking. For a chance to fight for you." He reached out, his fingers a ghost touch on my cheek.

I wanted to sink into the caress, believe every word, let him fight for me. But that black hole of anxiety, swirling with doubt, eclipsed that hope. I cared about him too much to let him take the fall for me. "I..." All the words I wanted to say choked me, locking in my throat, refusing to be uttered.

When I said nothing, Nash dropped his hand, his jaw working with unspoken words. But he ducked out of the room without another protest, his shoulders taut with frustrated emotion.

I trudged down the hall to Liz's room, where I'd be bunking. Usually I'd just take the couch, but she wanted a sleepover to debrief over the holidays. I was too tired to argue. Her cotton-candy pink room looked like Tinkerbell and her friends were in charge of decorating. The whimsical cottage room was tiny, barely big enough for the queen bed, leaving no room for a cot or pallet. Guess we were splitting the bed.

"Steph?" Liz's voice was soft behind me, like she was lulling a wounded animal into complacency before poking it with her own special brand of hardcore honesty.

"I'm fine." At least I still had Liz. *For a while, till she gets married and leaves you behind. Because everyone leaves you. You aren't worth it. And now Nash hates you because you're a coward*, that ugly voice whispered in my head. *Stop! Just... stop.*

I caught her frown in the mirror as she closed the door behind her. "Don't hide from me. I watched that man walk out of here with a smile while his eyes told me his heart was breaking. What did you say to him? I heard arguing, which is *so* not you."

I huffed, wrapping my arms around my middle, trying to stave off the growing sinkhole of panic threatening to swallow me. "I told him to fire me or let me quit. It'll get Hiram off his back."

"And he didn't agree?"

"Of course not! He asked me to trust him and said he wasn't leaving because—" I choked on a sob, the words tangling in my throat with no escape.

"Because?" Liz prompted gently.

"He said I'm worth staying for," I whispered the healing words, aching to believe them, but they hadn't sunk in yet.

"Good man." She nodded approvingly. "Then what's the problem?"

"This!" I shrieked, waving a hand over my body. "Me! I'm not sure I can do this. With him. He's so... so..."

"Steady?" Liz crossed her arms, tilting her head as if studying me at a different angle would help her figure out this mess of Stephanie I was emitting. "Steph, I say this with love, but you're the one pushing him away. Not the other way around. You're letting your fears speak louder than the truth and believing the lies of the ones who never loved you enough for their voices to matter in your life. Your fear of abandonment is valid, but it's ruling your present. You can't demand a man's loyalty only to be the one to get fickle at the first sign of a storm." Her posture softened slightly. "I know trust doesn't come easy—with men especially—but he's proved himself, Stephanie. Be brave."

The words ached like resetting a broken bone—painful in the moment but healing long term—and their truth rattled me down to my core. I'd been so terrified of Nash being like my father, leaving without a backwards glance, that I never realized my own tendencies to do the exact same thing the first minute I got scared. "I'm a mess," I croaked. "I thought I was past this."

Liz hugged me. "We all are, but the burdens get lighter when we share them. And maybe don't make life-changing decisions on a sleep deficit."

The raging emotion shook my insides, and I couldn't breathe. My lungs were tight bands of iron cladding, morphing my every breath into a wheezing gasp. The panic spread its tentacles through my body, starting to drag me over the edge of the abyss. *Oh no.* "Liz..."

"I've got you." She rubbed gentle circles over my back, humming softly. A hymn I recognized as "'Tis So Sweet to Trust in Jesus." Liz wasn't built for subtlety. But she'd been there for my panic attacks before, touch and sound being the biggest components to easing my episode.

I shut my eyes, focusing on my breathing. Feeling the rhythmic motion on my back and the tight squeeze of Liz's embrace. This attack wouldn't get the best of me. I just needed to breathe. *Breathe.* I focused on the words of the song. The sweet truths.

"Thank you," I whispered when the tidal wave ebbed into a trickling stream.

She smiled. "Always. Now get some sleep, you look like Wednesday Addams had a baby with a vampire."

I tried to laugh but couldn't quite manage it. It wasn't the first time I'd gotten that comparison.

"Things will look better in the morning." Liz drew the plaid quilt of yellow, cream, and pink back and let me slip under before she tucked me in. "Let me ask you, though: do you believe what Nash told you?"

"Yes," I murmured, and the admission rang true. I'd seen his sincerity, felt it to my bones. "I just... panicked."

Liz nodded. "Then sleep off this funk and go fight for your man in the morning."

"You're too good for me," I muttered, half asleep.

"And you're not getting rid of me. Ever. Got it? So don't even think about believing those lies that say otherwise." She draped a sherpa-lined throw over me. "That's what friends are for. You saved my sorry hide when I didn't deserve it. Remember he-who-shall-never-be-named-from-now-to-eternity?"

Despite my near-comatose state, I managed a snort. That particular breakup had won the record for worst in our friend group history, and Liz had turned into a Jekyll-and-Hyde situation. She'd narrowly avoided jail time with some of her retaliatory behaviour after she'd gone all Carrie Underwood on his truck. And friends didn't let friends go to jail.

But she was right. This was what we did for each other. The four of us were ride or die, speak the truth when you didn't want to hear it, and shoulder the burden types.

"Sleep," Liz commanded, clicking off the lamp and heading for the door.

"Liz?"

"Hmm?" Her lithe silhouette from the dim hallway filled the half open doorway.

"Did I break Nash too hard?"

When she didn't answer right away, my heart sank. I'd messed things up too badly, lashed out too desperately.

"I believe broken things can be fixed," Liz said at last. "And often they're more beautiful after because of the healing it requires. He's not a runner, honey."

Unlike me.

"You need to sleep this off," she continued. "Then talk to him with a clear head. The problem will still be there in the morning. Sweet dreams, Stephie."

I was asleep before the door closed, lost to a dark world of betrayal and toxic family relationships and the steadiness of a good man who stood in my corner. Fighting for me, fighting for us. Even when I didn't deserve it.

I would trust him like he asked. Now I just had to hope he could forgive me, too.

CHAPTER THIRTY-FOUR

Nash

I REMEMBERED NOTHING OF the drive home from Stephanie's. Just found myself sitting in the parking lot of my quiet apartment. Did I even stop at the stoplights? No clue. My chest ached with the swirling tension of our conversation. I hated seeing Stephanie cry, even if it felt so right having her in my arms. I'd put my heart on the line. I was all in to prove to her I wasn't a flake like her dad. But then she lifted those hazel eyes to mine, pooling with liquid and regret.

I don't know if I can stay. Talk about a sucker punch to the gut. She held my heart, and those seven words were a crushing weight against my sternum.

She's not Alexis. I ran a hand through my hair, shoving my glasses back up my nose before plunging outside into the nippy cold. She was hurting. Scared, even. And I didn't blame her for that. But Hiram's threat didn't scare me. No. What scared me most was losing his daughter. Because of that, I was going to prove myself to her. I'd sort this out exactly as I promised. I wasn't imagining the connection between us, the way she'd become an important part of my world. If holding onto her meant exerting more patience and self-control than I thought humanly possible, so be it.

Once I reached the third floor, thankfully without bumping into any of my neighbours, I slipped the key into the door and stashed my suitcase in the laundry room to take care of later.

I studied the apartment I'd called home for the last nine years with fresh eyes, and it was cold and empty after the warmth of Stephanie's cozy room and the nostalgia of the cabin. Look at me, calling that monstrosity a mere cabin.

My place had few personal touches. A stack of books on my nightstand and another on my coffee table. A few photos of Emmett's and Ryan's kids and several of their drawings littered the front of the fridge. The pops of colour from the Christmassy throw pillows on the couch and the navy rug on my bedroom floor were Stephanie's doing. She'd offered to spruce my place up when she first started working for me after taking one look at what she called my "jailhouse chic" style.

Steph.

For years, women had chased after me for my wealth. Never had I had to pursue a woman so deeply to give me a chance because of it. Now that I'd gotten a chance at forever with Stephanie, I couldn't go back to just being friends or boss and assistant. Not after kissing her. Not after holding her together while she fell apart.

I'd pursue the heck out of her.

First, I needed to run despite the late hour. Because I was still human, and the upheaval of the last twenty-four hours had me jacked up on adrenaline and more than a little anger. There would be no sleeping in my current state. Trading my jeans and sweater for sweats and a Henley, I hurried back outside, letting my feet pull me towards the center of town. I had no direction or destination in mind. Just me, the open air, and the rhythmic whoosh of blood in my ears

Before I got too far, I shot a text to THE WISE GUYS chat. If I was going to go head-to-head with a business tycoon like Hiram and not lose Stephanie in the process, I needed help. Thank the Lord, I had two friends I trusted with both my business and my love life... as reluctant as I was about the latter point at times.

ME

Dynamite

Meet me at Maisie's in an hour?

The use of our codeword was a rarity—almost sacred because it was a cry for help, no questions asked. Two thumbs-up popped up on the screen before I shut my phone off and started running, letting the cold air bathe my skin, cleansing my lungs as my arms pumped, my legs propelling me forward.

By the time I passed the clock tower in Riverfront Park and jogged farther along the river to the waterfall opposite the Monroe Street Bridge, I was feeling marginally better. A lack of oxygen replaced the pressure in my chest. I braced my hands on my knees, panting. Spokane in the post-Christmas haze was quietly beautiful. Like most of the world, that week between Christmas and New Year's was something of a twilight zone, but that didn't keep the holiday magic from the streets of our city. Setting up shop in Spokane had been something of an accident but not one I regretted. This was Emmett's hometown, and he was the one to lobby the location idea after college. We might have had better success in a bigger city like Seattle or Vancouver, but I didn't want to live in a rat race of never-ending bustle. Spokane offered us the best of both worlds—the busy hub between eastern Washington and the rest of the western states while retaining a quieter feel. It held a small-town charm without being a small town.

I made it back to the apartment with twenty minutes to spare. Sweaty, gross, and desperately in need of a shower. But less stressed.

My phone chimed as I jumped into my Jeep. Pathetically, I wondered if it was Stephanie. But I knew it wasn't. She'd looked exhausted and lost when I left her earlier. Hopefully she was getting some rest. But when I pulled my phone out, I did a double take. Because Gabe Carson's name was the last name I expected to see at this moment.

"Gabe," I said as the phone paired over my wireless speaker, and I backed out of the parking stall. "To what do I owe this surprise?"

"How are you holding up?"

I frowned, even though he couldn't see me. We'd traded numbers before I'd left, but I thought it more of a courtesy thing because I was dating his sister. Not that he'd actually phone me up for a chat. "Me? You mean Stephanie?"

"No, I mean you. I've got a good handle on how my sister is right now."

I huffed. "Liz call you?"

He gave a noncommittal grunt. Smart man. I couldn't see Stephanie being appreciative of Gabe probing her friends for updates, but my guess was she wasn't answering her phone, and this was a last resort. "My question stands."

I blew out a breath, turning into traffic and navigating the mostly deserted streets. "You were there. You saw what Hiram did."

"Mm-hmm. And I know what Steph did about it. Now I'm wondering how you're holding up."

I wasn't used to this big-brother routine. Gabe didn't just care about Stephanie, but he was calling to check in with *me.* Not threatening me not to hurt her—though I had no doubt he was capable of that. No, he was asking about me. "I'm royally annoyed with Hiram at the moment," I confessed. "As majorly as this messes me up from a business perspective, I'm more concerned with how it's impacted us. Me and Stephanie." I cleared my throat as her words skipped in my mind like a broken record: *I'm not sure I can stay.* "I'm not giving up on her. I'm just hoping she can hold on long enough for me to prove it."

Gabe was eerily silent. So much so, I had to check my phone to make sure we hadn't lost connection when I stopped at a red light.

"My sister loves you," he said, breaking the silence. "She's loyal to the point of martyrdom, which isn't her finest quality, and doesn't make smart life decisions when she's running high on stress and a lack of sleep. She's told you about her childhood?"

"Yeah."

"Trust doesn't come easy for her. But you're a good man, Nash. I saw the way she looked at you, opened up to you." He blew out a breath. "I doubt it feels that way right now, but she loves you. Problem being, she's convinced herself she's the problem and that the noble thing is to try talking herself out of her feelings. And she's a dang good negotiator." He chuckled mirthlessly.

"Any advice for me? Besides patience?"

"You love her." It was a statement, not a question.

"Pretty sure I should tell her that before I tell you," I said wryly. But would I get the chance?

"That's answer enough. Stability is the one thing Steph's always wanted. And yet she runs scared when it looks her in the face. All I can say is prove you're there and not leaving. Like you've already done."

"Pursue her."

"I knew you were a smart man."

Maisie's comforting blue building appeared in a sea of red and ivory brick, and I parallel parked in a rare front parking space. "Thanks," I said, leaning my head back on the headrest. I'd spent the majority of my life alone with a few trusted friends. Having Gabe call just to check in did something to my insides. My circle was expanding. I wasn't so alone. There were people who genuinely cared about me as a person, not just my wealth. Stephanie had given me that. "But aren't you supposed to be warning me off your sister? You know, threatening to bury my body where no one will find it after you feed my guts to the gators?"

Gabe chuckled, catching my lighter drift. "Guess it's a good thing I like you then. And the Marines tend to frown on homicide. Semper fi and all that. Now, go get your girl, Nash. We're all rooting for you," he said warmly. Well, warmly for him. "Take care of yourself and we're just a call away, okay? Don't forget that."

"Thanks." It took me a second to clear my throat of the clogging emotion. "Enjoy the game tomorrow night." Before I hung up, I had one more burning question. "Hey, Gabe, what's your actual military ranking? Or would you have to kill me if you told me?"

He laughed, loud and long. "I'm a First Sergeant, not James Bond."

"Good to know." We said our goodbyes and hung up.

Inside the coffee shop, only a few patrons lingered around tables, and the soothing hum of the machines blanketed the space. I found my friends at a booth in the back corner. Maisie's was only open for another hour, but it would be enough.

Ryan slid an Americano and a chocolate croissant across the table as I sat down opposite them. "Fortitude. You used the sacred word. What are your orders, O great one?"

Emmett flicked the back of Ryan's head. "Be normal for once, why don't you?"

Ryan shoved at him, but his face was solemn when he faced me. "Em told me about Hiram."

Emmett's eye twitched at the use of "Em," but he let it go. True tribute to how seriously he was taking this, and I appreciated it.

I told them everything—well, except for Stephanie's past since that wasn't my story. The Christmas shenanigans, the kiss—both of them, only because they were ridiculously nosy—Hiram's announcement. Getting it off my chest removed the weight even if it didn't remove the sting.

Per the rules of Code Dynamite, neither said a word until I dropped my head into my hands and sighed. "That's all I got." My world was imploding, but I had good men on my side to keep me grounded.

I might not get answers, but that was okay. For now, the burden was split three ways, letting me breathe more deeply than before.

"Sounds like we need a plan," Emmett said, sipping his frou-frou Frappuccino. The man was an anomaly, I tell you.

I grunted. "Maybe. Tonight, though..." I glanced between them and lifted my cup in a sort of toast. "Tonight, this is enough."

THE NEXT MORNING, I stepped out on Genesis's floor, the elevator doors whooshing closed behind me. Quietness bathed the office given the early hour and several staff still being on holidays. But I had a meeting with my legal team within the hour, and I needed some quiet moments to collect my thoughts. The time with Emmett and Ryan had settled the rising dread in my gut last night. I had a clearer head today, but the battle was still all uphill from here. With Nova and with Stephanie.

I paused a minute at Stephanie's empty desk. Should I text her? Maybe after the meeting, providing I had news. With thoughts still on my fake-real-maybe-nothing-at-all girlfriend as I pushed my office door open, I froze.

My office chair was pushed away from the desk, facing the window. Definitely not how I left it. I flicked the light on. "Hello?"

The chair swiveled, and my jaw dropped when Stephanie smiled softly at me. "Good morning," she said quietly. Redness rimmed her eyes, and her cheeks were extra pale. She looked... exhausted and broken. She lifted a to-go cup from Maisie's and a small pastry bag, holding them out to me.

"Steph," I whispered. *Please don't let this be a dream.*

CHAPTER THIRTY-FIVE

Stephanie

NASH GLANCED AT HIS watch, and I could see the thoughts dancing over his head. It was barely seven o'clock, and I wasn't a morning person. So why was I in his office before the sun was up? Excellent question.

"Thanks," he said, uncertainty tinging his voice as he accepted the proffered cup and snuck a peek in the paper bag.

I leaned back in his chair, running a hand over the soft leather of the armrest. "Your seat is much more comfortable than mine." Our chairs were identical, but I was scrambling for something to say. A way to ease into things. Because how did a girl start the conversation with the man she loved and needed to apologize to? Like a dork apparently.

Crossing the space between us, Nash perched on the edge of his desk, facing me fully with those intense eyes. "Then we'll get you a new chair."

I pursed my lips. "Nash."

"Stephanie." He sipped his coffee calmly, like finding a woman in his office at the crack of dawn was normal behaviour. Which, it better not be. Wow, I was in no position to be jealous. "What are you doing here?"

I swallowed hard, lowering my gaze to my lap. Needing something to do with my fingers, I brushed a nonexistent piece of lint off my black pencil skirt. *You can do this.* "I need to apologize for last night."

"Okay," Nash said slowly, waiting.

Here went nothing. "I was scared," I said simply, meeting his gaze. Not hiding behind my mask. Letting him see me. "And I still am, to be honest." My voice broke a little with vulnerability. The coffee sloshed in my cup as I took a sip to regroup. "But it's not fair for me to expect steadiness from you and then be the one to jump ship at the first rock of the boat." Setting the cup down on the desk, I braced my hands on my knees and dropped my chin. "I've been so scared of everyone else running from me that I didn't stop to notice when I was the one pulling away to protect myself." I puffed a breath. "I'm sorry for what I said and for running away instead of leaning in. I trust you, and I'm in. If you can forgive me?"

At the end of my little speech, I sagged back into the cushioned chair. It had taken all my strength and mental clarity to get that out. Doing hard things was exhausting—but worth it.

Nash reached out and cradled my hand in his. "Thank you. I could have handled last night better, too. Never will I hurt you intentionally, but I'm human, Steph," he said quietly. "I won't always have it together. I need permission to fail you. Knowing I'll always have your best interests at heart and that even when I fail, I'll never stop fighting for you and for us. That I'm not going to walk away at the first sign of trouble. I'm in this for the long haul, sweetheart. Going forward, can we agree to be honest and open?"

I smiled, a real smile—not a fake one. "I'd like that." Liz was right. No serious life-altering decisions should be acted upon without proper sleep. "I can't promise I won't panic again in the future. Unfortunately, things with my past and my dad bring the worst out in me. But I *am* working through things, and—"

Nash brushed his thumb over my cheek. "I don't mind reassuring you. As often as you need it. As long as we're a team, okay?" He chuckled when I practically preened under his touch. "And you really came here this early to tell me this?"

I laughed softly. "I wanted to prove to you I'm serious. That I'm tired of being a coward."

Nash lifted my hand to his lips, feathering a kiss over my knuckles. "You're not a coward, Steph. You're one of the bravest women I know."

My breath caught as he lingered in another kiss. "Brave? What woman have you been hanging around to get that impression?"

I felt his smile against my skin as he took me in. "The real Stephanie Addams without her professional mask. The brave woman who chose to do brave things in a world that didn't choose her. And kept choosing others, myself included."

My smile insisted on turning watery, but I had remembered waterproof mascara this morning. That was it. I was more than the girl who'd gotten left behind. More than just a discarded pawn in my parents' stories. There was more to me than that. It was a part of my story, but not who I was. I could be Stephanie Addams, the woman who chose to live bravely, trust a steady man, and let her walls down despite the heartaches. "Thank you. For seeing me, the real me. And not giving up when I gave you every reason to."

"You can't get rid of me that easily, Miss Addams," he quipped with a wink.

"Good. Does that mean you're open to an idea?" I arched my eyebrow, promising mischief and maybe some mayhem.

"With you? Always. You introduced me to pantry romance."

"Goodness, never say that again! That sounds way worse than it was." I tugged my hand from his, slapping it over my burning cheeks.

Nash had the audacity to sound amused. "What did you have in mind?"

I grinned. "Take me on a date tonight—a real one—and I'll tell you."

"You've brokered yourself a deal." Nash extended his hand, and I shook it firmly. I loved that this was our thing now. Leaning down into my space, our hands still clasped, he whispered, "In honour of retiring our fake relationship—for good this time because there's no going back—I propose we celebrate." He waggled his eyebrows.

Goodness, this man. My knees might not have had the gumption to hold me upright if I was standing. Trying to play off my fluttering pulse, I rolled my eyes and shoved his chest playfully, pushing the chair—and me—out of his reach. "I don't kiss till the third date."

Nash laughed at my retreat. "Oh, darlin', we're the rule breakers. *You* kissed *me* under the mistletoe before we ever had a real date."

LEAVING NASH TO HIS meeting with the legal team, I headed home, since there wasn't anything I could help with until he got answers from them. Nash promised to text me an update after and a time for our date. *Date.* Just the thought had me giddy. But first, I needed to come clean to Nana.

She was in the sunshiny kitchen, enjoying a cup of coffee with Liz at the breakfast table. "Things looking brighter in the morning, baby girl?" she asked, holding her arms out to me.

I sank into her embrace, letting her warmth and delicate lilac perfume envelop me. "I need to tell you something," I said quietly.

Liz shot me a knowing look and excused herself while Nana pulled back and eyed me with an all-seeing eye. I had no idea how I managed to pull this over on her for a week. I wasn't sneaky by nature, and Nana was the queen of sniffing out any and all sneakiness.

"About Nash and me…" I dropped into a chair, accepting the coffee Nana poured for me. "It was fake."

Nana froze mid-pour, some of the fragrant liquid sloshing over the rim of her own cup. "Fake?"

The word was bald and harsh, and I realized how ridiculous it sounded. Way to go, Hallmark, for giving us unrealistic trope expectations.

She wiped the table with a napkin. "Like one of those Hallmark hogwashes where he's an undercover prince and she's just a librarian, and they date to keep him from having to have an arranged marriage?"

I tilted my head back, as if thinking deeply. "You know, I don't think I've seen that one."

"Stephanie Mae Louise."

Ooh, full-named again. "Yes, sort of. Without the prince and arranged marriage drama."

"Why?" Nana's voice was deceptively soft.

I tugged at the cuff of my knit sweater. "I was tired of being alone and the odd one out," I confessed. "There were... some things said." The church conversation about my standards being too high and Anika and Samantha's whispers the night of the office party sprung to mind. "And Hiram texted, threatening to set me up with that Jarrett creep from last time. I panicked and just... thought it might help." My voice sounded small in my own ears, and my excuse was even lamer.

"Baby girl, I don't condone lying, and I had no idea he brought up that devil. I thought you were just supposed to bring a date." She reached across the table, squeezing my hand. "And while my eyesight may be going, I'm not blind yet. There was nothing fake about the way Nash looked at you, regardless of whatever plan you two might have concocted to the contrary."

I chewed my lip. "Yeah, I get that now. But if I'd never brought him, Hiram wouldn't have made that announcement and then—"

She stopped me with a hand lifted in a placating gesture. "Sounds like you're shouldering a load that was never yours to carry. Hiram's choices are his own, as are yours. You can't take blame for what you didn't do, only what you're responsible for. Last I checked, your father is his own man, accountable to God. Don't use misplaced guilt as an excuse to avoid what the Lord has in store for you." Love coated the firm truths, and she swirled an extra spoonful of sugar into her already sugary cup. "So you love Nash, huh?"

I choked on my coffee. Talk about conversation whiplash. We hadn't traded *I love yous*, but it felt like it. "It's only been two weeks," I deflected.

She raised a sculpted eyebrow in a way that looked eerily familiar to my own expression. "And the two years before that?"

"We were friends who..." Who were fighting an attraction because of our jobs.

Nana must have read my thoughts because she laughed. "Things have a way of working themselves out in God's timing. The hiccups along the way are opportunities for us to grow in faith, not wither in defeat."

This woman. Her advice was rock solid and grounded in truth. "I'm sorry I lied," I said. "There's a lot of things I could have handled better this week."

"Oh, baby." Nana's bright red lips curved with understanding. "That's part of living. Growing and failing and trusting in Jesus. Now"—she smirked at me—"tell me all about that gorgeous man and why I found flour spilled in the pantry."

I groaned and buried my no doubt scarlet face in my hands as my grandmother cackled. But my heart was lighter with the truth out in the open and hope on the horizon. We would make this work. Together.

CHAPTER THIRTY-SIX

Stephanie

"How many strings did you have to pull for this reservation?" I whispered in awe as Nash led me through a pavilion garden lit with dazzling white Christmas lights to the elegant, sandblasted scenery etched into Italia's front doors. The romantic atmosphere simply from the outside grounds had me swooning, even if it screamed luxury and exclusive, which made my skin prickle. I passed the Italian restaurant every day on my way to work, and my debit card had wept when I inquired about pricing last year.

Nash chuckled, his hand resting on my lower back as the warm air of the restaurant kissed away the harshness of the bitter wind. "The manager owed me a favour."

"I'm a little hurt that I'm not the only one you're making bargains with." I twisted my mouth into a disappointed pout while trying to hold back a laugh.

Nash had no qualms about laughing, though. He helped me out of my coat and handed it to an attendant. "Your bargains are the only ones that matter, Steph."

I could live with that. But also, an attendant *took* our coats? I may have technically been a billionaire's daughter, but I'd had a solid middle-class upbringing with my grandparents. More backyard barbeque than fine dining. Maybe I'd embarrass myself and Nash while I was at it. What if—?

"Hey." Nash's low voice skittered down my neck as he bent to meet my gaze. "Where'd you go?"

I laughed nervously. "Oh, you know, just imagining being thrown out on my ear for using the wrong fork or the elite patrons in the corner skewering me with condescension the whole night when I spill my water."

His lips twitched with a smile, begging to be let out. "We've got a private table. Don't worry."

Ha. That was easier said than done, my guy. But I did feel marginally better. If I messed up which fork to use, we could laugh about it alone.

"This way please, sir. Madam." The stone-faced maître d', starched within an inch of his life in his white shirt and black coattails, ushered us towards the back.

Nash's guiding hand on the small of my back was warm through the fabric of my dress as he steered me after the host. His instructions had been that he'd pick me up at seven and I had to wear something I loved. So I'd chosen my favourite teal wrap dress and paired it with some sparkly earrings. The appreciative gleam in his eyes when he picked me up was worth every minute. No doubt I had a similar look on my own face at the fine figure he cut in his navy suit.

I soaked in the rustic overhead beams, decorated with whimsical greenery and fairy lights. Festive yet classy. The whole room was dimly lit. Ironwork chandeliers dangled overhead. On the whitewashed exposed brick, wall sconces cast a soft light, and on every table sat a flickering candle. It exuded money. And romance. Definitely no complaints on the last part.

I adjusted my skirt before sliding into the chair Nash held out for me.

"Your server will be right with you, Mr. Prescott." The maître d' dipped his head and glided off across the room.

"You come here often enough to be known by name?" I whispered, even though we were alone.

Nash chuckled. "Not at all. Like I said, there was a favour called in. What would you like?" He opened the black leather-bound menu, flipping through the cream-coloured pages with interest.

Following his lead, I eyed the entrées listings, my mouth watering. The sheer amount of pasta listings ushered me into food heaven. *Choices, choices, choices.* Closing my menu, I crossed my hands over top.

Nash eyed me over his menu. "Decide already?"

"Nope." I smiled sweetly at him. "You pick."

His eyebrows flew northward. "You want me to pick dinner for you?"

I nodded. "Nothing on this menu sounds terrible, and frankly, too many options overwhelm me. I defer to your expertise." This was a big act of trust for me, even if it was in a small way.

"All right," Nash agreed with a slow nod. "And you don't have any allergies?" Once I confirmed in the negative, he perused the menu with much more intensity, like choosing the wrong dish might be a deal-breaker.

I touched the top of the luxurious leather, tugging it down a little so he'd focus on me. "I trust you, okay? It's not a big deal. Seriously, everything here sounds amazing."

Nash nodded and continued his search. It thrilled me he was so invested in this, even if it made me smile. When it came to food, I was easy to please.

After we split two appetizer trays—fried mozzarella bits and calamari—Nash ordered our main courses. And you know, it shouldn't have been so attractive to watch a man order for you. Especially with such ease. I hated ordering. Because despite always rehearsing my order beforehand, I still managed to stumble over my words—but only when it was a personal order. For work? No problem. Ugh. Alas, the world wasn't fair.

"We'll take a lobster ravioli and a Tuscan penne pasta, please."

Twenty minutes later, the waiter slid both dishes onto the table, and my mouth watered with delight. The smells alone were enough to satisfy me—except I really wanted both.

Nash reached for my hand across the table and offered a quick prayer over our time and our meal. Then he smirked at me. "Ladies first."

I whimpered, glancing between both plates. How to choose, how to choose?

A laugh tumbled out of Nash. "You'd think I was asking you to pick a favourite child. Here." He scooped up a forkful of the lobster ravioli. "Taste test."

I opened my mouth, humming as my lips closed around the deliciousness. The explosion of flavours danced on my tongue, and I groaned, eyes sliding shut in delight. The heartiness of the lobster chunks blended with the creaminess of the mozzarella, perfectly topped with a gorgonzola sauce. "That was beautiful." I sighed as I swallowed, the taste lingering on my palate. I'd grown up with Nana's Italian cooking, which was homey comfort food. But this... This was elegant and exquisite. Absolutely divine.

Nash had a forkful of Tuscan penne ready next. And it was heavenly. Creamy with delicious hints of savoury artichoke and fresh bursts of sun-dried tomatoes, soft pasta with goat cheese and wilted spinach.

"You're really going to make me decide?" I groaned, leaning back in my chair.

"That or we split the plates half and half."

"I can live with that." I grinned at him, adjusting the napkin on my lap. "Told you I trusted you. You have good taste."

"I'm getting the impression you're a foodie, and I could have put anything in front of you, and you'd have been happy."

"Sir, how could you say such a thing?" I placed a hand to my chest in mock horror.

We enjoyed our food in comfortable silence for a few minutes, appreciating the skills and blends of the dishes. The soft lighting really set the mood, and the mellow jazz music crooning in the background was a nice touch.

"So, are you ready to tell me about this plan of yours?" Nash asked, handing me the plate of lobster ravioli to finish.

Sliding him the Tuscan penne, I grinned widely. "You sure you're ready? 'Cuz you're gonna hate it."

Nash's espresso eyes glinted with contentment in the candle-light. "Try me."

CHAPTER THIRTY-SEVEN

Nash

STEPHANIE WAS ABSOLUTELY RIGHT. I hated this plan. But I had to hand it to her—it was clever. Brilliant. And maybe a touch insane.

"You think we can move the launch up by that far?" I asked slowly.

She shrugged. "It's possible. We get a shorter promotional time, but we're ready, and it gets the software program public."

"True." I reclined in my chair. "And the second part of this plan?"

"I stop working for you," she said bluntly, scooping a mouthful of ravioli into her mouth like she didn't just drop a bomb.

"No!" I scowled, shooting forward with bullet-speed intensity. "Absolutely not."

Stephanie chewed faster, shaking a finger telling me to wait. "Hold your horses," she complained after swallowing. "I did something this morning. Something I should have done a long time ago." She rummaged in her purse and pulled out her phone, swiping before handing the device to me.

I studied the screen. Was this what I thought it was? A social media page with a picture of Stephanie and a bio describing her as a photographer in the Spokane area. She'd posted a few pictures already, mostly from Liz's engagement shoot, and my jaw dropped at the number of likes and follows—impressive numbers for a new account. "Steph, this is amazing!"

She blushed rosy pink under the praise. "There's been a ton of booking requests and... Cal Satterfield got wind of it, and he reposted it. Apparently the name of a photographer coming from a professional athlete holds some weight."

I chuckled. "Why have famous friends if you can't toss their names around once in a while?"

"You're terrible, and I didn't ask him to do that." Stephanie smiled wryly. "My money is on Juliet. She's scary when she turns on her lawyer voice."

"So you're gonna do this?" I fiddled with my fork.

Her nod was jerky but determined. "I need to chase this passion. Stop being afraid and take a chance."

"I'm proud of you, Steph."

Her face glowed with pleasure at the words. Maybe she hadn't heard them enough, but I'd keep telling her until she believed it.

"But I'm not leaving you in a lurch," she said.

I shook my head. "As much as I love having you make my life simpler, I'm not going to stand in the way of this new venture. You can work as long as you want, and then we can find a replacement when your bookings get full-time."

"When?"

"Of course. There's no *if* about it, darlin'." I smiled encouragingly and finished my last bite of penne. "How about dessert?"

She leaned back in her seat, hands draped over her stomach as indecision warred on her face. "You have no idea how much I want to say yes." Her cheeks puffed adorably. "But I don't think I could eat another bite."

"To go then?"

"I love you." Stephanie froze, sparkling eyes wide. Her mouth softened into a perfect O. Perfect for kissing.

My pulse thrummed in my ears, and I swallowed hard. *Wow, what?* Was that just an expression because of the dessert? Did she actually mean it? I'd wanted to hear those words for what felt like forever.

Stephanie's expression shifted from surprised to gentle, her posture relaxing. "I love you, Nash Prescott. I know it might be too soon to say it, but I've known it for a long time."

"It's definitely not too soon," I said huskily. "Because I love you, too. And my one Christmas wish was to make you fall in love with me." Lifting her hand to my lips, I kissed her knuckles because we were in public after all. Then I motioned to our waiter. "What do you say? One lime white chocolate cheesecake to go?"

She laughed, and I could get drunk on the sound. It was heady and addicting, and I wanted to listen to it for a lifetime.

When I walked her to her door half an hour later, she wrapped her arms around me in a tight hug. "Thank you," she whispered into my woolen coat.

"For the cheesecake?"

Stephanie snorted. "For tonight. For everything." She tipped her chin up to meet my gaze, her features soft in the warm porchlight. "For fighting for us."

"Anything for you."

"Anything?" she challenged, arching an eyebrow.

"Anything," I affirmed. "Even a new last name." This was daring territory. Our relationship was still new, and I was trying not to push her too hard.

"Oh?"

"I know of one up for grabs. It's just waiting for the right woman."

Her jaw slackened, and I caught the sharp intake of air, but her lips twitched in a hidden smile.

Leaning down to whisper in her ear, I added, "Now, about that kiss?"

Stephanie huffed a laugh and shoved my chest lightly. "I have one more surprise for you first."

Our noses brushed. So close. "Not sure I can handle any more shocks, darlin'."

"Oh, you'll like this one. I told you I had information, and it's the name of the mole in Genesis."

I froze, ice and fire licking my veins. "You got a name? How? The IT guys couldn't come up with anything."

She dug around in her purse and held up a folded pink sticky note and a USB stick in the faint light. "In a surprising turn of events, Zara left these in my bag. I checked it out, and it's legit." She paused. "It's Samantha."

Stephanie shrieked when I swung her up into a hug and kissed her, relief coursing through me as I cupped the curve of her cheek. Savouring the moment. Relishing in her sweetness as her hands slid over my shoulders to my neck.

When I leaned back to catch my breath, I kept my forehead pressed against hers. "Have I told you how amazing you are?"

"Not today," she whispered, and I could hear the breathlessness in her voice.

"Let me remedy that then." And I kissed her again. Thoroughly.

CHAPTER THIRTY-EIGHT

Nash

"ARE YOU SURE THIS will work?" Emmett asked, crossing his arms over his broad chest as he stared down at the papers littering the end of the conference room table.

It was late. City lights winked across the darkness outside the wall of windows as Emmett and Kelsi joined Stephanie and me for a debriefing. For Stephanie's plan to work, we needed to crunch numbers and build a team. Not at all how I'd planned to spend the night before New Year's Eve. But we were running out of time and options.

"I'm not sure of anything right now." I heaved a sigh, messing with my hair. Pretty sure I was going to resemble Einstein at this rate. "But it's this or settling for Nova potentially beating us to market without a fight. We've worked our tails off the last year for this. I'm not going to let that happen."

"Could Hiram in any way be bluffing?" Kelsi asked from opposite me, beside Emmett. She tugged a loose piece of her ginger hair in concentration while she scanned another document.

"Doubtful," Stephanie cut in from my side. "This was a calculated move and not the first time he's pulled this stunt. There's a pattern of corporate espionage. SkyLark, MLC. All circumstantial at best but—"

"With no paper trail," I finished. "Until now."

"Did you at least fire the traitor?" Emmett growled.

I thought about Samantha. She'd been so clever, and there was no direct proof linking her to Hiram on the Genesis servers yet. But Zara's sticky note and USB drive had given us the clues we needed. Emails between Hiram and Samantha, a phone recording, and several pictures of them together. All because Zara had been worried he was having an affair. After the announcement, she'd connected the dots and decided she liked us enough to risk ticking off her husband.

It was enough of a connection for us. The hard part was not tipping Hiram off, but our early departure had likely already done that. "Her severance was effective immediately." It'd taken a bunch of help from HR, but I'd paid her out handsomely—more than she deserved. I wanted her out of the office while we pulled this launch off. Anything to keep Hiram from knowing we were going to outmaneuver him to the finish line.

"So, you have a plan." Kelsi waved a hand over the paper-littered table. "Where do we fit in? I know he's Mr. Pennybags"—she jabbed a thumb at Emmett—"but what about me?"

I grinned as Emmett huffed at the moniker. "You, Kels, are the missing link. You're the one with connections. You *are* the market."

Her grin was feral, her eyes bright. "Oh, I like the sound of that."

"Thought you might. And I'm not expecting you to do this for nothing, so name your price—"

"As if," Kelsi scoffed. "I want this program to succeed as much as you do because selfishly, I refuse to give money to that egotistical tyrant." She shot Stephanie a grimace. "Sorry, not sorry."

Stephanie waved her off. "No offense taken."

"I know twenty author and creator names in the field I could get on board, right now," Kelsi continued with a snap. "Tell me when and you've got yourself an army of campaigners."

I glanced at Emmett, the strongest voice of reason in the room. We had a plan. We had a team. But he was head of finance, and that was an avenue we had to consider.

He stood with his arms still crossed, silently assessing the paperwork in front of him, forehead etched with deep frown lines as he no doubt weighed every angle. "It's insane," he said at last, glancing between the three of us. "But a little insanity never hurt anyone."

Something eased in my shoulders. We had a green light. An accelerated timeline wouldn't be the end of us.

Stephanie slipped her hand into mine, lacing our fingers, giving them a squeeze. "We can do this. Not alone, but with all of us."

I nodded, my mind sparking with a dozen next steps. "Now that it's doable, it'll go to the board in the morning. We'll hit the ground running with marketing the day after New Year's. I'm confident we can launch by the end of January. Thank you. Both of you."

Kelsi offered a grin and a jaunty salute. She rolled her shoulders in a stretch and glanced out the massive windows lining the north wall. "Wow, it's later than I thought."

Emmett grunted. "Ryan watching the boys?"

"Yup, it's pizza night and an action movie. I dodged a bullet." Kelsi shuddered.

"You prefer corporate espionage to movie night?" I asked, biting back a smile.

Kelsi rolled her eyes, hefting her Delaware-sized purse over her shoulder. Seriously, what did she have in there? It wasn't even the diaper bag she usually carried. No wonder she had muscle tension. "I prefer my espionage fictional and not threatening my friends." She flashed a wicked grin. "But it's given me a whole new villain profile for my next book. We're gonna nail him—or at least beat him in his own game, Nash."

I dipped my head in thanks for her supportive gesture, not in the least offended over her thrill at getting new story fodder. Because the thing about Kelsi was that she was a multigenre author—rom-coms and suspense. Everything was potential book material. Which meant Hiram was for sure going to land himself on an FBI watch list in one of her books. And I could guarantee it wouldn't be a rom-com special.

And I, for one, was already looking forward to reading Kelsi's fictional plans for his demise—theoretically, of course.

"We just need to get through New Year's." Stephanie squeezed my hand again.

"Speaking of." Kelsi adjusted her monster bag as she paused at the door. "We're still on for tomorrow. Four couples and half a dozen kids. Should be great."

Stephanie made a small noise. "Actually, my nana's here and—"

Kelsi shrieked. "Charmain Russo Addams is in town?!"

Somehow when referring to Nana, you needed all three of those names to fully capture her essence. And then some.

Stephanie laughed. "In the flesh."

"Bring her!" Kelsi glanced at Emmett. "You and Danielle don't mind, right?"

This year our festivities would be at the Mitchell residence because we traded holidays between the three of us.

Emmett shrugged, running a hand over his beard. "Don't see why not but check with Dani."

Kelsi cackled. "Oh boy, Steph, after hearing all your stories about her, I can't wait to see her take on Ryan."

It was my turn to snicker because as much as I loved my best friend, he was no match for Nana. And it would be a glorious thing to witness his set down.

Stephanie's elbow jabbed into my ribs, cutting off my strangled laughter. "I'm sure she'd love to come. She's a big fan of yours."

A genuine smile touched Kelsi's face. "That might be the nicest Christmas gift I got this year."

"Compared to the new walking pad I happen to know Ryan surprised you with?" I cut in, teasing.

Kelsi huffed. "And I'm out. Later, boys. I'll confirm with you when I get home, Steph. Goodnight!"

Emmett shuffled the papers together, semi-neatly. "Hold up, I'll walk you out."

"See you tomorrow, Nerf guns blazing," I called after him.

Emmett stumbled, whirling to face me. "You're kidding."

I crossed my arms. "I promised the girls I'd have a surprise for them after Christmas. You wouldn't want me to break a promise to your young, impressionable daughters, would you?"

"And you thought Nerf guns were the way to go? With six kids in the house? Why would you do this to me?"

My grin sharpened, and I struggled to rein in my laughter. It wasn't often I got my unflappable friend ruffled. "Oh, a little something you might remember as the Freshman Shower Escapade."

Emmett's face slackened, nostrils flaring. "You're serious right now?"

"As a tombstone, Pennybags. I get my revenge fifteen years later, and it is *sweet*."

Kelsi cackled from the hallway, clearly in on the joke. No doubt thanks to Ryan spilling the details.

Stephanie's curls bounced as she watched our conversation shoot back and forth like a ping-pong ball. "I have so many questions right now," she said, hazel eyes dancing.

Emmett growled like the bear he was. "Don't you dare, Nashville."

"Ooh," Stephanie teased. "Nashville, huh?"

"Don't start a war you can't finish," I said, adding to Stephanie, "I'll tell you in the car."

Emmett's steely grey eyes narrowed. "Foul play."

"Hey, you can't rain on my parade when I finally get a girl I can tell secrets to, when you two have been happily married and spilling my secrets for nearly the last decade."

"Nine years and counting!" Kelsi called from the hallway.

"Semantics." Emmett sighed but turned back to the doorway.

"That's not a no, Mitchell," I taunted.

Emmett shook his head as he left mumbling, "The price I pay for a misspent youth. I apologized... eventually."

Once he was gone, I caved to the laughter pressing on my chest. It was refreshing, like shedding the weight of the world for a few minutes.

"The Freshman Shower Escapade?" Stephanie questioned as I wiped my eyes.

Catching my breath, I shuffled the remaining papers into a folder. "Emmett had a bit of a wild side in his younger years, and I was the collateral damage on one of his pranks."

"I can't see that. He's so"—she waved vaguely—"straitlaced."

"Don't let that suit fool you."

"And just how bad was this prank for you to be subjecting him to a bunch of screaming kids hyped up on sugar on New Year's Eve, duking it out with Nerf guns?"

"Let's just say it involved a shower caddy, a can of shaving cream, a cockroach, and a near case of public indecency. Seeing him squirm will be worth it."

Stephanie bit her lip, scrunching her nose. "I don't need any more details."

No, she really didn't. Especially since it was my own dignity on the line.

"Want to head back to my place?" Stephanie asked as we entered the elevator, and I punched the ground floor button. "We can hang out and finish finalizing our battle plans. Liz made sticky toffee pudding."

"You had me at *we*." I tugged her into a hug as the elevator whirred into motion. "And I'm glad you're on my team."

"Always." Stephanie smiled sweetly up at me, and could you blame me for stealing a kiss?

"Anyone ever tell you you're a romantic?" she whispered, when the doors whooshed open, ushering us into the quiet lobby.

I laced our fingers together and winked. "Only for you, sweetheart."

CHAPTER THIRTY-NINE

Stephanie

"Who needs Times Square when you've got this?" Nana said as we ducked into the brightly lit-up Mitchell residence with the bitter north wind chasing our heels. The powdery blowing snow was nearly blinding on the drive here after Nash picked me and Nana up. But Emmett and Danielle's house buzzed with warmth and comfortable conversation. We rang the doorbell twice and knocked but no one answered. So we let ourselves in.

I kicked off my sensible Chelsea boots, shivering as the warm air thawed my core. Ryan and Kelsi and their kids were already here, judging by the level of kid chatter and the trail of small shoes littered across the split-level house's landing. Liz and Ben were here, too, given the sparkly silver heels in the mix.

"Come in, come in!" Ryan hollered from the foot of the basement stairs. "Mi casa es su casa!"

"Don't let Emmett hear you say that," Nash joked, helping me out of my coat.

Ryan trudged up the stairs dramatically. "As the extrovert of this brotherhood, the welcoming committee falls under my jurisdiction. Emmett can grouse all he likes, but someone's gotta do it."

Danielle appeared at the top of the stairs, trying to pry her blonde ponytail from being held hostage by Ryan and Kelsi's ten-month-old baby perched on her hip. "So glad you guys could make it! I'd apologize for the noise, but it's pretty standard around here these days."

Nana started up the stairs. "Nothing wrong with the sound of children. The world could do with more of it." She shot Ryan a reproving look over her shoulder, but her eyes sparkled. "Even if a few of them never grow up."

Ryan blinked. "Was I just schooled by Charmain Russo Addams? And was that a compliment on my youthful heart or a diss about my exuberance?"

I laughed. "Both, simultaneously. Get used to it."

Nana ignored us and paused in front of Danielle to coo over the baby. "Now, who is this cutie?"

"Meet Sebastian."

Nash hung up his coat and ushered me up the stairs while Nana and Danielle disappeared farther into the house talking all things baby, and Ryan lumbered back down to the basement.

"Is the Nerf gun still in my purse?" I whispered.

Nash nodded. "Can't give it away too soon. I'll grab it a bit later, if you don't mind."

"Emmett sounded less than thrilled about this particular surprise."

"Oscar the Grouch Emmett is less than thrilled about everything and hates all surprises."

I snorted as we entered the living room. A yule log flickered and crackled on the TV screen in the corner, giving a nice ambiance to the cheerful room. It was the next best thing to a real fireplace.

Nash and I had been at the office all day, scheduling meetings and ironing out the next three weeks of our campaign before the launch date at the end of January. We'd gotten as far as we could for now, and a night of fellowship was the perfect breather before the craziness of the launch would take over our lives the next couple of weeks. A calm before the storm.

Liz swished beside me, decked out in a gorgeous blush-pink cocktail dress with sheer long sleeves and sparkly sequins. She took the platter of meats, cheeses, and crackers I was carrying.

"I didn't think there was a dress code," I said, glancing around and feeling a little underdressed in my jeans and aubergine cable-knit sweater. But Liz was the fanciest of the lot.

She laughed. "There isn't, but I'll never get to wear this once school starts, so I'm taking advantage."

I smiled slyly. "I'm sure Ben approved."

"Of course he did." She shimmied her shoulders. "He bought the dress." Shifting the platter in her arms, she grabbed my hand. "Now, come on. I've been dying to give you this surprise."

"I didn't think you were capable of secrets," I teased. Which, to be fair, was half true. If I had to pick a secret-keeping friend, Liz was at the bottom of the list most of the time. But she had an air about her that persuaded you to open up to her anyway. If I wanted a secret vault, it would be Paisley. She could give Fort Knox a run for its money.

"Har, har." Liz set the platter on the table and shoved me into the kitchen ahead of her.

"Surprise!"

I blinked. Once. Twice. Nope, I wasn't dreaming.

Two very dear and very familiar faces grinned back at me from the middle of the kitchen, and I couldn't help the yelp of shock that tore out of me.

"Pais? Jules? Are you serious right now?" I demanded, laughing. They were *here*. Not on my phone screen hundreds of miles away.

The four of us flung into a group hug. Tears stung my eyes, and for the first time in the last week, they were the good kind. I needed this hug. These women.

"Best surprise ever," I said, swiping at my eyes, relieved to find my mascara had decided not to smudge. "But how...?"

Liz grinned mischievously. I should have guessed. Under all those floral head scarves and cute embroidered overalls, she was a devious mastermind. "I may have asked Dani if she'd be opposed to some surprise guests, for your sake. She was happy to oblige."

"Dani, you're the best!" I called over the hubbub to the corner where she and Nana were chatting with Kelsi.

Danielle threw me a wink, her smile warm with understanding.

"Nash, this is—" But he wasn't behind me like he had been a minute ago. This house wasn't huge, so where had he vanished to?

An undignified—very masculine sounding—scream erupted from the living room where we'd come from, and I darted towards the noise.

And there in the center of the blue-carpeted floor was Nash. At the bottom of a dog pile of five kids, with Emmett holding him at Nerf gunpoint.

"What the… Nash?" I choked on a laugh, but Liz didn't bother refraining hers.

Four small children each pinned one of Nash's limbs, and Emmett's preteen stepdaughter perched directly on top of him. He wasn't going anywhere.

At my question, Nash's head popped up, his hair deliciously disheveled and his glasses askew. "What's going on? I was ambushed, that's what." He glared at Emmett. "You double-crossing surprise ruiner."

Emmett only smirked and shot him in the forehead with a dart.

"Dad said no head shots, Uncle Em," an eight-year-old boy, Ryan and Kelsi's oldest, draped over Nash's left leg hollered.

Emmett winced at the nickname, and Nash howled in laughter. Which only made Emmett shoot him again. In the torso.

That curbed his laughter, and Nash grunted. "Seriously? All because I mentioned I was bringing a Nerf gun? I had no plans on shooting you, just surprising the kids. Did you even have a Nerf gun before this?"

"Nope," Emmett's daughter declared, shoving a loose piece of blonde hair out of her face as she sat on Nash's chest. "He went out and bought it this afternoon."

Emmett frowned at her. "Way to keep a secret, Sadie girl."

Sadie just giggled, eyes dancing. She was the mini version of her mother. "Off with his head!" Her Queen of Hearts impersonation was flawless—Kelsi, theatre nerd she was, clapped loudly—but it was lost on the younger kids who immediately burst into an argument.

"We're not cannibals!"

"You mean murderers. Cannibals eat people."

"We don't do that either!"

"Nobody's eating or killing anybody," Emmett grunted in confirmation before the conversation completely spiraled out of control.

"Are they for real right now?" Juliet whispered behind me.

"Oh yeah," Liz confirmed, choking on a cackle.

"Can I get up?" Nash asked, the barest hint of frustration leaking out of him. "I'll admit I'm beat, say uncle, or whatever other sadistic demand you have. I can't feel my legs."

"Juliet here's a lawyer if you want to sue for damages or need a hostage negotiator," I offered.

Juliet snorted. "I do contract law. Rogue children and foam darts are not my wheelhouse."

Nash just groaned and flopped his head back. "Not exactly how I envisioned this meeting going, ladies."

"Aww, he thought about meeting us." Paisley transformed into a giant heart-eye emoji, clasping her hands under her chin.

"Daddy?" Sadie asked, glancing at Emmett for permission to release the hostage.

Emmett sighed and lowered the weapon. "All right. Thanks, kids. Your doughnuts are in the kitchen as promised."

"You bribed them with pastries?" Nash huffed, sitting up.

"It worked."

The kids darted past us, arguing over who wanted sprinkles or jelly-filled, then Emmett fired one final shot at Nash. Right in the chest. "Now we're even," he declared.

Nash scoffed and straightened his glasses. "Not even close. This was supposed to be payback for the Freshman Shower Escapade. Now, I'll have to think of something else."

"It was a terrible prank, and you never reveal your plans to the enemy. Live and learn." Emmett shrugged. "You've had fifteen years. Another fifteen won't kill you."

"You're the worst," Nash grumbled, giving Emmett a shove as he passed. Stopping in front of me, he offered a heart-stopping smile. "I'm sorry you had to witness my humiliation and utter betrayal at the hands of a rogue army."

I grinned up at him. "Oh, I don't know. The karaoke was probably worse. Gabe sent me the video footage for a memento. So, I guess you'll have to figure out a way to redeem yourself."

"I'm sure I can come up with something." He leaned towards me, probably to kiss me, but I'd never know since a distinctive throat clearing that could only be Juliet interrupted us from behind. Right, we had an audience.

Warmth flooded my cheeks, but I laughed sheepishly, motioning towards them. "Sorry. Ladies, this is Nash. Nash, these are my friends. Liz, you know. Juliet, our resident storm cloud, and Paisley, our hobbit and literary genius."

"It's a pleasure. I've heard a lot about you," Nash said warmly, nodding. "You're Myles Delavan's wife, right?" he asked Juliet.

Juliet visibly softened at her husband's name. "Yup."

"And you married Greyson Satterfield, yeah?" he said to Paisley.

She laughed. "Did you give him a cheat sheet, Steph?"

"Nah, she just talks about y'all that much." He smiled at me, dimples and all, melting my insides like butter. *Darn those dimples.*

"Did the guys come up, too?" I asked, shifting the conversation away from myself and giving my face a chance to cool its Sahara Desert temperatures.

"Yeah, Ryan kidnapped them to show them something downstairs. I heard rumours of a garage and a motorcycle..." Liz said.

Emmett growled and stalked away, thumping down the stairs. "Ryan Jacobs, I swear if you touch that thing—"

"Serves him right," Nash crowed.

Emmett and Danielle might be more introverted compared to Ryan and Kelsi, but they sure knew how to throw a party. Light jazz music crooned in the background, the TV fire flickered, the Christmas tree still twinkled with lights, the table groaned with the platters of appetizers and snacks, and despite the abundance of new faces added to the group, nothing felt weird or awkward.

Particularly after our first ice-breaker game—two truths and a lie.

Nana stared Ryan dead in the face, her red lips twitching as she rattled off her three facts. "I never cried during the movie *Up*, I had a lovely chat with Grace Kelly when she visited New York City in 1959, and I had a Japanese pen pal as a teenager."

She was remarkably well prepared for a woman who'd had no warning about this game. But she was Charmain Russo Addams. Should I really have been surprised? She was prepared for everything.

"Aha!" Ryan leapt from the couch, pointing at her. "The first one has to be a lie. No one doesn't cry through *Up* unless they're a psychopath. Which, you don't strike me as."

Kelsi snickered. "Nice save, babe."

From where I was curled up next to Nash on the loveseat, I shook with silent laughter. This was so much better than what Kelsi hoped for. I knew the answer, of course, but Nana was sneaky. I'd give her that. Ryan wouldn't know what hit him.

"Well?" Ryan grinned with the air of a man fully confident in his reasoning. Too bad he was about to be outsmarted by my octogenarian mastermind of a grandparent. "I have my doubts about the other ones, but—"

"You calling me a liar, sunny boy?" Nana raised a feathered eyebrow.

Ryan's eyes went dinner-plate wide. "Eh... no, ma'am, just... questioning the sheer... expansive experience of the life you've lived."

Nana cackled. "Oh, you're smooth." She shot me a wink then dropped the bomb. "I never cried through *Up* is true."

Everyone gasped.

Ryan blinked at her. "But... you don't have the eyes of a psychopath."

I couldn't hold it in any longer and burst into loud snorting laughter, clapping a hand over my mouth. "I'm sorry... sorry," I wheezed, trying to control my hysterics. "She's never seen it."

"What?" Ryan demanded, glancing between us.

Nana smiled impishly with a toss of her permed head. "Can't cry over a movie you've never seen." She tapped her temple with her pointer finger, nodding knowingly.

Ryan stared at her in unabashed admiration. "I want to be you when I grow up."

"Looks like you'll be waiting a while." Nana winked at him, and they shared a chummy smile.

"Then what's the lie?" Kelsi asked, eyes wide. "Please tell me you did meet Grace Kelly."

Nana folded her hands, eyes going soft with remembrance. "That's also true. She was a lovely woman. Very kind. My cousin was the one with a Japanese pen pal."

Because of course she was.

By nine o'clock, the littles were camped out asleep in their sleeping bags in the basement. Except for Sadie, the Mitchells' oldest.

"Mom, can I please go read now?" Sadie begged as we hung out in the living room.

Danielle shifted baby Sebastian on her shoulder and smiled. "Sure, sweetie. Are you sure you want to stay up?"

Sadie's blonde head bobbed as she leaned on the arm of the couch. "But I want to read my new books. And Neverland is *perfect*. Daddy set up the fairy lights."

"Of course he did." Danielle chuckled. "Off with you then."

"Thanks!" Sadie bounded across the room and, after loading up a plate of snacks, hurried down the hall.

"Neverland?" Paisley asked curiously from beside me on the couch.

"Yeah. This house has... quirks. There's a weird little hidey-hole in her room that Emmett turned into a reading nook for her, and she's obsessed with all things Peter Pan."

"Aw, how sweet. And now I'm a little jealous."

"Need me to take him, Dani?" Kelsi asked from where she was curled up on the brown leather recliner. Her ginger hair was knotted into a messy bun, and she cradled her cup of hot chocolate like a lifeline.

"Only if you want to, otherwise I'm good."

"No complaints from me. We've got time before he needs another feeding." Kelsi stifled a yawn, then grinned wickedly. So typically Kelsi. "You got baby fever?"

Instead of laughing at the teasing, delicate pink flushed Danielle's cheeks, and she shot a glance in Emmett's direction, biting her lip. He and the guys were clustered around the dining room table with a card game, which from the groans and cheers, someone was losing badly.

"Oh my gosh, are you pregnant?" Liz hissed around a mouthful of carrot sticks and dip.

Danielle tucked her chin against the baby's downy head, smiling. "We weren't going to announce it yet, but yeah. Due in June."

I slapped a hand over my mouth to keep in a squeal as I bolted upright. Liz was under no such compulsion and whooped as she and Kelsi jumped to their feet. If Dani wanted to play it cool, she'd picked the wrong group of friends. Because we were the furthest thing from chill about this.

Liz plopped down next to Danielle, squeezing her into a hug, while Kelsi perched on the couch arm, hand on Danielle's shoulder. Even crusty Juliet smiled, eyes shining. Babies were to be celebrated, and our friend group did that well.

Amid the well-wishes, dozens of questions, and hushed screaming—baby Sebastian *was* sleeping after all—I glanced at Paisley next to me. "Pais, you okay?"

It'd only been just over a week ago she'd talked about not being pregnant herself.

"Hmm?" She shook her head, dazed, as if returning from a different world.

"Where'd you go?" From the first moment I'd met Paisley, I'd become acquainted with the top of her head because her nose was always in a book. She lived and breathed literature—no doubt why she'd become a librarian. And part of that was the occasional wistful look that snatched her from the reality of us into some far-off land. Was that where she was now—trekking the depths of Middle Earth or some other such place? Or was she hiding some deeper hurt?

Paisley smiled softly, and I didn't detect pain in the gesture. But a longing lingered in her emerald eyes behind those too-large frames. "I'm still here. Just... basking in the wonder of reality. Soaking in the moments, you know? Sometimes it feels too good to be true..." She swallowed hard.

I clasped her hand. "I know a little about the ache when it comes to watching others get what you're wishing for."

Sympathy touched her smile. "You waited a long time for him"—she tilted her head in Nash's direction—"all the while celebrating with us."

"Yeah." I shifted so our heads leaned together. "Doesn't mean it wasn't hard. And it's okay to be honest about that."

"It's trusting God's timing, right?" she said softly. "His ways and plans are better than our wildest dreams. Even if the moments feel bleak."

"Always."

We stayed that way for a moment. Until she added, "We met your brother and his family. Mama D had them over for dinner the day after the game. The showdown between Cal and Myles getting Jackson's attention was epic."

I snorted. "Please tell me you got video footage."

Juliet scoffed, and I wondered how long she'd been listening even though we'd been quiet. "Of course we did. What, do we look like amateurs?"

"Jackson called me that night and couldn't string two words together in his excitement."

"They won, thank goodness," Paisley said, stretching her back. "And Cal got him a locker-room tour."

"Why that's appealing is beyond me." Juliet shuddered. "They're grown, sweaty men. Who stink."

"And yet you married one," Liz teased.

A goofy smile that looked so out of place on Juliet's usually stony expression touched her lips, and her aquamarine eyes softened as she found Myles watching her across the room. They were such newlyweds. "The perks outweigh the cons."

A hand cupped my shoulder, and I tilted my head back. "Hi," I said as Nash smiled down at me.

"Hey."

"Did you win?"

"You bet." His lips curved in a smirk. "Emmett even helped a bit."

"In your dreams," Emmett grunted, tromping across the living room and settling in beside his wife. His face relaxed as his arm settled around her, and he studied the sleeping infant, drooling on her shoulder.

"Such confidence," I teased.

"Never thought I'd say this, but time out, you two," Ryan called from packing up the card game. "We're not used to this level of flirting from you."

"You're one to talk after the display you put on the other week," Nash shot back.

"All right, boys, time for bingo!" Danielle announced, rolling her eyes like she'd refereed their bickering a hundred times. Which, to be fair, she had.

We played countless bingo rounds, each winner getting to pick a prize from the gift bin. Just like Christmas Eve, we all brought a small wrapped gift for the winners' bin. Thankfully, there was no stealing this time and no weird family dynamics with siblings who ganged up on you. If you got bingo, you picked a prize. Pure and simple.

At five minutes to midnight, we crammed into the farmhouse-style kitchen. Emmett poured glasses of sparkling apple-cranberry juice and Danielle passed them around. Sadie emerged from Neverland with droopy eyes and a crease on her left cheek, book still tucked under her arm, like she couldn't bear to leave it behind.

Paisley scurried over to her, and the two bent heads were instantly best friends discussing far-off worlds of imagination.

Nash draped an arm around my shoulders, tucking me into his side. A perfect fit.

I smiled up at him, glass in hand. "Are we supposed to make a wish or something? Or is that just for birthday candles?"

He chuckled. "Wish away."

"Are you going to?"

"Don't need to, darlin'. I got everything I wanted this Christmas." His warm espresso eyes melted me, and I leaned farther into him.

Emmett glanced at his watch. "All right, in ten... nine..."

The rest of us took up the count, and happiness fizzled in my veins as I surveyed our little group. Despite the uncertainty on the horizon with the launch, this moment was golden—a treasure. My eyes slid shut, taking a mental snapshot. It was one worth holding onto.

"Three... two... one... HAPPY NEW YEAR!"

Nash lifted his glass to mine and clinked it gently, then bent down and kissed me gently. "Happy New Year, Steph."

I kissed him back. "May it be our best one yet."

"Hey, there's fireworks!" Sadie cried, pelting down the stairs and out the front door.

Nash and I followed her, a few others trailing behind us. The wind was still biting and frigid, despite the layers, but the whistle and crack of the fireworks going up the next street over were worth it. The colours danced overhead in a tapestry of red, green, and silver.

It was just starting to snow again, the snowflakes catching in our hair. I stole a glance at Nash and watched the way the flickering fireworks cast shadows on his face. His grin was boyish and adorable. Strong and steady. I slipped my icy hand in his and squeezed it lightly.

He squeezed back. Three times.

I tilted my head at him curiously. Despite Gabe's best efforts, I hadn't mastered Morse code.

"I love you," he whispered.

Happiness trickled through my fingers and all the way down to my toes. I was... content and a little giddy. And I loved it. Loved him.

I sent a return message of my own with four squeezes. *I love you, too.*

Nash smiled down at me, the streetlight's soft glow winking off his glasses and the powdery snow sticking to his hair and coat. Despite the nipping wind, his gaze was warm. He lifted our entwined fingers and kissed the back of my hand. "Steph," he whispered, leaning down till our noses nearly touched.

I loved when he said my name, but the swoosh of a window opening above us cut off our moment. And when we looked up, Emmett was hanging out the window with a Nerf gun.

"Please remember your audience," he groused, waving the gun towards Sadie, who was still mesmerized with the pyrotechnics display. "I will use this if you get mushy." But his lips were twitching with a hidden smile beneath his beard.

For all his grumbling, he was happy for us. Unable to resist a tease of my own, I stood on tiptoes and kissed Nash's cheek, dragging him towards the door out of the way as Emmett let out a shot.

"Bah humbug!" Nash called out to him.

"Wrong holiday, Nashville."

I laughed till my sides ached in Nash's arms, under the streetlights and the pop of the fireworks. And it felt right. *Like home.*

Epilogue – Stephanie

APRIL—FOUR MONTHS LATER

"Right there, perfect!" I clicked the shutter button, its rapid purr a familiar friend. Checking my screen, I scrolled through the shots to make sure I'd captured enough before changing positions.

The heady aromatic smell of lilacs hung heavily around us as the late-April breeze mussed my curls, tickling my cheek. I inhaled deeply, savouring the scent of my favourite flowers. Pity they bloomed for such a short time.

I refocused on my subjects. "All right, face each other. Paisley, wrap your arms around Greyson's neck. Grey, place your hands on Paisley's hips." The evening sun diffused through the maple leaves overhead, giving a soft, golden-hour glow to the pictures. This copse of trees with an old wooden swing was my favourite part of the Satterfield property. It had always screamed romance to me. Perfect for a wedding. Or an engagement. *Focus!*

My models complied, looking absolutely adorable. Nash had surprised me with a spontaneous trip to Serenity Springs, Idaho, to visit friends for the weekend, and I was itching to whip out my camera. Paisley and Greyson were my willing—or mostly willing, since they were both camera shy—test-run models. Getting to shoot my bestie and her husband filled my heart. Paisley had had a rough go of life but watching her throw her head back with laughter as Greyson whispered something in her ear was a precious honour as a photographer. And being back in Idaho fed my soul. I was back with my people. Once I'd called it home-away-from-home, and in a way, it still was. But in the last five months, I'd found home had shifted from a place to a person. Spokane was truly home because Nash was there.

I was four months into my photography career, and just last month, Nash and I started a hunt for my replacement as a PA. Bookings had skyrocketed, and I'd settled into my rhythm in shooting and editing. From family shoots to senior graduations to engagements, I'd found my footing. For now, weddings were a no-go, at least not without a second shooter. But I was happy.

"Give her a kiss—no making out!" I called.

Paisley shot me a disapproving look, one I was sure she'd honed the use of as a librarian. "Do we look like Myles and Juliet?"

I laughed. "Touché. Carry on." I snapped a few more candid shots before taking another sneak peek at the screen.

"Can we finish our shots on the back-porch swing?" Paisley asked, beaming up at Greyson. "We had our first kiss there."

"And several more after that," Greyson said quietly, smirking.

Paisley's face flushed and she laughed, swatting his chest. Almost four years into marriage, they still had that spark and banter. I loved that for them.

"Of course. Let's go!" I glanced around. "Wait, I left my bag at the swing. I'll meet you there in a few."

Hand in hand, Paisley and Greyson headed for the house, whispering. I glanced over my shoulder and saw him reach for her hand, pressing a kiss to her temple before they disappeared around the bend. Something was up, but I couldn't put my finger on it.

Hurrying to the rustic swing, I nestled the camera into my bag. It was easier to transport that way since I'd have to change my lens at the porch, and I didn't want to do that right here and risk any floating dust particles. I ran a hand over the braided old rope. Still sturdy. I'd spent countless hours on this swing whenever I was in town. Thinking. Praying. Daydreaming. I zipped the bag and straightened, pausing a moment to breathe in the fragrant perfume of lilacs.

"Steph?"

I yelped, whirling around with a hand on my heart as Nash stepped out from behind a tree. "Jeepers, you've got to stop that!"

He chuckled apologetically. "You're pretty cute when you're scared."

I snorted. "Maybe, but that jolt to my blood pressure may lead to fainting." It had, one time in the office. And I wasn't about to let him forget it. "Why are you here? I thought you were waiting for me at the house. Got tired of Cal's hockey lingo? I know you're secretly fangirling," I teased.

Nash smiled and cleared his throat.

Was he… nervous? I'd only seen him wear that expression once before—on launch day for Genesis's new software program in January. But we'd been successful. Wait. "Did something happen with the lawsuit with Nova?" Panic licked through my veins. "I thought it was a straightforward case, especially with other victim companies working with us?"

"Steph." My name was a caress in his low timbre, and it stilled my ramblings. "Everything's fine. That's not why I'm here."

"Oh?"

He stepped towards me, taking my hand in his. The dappled sun highlighted the reddish tints in his dark hair only visible in certain light. His Adam's apple bobbed as he smiled down at me. "I've got another bargain for you, sweetheart."

"Should I feel special?" I quipped. "You kept making deals with Italia's after all." We'd been back to the Italian restaurant where we'd had our first official date a few times, and we'd been eating our way through the menu. But the lobster ravioli was still my favourite.

Nash smirked, dimple popping. "This is an exclusive deal, so it's special all right." Releasing my hand, he sank down on one knee and opened a ring box.

Where had he hidden that? My hands flew to my mouth. This was real. It was happening. "Nash," I whispered hoarsely.

He smiled up at me tenderly, a steady presence. "Stephanie Addams, you are the most amazing woman I've ever met. I've loved you for years. Will you do me the honour of being my wife so I can love you for a lifetime?"

Cue the waterworks. I sniffed, swiping at a tear that pushed past my defenses. And once again, no waterproof mascara in sight. "Yes! Yes, of course I'll marry you!" I threw myself into his arms, landing on his knee. Half laughter and half tears shook my frame as he held me tightly. "Thank you," I whispered against his neck.

Nash pulled back slightly and held the ring box out. I peered at the ring for the first time since I was paying more attention to the man than the ring in the actual moment. It was exactly what I'd dreamed of. A single circular diamond solitaire set in a silver band. Classic and elegant.

"It's perfection," I breathed as he slid the ring over the knuckle of my left ring finger. A perfect fit. No doubt my friends were to thank for that.

Nash lifted my hand wearing his ring to his lips, pressing a kiss there. "I love you."

I looped my arms around his neck, gazing into those rich, soulful eyes, overflowing with love and emotion. For me. I'd spent my life trying to feel accepted and wanted, only to find a man whose steadfast, present nature was beyond what I'd ever dreamed. "And I love you. Forever and always." Feeling impish, I added, "Shake on it?" I held out my hand to shake, like we'd sealed our previous bargains.

Nash ignored my proffered hand and his dimple deepened with mischief. "I can think of a better way to seal the deal, darlin'." And he kissed me, long and slow. Full of promises.

Wrapping my arms around his neck, I smiled into the kiss. I was home.

Bonus Epilogue – Paisley

END OF JANUARY (BEFORE Stephanie and Nash's engagement)

I burned dinner.

No. That sounded too tame. Too benign.

I *scorched* dinner beyond recognition. Like Smaug would have done to the dwarves if Bilbo Baggins hadn't snuck into Mount Erebor first.

Our guests—my best friends Liz, Juliet, and Stephanie plus their fellas—were arriving within the hour, and I now had nothing to serve them. After assuring my besties at Christmas that I hadn't burnt a meal since Greyson and I got married three years ago, Murphy's Law would come back to bite me when it counted most.

I threw the windows open to clear the billows of smoke as the detector screamed at me. "I'm doing the best I can!" I yelled to no one in particular.

Rosie Cotton, our beloved Golden Retriever, hunkered in the corner of the living room having a meltdown. She hated all beeping noises but especially the smoke detector, and that was all it took to turn her into a nervous wreck of the shakes. But I couldn't comfort her while I had Mount Doom erupting inside my oven.

The fire extinguisher was not in its designated home under the sink, so I grabbed the mason jar of baking soda from the cupboard and hucked the contents into the oven. The fire spluttered down enough for me to rescue the dish and set it in the sink, in all its smoldering glory. Therein lies the remains of a roast dinner—may it rest in peace.

Tears stung my eyes, and heat prickled the back of my neck. One time. Could something go right in my life just one time? And today of all days with my friends coming over, and... and... I studiously avoided looking at the calendar. I didn't need a reminder of the date. The day I'd married the first man I'd ever loved. A man who wasn't Greyson Satterfield.

"Rosie, chill out!" I snapped over her frenzied barking.

It had been years. Jared didn't deserve any more of my head space. And he certainly wasn't worth burning a meal over. *Get your head in the game, Paisley Grace.*

Dragging a stool under the kitchen smoke detector, I climbed up and yanked it from the ceiling, killing the high-pitched shrill. Silence fell over the house, still thickly choked in smoke.

Surveying my smoky domain from the loftiness of the stool, I pinched the bridge of my nose, and my chest heaved in a silent sob. I wanted tonight to be special. Perfect. Nash, Stephanie's boyfriend, was a millionaire for goodness' sake. Not that I thought he'd be a snob. I didn't get that vibe from him when we met on New Year's Eve almost a month ago. But still. It had taken forever to finagle this dinner onto the agenda with Nash and Stephanie's work schedule in their race against the clock to get Genesis's new marketing program launched by end of January. Their official launch was yesterday. Tonight we'd hear how successful they'd been.

My shoulders drooped. I'd wanted this dinner to be a celebration. Not a letdown.

Warm hands grasped my waist, and my eyes flew open. It was Greyson. Shirtless with a towel around his waist, still wet.

"What are you—I thought you were in the shower," I spluttered, glaring down at him. "You're dripping on my clean floor."

Greyson studied me for a minute, then lifted me down off the stool with ease, muscles rippling. It wasn't fair how simple he made it look. Sure, I was a bit of a lightweight who needed some more meat on my bones, but did he have to rub it in? Didn't stop me from appreciating it, though. No, ma'am. Time in the military had done wonders for my husband's physique. Even though he'd retired a few years back to come home as the new local mechanic.

"I heard the fire alarm and Rosie. Thought something was wrong," he said in that husky voice I loved.

Did he have to be so sweet about it when I practically bit his head off? "Oh, something's wrong all right," I snapped. "Look in the sink." It was a silly thing to say since the cloying perfume of smoke made it obvious *charcoal à la mode* was on the menu tonight.

Those stupidly persistent tears kept knocking on my tear gates, but I ignored them even as my chest ached with pressure from the build up. I didn't have time or the emotional bandwidth for tears. I needed a plan.

Or more accurately, dinner for eight in the next forty-three minutes.

"What's going on in that mind of yours?" Greyson asked, his rough voice gentle as he turned me towards him.

"Oh, I don't think you can handle all that."

He made an amused hum deep in his throat, leaning down. I thought he was going in for a kiss, but nope. He bypassed my willing lips and traced his nose over my jaw before kissing down my neck. "You know what they say about assuming."

"What's that?" I asked, way more breathless than I intended. He was playing dirty, kissing me to steal my anger—and my snark. Infuriating man.

Greyson chuckled again. Another kiss over my pulse.

"Grey, we have company coming," I whispered, my voice nearly strangled.

"I know." He sighed, warm breath feathering my skin. "But you're deflecting, because I can feel those thoughts in that beautiful brain whirling at the speed of light. What's going on? Are you nervous about tonight?"

"Maybe." I fiddled with his damp sandy-brown hair. "We're about to have a millionaire in our house."

"We have Cal and Myles here on a regular basis."

"Not the same thing. They're family."

"Nash didn't strike me as the pretentious type."

I rolled my eyes. "He's not. Steph would have chewed him up and spit him out if he were."

Greyson choked on a laugh. We both knew I wasn't wrong. "Then what's the real problem? Because I have a guess, if you care to hear it."

"I'm fine. No problem."

"Pais." Greyson's voice took on a serious edge, different from the playful, flirty tone he'd been using before. "The date. You're overwhelming your brain with thoughts and tasks to avoid thinking about it."

Nope, we were not talking about this right now. I shoved his chest, and he released me. "Don't be ridiculous. And go put some clothes on." I ran the cold water in the sink, letting it cascade over the blackened mess. What did I have in the pantry for short notice? Tacos? Quesadillas? Frozen pizza? *Way to make it special, Paisley Grace.*

Greyson's arms slid around my waist from behind, and I reluctantly sagged against his chest. "If you want to talk about this later, we can table it. But we have to talk about it sometime, Pais."

"But I'm *fine*," I tried to insist, though it sounded wobbly.

He sighed and kissed behind my ear. "Pull out some ground beef from the freezer. I'll make spaghetti. We can use the sourdough you made yesterday for garlic bread, and there's lettuce for a Caesar salad."

That... would work. And Grey's spaghetti was to die for.

I spun in his embrace, looping my arms over his broad shoulders. "I love you. Even if you're just trying to distract me."

He smirked, nudging our noses. "Is it working?"

I bit my lip. "Maybe. I just..." I dropped my hands to his chest, his skin warm under my touch and smelling divinely like soap. His heart beating in a rhythmic thrum under my palm. That was one of the things I loved best about this man. He was rock-solid steady. And after the life I'd lived, nothing in the world was more attractive than that.

Greyson gently tilted my chin up with his finger. His piercing blue eyes—a shared trait among all the Satterfield offspring along with their all over-six-feet heights—waiting patiently. Encouraging me to open up.

"I hate that *he* still takes up space in my head after all these years," I whispered. "I don't want to think about him. It hurts."

Greyson pressed an achingly sweet kiss to my forehead. "Then don't. Tonight, laugh with our friends, forget about him and this... soggy mess." He reached behind me and flicked off the tap. "And remember you're loved. Right here." His lips moved gently over mine as he kissed me, punctuating his words. "Right now."

This time I was the one urging him closer, but he tugged back with a cocky grin. "We have guests coming, Mrs. Satterfield."

I groaned. "Rake. Fiend. Rogue."

"I love your vocabulary." He laughed and chucked my chin. "Grab the beef. Give me five minutes, and I'll be back."

And he was. Together, we assembled the spaghetti, garlic bread, and Caesar salad then chilled out one big baby of a dog. By the time the doorbell rang at six o'clock, the smoky haze ceased to exist, and Greyson's spaghetti was ready.

Liz and Ben stood on the porch, bearing gifts, and Juliet and Myles climbed out of their truck in the driveway.

"Ooh, spaghetti!" Liz exclaimed, stepping inside and flinging her arms around me.

"Where's Steph and Nash?" I asked, returning the hug.

Liz laughed. "They're just behind us. Now where's that fur baby? Auntie Liz has gifts." She jiggled a baby-pink gift bag.

"I put her in the laundry room," Greyson said from behind me. "She still gets too excited when the front door opens." And as if confirming his words, Rosie's excited bark from the back of the house proved it.

Juliet trudged up the steps, Myles behind her.

When they stepped out of the shadows into the entryway, I gasped. "Myles! Your face!"

In addition to his usual man bun, he sported a black eye and a three-inch cut across his left cheek, held together with stitches. "It's not as bad as it looks."

Juliet scoffed and hung up her coat on the vintage coat stand. "That's what they all say."

Myles's smile was slightly strained, like smiling pulled on the wrong muscles, and I got the sense this was a conversation they'd been arguing for days. "You should see the bruise on my side."

"They should *not*."

Myles grinned at her, brown eyes twinkling with mischief. "Ladies love a man with a scar, Jules."

"Oh, you have a lot of experience with that?" she countered, blonde eyebrow arched perfectly.

Greyson snickered and punched his brother-in-law's arm. "Walked right into that one, man." He hugged his younger sister. "Go easy on him. The man's injured. For a good cause, too. I saw the game."

"He'll live," Juliet deadpanned and wriggled out of the hug, pushing past him like only a younger sibling could. Not that I'd know since I didn't have one, but I'd hung around the Satterfields—Juliet, Cal, and Greyson particularly—long enough to have noticed these things.

"Heard that, babe," Myles called after her. "She took that stick to my face more personally than I did."

"Wait, hockey!" I said, things clicking in my brain. "We're having spaghetti. Does that work with your diet? I know you're not supposed to have high carbs during the on-season." With it being the middle of the hockey season, Cal and Myles were pretty regimented with how they ate. The original roast dinner with salad and roasted veggies would have been ideal, but would a carb-heavy pasta be too much? I mean, we still had salad, but...

Myles grunted, but reassurance lined his light smile. "It'll be fine, Pais. I'm not turning down Grey's spaghetti, no matter what Coach says."

"Where can I put these?" Ben lifted a plastic container of what looked like pastries.

"Oh, sorry, Ben. Anywhere on the counter's fine. Make yourself at home," I said, and he disappeared into the kitchen.

A car door slammed outside, and a minute later, Nash and Stephanie hurried up the front stairs.

"Wow, it's cold! Pretty sure my nose froze between here and the car." Stephanie gave her head a little shake, bouncing her curls.

"Three words. Fleece-lined tights," I said simply, taking her coat and giving her a quick squeeze. "Oh, you guys look tired."

Stephanie snorted. "Just what every woman wants to hear, Pais."

"Does this mean the launch was successful?" Greyson asked at my back. The rest of our friends crowded closer to hear the news.

Nash and Stephanie exchanged glances, dark-rimmed eyes shining. Sharing a hundred thoughts and no small degree of elation.

"Short answer, yes," Nash said. "Long answer over dinner."

The guys did the standard man greeting with nods, handshakes, and backslaps. We were lucky that our guys got along almost as well as us girls did.

Greyson let Rosie out of the laundry room, and introductions were made. She fell instantly in love with Liz—no surprise there, kids and animals adored her—and demanded pets from everyone, even Juliet, who only tolerated animals because *hair*. Okay, and allergies. She wasn't a diva.

Eight was a tight squeeze around our little dining room table in the nook off the kitchen, but we managed, and after Greyson said grace, conversation ebbed and flowed punctuated by jokes and laughter. We'd done friend dinners before, but tonight was the first time Nash was joining us, and he fit right in.

"So, the impromptu launch?" I prompted, sliding a piece of garlic bread onto my plate. "You made it!"

"Congratulations for pulling off the insane!" Liz said between bites of salad. "Any hiccups?"

"Nope." Nash grinned down at Stephanie. "Thanks to my brilliant girlfriend, we beat her father at his own game."

"And it was really his own wife who gave you the missing information?" I asked.

Stephanie hummed, twirling noodles onto her fork. "I'm not sure how long that wife status will last, but Zara's got a good heart. Without her, we wouldn't have had the identity of the mole. Or any evidence to start a lawsuit against Nova."

"You're really taking on your dad's company?" Myles asked, looking impressed.

Stephanie nodded. "It's not personal. Well, it sorta is. But from a business outlook, we're not the only ones he's tried to sabotage."

Nash sighed happily. "For now, we're all just grateful it's done and out. Pretty sure we're going to need a vacation after those crazy hours."

"They weren't *all* bad," Stephanie said, a flirty edge to her words.

Wow, I was still so not used to seeing Stephanie date. Or flirt. Or kiss. Which was what Nash was doing now. On the cheek, but still.

"But enough about us," Stephanie said, straightening. "Thanks for hosting this, Pais. Grey. It's nice to get out of town and relax for the first time since Christmas."

Liz offered humorous escapades of the return to school of her kindergarteners. Ben recounted a tow he'd done recently involving an elk and the front end of a car that miraculously still drove... until it didn't. Juliet mentioned she'd be going on the road with Myles and the guys next month to negotiate a brand deal for a couple of the players as part of the Chargers' legal counsel. Then talk shifted to Liz and Ben's wedding.

"Two months," Liz said grinning. "It'll be great."

"Any more hiccups with the planning?" Nash asked, taking a sip of water and using his free hand to pet a persistent Rosie who sat between his and Stephanie's chairs, soaking in the love. She wasn't begging so I couldn't really fault her.

Ben shook his head. "For now, things are in order. Next week? That's anyone's guess."

Liz elbowed him. "Don't say that. Any more hiccups, and we're eloping."

"You say that like it's a bad thing." Ben smoldered, making Liz titter.

I watched Nash and Stephanie and had no doubt they'd be next in line for the wedding hoopla. In the ten years I'd known her, Stephanie had never been this relaxed. And there was a soft glow to her face, a lightness.

"They'll be next," Greyson whispered in my ear, setting a pile of plates beside the sink while I soaked the spaghetti pot a few minutes later.

"Oh? Nash tell you something?"

Greyson smiled smugly. "Nah, but she looks at him the way you look at me, so..."

"Your powers of deduction are profound," I deadpanned, hip-checking him. But of course, he didn't budge, and I ricocheted off of him like a bouncy ball. "'Don't spoil the wonder with haste.'"

His warm chuckle skittered over my skin. "Quoting Tolkien to me again, Mrs. Satterfield?"

"Hey, Greyson, can I pick your brain for a minute about an old Thunderbird that came into the shop this week?" Ben interrupted from the table. Which was probably a good thing.

"What year?"

"'55. Beautiful shape."

"You're speaking my language." Greyson kissed my temple before moving back towards the table.

When I turned around, the girls were watching me curiously. "What?" I asked, flicking off the water.

"Nothing." Liz drew the word out, eyes sparkling with pixie dust. "Sometimes I just forget how cute you two are."

"And we're making sure you're okay. *Today.*" Juliet pinned me with a hard, no-nonsense look.

They'd walked with me during my relationship and brief marriage with Jared. They'd helped me pick up the pieces of the broken woman he'd reduced me to. I straightened my shoulders, deciding to be honest. "I'm done giving him room in my head. It's in the past. I can't rewrite the chapter. And he doesn't deserve my thoughts."

Stephanie nodded sagely. "You've grown a lot since then, Pais. And I know it's hard to come to terms with a relationship that should have worked but didn't."

After Christmas, Stephanie had shared with us what Liz was calling the "final showdown" with her dad. Even if our situations were different, Stephanie knew what she was talking about. She'd been abandoned and manipulated by her dad, and I'd been betrayed by the man who had vowed to love me till death did us part.

Grief was messy. One day you felt fine, and the next the past crept up on you like a ghost. Chilling fingers of a phantom gripping your neck in the dark. But we were healing. We were pressing forward in faith towards the light. Our dark chapters were just that—chapters. Not the end of the story.

"Hey, you up for guys versus girls Settlers of Catan?" Myles asked, coming in with the bread basket from the dining room, breaking up the moment.

"Ooh, bring it on!" Liz fist pumped.

"You're so going down," Juliet vowed with a smirk.

"Y'all are something else." Stephanie shook her head.

I smiled at them. "Let me put the coffee on."

LATER THAT NIGHT, AFTER Liz and Stephanie were holed up in our guest room and Ben and Nash left to crash at Myles and Juliet's, the house was quiet. I cuddled against Greyson in bed, my hand resting on his chest, feeling the steady thrum of his pulse and his even breathing. Rosie snored lightly at the end of the bed.

Originally, she was supposed to sleep in the laundry room. That had lasted all of two nights when Greyson caved to her soft nightly whimpers and let her into our room. She hadn't jumped into bed with us, just curled up on the rug at the foot of the bed and drifted off to dreamland without a sound.

"Grey?"

"Hmm?" It was more a noise than a reply, and I could tell he was nearly asleep, even though his thumb rubbed soft circles over my shoulder.

"Thank you for tonight. You're amazing. And I don't think I say that enough."

He stirred slightly. "My spaghetti does it for you, huh? More than the dress blues?"

I laughed, turning my head to muffle it in his shoulder since we did have guests after all. "It was incredible as always, and I do love a man in uniform, but that's not what I meant."

The bed creaked as he rolled towards me, tugging me more firmly into his arms. "Then don't let me stop you from whatever you had to say."

I pressed my cheek against his chest. "No conversations tonight. Just... can you hold me for a while?"

"Forever," he slurred, and I knew he was slipping away again. Marines (even retired ones) and their freaky ability to sleep within seconds. Me? Only if the room temperature was sixty-eight degrees, I had a weighted blanket (or Grey's arm, I wasn't picky), fluffy socks on, and white noise running. Even then my brain would kick into overdrive and overthink *everything.*

Greyson's arms tightened slightly. "You're making me dizzy with all that thinking, Pais."

"What are you going to do about it?" I teased.

He kissed me. And I forgot about everything else.

THE END

The story continues with Paisley and Greyson, coming Spring/Summer 2026!

But wait!

Want to see more of Nash and Stephanie?!
Keep reading for Nash's POV of the engagement scene (and a chance to meet the cast's favourite hockey player)! And if you want even *more,* sign up for my newsletter here to receive the meet-cute scene (aka the Interview) from 2 years earlier!

Bonus Scene – Nash's POV of Engagement Day

I ROLLED MY SHOULDERS as I stood on the whitewashed back porch of the Satterfield house, surveying the yard and the copse of trees where Stephanie was doing a photo shoot with Paisley and Greyson. She'd been itching to photograph her friends, and they'd agreed. Little did she know it was all part of my plan.

About a month ago, Stephanie had let it slip that this was her favourite spot in Serenity Springs, and she'd love to get married here if she were a local. It might not have been practical for a wedding, but I could manage an engagement. And today was the day.

With nearly five months of real dating and a week of fake dating behind us, today I'd ask Stephanie to be my wife. I patted my jeans, reassured that the box was still bulging in my jean pocket. Was it possible to be nervous and excited at the same time? Having my mom call on the drive up here with Stephanie probably didn't help. It was the first time she contacted me after checking out of rehab just before Christmas. I'd half hoped maybe no news was good news. But no.

She wanted money for rent, she said, but I knew better. Rent money had a way of turning into drug money, and she'd be on the streets for a while until she called me and agreed to rehab again. In the past, I'd have given it to her. But something I was learning—Stephanie, too—was about familial boundaries. I would stand by my mother and fund rehab as many times as it took for her to stick it out... but I couldn't be her enabler. It was a hard conversation to have the morning before proposing to my girlfriend. Taking this step was necessary. Even if it gutted me. Even if my mom had cussed me out until Stephanie hung up.

Hands clapped on my shoulders from behind, snapping me out of my thoughts. "Feeling ready, man?"

It was an odd thing for a man to meet a famous athlete—my favourite athlete if I was being completely honest (don't tell Juliet). Cal was the second most down-to-earth famous person I'd met, and in my position, I had met several. But first place would always belong to Stephanie's cousin, Hailey Bishop, because Hailey was family. And also, completely awesome.

Where Greyson, as the older twin, got all the older brother intensity and military bearing, Cal joked and ribbed without mercy. It never ceased to amaze me how much my circle had grown in the last four and a half months of dating Stephanie. From just Ryan and Emmett in my corner, I'd gotten Stephanie's friends and their partners, the Satterfield clan, Gabe and his family, Hailey, and Nana.

I cleared my throat and cuffed Cal's shoulder. "As ready as a man ever can be in this situation. It didn't work out in my favour the first time."

A shadow of pain flashed in his eyes. "I know the feeling. My fiancé left me a month before our wedding."

Say what now? "I didn't realize you were engaged before Khia's mom."

He shrugged, staring out in the distance with the air of a man seeing ghosts, what-ifs, and a thousand memories. "She'll always be the one that got away." Shuffling his feet, he cleared his throat.

There was more of a story there, I could tell. But I wasn't one to pry, knowing firsthand the complicated emotions that came with exes and disappointed dreams.

"You're even worse at pep talks than I am, my man," Ryan called from behind us, breaking the tension.

"Never thought I'd see the day that happened," Emmett grunted, joining us with Gabe on his heels. "Somebody write this down."

Stephanie was loved by a lot of people, and while I knew she wanted a private engagement because she hated being the center of attention, I couldn't say no to our tribe wanting to throw a surprise party afterwards. So everyone involved had trekked out to Serenity Springs unbeknownst to her. Including my best friends. Actually, Emmett was the one to cajole Ryan into it. Emmett could huff his way through an argument about how much he hated drama, but as long as it wasn't *his* drama, the man took a front-row seat and brought snacks.

I glanced at my watch. According to the time we'd agreed on, Greyson and Paisley should be making an excuse to leave Stephanie alone any minute. "It's time," I said at last.

Gabe slapped my back. "Go get your girl." Approval crinkled around his amber eyes. For all the talk about protective older brothers hating their younger sisters' boyfriends, Gabe had honestly been my biggest supporter through our entire relationship.

I patted my pocket one more time, discreetly wiping my damp palms on my jeans. I could do this. Amid the hoots and hollers of the guys, I strode across the lawn and into the trees, keeping to the edge to avoid giving my presence away too early.

Nearing the rustic swing, I caught a glimpse of Stephanie, Greyson, and Paisley and ducked behind a maple. Waiting. Nerves tingling with anticipation. Heart pounding. *What if she says no?*

"Wait, I left my bag at the swing. I'll meet you there," I heard Stephanie call.

Paisley and Greyson exited the trees at a slightly hurried leisurely pace so Stephanie wouldn't follow them too quickly.

But Stephanie wasn't in a hurry. She zipped her camera into her bag and stood for a moment, tilting her head back and inhaling deeply, her eyes fluttering shut.

This was it. I wiped my hands on my jeans again and twitched my shoulders. Then I stepped out from behind the tree. "Steph?"

She jumped, whirling around with a hand to her heart. "Jeepers, you've got to stop that!"

I chuckled apologetically. "You're pretty cute when you're scared."

She snorted, pouting a little "Maybe, but that jolt to my blood pressure may lead to fainting."

Which, to be fair, it had happened once at the office. Thankfully, I'd caught her before she hit the ground, but I definitely wasn't auditioning for a repeat performance, and she didn't let me forget it.

"Why are you here?" Stephanie asked. "I thought you were waiting for me at the house. Get tired of Cal's hockey lingo? I know you were secretly fangirling." Her eyes danced with amusement.

Cal and I got along just fine, and he'd barely mentioned hockey all day actually. I smiled and cleared my throat. I hated nerves. I never got them. But this was important. Really important. Stephanie wasn't Alexis. Wasn't my mother. These women couldn't be more different, and I was done with a ghost living inside my head. It was time to let go once and for all.

But panic morphed Stephanie's face. "Did something happen with the lawsuit with Nova? I thought it was a straightforward case, especially with other victim companies working with us?"

"Steph," I said, my voice low, and she looked up at me with such devotion and assurance, I nearly forgot where I was going with all this and just skipped to kissing her. *After. First things first.* "Everything's fine. That's not why I'm here."

"Oh?"

I moved towards her, taking her hand in mine. Running a thumb over the smooth skin of her knuckles, I admired the way the sunlight warmed her fair skin, bringing out the green tints in her hazel eyes. This woman had my heart. I swallowed hard, then smiled down at her, finding the words I needed. "I've got another bargain for you, sweetheart."

"Should I feel special?" Her tone was teasing. "You kept making deals with Italia's after all."

I smirked. "This is an exclusive bargain, so it's special all right." Releasing her hand, I took a deep breath and slipped the box from my back pocket, dropping to one knee as I opened the box.

She inhaled sharply, hands flying to her mouth. "Nash." My name was a whispered plea on her lips.

Kneeling at her feet, I laid my heart bare. "Stephanie Addams, you are the most amazing woman I've ever met. I've loved you for years. Will you do me the honour of being my wife so I can love you for a lifetime?"

Stephanie sniffed and a single tear trickled down her cheek. "Yes! Yes, of course I'll marry you!"

And just like that, history was rewritten. The love of my life said *yes* and threw herself into my arms. My heart soared, and I crushed her to my chest as she perched on my knee, laughter and tears shaking her frame.

"Thank you," she whispered against my neck.

I pulled back slightly, showing her the ring box again. Her eyes sparkled as she stared at the ring. A round diamond solitaire set in a silver band. It was classic and elegant, just like her. And I had her friends to thank, especially for figuring out the sizing.

"It's perfect," she whispered as I slid the ring onto her left ring finger.

I lifted her hand, still in awe at her wearing my ring, and pressed a kiss to her soft skin. "Thank you for saying yes," I whispered. "I love you."

Her arms looped around my neck, filling my nose with her heady vanilla scent. I loved that smell. Loved her. Her gaze shone with emotion. I'd found a woman who accepted me as I was, who saw me as enough despite my imperfections and flaws. A woman who was my forever.

"And I love you. Forever and always." She waggled her hand with an impish grin. "Shake on it?"

I ignored her hand, smirking as I leaned in. "I can think of a better way to seal the deal, darlin'." And I kissed her, long and slow. Cherishing the moment. Cherishing her.

"As much as I'd love to keep you here to myself," I said after reluctantly breaking the kiss several minutes later, "we should head back."

She sighed and rose from sitting on my knee. "How horribly responsible of you," she teased.

I laughed, taking her hand and weaving our fingers together as we walked. "I'm in favour of short engagements. What do you say?"

She blushed peony pink. "Please."

Our surprise entourage erupted into cheers and clapping as we emerged from the trees, and I raised our laced hands overhead.

Stephanie jumped in surprise, then laughed. "They all came for this?"

"Not for this," I whispered. "For us."

She studied the crowd clustered on the porch, the familiar faces of friends and family. Her hazel eyes sparkled with unshed tears.

Fishing a free hand into my pocket, I twirled a piece of disfigured mistletoe between my fingers. "For old times' sake?"

Stephanie eyed it, biting back a smile. "Is that... plastic?"

"Don't ruin the mood, woman," I growled playfully, looping a finger through the belt loop of her jeans and tugging her closer. "Do you know how hard it is to find real mistletoe in April?"

She just laughed and rocked up on her tiptoes, pausing a breath from my lips. "You're really a romantic, Mr. Prescott."

"Only for you, darlin'."

And just like the first time on Christmas Eve, *she* kissed me.

Author's Note

To borrow from the ever-eloquent Princess Mia in the iconic *Princess Diaries*: "Me? Write romance? Shut. Up."

This story was equal parts fun and therapeutic. It was a story for me as well as for you. Stephanie is the most "like-me" heroine I've written to date. And while it's not autobiographical by any means, so much of this book was rooted in reality. The happier parts of the Addams' family traditions were borrowed from the magical memories of my childhood, and bruschetta is something we take very seriously in my house. Other small tidbits of real-life were fun to slip in, too (e.g. the fifteen-dollar-gift rules, Spokane—because I played tourist there in 2019 and loved it, the car that hit an elk and still drove... until it didn't. True story). I love Christmas and this was a fun way to capture the nostalgia in black-and-white.

Full confession: I'm not a romantic person by nature. At least not a hopeless romantic. (As you may have guessed by this point...

or maybe the series title gave you a clue.) A dear friend once used the term *melancholy romantic*, and that's where I fall.

I love rom-coms as much as the next girl, even if I never quite saw myself in the shoes of the heroines obsessed with love. And so this book was born. For the girls who want to be someone's person, who like the idea of love, even if the bruises on their hearts make them wonder if that's even possible after heartache.

Whether you're like Stephanie and waiting for the shoe to drop, terrified of opening yourself up to be being left by the person supposed to love you the most. Or whether you felt like Nash, only worth keeping around because of what you have to offer, never for who you are. For all the single girls who have watched their friend group get their happily ever afters and wonder if it'll ever be their turn. This one's for you with all my love.

If that's you, I hope you find a home here between the pages. And know as I scribbled away at this little Christmas escape, I've prayed you'll find the staying kind of love, too. Most importantly though, I've prayed you find a lasting kind of love, first and foremost in Jesus Christ. His love is greater than any romance can ever be.

Rest assured, this is only the first book in this world of friends and their reluctant love stories. So if you found a character who made you say, "Man, I wish we got their story," stick around! There's a good chance you'll be getting it in the days ahead. <3

Acknowledgements

Writing is often a lonely endeavor only made possible by the support and encouragement of the real VIPs. Without you, this book wouldn't have existed. My name may be on the cover, but it's all thanks to the amazing team standing behind me. So much love for you all!

Marissa Adams, who is the president of the Emmett fan club. And also read the very first copy of the first draft in instalments. I've never shown my work to anyone that early, but I'm so glad it was you. Your insight was invaluable, and you convinced me this wasn't a dumpster fire worthy of the trash heap on more than one occasion. Readers have you to thank for all the extra Emmett content. His book is coming, I promise.

Kysa, Hannah, Amanda, and May—thank you for beta reading and fangirling over a *very* early draft of Nash and Stephanie's story and giving so much feedback. The story grew almost 25K words thanks to your insight, haha, and I'm so grateful for all the plot holes you caught.

Leah, my gold star editor. Girl, working with you was a dream! You sharpened the story into something magical and completely caught my vision. I can't thank you enough! Reading your comments had me in stitches and was a highlight of my summer! Thanks for loving the story—and me—so well! Seriously, you're amazing. Love you, girly! <3

Alicia, thank you for being the last line of defense against all the pesky typos and for saving me from my hyphen-happy self. Your excitement for the story and your sharp eye were so appreciated. I'm so grateful our paths crossed!

Emily, my cover designer. You're amazing and brought my vision to life better than I could have ever dreamed—I still can't get over how GORGEOUS it is. Thanks for making my dreams come true!

My hype and ARC team in the Bookstagram community—you're the bestest. Thanks for taking a chance on me and this little Christmas adventure. This girl is so blessed by each of you.

Drew Taylor and Hailey Gardiner Brown: You were both the first rom-coms I ever read and enchanted me forever—so much so, you inspired me to write one of my own. Hailey: The Bookstagram/Authorgram community was devastated to lose you too soon this year. I wish I could have met you in person, but your beautiful light impacted my life just the same. I hope I can be half as funny as you one day. You're responsible for the surplus Jesse McCartney songs in my playlists, and I loved our shared appreciation of early 2000s pop culture (you're 100% right, Lizzie absolutely deserved better than Paolo). Every world needs a Hailey, and I'm so glad you've been a part of mine. Miss you, sweet friend. <3 Drew: I've had the immense joy of watching your stories grow from the first book till the present, and you amaze and inspire me. The way you tackle hard topics in a light-hearted rom-com setting is beautiful. And I can't wait to see where your new genre shift takes you. Keep shining the Light!

And Jess Mastorakos, who made me fall in love with Marines in the first place. I've been sitting on this secret for a while. It needed to be said, haha.

For the gals of the Glory Writers Princess Diaries & Little Women summer writing cabins. Y'all kept me sane! I couldn't have made it without your encouragement & those late-night sprints that turned into unhinged rambling. You're the best. Let's do it again!

My author friends and book community—Anna Christine, Val, Drew, Faith, Alissa, Britt, Catie, Elisabeth, Stephanie, Victoria, Emily C, Emma, Leah, Rebecca Jo, and well, there's too many to name! You know who you are, and you inspire me to excellence—thank you. I'm so glad we're in this together. You pushed me over the finish line with the sheer force of your encouragement and prayers as I navigated this genre shift. Thank you from the bottom of my heart. <3

My family. Well, I did it—made it though an entire story without main character/major side character casualties! Who'd have thought? Can't guarantee a repeat performance so let's take this as a win! Thanks for the Hallmark marathons (Mum), the hypothetical "if the transmission went...?" conversations (Dad and the little bro), and respecting the door being closed during work hours. It's nice to see you all again after that insane season of deadlines. And thanks for being so supportive, even though none of you are romance readers, haha.

For the Bilinskys, thanks for all the childhood Christmas memories; I loved them for us. And especially for Nana and Papa—love you forever and Nana, may your orange cardigan live in infamy—and my cousin Alex, thanks for being the Hailey to my Stephanie growing up, even if you are the older one. Can we agree after over 20 years that the toy smuggling scheme was your idea? I take full responsibility for the spa set—call it even?

You, dear reader. Whether you're a hopeless or a reluctant romantic, I'm honoured you picked up this story, and I hope you leave with a piece of Christmas magic.

The best for last, my Heavenly Father. Thank you for making me brave, Jesus. For loving me despite my own fears and hang-ups. For modeling unconditional love and grace. For being the staying kind. I love getting to do this journey with you. Soli Deo gloria.

Loved the story?

Consider leaving a review on Amazon and Goodreads!

Also by Morgan Taylor Giesbrecht

<u>Newhaven Secrets Series</u>

The Lies We Live

(World War One Spy Mystery)

About the Author

Morgan Taylor Giesbrecht fell in love with fictional realms at a young age and quickly began writing tales of her own—full of hope, brave living in a dark world, and unexpected love stories for the crusty romantics (like herself). She's a hobbit at heart (but not in height) with deep roots in the past, who loves the occasional adventure and exceptionally dry humour. British Columbia, Canada is the place she calls home, nestled in the foothills.

You can find Morgan here:
Instagram: @authormorgantaylor
Facebook: Morgan Giesbrecht, Author
TikTok: @authormorgantaylor